Praise

NICK CU

and

LITTLE HEAVEN

"A grotesque masterpiece that sets the bar high for horror fiction."

—*Cemetery Dance*

"Cutter proves yet again that he is a master of thoughtful pulp horror. . . . Drips with dread from the very first lines. With its claustrophobic, isolated setting, gory details, and strong action sequences, this book is sure to win over horror fans, but there is also a powerful underlying philosophical aspect here, which ponders the meaning of family, love, and community. . . . Imagine that Bentley Little or the late Richard Laymon tried their hand at writing a Cormac McCarthy novel, and you understand who will enjoy this story."

—*Booklist* (starred review)

"For all horror fans, this is the latest—maybe *greatest*—novel to come from the mind of the frightening Nick Cutter to date . . . portraying images, as always, that stay in your mind and stop calm, peaceful sleep from coming."

—*Suspense Magazine*

"A sprawling epic that can stand alongside the best of '80s King, Barker, and McCammon. . . . Fun, nasty, smart, and scary, and in all the right places."

—Paul Tremblay, acclaimed author of
A Head Full of Ghosts and *Disappearance at Devil's Rock*

"Terrifying. . . . The kind of horror that remains in the room of the reader. It's as if Nick Cutter spun a very human yarn into the myriad folds of a monster."

—Josh Malerman, acclaimed author of *Bird Box*

LITTLE HEAVEN

A Novel

NICK CUTTER

ILLUSTRATIONS BY ADAM GORHAM

GALLERY BOOKS

New York   London   Toronto   Sydney   New Delhi

G

Gallery Books
An Imprint of Simon & Schuster, Inc.
1230 Avenue of the Americas
New York, NY 10020

First Gallery Books trade paperback edition July 2017

GALLERY BOOKS and colophon are registered trademarks of Simon & Schuster, Inc.

Excerpt from *House Made of Dawn* by N. Scott Momaday. Copyright © 1966, 1967,
1968 by N. Scott Momaday. Reprinted by permission of HarperCollins Publishers.

For information about special discounts for bulk purchases,
please contact Simon & Schuster Special Sales at 1-866-506-1949
or business@simonandschuster.com.

The Simon & Schuster Speakers Bureau can bring authors
to your live event. For more information or to book an event,
contact the Simon & Schuster Speakers Bureau at 1-866-248-3049
or visit our website at www.simonspeakers.com.

Interior design by Davina Mock-Maniscalco

Manufactured in the United States of America

20 19 18 17 16

The Library of Congress has cataloged the hardcover edition as follows:

Names: Cutter, Nick, author.
Title: Little heaven : a novel / Nick Cutter.
Description: First Gallery Books hardcover edition. | New York : Gallery Books, 2016.
Identifiers: LCCN 2016000320 | ISBN 9781501104213 (hardcover : acid-free paper) |
    ISBN 9781501104237 (softcover : acid-free paper) | ISBN 9781501104220 (ebook)
Subjects: | GSAFD: Horror fiction. | Suspense fiction.
Classification: LCC PS3603.U883 L58 2016 | DDC 813/.6—dc23
LC record available at http://lccn.loc.gov/2016000320

ISBN 978-1-5011-0421-3
ISBN 978-1-5011-0423-7 (pbk)
ISBN 978-1-5011-0422-0 (ebook)

There was a house made of dawn. It was made of pollen and of rain, and the land was very old and everlasting. There were many colors on the hills, and the plain was bright with different-colored clays and sands.

—N. Scott Momaday

TAKEN

1980

1

THERE IS A SAYING THAT GOES: *Evil never dies; it merely sleeps.* And when that evil awakes, it can do so soundlessly—or almost so.

Even insects can scream.

The little aphid did, though at a register too high for any human ear to perceive. It toiled in the root system of a cactus plant growing on the edge of the New Mexico desert. An insect so small that it was practically invisible to the naked eye.

This was how it would begin again. The wheel coming around.

While the aphid fed on sugars deposited in the cactus roots, something curled up from the blackest recesses of the earth. It slipped inside the aphid's body. If there was any pain—and yes, there would be—the insect was unable to articulate its agony beyond that thin scream.

The aphid trundled up the root stem, through the loose-packed sand, up onto one of the cactus's fleshy leaves. There it encountered a honey ant, which fed on the honeydew that aphids produce.

Their antennae touched briefly. Whatever had stolen inside the aphid slipped soundlessly into the ant—something as inessential as the smoke billowing from the chimney of a charnel house.

The aphid erupted with a tiny pressurized hiss.

The ant returned to its hill, skittering through a fall of lemony afternoon sunlight. It disappeared down the hole. Shortly afterward, the hill emptied, ants pouring forth in furious multitudes.

The ants organized themselves in a skirmish line like soldiers on the march, and proceeded determinedly until they came to the burrow of a meadow mouse. They filed down the burrow, thousand upon thousand. There came an agonized squeal.

Presently the mouse emerged. It hopped and shook, its skin squirming. The mouse spun a few agitated circles before righting itself and dashing into the dry grass. It paused here and there to gnaw at its flesh, drawing blood. In time, it crossed paths with a desert shrew. Moments later there arose a high, mindless shriek.

The shrew encountered an opossum, which in turn encountered a black-tailed jackrabbit, which hurled itself screechingly into the jaws of a kit fox, which thrashed and gibbered and scurried into a den that housed a family of jaguarundis. More shrieks cresting across the arid expanse of sand.

Night fell over the desert. In the darkness, something shambled from the den. The moon touched upon its strange extrusions, its flesh shining wetly in the pale moonlight. It breathed through many mouths and gazed through a cluster of eyes lodged in a knot of fatted, blood-streaked fur. It locomoted on many legs, each of them foreshortened, compressed like the bellows of an accordion; the creature, whatever it was, scuttled in the manner of a crab. This abomination carried itself across the sands, moving stealthily, its quartet of snouts dilated to the breeze.

A solitary gray wolf sat on a rocky outcropping, scanning the mesa. An old wolf, much scarred, an ear torn off in some long-ago territorial battle. The wolf spotted movement. A shape shambled into view. This thing moved as though wounded, and yet the wolf's predatory instincts said, *No, no, no*—this thing was not hurt. It was . . . something else.

The wolf loped off to investigate. It was wary but unafraid. If this other creature could bleed, the wolf would bleed it.

It had no fear. The wolf was apex. It had never encountered a creature that was its equal, not once in its long life.

HOURS LATER, the thing, now substantially larger, shuffled to a patch of sand. A patch dramatically darker than the surrounding earth. The trees sprouting from its black and oily surface were gnarled and stooped, yet grimly alive in a way that indicated suffering.

Diligently, the thing began to dig. The hole widened and grew deeper. The sand became darker until it was obsidian, as if it had been soaked in tar.

The creature encountered something buried in that unnatural blackness. Its many snouts snaffled, its mouths groaning and squealing.

Then: that something moved. A great shuddering exhale. The creature backpedaled madly, scrambling out of the pit.

From someplace in the vaulted sky came the screech of a bird of prey.

2

PETTY SHUGHRUE awoke in the still hours of night with her skin rashed in gooseflesh.

Pet. My sweet Pet.

She sat up. The wind hissed through chinks in the farmhouse walls, between the joists her father had imprecisely hammered home.

Come, my Pet. Come see, come see, come see . . .

The voice was inviting, honeyed. Yet something lurked behind its sweetness. Corrupted and lewd, like a dead man's face staring up from the bottom of a shallow pool.

She swung her legs off the bed; the pine boards were cool on her bare feet. She wore the nightdress her mother had sewn for her before she was even big enough to wear it. Her mother had always been two steps ahead—it was in her nature to make Petty a new nightdress before she had outgrown the old one. Her mother wasn't like that anymore, but Petty preferred to remember her that way.

Her throat itched with thirst. She walked into the kitchen, passing the support post where her father recorded her height every birthday, notching it with a Magic Marker. Petty's feet whispered on the floor— odd, as usually the creaking timbers woke her father, who was such a light sleeper that the sound of a sparrow settling on a windowsill was enough to stir him.

From somewhere far away—like a musical voice from the edge of a dream—she heard the trilling notes of a flute.

She stepped outside. The night was cool, the grass silky under her bare feet. The moon was slit by a thin night cloud. She walked to the water pump and set the bucket under its spout. The pump squealed as she worked its handle. Water sloshed out, silvered by the moonlight as it splashed into the bucket . . . except it didn't look like water. Too *thick*, with a coppery undernote.

My Pet, oh, my Pet, sweet as sun-warmed honey . . .

She dipped a ladle into the bucket and raised it to her lips, although something buried deep inside her fought the instinct. Heavy, salty, metallic, the way she imagined molten iron might taste. She drank more. It was good, though it did not slake her. If anything, her thirst intensified.

Scuttling movement to her left. She swung toward it, alarmed.

Something was standing there. *Standing?* No, it slumped. Huge and shapeless, like a heap of quarry stones covered in burlap. Its parts appeared to move independently of one another, the whole mass hissing and emitting thin squeals and murmurs. The head of a wolf hung off its flanks—it looked as if it had been killed and decapitated and slung on its side . . . but Petty sensed the wolf's head was somehow a part of this thing, of a piece with the rest of its lunatic assembly.

This living nightmare shambled closer. Petty's skin went cold all over.

Something else was standing behind that awful mass. A long weedy shape, more human than not, a twist of living smoke. It looked a little like a man's body that had been melted and elongated like taffy.

This figure did not speak, but Petty could *feel* it. The thing gave off a brooding wickedness—yet it also struck her as somehow bored, as if it had grown weary of all the horrible things it had seen and done. Petty was filled with the sense that this thing was utterly, fundamentally malevolent—shot through to the core with it—and so, weary or not, it could only continue to be and to do what it had always been and done.

"My Pet," it said. "Ooooh, my sweet morsel . . ."

It lifted something to its lips. A serrate-bone flute.

When it began to play, Petty had no choice but to follow it.

PART ONE

THE

SUMMONING

1980

1

THE LION IN WINTER

MICAH HENRY SHUGHRUE awoke into a darkness so thick it was like all nights folded together.

He sat up in bed with an unspeakable fear crazing through his vitals—a stark wash of terror, bubonic rats scuttling through his veins. He reached for his wife. Ellen's breaths came unrushed, the bones of her wrist frail and birdlike under the thin stretching of skin.

He plucked his eye from the bowl on the nightstand. He never slept with it in. But he didn't like Petty to see him without it in—the flesh inside the socket cured like pig leather. He thumbed it into place and said, "I will look in on Pet."

Ellen would not answer. She never did. Her eyes were open—they almost always were nowadays—but invisible under the two moisturized pads wedged beneath her eyelids.

Micah stood in his sleeping flannels. Their daughter, Petty, slept in a room off the kitchen. The house was silent as he made his way through it. He eased his daughter's door open. Instantly he felt it. An absence. That clotted, stinging darkness holding nothing at all.

Micah's breath rasped as his remaining eye adjusted. The blankets had been folded back at one corner, as if his daughter had slid out for a drink of water—she did this sometimes in the summer when the heat lay leaden inside the walls. One evening he'd found her at the pump, the hem of her nightdress wet with water. He had chastised her, not wanting her to make a habit of being out of doors at night. But the water was cooler from the pump, she'd said, so much better than the tepid stuff that ran from the kitchen tap.

"Pet?" he said, sure that he would get no reply. His mind was quickly turning to the solidity of her disappearance.

He had been dreading this moment since the day she was born.

He moved swiftly through the house. She was nowhere inside. The back door was ajar. He stepped outside. The fields rolled away under the moon, flat and endless. The Black Mountain range tilted against the horizon.

"Pet?" he called.

The wind curled around his ankles. He went back inside. He stepped into his boots and donned his duster, then went back out.

He gazed across the moon-silvered field. Beyond it, miles off, rose knuckled hillsides that, come summer, would be clad in flaming poke-weed. The barn door was open—had he forgotten to shut it? He crossed the field and stepped into the barn. He felt his way through the shuddering horseflesh and climbed a ladder to the hayloft.

The trunk was where he'd left it, covered in a horsehair blanket. He had not gazed upon it in years. It held his old life. That was a time best left shut.

The trunk's innards smelled of gun oil and old blood. He retrieved one pistol, then the next. They felt good in his hands. Like brothers, like sisters, like homecoming.

Both guns were highly modified. Russian Tokarevs bored out to chamber .45 rounds. Their barrels had been filed to four inches. Micah had also ground off the sights—sights were useless at close range, and anyway, they might snag when clearing concealment. One gun had a mother-of-pearl grip; the other, sandalwood. He loaded them and slid them into the pockets of his duster.

Outside, the fields lay spectral in the witching hours. Ground fog ribboned along the earth. Micah marched toward a forest of piñon and ponderosa pines at the edge of his property—past the tree line, the land was still wild.

I should not have closed my eye, he thought. *Should not have let my guard down.*

Fifteen years. A long time to keep one's guard up. Hellishly long for even the hardest of men. That man can try to sleep with one eye open, keeping watch over those he loves and fosters . . . but every man has to sleep sometime.

And he'd felt it coming, hadn't he? Something gathering toward his family—a feeling not unlike the thunder of hooves as a stampede approaches. He might as well have tried to outrun his own skin. You cannot outfox the devil. You may be able to stay his approach if you're lucky and a little crazy, but in the end, his black eye will ferret you out.

A tatter of cloth hung from a piñon branch. A pattern of cabbage flowers, faded from washing. Petty's nightdress.

Micah stepped into the trees, treading on a carpet of brown needles. His body ached. His knees were about cooked and his arms felt heavy. Age makes fools of us all. There was nothing to track—no blood, thank Christ, and his daughter's bare feet would leave no impression. His heart thumped ponderously in his chest, but he walked with care, his working eye half lidded as though he might fall back asleep. The fear he had felt upon waking, the fear that had spiked when he discovered his daughter's bed empty, was now gone. He cursed his own inner coolness—the very trait that had distinguished him in his past life.

Do I not care enough for my daughter to feel true panic? What other father would react this way, under these same circumstances?

He came upon a clearing. A shape stood in the fall of moonlight. It was black, as if its body had been carved from the surrounding night. It was unmoving, but Micah could tell that its eyes, so many of them, were focused on him with a commingling of baleful mockery and something that smacked of pity: the flat stare of a cottonmouth as it gazed upon a field mouse.

"Give her back," Micah said.

The thing shuffled forward. Its body rippled as if in delight. It gave off an odor that reminded Micah of the night, years ago, when he had awoken to hear scratching inside the walls at a hotel in Carson City. There was a hole the size of a thumbnail where two walls met; carpenter ants—the most enormous he'd ever seen—spilled through the hole, numberless in their multitudes, sheeting down the plaster like bristling dark molasses. They carried with them the same dry, festering stink he smelled now—metallic, vinegary, somehow vulgar.

The thing issued a gargling hack. Was it trying to speak? It capered and sloshed; its body teemed with quarrelsome movements. The sense of déjà vu was overwhelming; he was nauseated by it. This had happened before, all of it. Yet it had the feel of a dream, something that had once occurred in a fantasyland—someplace far away and long, long ago.

"Give her back," he said again.

The thing made a clotted rattle that might have been its attempt at laughter. Its head, or one of its heads, cocked to one side—*too far*, as if its neck had been snapped and had surrendered to the bulbous weight of its skull . . .

But Micah knew it wasn't a head he was looking at—heads were appendages gracing men and beasts, and this thing was neither of those. Micah had not dealt with such creatures in so, so long. Staring at its shuddering shape filled him with exhaustion so dreadful that it was as if the hollows of his bones had been flooded with lead.

The thing shook with what could be mistaken for mirth, the ribbed and fatty texture of its body jiggling. Why was he speaking to it? He knew where Petty was—or would soon be, anyway. He spat on the browned pine needles and reached for his smoke wagons.

"What in hell do I need you for?"

His hands lit up with thunder. Bullets tore into the thing. Parts of its body ripped free and spun into the dark. The creature slumped to the ground and attempted to crawl or flop toward Micah, heaving itself forward in torturous paroxysms. Micah paused, the gunpowder stinging his nose, and took careful aim. He plugged the final four rounds into what he felt to be its skull, or skulls. The thing jerked and bucked. Then it stopped, all told.

Micah slammed fresh clips into his pistols. He holstered one and approached the thing with the other one drawn.

The creature lay prone, its body issuing a queer hum. Putrid fumes carried off it. Meat from many species of animal all crushed together, the bones jutting slantwise and the exposed fatty tissues shining butter-yellow in the moonlight. He spied the crumpled head of a jaguarundi that had been stitched through some horrific process to the shell of an armadillo. There were elements of birds, of fish, of serpents—and a swath of tawny flesh that might have once draped the skull of a luckless hiker. The corrugated canvas of flesh and fur was maggot-ridden and pocked with ichor-filled boils.

The head of a wolf hung off one side; its eyes had been sucked out and added to the muscat bunch that stared woodenly from the middle of the thing's chest.

Micah had no inkling how these atrocities came to be. He knew them only as the handmaidens of his old nemesis. He couldn't guess at the wicked animus filling their bodies. The hum intensified. The heap of corrupted meat convulsed. Micah stepped back. One of the thing's skulls—eyeless, featureless, nothing but a bloated bladder of mismatched organ meats and pelts—swelled and threatened to burst . . .

And then it did. It ripped raggedly apart. Insects poured out. Weevils and bark beetles and deer ticks, millipedes and sightless moths, ladybugs with blackly diseased wings. The thing deflated as the bugs deserted it in a scuttle of legs and carapaces and wriggling antennae—

From somewhere in the night, distant and dimming:

The trill of a flute.

2

THE HIRED GUN

WHEN YOU WHITTLED right down to the nub of it, killing yourself was a matter of will. You had to find that iron in your spine. The gumption to carry your soul into the dark.

Minerva Atwater sat at the desk in her room at the Beldings Motel in the one-horse town of Ludo, Nevada. She nursed the hope that the man she had come to see would be the one who killed her.

The motel was a cesspool. Appropriately, her room was a dump. At least the place stayed on theme. The orange shag carpet was studded with cigarette burns. An arrogant roach skittered across the popcorn ceiling like an ambulatory scab. Minerva could afford better, but this room suited her present temperament.

On the desk sat a box. Inside the box was an old-style syringe kit. Early 1900s vintage, before companies began manufacturing disposable needles. She'd found it in an antiques store in Sedona, Arizona. It was the sort of thing she could imagine a genteel morphine addict using—a brain surgeon or a bank manager. The initials G.P.G. were stamped on its copper plating. Who the hell bought a monogrammed drug needle?

The syringe was two inches long, polished steel, with a large-bore needle. The antiques store owner had sold it to her for twenty bucks. He said she had a fine eye for this sort of thing.

An eye for what, needles? she had thought. *Oh yeah, you betcha.*

Seven or eight thermometers also sat on the desk. She'd bought them at a Rite Aid earlier that same day. Inside each was a drop of mercury. She remembered her father telling her a story about the medicine men who used to travel around in the Old West days, selling mercury as a restorative. Laird's Bloom of Youth, goofy names like that. Those quacks would claim it'd put the apple back in a woman's cheeks and restore the ruby to her lips. Which was pure horseshit. Painting your face with quicksilver was about as restorative as gargling pony piss—but at least piss wouldn't kill you.

But then, Minny did want to die. It was just about the only thing she wanted out of life anymore.

She set a plastic spoon on the desk and cracked a thermometer open over it. The glass snapped crisply, depositing a bead of silver into the spoon. She did the same with the rest of the thermometers, then drew all the mercury into the syringe. She looped a bootlace round her arm above her elbow, clamped one end between her teeth and cinched it. Her arms were thin, so it didn't take much to raise a vein.

Once upon a time she'd heard the whispers. *That girl's so skinny she could take a bath in a shotgun barrel.* Or: *Like a snake on stilts, that one.* But she hadn't heard those whispers in many a moon. In a weird way, she missed them.

The needle slid into a fat vein. Her skin dimpled, and the tip punched right in. The first time she'd tried swallowing the mercury, but she'd just gone dizzy and thrown up. No, right into the bloodstream seemed best.

She inhaled deeply—she could taste the poison at the back of her mouth: warm, with a metallic edge—and retrieved her pistols from their case. They slid into pancake holsters on either side of her rib cage. She pulled her long duster coat on over them.

Maybe tonight. She hoped to Christ so. Christ or whoever might be up there looking down on her small life, on all humanity, our every sad endeavor.

Please, she thought, *show some mercy. Just a little. Haven't I earned it?*

The answer came on the wind that fussed with the drapes edging the open window.

Oh no, my child. You haven't suffered nearly enough yet.

THE MOTEL BAR was practically empty. A stag-antler chandelier cast its glow over the interior. The sound system was playing "Boogie Oogie Oogie" by A Taste of Honey. A pair of rubby-dubs occupied seats in opposite corners, where they drank with quiet desperation. A third man was shitfaced, smoking a cigar at the end of the bar.

"Whiskey," she said. The barkeep brought a glass.

Minerva said, "Leave the bottle. *Oogie oogie.*"

The bartender was heavy, with a walrus mustache and old-timey sleeve garters. He looked like a big fat idiot, and she almost told him so. She could feel him clandestinely taking her measure. What he saw was a tall woman of tubercular slenderness, pale eyes, dark hair shaved nearly to the skull. But if he considered her closely—if he looked directly into her eyes, so different from those of the four-bit whores he doubtlessly trafficked in—he would see . . . well, *something*. It spun and capered behind her golden irises, which seemed to tick clockwise, snipping off each second.

But he would not look too closely—no man ever did—because Minerva's gaze had a withering effect; it seized something precious inside of you, shriveling it like a cellophane wrapper tossed onto an open flame.

Minny drank a shot of whiskey, another, another. Her arm pumphandled the hooch into her mouth. She felt good—more to the point, she felt like day-old owl shit. The mercury was percolating merrily through her system. It hurt quite badly, but she'd withstood much worse. She hoped she could force enough whiskey into herself to dull things further without throwing up.

If I do this right, she thought, *any donkey dick with a gopher gun should be able to irrigate me right between the eyes.*

Minny had made other attempts to do herself in. The first time had been . . . Christ, when was that now? A pauper's cemetery near the Mexican border. She'd killed a man, or maybe it was two or three. They died as they always did, with screwed-up looks on their faces that said they had witnessed a terrible reckoning just before the door slammed shut. Afterward, Minny had perched on a tombstone and socked the barrel of her Colt M1911 under her chin. She cocked the hammer, wanting it so badly but knowing—without even pulling the trigger—it wouldn't work.

The deal didn't work like that. It was a compact etched in blood—hers and the Englishman's and Micah Shughrue's, too. Their blood, and the blood of the black thing that had tendered the deal.

You can't walk it back. You can't welsh on a deal that fills your very veins.

She'd pulled the trigger anyway. What was the harm in trying? Hah! There had come a lifting sensation, her body a sail filling with wind . . . She came to sometime that night, though it could've been the next. The moon shone over the gravestones. Her hair was matted with blood and hardened curds that she instinctively identified as her own brains. But she was fine. Intact. Nothing but a small coin-shaped scar on the top of her head where she used to part her hair before she'd taken to shaving it.

She'd tried other ways, sure. Pills. Hanging. Slitting her wrists with a barber's straight razor. One night she paid a man eighty dollars to stab her out back of a porno theater. The man had seemed the sort to stab a woman for eighty dollars, though he might have done it for free if she'd proposed it. There was little negotiation or discussion. He'd just smiled and begun to stab her with a bone-handled fillet knife, powerful thrusts to her belly and chest. The pain sizzled through her as the knife sliced sideways, sawing through velvety muscle. The man was a dab hand with a blade; he might have had some butchery training. They were both grunting: she from the pain and the air whoofing from her lungs with each knife thrust, he from plain old exertion. Minny had braced her hands on his shoulders to stay steady and aid him at his task. She'd stared into the man's bright magpie eyes as her blood splashed the oily cement, until she slipped gratefully into the black . . .

When she came to, the man was dead, his neck slit so deep that Minny could see the gleam of his severed windpipe. She was fine, of course. A few shallow scratches on her stomach. She had then dragged the man's body behind a dumpster, leaving him beside a box of sun-bleached porn magazines with titles like *Old Farts* and *Fifty and Nifty*.

But right now, tonight . . . yes, it would be different. She couldn't kill herself, and she couldn't induce someone else to do it. The deed had to be committed fairly. She had to lose. Well, she wasn't a sore loser. Tonight she'd get herself good and properly killed.

"Boogie Oogie Oogie" segued into "I'm Your Boogie Man," by KC and the Sunshine Band. Had she stumbled into some kind of half-assed theme night? Minerva dropped another shot of whiskey down her throat. A woman came out of the men's bathroom. A jaundiced-looking businessman followed her out, hitching up his slacks.

The woman elbowed up beside Minny.

"How about it, pal—you want a ride?"

Minny turned to face her. The whore leaned back.

"Ah, shit," she said, pronouncing it as *sheeee-it*. She was stoned out of her gourd. "I thought you was a dude."

Her laugh was nasty. Her hands were covered in scabies, and her nose had been busted a few times. "Well, so what?" she said, more to herself than Minerva. "It wouldn't be my first time with a chick." She wiggled her hips. "What do you say?"

"Oh, I imagine not," Minny said breezily. "I'd rather eat cat shit with a pair of chopsticks, to tell you the truth."

"I will leave you to it, then," the whore slurred, unfussed, and sidled down the bar toward the drunk smoking the cigar.

Minny heard the growl of a pickup truck. The light of headlamps washed over the bar's dust-clad windows. She tossed another shot down her throat.

The door squealed open on its rusted hinges. The clopping of boots.

"You the one they sent?"

Minerva turned sluggishly. Dizzy, sick, drunk. *Good.*

"Yuh," she said, and burped. "I'm all of it."

The man looked like they always did. Leathery, rawboned, a face raked by the wind. A hard man made harder by the awfulness he had committed. A man untroubled by his past. She could not tell by looking if he felt any remorse for the things he had done—the things that had put his name on the breeze, put him in the wheelhouse of her employers, put her on a path to this very meeting. She did not rightly care. He probably saw himself as a fox set loose in a sheep pen—how could he be blamed for doing what came naturally to him? And who knows? Maybe he really was that fox. Sadly for him, she was a wolf.

"The lady shootist," the man said. "I heard of you, but I thought you wasn't real. Just a spook story."

Minny said, "You will find that I'm real enough."

The man's gaze was cold, but then they always were right up until the end, when they turned fear-struck and childish.

He smiled. "I hear my head's worth twenty grand."

Minny shook her head. A heavy lead block had replaced her brain. "You'll fetch five grand per ear, if I'm lucky."

"That's not too shabby," the man said, proud at the price.

"I've done better."

The man's smile evaporated. "I'm sure you have. But what about taking me alive—you get any more for that?"

Minny said, "Never bothered to ask."

The man's jaw set. "What if I go without a fuss?"

"Do you have a mind to do so?"

The man shook his head.

"Then I saved myself the haggling," Minny slurred.

The man said: "Look at you! You're drunk as a tick!"

Minny laughed at the odd turn of phrase. Then she spoke so everyone else in the bar could hear. "You best all clear out. And none of you even think about calling the authorities. This will be done soon enough."

The patrons obediently departed. Minny's sight was failing, but she could see shapes behind the bar's front windows. The parking lot lights glinted off shotgun barrels.

"You brought help."

"I heard about you, was all," the man said evenly. "Got the devil's own luck."

It isn't luck when all you want to do is die, son.

"What do you say we part company in good faith?" the man said. "You go your way and we ours. There are other bounties, aren't there? Other men."

"The only time I ever shot a man in the back was when he was running away." She opened her palms to him. "There are things a man can't run away from, boy. And I am sorry to say that tonight you've run clean out of road."

The man opened his leather bomber jacket. A pistol was tucked into his belt above his Confederate Eagle belt buckle.

"I ain't your *boy*, bitch. I'll kill you," he said. "Dead as a beaver hat, that's you."

This fellow was a fount of old-timey sayings, wasn't he? Instead of laughing, Minny swooned. Guts heaving, bowels thudding, eyes screwed tight like pissholes in the snow. *Dead as a beaver hat? How quaint. I like your spirit, boy.*

She made no move for her pistols. Her arms were crossed. The man's hand twitched above the grips of his own gun.

Be a crack shot, she prayed. *Put one slug through my pump house, another through my brain box. That would meet the terms of the pact. All fair, all final.*

It happened then—right that very instant—even though she did everything to fight it.

The Sharpening.

That was what she called it. Some natural mechanism snapping on. Her every sense became more attuned. Her view of the world expanded and shrank at the same time—she could see everything, the tiniest detail. The sweat on the man's forehead, each bead set to pop from his skin. The curve of the men's jaws beyond the windows, the tension of their fingers on the triggers of their scatterguns. Everything came into perfect focus: it was like staring at things through a huge magnifying glass. And she could operate within this view with total confidence and speed while everyone around her struggled like ants in molasses.

The man went for his gun—too slow, too goddamn fuckingly cocksuckingly slow.

Come at me, man! Quickly! Fill your Christing hand!

Her own hands uncrossed and moved toward her weapons with sickening swiftness. The next moment her fingers had wrapped around her Colts—*I should have fixed them in the holsters with Krazy Glue*, she thought—the barrels coming up smoothly. The guns kicked as bullets leapt from their muzzles, wasping through the air and hitting the young man spang in the heart and head, flinging him backward before his pistol had even cleared his hips.

Minny swiveled, no longer fighting it, giving herself over to the devil in her bloodstream. Perfect holes snapped through the windows—*pip! pip!*—as bullets drilled through the glass and into the men outside, slugs slamming into their bulging eyes and coring through the obliging softness, then out the backs of their skulls in a gout of sticky pink.

By then the Sharpening was already retreating. Like a sneak thief, it came and did its filthy business and left without a trace.

The young man's body had been blown clean out the door. His boots stuck straight up in the air. Something between a sob and a scream built in Minny's throat.

Goddamn you. I've had enough. Goddamn you. Let me die.

The answer came in the wind curling between the dead man's boots.

Suffer. Suffer as you have made me suffer . . .

She shouldered the door open, stumbling outside. The dead man's skull shone in the moonlight, the scalp blown apart and a bubbly purple foam emitting from the brain with a pressurized gurgle. His wide-open eyes stared at the sky, the corneas gone milky in death.

. . . or you may come to me, child, the voice taunted. *You still know the place, don't you? We can face each other as deal makers do. Strike a bargain.*

Her marrow went cold. She felt it that way exactly: the brown bone soup crystalizing into ice inside her bones, as cold as hoarfrost in a mountain pass.

Come to me, girl. Why play at this? Let us end these silly games.

She walked in the opposite direction of that voice—which was impossible, as it came from all points of the compass. It whispered inside her head in a voice she dared not name.

3

THE GARDENER

THE MAN the townsfolk knew as Gardener walked into the Glory with a Deathstalker in a glass jar.

The man had gone by other names in other places. Some had known him as English Bill (though his name was not William) or simply the Englishman. Others had known him as the Whispering Death. Still others had known him by no name at all—his presence had been nothing but a shadow darkening their periphery before their lights were snuffed out.

But the people of Old Ditch, a decaying boomtown on the border of California and Arizona, knew him as Gardener. If townsfolk insisted on a proper name—and sometimes they did, as folks in small towns can be suspicious of nameless people—he would answer to Elton, though this was no more his name than William was. The mail that arrived at his house was often addressed to other names, too, none of them his own.

But the people of Old Ditch knew him as Gardener. The fact that he was black helped in this regard—in the South, it was not uncommon for black men to be hailed by their jobs rather than their birth names. It might be Cook or Baker or, yes, Gardener. There was rarely any cruelty to it, despite the fact that it was dehumanizing. It was simply how things were done. Everyone accepted it, more or less. Even Gardener did, now. Years ago he would not have been so obliging—in fact, he might have cut your tongue out if you refused to call him by his Christian name, or whatever name he commanded.

Gardener had earned this name in the common way. He *was* a gardener. When he'd arrived in Old Ditch, the Rawlston Paperworks was going great guns; the surrounding woods were harvested, pulped, rolled out in sheets of clean white hundred-bond and shipped off to the ivory towers of academia, to Wall Street, to mom-and-pop shops around the country. The women married to the Paperworks executives hired him to tend their flower beds while they fanned themselves on their whitewashed porches and said, "Good work, boy, very good"—calling him *boy* despite the fact that he was often their elder. He tended the grounds at the Mission Church, making sure the marigolds and snapdragons were in full bloom from spring through early summer, and the orange glories and peonies on into the fall. Come the cooler months he'd sweep the church and do odd jobs for the pastor. It was a good and quiet existence . . . in the daylight hours, anyway.

The Glory, a bar at the end of Old Ditch's straggle-ass main street, was deserted when Gardener stepped into it that day. It was not long past noon, an unseemly hour to be seen inside a drinking establishment. Many of the buildings lining Old Ditch's main thoroughfare lay empty, their doors boarded over. The Paperworks had eaten the woods and shuttered its doors before moving on to another patch of unsullied wilderness, leaving the town to rot into itself.

Gardener limped to the bar and sat down under a poster for Camel unfiltered cigarettes; it featured an overweight police officer smoking against the door of his patrol car, the sun sparkling off his aviator sunglasses. *Have a REAL cigarette—have a CAMEL.* Gardener could see his own reflection in the fly-spotted mirror behind the bar. His hair, which he had once worn long and straight, was clipped close to his skull and flecked with gray. His skin was ashy dark, as it had been uncommonly warm of late and he washed with carbolic soap, which dried his skin. He set the glass jar with the Deathstalker on the bar.

"Whiskey," he said.

The tender was a God-fearing man named Clayton Suggs. He had bought the bar and its stock a year ago for a pittance—it took no time at all to discover he had been rooked, but by then, the bar's old owner was miles clear of Old Ditch and surely laughing like a bastard. Suggs's only hope of financial gain would be to sell the place for its wood, but there was nobody to buy it, seeing as the Paperworks had fucked off and left.

"Bit early for the hard stuff, wouldn't you say?" said Suggs.

"I haven't touched a drop in fifteen years. But time makes liars of us all, Mr. Suggs." Gardener's words held a trace of the English accent he'd carried across the Atlantic many years ago. "You need not trifle yourself over it."

Suggs frowned. It wasn't that he didn't care for blacks in his establishment—beggars can't be choosers, and if the man had folding money, he was welcome to a stool. But he knew Gardener only slightly, having seen him hunched over in yards around town, and the man had never looked entirely healthy. It wasn't just his pronounced limp, the way he dragged that one gimpy leg behind him like a curse. His body was skel-etal inside his overalls, his wrists and ankles birdlike and queerly femi-nine. Suggs suspected his ill health was a product of those pansy *British* genes. Englishmen always appeared cadaverous to Suggs. And Gardener looked particularly bloodless at the moment, as if vampire bats had been at him. More than that, he appeared . . . haunted. His eyes sank far into his sockets, as if they had witnessed an event of such horror that they had retreated into his skull.

Yet Suggs had always sensed a strength in the man, too—dormant, but bubbling just under the surface. A *wrath*, Suggs suspected, even a dangerous malignancy of character that the man struggled to keep bottled up. Old Ditch was a harder place now, populated by men who'd snatch the pennies off a corpse's eyes . . . but nobody ever laid a hand on Gar-dener. There was this gut instinct that if any man were to do so, that man might draw back a stump.

Suggs set the whiskey bottle on the bar. "I'll put it within reach, champ, but I am for damn sure not pouring it."

"Good man. I shall administer the dose personally. *Cura te ipsum.*"

"Whuh?" Suggs said.

"Physician, heal thyself."

Gardener poured a heroic measure. Suggs made a mental note to charge him double for it. His eyes fell upon the Deathstalker. The scor-pion was eight inches long and dark as midnight. Its claws clicked upon the glass jar.

Suggs said, "I can't imagine why in hell you'd bring that in here."

"Well." Gardener nodded. "It is here now, as I have brought it."

"And you'll keep it in the damned jar, too," Suggs said.

"Fifteen years," Gardener said, speaking more to himself than to Suggs. "It's a very long time to go without a drink. And my life has been much improved for it."

"Let me take the bottle away, then. Let that improvement continue."

Gardener gave Suggs a look. The spit dried up in Suggs's mouth—something in his spirit fled from the dark holes that sat at the center of the black man's eyes.

"I'd be obliged were you to find it in your heart to leave it, Mr. Suggs. It will be a balm to my wounded spirit."

Gardener took a sip of whiskey. He winced.

"Tell me, Mr. Suggs. Perchance, did you use this swill to strip the old paint off your car?"

"Don't have a car anymore," Suggs said woodenly. "Bank took it."

Gardener unscrewed the jar's lid. He set the jar on its side. The scorpion crept over the rim and hesitated two inches from Gardener's hand, which lay palm-down on the bar.

"What the hell's got into you?" said Suggs.

"Have you ever seen the face of the devil?" Gardener asked quietly.

Quite suddenly, Suggs felt a strong urge to urinate. He no longer wanted to be in this place with this man.

"It is my judgment that people believe they have seen the devil." Gardener drummed his fingers on the bar. The Deathstalker reared back, poised to strike. "They have seen the devil in the faces of wicked men, and at the sight of murdered women and children. But they have no inkling of the real devil and the horrors he can bring."

Gardener's voice had gone breathless and dreamy. His fingers tap-tapped . . .

The scorpion darted forward and jabbed its stinger in the back of his hand. If Gardener's features twitched, Suggs did not notice it. The Deathstalker's body flexed as it pumped in poison. Gardener picked up the whiskey glass with his other hand and drained it at a go.

"Mr. Suggs, the quality of your whiskey is poor, and so truly, I cannot tell you what is worse. Drinking this"—he held up the empty glass—"or enduring this." He tapped the glass on the scorpion's exoskeleton. It made a sound like champagne glasses clinking during a toast.

Gardener sloshed more whiskey into his glass, pouring with his free hand. The scorpion gripped his other hand in its pincers. It was beginning to draw blood.

"You have been envenomed," Suggs said hoarsely.

Gardener closed his eyes. He raised the glass to his lips. The gutrot washed down his throat with a fiery itch. The scorpion's stinger was embedded in his skin. The creature struggled to pull itself free but could not—Gardener's flesh was swollen tight, trapping it.

A miscalculation evident in men just as it is in beasts, he reflected. *The urge to kill can be so great that a creature overextends itself, and in so doing threatens its own life.*

Gardener had served the citizenry of Old Ditch faithfully for many years. He had served it in clandestine ways, too. Four years ago, a pair of petty drifters and brothers named Horace and Eldred Bilks had raped a prostitute at the old Fairfax motel. They had been hell-raising around town a few days by then. Evidently the girl had made some offhand remark about Eldred Bilks's harelip, about which he was sensitive. The younger and more sadistic of the two brothers, Eldred had lashed the woman to the hitch of his pickup and dragged her five hundred yards down a gravel road, busting her elbows and one kneecap. She was twenty-two and considered a looker before the incident.

Gardener had been planting pansies at a house a block or so from the Fairfax when the screams broke out. A few minutes later came the screech of tires as the brothers laid tracks. Next, an ambulance screamed past. What Gardener didn't see, and knew he would not see, was a police car. Not anytime soon. The sheriff, a sniveling wretch named Gorse Ellson, had no taste for the kind of violence those brothers could bring. *It's just some whore*, Ellson would tell himself. *No use getting hurt over it.*

Knowing this, Gardener fell to grim musings. The woman worshipped regularly at the Mission Church. Her soul was clean, if not her body.

Gardener walked to his small home and lifted a loose floorboard under his bed. Underneath were three pistols: two German Mausers in a beechwood box, plus a smaller Paterson model. He had arrived in Old Ditch with these and little else years ago. The sole tether to his old life. He would take them out to clean and oil them every year, only to rest them back beneath the boards. But that day he holstered one of the Mausers and hung the Paterson on a length of wire descending from his left armpit. He pulled on his felt coat and set off.

He did not own a car. But he was adept at hot-wiring them—a trick learned in the sad old, bad old days. He found an unlocked Dodge Dart behind the coin laundromat. Easy as pie, as the Yanks say.

That evening he found the Bilks brothers along the creek ten miles outside Old Ditch. Their car was parked at the end of a rutted wash under the sweeping limbs of an oak tree. Gardener waited until nightfall before creeping up on them. By the light of a harvest moon he could make out a body curled by a guttering fire. He tensed, reaching for his pistol—

He caught a noise in his blind spot—the clicking sound a rider makes to urge a stubborn horse forward. Gardener turned to spy Eldred Bilks sitting in the crotch of a tree with a revolver trained on his chest.

"Lookee, lookee," he said. "If it isn't Hopalong Nigger."

Gardener cursed himself; as a younger man he would not have been so easily ambushed. The second brother awoke and joined his sibling. Their eyes shone with bright avidity, two cruel boys who had come across a crippled bird.

"I seen you around town," said Horace, the more observant of the two. "Mowing lawns for nickels, huh?"

"I do that, yes," Gardener said in his smooth British lilt, which took the brothers by surprise. "But I do not come to you under that guise."

"What the hell—*what* guys?" said Eldred.

"Hush," Horace told his brother. His gaze was sharper now. "What guise do we entertain you under, pray tell?"

"I come as a death angel, Horace Bilks. Yes," he went on, seeing their startled looks, "I know your names. But they will be unattached to you soon enough. I've come to kill you, Horace. You and Eldred both."

The Bilks brothers laughed . . . until something in Gardener's eyes rendered their mirth stillborn. They thought they had been dealing with a middle-aged gimp. But it was dawning that they were in the presence of something else—something that had learned to hide its true face.

"You are poor representatives of our species," Gardener went on. "I do not know how you came to be as such. A man cares not if the mad dog was once a good dog. He cares only that the dog has gone mad and that it must be dispatched."

Dispatched. This was how Gardener had once viewed his bloody work. Dispassionately, as a mailman viewed his job. The mailman delivered letters into mailboxes. Gardener had once delivered men into coffins.

"You do us a grave disfavor," said Horace mockingly.

Gardener opened his coat to show them the Mauser holstered on his right side. Horace Bilks angled his head to that same side, the cartilage cracking in his neck, eyes wolfishly set.

"Tell me, nigger," Eldred said with casual venom, "do you stick up Texaco stations with that lump of pig iron? A-cause we ain't no Texaco."

"You joke to cover your fear," Gardener said. "But I can smell it."

Eldred's pistol hand came up, pinning Gardener between the eyes. "I will kill you," he said bluntly.

"Ah. But will you act honorably?" Gardener asked. "Shall you be sporting, as your forefathers were? The great men who first colonized these empty lands?"

"Wait, are you . . . are you challenging me to *draw*?" Eldred barked laughter. "What year do you think this is, y'old fart?"

"How old-fashioned," said Horace. "But you have to understand, my brother and me, we do everything together."

"Including raping and mutilating women," said Gardener.

"Oh hell yeah, especially that," Horace said. "So what I'm saying is, you'd have to be faster than both Eldred 'n' me."

Gardener kept his peace.

"Okeydokey." Horace cracked his knuckles, enjoying this game.

"You mowed your last blade of grass, jig," said Eldred.

"Are you square with your creator?" Gardener asked them both. "I can give you some time to make that peace."

"No need," said Horace. "It's you who's gonna stop breathing."

Gardener nodded evenly. "Shall we settle on a count of three?"

Eldred holstered his gun. The brothers stood side by side, fingers twitching near the butts of their pistols. The sweat shone on their foreheads like diamond dust.

Gardener's right hand hovered over his Mauser . . .

. . . while his left slipped slyly through a vent on the opposite side of his coat for his hidden gun.

"Who will count?" Gardener said.

"You do the honors there, old man," Eldred said. "Can you count that high?"

Gardener began. "One . . ."

He fired the Paterson twice. The slugs ripped through his coat and slammed into the brothers a split second apart. The men staggered and fell into each other, their skulls knocking together. Gardener unholstered the Mauser swiftly and emptied its clip, for he was lethal with either hand. One bullet tore Eldred Bilks's jaw off, spinning it across the dirt. The man toppled and fell with his tongue hanging out of the fresh hole in his face, purple-rooted and unsettlingly long, like a skinned snake. His brother died with a little more dignity, but he died.

Gardener had used this trick in his old life. It wasn't sporting, but then neither was dragging young girls down gravel roads by a trailer hitch.

It was this night—the night he'd killed the Bilks brothers—that Gardener mused upon as he sat in Clayton Suggs's bar with a scorpion's stinger buried in his hand. He had killed many men in his lifetime, both deserving and less so. The fact rested uneasily within him, yet he could do nothing to dislodge those acts from his past.

"There is a sect of monks who make an art of the act of self-flagellation." Gardener squinted at Suggs, the venom and liquor blurring his sight. "Do you know this word, Mr. Suggs? Flagellation?"

Suggs swallowed with great effort. "I do not."

Gardener poured himself another drink. He gripped the glass with his scorpioned hand this time, raising that hand to his mouth. The Death-stalker thrashed, pincers snapping. Gardener drank. His hand did not shake.

"They thrash themselves, yes?" he said. "Using short, many-tongued whips tipped with metal spurs. They walk the streets, uttering psalms and rending their flesh. The gutters run red with blood. It's penance, Mr. Suggs. They do so to alleviate the stain of sin from their corporeal body, letting those sins escape through the flesh."

"Your neck, man," Suggs said queasily. "It is plainly bloated. I'm thinking it'll make breathing a chore."

"Penance is a very human need, Mr. Suggs. Yet I fear it is useless. A man does things in his life. Things he cannot repay or outrun. That man can spend the rest of his life paying and running, but he can never quite find the required distance. The toll is too high, because that man set it that way."

Gardener reached over the bar and coiled his fingers around Suggs's wrist. Suggs stared down at the man's fingers, hard as obsidian, digging into him. It was all he could do not to cry out.

"Do you understand, Mr. Suggs? Do you share my view on this matter?"

When Gardener released him, Clayton Suggs fled the Glory. Gardener let him go. Perhaps he would run to the pharmacy and return with antivenom. But the sting of a scorpion wasn't nearly enough to kill Gardener. There were some things, terrible things, that preferred to kill you slowly—over a lifetime, or perhaps even longer.

He wished Suggs had not left. He wanted to tell him of the dream he'd had just last night. It was the same one he had dreamed every night for the past fifteen years. He awoke each morning with his skin screaming as the terror fled from his veins.

In this dream, he saw the face of God. For this had been his wish—the deal he'd made with that thing that lurked in the black rock.

Show me the face of God.

And Gardener saw it. Every time he closed his goddamn eyes.

God's face was vile. The first few times, Gardener had suspected trickery—the black thing invading his head and twisting his thoughts. But in time, his soul moved against this proposition. He had been granted his wish fairly. And now he had to live with it.

God's face was that of an idiot. The moronic, drooling, palsied face of an enormous infant. A face covered in seeping boils and a-crawl with insects not to be found anywhere in nature. God's eyes stared with malicious cruelty—and there was vast power in that gaze, yes, although it was witlessly applied. That gaze took aim at anyone, disregarding goodness or worth. It ruined people chaotically, without wisdom or just cause. This was the purest terror Gardener felt each time he shut his eyes: at the fact that the universe was lorded over by an infant of incalculable wrath and directionless evil who had not the slightest sense of right or wrong, guilt or innocence, or the hope of a better life.

And all of humanity worshipped that mindless, gibbering *thing*.

When he awoke this very morning, Gardener had found the scorpion sunning itself on the front steps of his home. As if it had been waiting for him. And Gardener had known, with a certainty that lived someplace outside his flesh, that his old friend was coming. With that, he understood that the days marking his existence could perhaps be counted on the fingers of two hands. Perhaps only one.

Pinching with his fingers, he finally released the scorpion's stinger from his flesh.

"Go on, now," he said to it, setting it on the floor. "You have had an eventful day."

PART TWO

BEGINNINGS

THREE SHOOTISTS COME TO TOWN

1965

1

THE ENGLISHMAN'S CAR was in atrocious shape, but he had been tasked with killing a man that day, that *very* day without delay, if possible, so there was nothing to be done about it—the car and its driver would both have to cope.

He had stolen the car, a Ford Galaxie 500 with red leatherette upholstery and faux-marble door panels, from a traveling salesman working the southern territory. The salesman picked the Englishman up on the side of the road, where he'd been thumbing a ride. After a half hour of polite chit-chat, the Englishman drew a pistol and ordered the man to pull over and get out.

"But," the salesman sputtered, "I did you a favor, for God's sake!"

The Englishman said: "Yes, and that's irony for you, chum."

"I didn't have to, you know," the salesman said, getting out of the car. "A lot of people wouldn't pick up a man of your coloration."

"You are a gentleman and a prince," said the Englishman, and drove away.

The salesman trafficked in encyclopedias. The trunk was packed with them. The Englishman stopped and tossed them into the weeds. After a hard afternoon's driving, the car developed a persistent knock. The Englishman drove on and a few hours later ran over some debris strewn across the road that tore the fender molding half off. The loosened metal flapped against the frame, which, in addition to the engine knock, created a din that he could not alleviate even by cranking the radio up and blasting "Be My Baby" by the Ronettes.

He tried to ignore it and focus on the task at hand. He had been hired for a ticklish bit of work by a man named Seaborn Appleton. He had made Appleton's acquaintance following another bit of business he had done for his primary employer, who would remain nameless. Said business involved killing one Mortimer "Bladder" Knipple of Marfa, Texas, who had stabbed a man in a drunken fracas. The dead man happened to be kin to the Englishman's employer. Restitutions needed to be made, and such debts could be paid only in blood.

The Englishman discovered Knipple brandy-drunk in a flophouse outside of Wimberley, where Knipple pulled the same dagger he'd used to kill the other man. The Englishman's employer would have preferred Knipple be delivered alive—and if he had been, his sufferings would have been legendary—but as the Englishman had no inclination to tussle with a stabby drunk, he shot Knipple in the brain with a silenced pistol and took a Polaroid of the corpse.

When he telephoned his employer to say the job had been done, he was given Seaborn Appleton's contact details with the assurance that any job would net a handsome payout. He called Appleton. Appleton spoke a name. It was a name the Englishman was acquainted with, in the way a territorial wrestler is familiar with the work of a man toiling in another region. The name sent the slightest twinge up the Englishman's spine, which was a sensation he had not felt in years. He didn't mind it at all. It told him he was alive.

It was that man the Englishman was presently making fast to murder. But again, there was the small matter of the car. It was shaking to pieces. There was a plastic hula dancer on the car's dashboard; its hips swayed with every shake and judder. That dancer was crass, like so much of Americana. The Englishman occasionally missed the stolidity of his home country here in the land of neon and silver lamé and velvet Elvis paintings. That garishness sat against both the Englishman's temperament and his adopted appearance—he favored well-cut suits and snappy hats, and wore his hair long and straight with the aid of a relaxing solution.

He ripped the dancer off the dash—the suction cup came free with a loud *pok!*—and tossed it out the window. His mind returned to the small matter of killing a man.

The Englishman was so preoccupied with the matters of the car, the man, and that man's death that he took no notice of the person hopping antsily from foot to foot at the traffic light where he had stopped. The Englishman had needed to pull off the freeway into a sleepy burg in order to fill the tank. It was night by that point, the streets deserted save for this lone person—a man hopping about as if beset by the dire need to piss. So preoccupied was the Englishman that he didn't even see the man snake up to the car. He took notice only when the man stuck his arm through the open window. At the end of that arm was a rusted pistol that looked to have been salvaged from a lake.

The man holding it had the skin of a decaying apple. His eyelids fluttered with some kind of sickness. Rusted or not, the gun looked powerful enough to tear the stranger's stringy arm off if he elected to pull the trigger.

The Englishman reached to one side. The man waggled his gun in warning.

"You want money, I'm guessing?"

"That's right," said the man, breathing his mouth stench onto the Englishman. "You's pretty smart, ain't ya?"

"Bright as a penny, old chap."

The man licked his lips, cracked and salt-whitened. "You talk stupid."

The Englishman retrieved his wallet, fat with bills—he did not believe in banks, or of records of any sort—and handed it out the window. The man was so taken with the wallet's plumpness that he did not see the Englishman reach for his own weapon, a silenced Colt 1903 that lay beneath a folded copy of the *Hobbs Daily News-Sun* on the passenger seat.

The Englishman shot the stringy fellow through the car door. There came a sharp report as a slug drove through one-sixteenth of an inch of Detroit rolling iron. A hole sprouted as if by magic in the man's belly. He fell onto the street, shrieking and clawing at his stomach.

"Give me back my billfold," the Englishman said calmly.

"You shuh-shuh-shuh-*shuh*—!"

"Shot you. Yes, I did. The wallet, man. Give it to me now, or I will put the next one in your wrinkly bollocks."

The man's face twisted in agonized incomprehension.

"Your *balls*, sir. Your oysters. Again, and for a final time, the wallet."

The man managed to scrape it up and, groaning, blood pissing through the hole in his gut, handed it through the window. The Englishman glanced in the rearview mirror, saw nobody had witnessed the event, and tipped an imaginary cap to the man he'd shot.

"Heigh-ho."

"I need a doctor!" the man wailed.

The Englishman said, "You'll need an embalmer."

The man sat on the street. Blood burped from the hole in his stomach. His mouth hung open in horror, spittle foaming on his lips.

"I suggest you crawl to the nearest clinic," said the Englishman. "Or wait it out where you're sitting. Either way, it oughtn't take long."

THREE HOURS LATER, the Englishman piloted the car up a hill that crested onto a plateau staggered with bur oaks. To the west lay the razor-backed peaks of the Mogollon Range. The San Francisco River valley spread out beneath him. The lights of Mogollon township glittered in the new dawn.

2

MICAH HENRY SHUGHRUE had come to Mogollon to kill a man.

Seaborn Appleton was that man's name. The Chemist, as he was otherwise known. Einstein with a chemistry set. Appleton created acid that could rip your scalp off and fill your brain with fanciful visions. Supercharged PCP that would keep you high a full day. Wild and wonderful stuff that had the dope fiends, speed freaks, and needle jockeys lining up down the block for a taste.

Appleton had acquired Micah for protection. Appleton did not maintain a home base. He preferred the life of the traveling snake oil salesman. Appleton went from town to town in a VW camper van, peddling his wares. It seemed a perverse way to live, but upon scrutiny it made sense. The supplies he required were often available only with a prescription, so they had to be procured from pharmacies and hospitals—at night, after hours, with the help of a lockpick set. Following these thefts, those places adopted better security measures. Then it was time to move on to another town.

Seaborn Appleton was also a suspicious sort. A paranoiac, you might even say. He'd adopted perpetual motion as a lifestyle—his enemies, of which he was convinced there were many, would find it harder to zero in on a moving target.

Part of Micah Shughrue's job was to drive the VW camper from town to town while Appleton dozed fitfully on the foldout cot, occasionally screaming out as if in pain. Micah drove in silence at Appleton's behest— no radio, only the musical tinkle of Appleton's powders and liquids, all housed in glass bottles, rattling in the back.

Appleton preferred to sell directly to his clientele. Most drug lords— and Appleton was that, if one of minor regard—usually tasked low-level flunkies with the selling. Who wanted to deal with the scabby-faced, buttery-skinned addicts themselves? Who wanted to confront the physical manifestation of the poison they profited from? But Appleton got a kick out of it. He enjoyed the craven need in all those twitching, bloodshot eyes.

Appleton himself was a dour, funereal, and jarringly skeletal man. But put him in front of a gaggle of crankers, and his limbs loosened, his dourness receded, and his voice took on the rich, plaintive tones of a lay preacher.

"Ooooh, yes," he'd say, displaying his newest wares. "You will be astonished, my pretties. This magical stuff will take you places you never dreamed existed."

By the time Micah joined him, Appleton was beloved by the addicts of the towns he cycled through. They would catch wind of his arrival and do everything short of roll out a welcome mat. When it was time to move on, they practically clawed onto the bumper of his van, wailing at him to take them with him. For Micah, the work was easy. There were the expected scuffles. Jittery addicts brandishing box cutters, demanding money or product. An upstart rival asserting claim over a territory that had been the Chemist's for years—but Appleton had let it go with a shrug. "This country is too vast, and too full of paying customers, to go to war over one tiny patch of it," he'd said. For eight months, Micah kept Appleton from bodily harm, and was compensated handsomely for his efforts.

Then Micah met a woman. They had been looping back down into Oregon at the time, plying their trade in familiar ports of call. The woman showed up at the abandoned soap factory where Appleton was entertaining clientele. She was carrying something.

Micah approached carefully, measuring her intentions, one hand on the butt of his pistol. Maybe she was carrying a gun—in his experience, sometimes the direst threat came in the most unlikely package. He roughly caught her arm.

"Show me," he said.

The woman twisted painfully to reveal her sleeping infant daughter, partly swaddled in a grubby fleece blanket. The baby's arms . . . well, that was the trouble. The little girl had no arms. Only a pair of melted nubs like amputation remnants jutting from her shoulders.

"She was born this way," the woman said quietly. "And blind, too."

"I am . . . sorry." Micah didn't know what else to say.

"It was the drugs that did it." She looked wretched, cored out by grief. "I shouldn't have taken them with her in my belly, but I was weak."

The babe awoke and began to mewl. Its eyes were a featureless gray, as if molten pewter had been poured into the sockets.

"Would you shut that up?" Appleton called over. "It's ruining my mood."

After the last bug-eyed scrounger had left, Micah detailed this encounter to Appleton while they sat inside the van. Appleton's response was in keeping with his nature.

"I sell drugs, man! Drugs hurt people. They hurt the trembling lives inside those people, too. They also make people feel wondrous and let them escape the horror of their inept, ridiculous existence for a while. I can't be responsible. I *won't* be!"

On the most basic level, Micah understood Appleton's point. People were responsible for their own lives. But still, he couldn't shake the sight of that tot.

"From what depths of soul do you dredge up this moral outrage, anyway?" Appleton said with a mocking laugh. "You've probably killed more men than my products ever will. Why else would I have hired you?"

"Not women, not children, not the unborn."

Appleton shrugged. "It's settled, then. We're both killers."

"Most every man I have ever killed was trying to do the same to me at the time."

"That infant isn't dead," Appleton said petulantly. "She will simply have more challenges to face than other youngsters."

Something snapped inside Micah right then. It happened from time to time, often without warning. He couldn't help it and didn't even try to—it came as a release of all that pent-up pressure.

Micah stepped outside the van. He grabbed a box of the Chemist's newest, dandiest product and hurled it onto the cement of the soapworks. He set about stomping on it, grinding the bluish powder into the oily floor, reducing it to worthless paste.

"What are you—?" Appleton cried. "You cocksucking sonofa*whooooore!*"

Micah kept at it, laughing like a satyr. So intense was his rage that he did not notice Appleton reach under his cot for a small-bore pistol, which he quickly fired.

The slug hit Micah under the armpit, both his arms being raised in a gleeful jig. He was thrown down and the wind knocked out of him. He reached for his gun, but Appleton was already behind the wheel. He fired the van up and tore out of the soapworks, leaving Micah on the floor with the silvery tang of the crushed drug sharp in his nose.

He lay bleeding for several minutes. He thought: *It is always the goddamn amateurs who score the luckiest hits.* He stood and staggered five long blocks to a pay phone. He could not call a hospital. They would fix him up, but they would also send for the police. So he called a veterinarian, a man who owed Micah a favor. The vet arrived some time later to find Micah passed out in an alley not far from the phone booth.

The vet drove Micah to his office. He dug the bullet out and inserted a stent into Micah's chest to vent the blood. For many days, Micah lay in the garden shed out behind the vet's house with that stent jabbing out of him; he twisted a spigot to drain his own blood. He coughed up pints of blood, dark and thick as pancake batter, and descended into hallucinations.

Once he healed, he embarked upon a relentless pursuit of Seaborn Appleton, who was by then miles away in the company of new henchmen. Micah shot two of those new men in a cathouse in Elko, Nevada, but Appleton escaped with his third hired gun. After that, Micah caught wind that Appleton had put out a call for harder men—professional mercenaries, ex-military—and put a bounty on his former protector's head.

Undeterred, Micah headed to Mogollon. He suspected it would be the bastard's next stop, following his migratory pattern.

And when Appleton arrived, Micah Shughrue would kill him dead and that would be that.

3

MINERVA ATWATER had come to Mogollon to kill two men.

Her contract called for only one individual, a man named Micah Henry Shughrue. A veteran of the Korean War who had spent the ensuing years on the shadow side of the law. A gun for hire. A merc. Of late, he'd been loosely associated with a criminal enterprise operating out of Kansas City. He wasn't a member of that particular outfit—more of a stringer. Five years ago, he'd been set upon by Deputy US Marshal Clint Smith, who rousted him in the bathtub of a Topeka whorehouse; Micah Shughrue shot Smith in the leg with a zip gun stashed under the towel folded neatly next to the tub and alighted on foot, running down the street and into the Topeka gorge naked as a jay. Evidently he'd survived. Shughrue seemed to be that, if nothing else. A survivor.

Micah Shughrue. By many accounts, the nastiest goddamn sonofabitch walking this earth. He was the first man she would kill.

The second man was a foreigner. The Englishman. The Whispering Death. An assassin. Remorseless, dead-eyed, black-skinned. Talked with a funny accent. Wore a fancy suit, fancy hat, grew his hair long like a woman. Carried pearl-handled pistols and, it was said, could knock the wings off a bumblebee's back with either hand. His shadow was the last thing you saw before your brains fanned out the front of your skull.

He was the second man she would kill. Though in truth, the exact order was not so important.

Minerva had no contract for the Englishman. In point of fact, both Minerva and the Englishman had been hired by the same man: Seaborn Appleton. Both for the same task, killing Micah Henry Shughrue.

"The man has gone feral," was how Appleton phrased it to her. "I knew of Shughrue's past misdeeds, but he was valuable to me. Yet in time, he was once again given over to wickedness."

Appleton had repelled Minerva at first glance. A jangly skeleton draped in cheap seersucker with a face like a dime's worth of dog meat. She boggled at his success in the pharmacology trade; the only thing she'd ever buy from Appleton would be a sack, which she would slip over his head so as to spare herself the sight of his puckered bunghole of a mouth and his snake handler's eyes. But a job was a job, and Appleton was paying cash on the barrelhead. As well he ought to, considering the man he was asking her to snuff.

"Why the two of us?" she asked.

"Insurance, my dear. If the Englishman fails, you will finish it. Or the other way round, as may happen."

"I don't need his damn help."

"Oh yes, and he doesn't need yours. But who can say? Mr. Shughrue is a very . . . ah, he is a man to whom completeness is key."

"What in hell do you mean by that?"

"I mean he is a *completist*, my dear. He holds the most fastidious sense of it. A thing is only done once Micah Shughrue has rendered it so, and it is he alone who concludes when those ends have been met. He is a finisher, in all. A more scrupulous sense of finality than any man I have ever met."

The poached eggs of Appleton's eyes quivered fearfully. Minerva found yet another reason to be revolted by him.

"He's just a man," she said. "A bullet will end him, same as anyone else."

Appleton didn't seem so sure. What did he think this Shughrue was, some deathless devil?

Appleton said, "How many men have you killed?"

"Enough," said Minerva.

"Don't lie to me. How many?"

Minerva cut her gaze at Appleton—her pale eyes were ringed with gold, but were not yet those of a killer. She had hurt men, quite badly in fact, but . . . it was not that she was chicken-gutted. It was simply that the opportunity had not presented itself. She was a bounty hunter. The men she'd pursued to that point were meek creatures: debt shirkers, those on the scamper from their creditors. One of them had come at Minerva with a knife; she'd busted his knee with a length of stovewood. She'd peppered another one's buttocks with wolf shot when he tried to flee. And she'd crippled a bookie named Thelonious Skell for nonbusiness reasons.

But kill a man? End his life? No, not yet. But she was good and ready.

"I've killed three men," she lied.

"And did they die quickly?"

"Slower than they would have liked."

"You'll want to finish Shughrue fast," said Appleton. "As quick as you can pull the trigger. 'Cause he won't stop until he's killed you. And depending on his mood, which is poor at the best of times, he might move on to your mother, your father, and your children."

"Do I look like a mother to you?" she said.

After wrapping affairs with Appleton, Minerva retired to her fleabag motel. It was a day's drive to Mogollon. Appleton intended to delay his arrival there to ensure that Shughrue—whom Appleton could feel breathing down his neck—would show up the day before. Minerva and the Englishman would also come that same day. All things being proper, Micah Shughrue would be dead by the time Appleton's VW van crossed the town line.

"Maybe you and the Englishman can work together?" Appleton had suggested.

Minerva demurred. More precisely, she'd said: "I'd rather fall off the roof of a whorehouse and catch my eyelid on a nail."

She had plans for both men.

Micah Shughrue was all business.

The Englishman? That was entirely personal.

4

MICAH HENRY SHUGHRUE encountered the Englishman in Trotter's Stables at the end of Mogollon's ramshackle main street around mid-morning.

Mogollon was a scratch-ass town of less than two thousand souls. It was afflicted with the same leprosy as a lot of these decaying New Mexico boomtowns. A century ago, men had descended upon the area to pan for gold and silver. Claptrap camps went up to service the prospectors—saloons with faro tables, brothels, joints where men spent the gold dust sieved out of the rivers. But nobody was really *from* a place like Mogollon, and when the gold dried up, towns like it mostly emptied out. Now all that remained was a shell, hollowed out, populated by those too stupid or lazy to move someplace better.

Micah had taken a room at the Two Points, the only motel in town. He did not sleep, but even on a normal night, Micah slept only a few hours. He had flicked on the black-and-white Zenith and watched until the Indian's head came on and the words beneath it read: *Your Local News at 7 AM!* When dawn broke over the swaybacked roofs of Mogollon, he dressed in fresh clothes and holstered his pistol inconspicuously and made his way to a coffeehouse that was just opening. He drank bad coffee and ate a honey bun that tasted too much like the Camels the man behind the counter smoked, but still, he ate another as he read a big-city newspaper cover to cover. He scanned the street every so often. The town awoke sluggishly; nobody seemed to have much to do or any intensity about them.

He spotted a man walking down the opposite sidewalk in the direction of the horse stables. Micah had heard about a black pistolman with long ladylike hair and English manners. The exact sort of man Appleton might have hired.

Micah ordered another coffee to go and carried his paper cup out onto the street. He tucked his body behind a wooden column propping up the veranda and watched the black man disappear into the stables. He crossed the street and tossed his coffee cup behind a shrub. The street was thinly trafficked, only a mother pushing a stroller down the opposite sidewalk.

Micah unholstered his gun and eased around the open stable door. It was dim; feathery shafts of sunlight slipped through the wooden slats, picking up a patina of dust. The air smelled of hay and of horseflesh. The Englishman was bent at the feet of a horse. He seemed to be examining a malady on its hoof. He made a sweet clicking noise that came from deep in his throat. Micah slipped behind another horse ten feet away from the man.

"Hello," he said.

At first, the Englishman remained bent at the horse's feet, its hoof clasped in his hands. Then he shook his head in a slow side-to-side as if chastising himself. When he stood and turned, his own pistol was drawn. He was met by the sight of Micah, the majority of his body—his center of mass, as a rifle instructor would say—shielded by a dappled roan. Micah was aiming his Colt at the man from under the horse's belly.

"Ahem," said the man, "you've put me in a spot, old bean."

It was him. The Englishman. The Whispering Death. And he was right: all he had was a tricky shot at Micah's head or his legs. Micah had the Englishman's whole body to hit.

Of course, Micah knew that the Englishman must have already considered simply shooting the horse. But the bullets would craze through the beast's heavy vitals, or be flattened on its bones. A gut-shot horse would buck and fuss, giving the Englishman an opportunity, but there was a much better chance that Micah would irrigate his opponent's chest well before that.

Micah said, "I have never met a black man with straight hair. How do you do it?"

"Relaxer," the Englishman said. "Enough to float a coal ship."

The horse's cock slipped from its sheath. Micah could not see its entire length due to his positioning, but what he glimpsed put him in the mind of a thick rubber hose. Not quite a fireman's hose, girthwise, but not far off. Micah angled his gun away from the horse's comically large member. He did not want to accidentally blow a hole through it.

"I will not lie," the Englishman said, looking at it. "I feel unmanned. It's not good to feel that way before a gunfight."

"It is an animal. Our anatomies do not square up."

"You make a good point. And yet—"

The horse pissed. Long and loud and luxurious. Droplets of urine splashed up to wet Micah's trousers.

"My God," the Englishman marveled. "Do you think it's been given a diuretic?"

The horse finished. It shook contentedly and began to eat hay. This interlude having concluded, the men returned to their own business.

Micah said, "I take it Appleton hired you?"

"He did. He claims you killed two of his men."

"I never killed a man who didn't deserve it."

"Bully for you."

"And you?"

The Englishman said, "I hunt people for money. I imagine most of them have been bad eggs, but I never bothered to read their diaries."

Bold was the man who could joke with a pistol pointed at his belly.

"It's a job to me, nothing more," the Englishman went on. "But according to Appleton, you've been asking for it."

"Who of us is not asking for it?"

"So then, why not let it go?"

"Appleton dealt me a bad turn," Micah said simply. "I will not be done wrong."

"Ah. You're one of those."

Micah set his jaw. The Englishman did not know about the baby with no arms. Micah had dreamed about that child. She was the reason, more or less, why he had to kill Appleton. He could even set aside Appleton's treachery in dry-gulching him. That was business. But Micah hoped he'd sleep better with Appleton gone.

For this reason, he did not wish to shoot the Englishman. Not because he was scared of the man's skills. The Englishman was a trained killer, but Micah had his own abilities in that area. He was not anxious about taking out the Englishman on moral grounds, either—he had murdered for lesser cause, sadly.

No, Micah didn't want to fire on the Englishman because something might occur during the course of events to stop him from finishing what he'd come to Mogollon to do, that being to kill Seaborn Appleton. Kill him for that little baby with no arms.

Such was Micah's mind-set when a woman rushed into the stable with two pistols drawn and firing.

For a split second, Micah assumed she was an apparition. He used to have similar visions when drunk, though in those, the woman was stepping naked out of a lake or naked into a bedroom—in any event, naked. But this woman was clothed in a duster the color of old fingernails and alligator-skin boots. She carried a pair of Colts that kicked skyward as she squeezed the triggers.

The stabled horses reared at the deafening gunshots. The roan slammed into Micah, knocking the wind out of him. His gun fell to the dirt. He saw the Englishman catch a slug through his shoulder. It reeled him in a sloppy pirouette. Micah grunted and knelt for his gun, spinning toward the woman—a *girl*, really—to return fire as the horses stampeded out the stable doors. His bullet struck a post near her head, spraying splinters. She flinched at the flying wood and fired ploddingly from the hip.

Minerva couldn't have hoped for better luck. She had been sitting in her car scoping the main drag when, at precisely ten o'clock, she'd spotted the English twit. At two past ten, Micah Shughrue followed the British fuck into the stable. Two bugs in the kill jar. She had a mind to let them shoot each other dead, but that would not satisfy her. *She* had to flatline the Englishman. He would have to die first; he struck her as the sharper shot. Once he was dead, or at least down, she could focus on Shughrue.

But things began to spin out of control the moment she stepped into the stables. She'd intended to surprise them. Unsporting? Granted. But she needed every advantage against such experienced gunmen. Minerva expected to take return fire. She might even be hit. But she could withstand that, she figured.

This belief had persisted up until the moment the bullets began to sing through the air. When she charged into the stables, everything sped up. She pulled the triggers and could feel the Colts' hammers cocking back as the springs compressed. She could even feel the firing pins strike the flash holes, igniting the powder in each round. But her own movements were lethargic—her veins running with molasses, her arms leaden.

Oh Christ oh Christ, she thought. *This is happening too goddamn fast—*

Micah Shughrue saw this woman coming and he did not blink. He thumbed the hammer of his own Colt and put his first shot into the Englishman's side. Gray smoke mushroomed from the barrel; the Englishman's tailored shirt blew inward, then out again as the bullet jolted through his innards. Turning then, his mind clear and his breath quickening, Micah fired at the woman, whom he assumed to be the Englishman's partner despite the fact that she was firing *at* the Englishman, determinedly so, her lips skinned from her teeth. His bullet winged her left leg down at the calf. She continued to advance, teeth bared and wolfish, her Colts thundering.

In the midst of all this, the Englishman sat confused. A rare inertia gripped his mind. Such sudden violence when he had been anticipating a gentlemanly tête-à-tête, followed by him dispatching Micah Shughrue and collecting Appleton's reward. But then . . . this *harridan*. An appalling harpy with murder on her mind. At once he had been winged; moments later, he was hit again, this time by Shughrue. Only then did he pull his pistol and take aim at the murderess. A bullet whizzed past his skull, making the sound of an angry hornet. One of his own bullets struck her. She collapsed behind the water trough . . .

Minerva crumpled behind the trough, clutching her belly. It felt as if she'd been kicked by a donkey, and yet there was no real pain—only the sudden and somehow blunt force of impact. The fact blitzed through her brainpan: *I've been hit!* She'd never been shot before. So this was how it felt. She had expected worse. All she sensed was a cold disconnect between her chest and legs, like a bunch of threads had been cut.

Miraculously, Micah Shughrue was unhurt. The Englishman had eaten considerable lead, and the woman, too. Micah could see the black man on his back with blood running out of his shirt. A fine layer of dust and hay was stuck to his face.

"Oh," the Englishman said. "Gents, I am killed."

"I'm sorry for shooting you like that," Micah said to him. "It was not my intent."

Micah approached the trough. The woman lay behind it, grasping her side and retching. He turned back to see the Englishman sitting up. Too late, he noticed the dainty derringer clutched in his hand—

The lead ball struck Micah in the left eye. He fell straight back. A fine mist of blood hung in the air. He knew nothing else.

5

MICAH AWOKE BLIND.

He sat up with a jolt. Where was he? His final memory: the Englishman's bullet snapping his skull back, followed by a terrible *squelch* inside his head.

He lay on a threadbare mattress, or so it felt. He could tell he was naked save for a pair of underwear.

Sightless.

An icy thread of fear spun around his heart. What goddamn use was a blind gunman? Forget killing Appleton—if he was blind, he could be killed by a child. A beggar could sneak up and slit his throat.

His fingers spidered up his chest, his face . . . he felt the bandages wound over his eyes. He unraveled them. Oh, thank Christ. He could *see*. He blinked. His view improved. He was in a makeshift infirmary. White privacy curtains were draped around his bed. He ran his fingertips around his right eye socket, the eye he could see out of. His fingers investigated the left eye next, figuring that the eyelid was gummed shut with blood or was otherwise occluded—

His index finger pushed past the sagging lids and into the sticky vault where his eye had recently resided. His fingertip grazed the raw flesh at the back where the nerves collected. He gasped.

"Christ, careful what you're doing!"

A man had stepped through the curtains. He wore a much-bloodied shirt and a hat with a beaten crown. Needles of sweaty hair protruded under its wide brim.

"Quit poking at it. It'll get infected, turn to sepsis. And you see, I can't very well amputate your head. That would be what you call a terminal decision."

"You a doctor?" said Micah.

"Who the hell else would I be? Who else goes around fixing shot-up morons?"

"You took the eye?"

The doctor nodded. "I took the eye."

Both men were silent a spell.

"It does not hurt," said Micah. "It . . . tingles."

"I flushed the socket with a numbing agent and gave you a shot for the pain. But you'll feel it soon enough. It won't be pleasant."

"Did you have to take my eye, Doc?"

The doctor removed his hat and ran a hand through his hair. His hands were stained with blood the way a mechanic's hands can get with axle grease—the skin takes on the tincture of the substance that he works with all day.

"I am no surgeon. I administer to the men and women around here, most of them farmers or ranchers. If a hand gets crushed and we can't get them to the hospital two towns over, I take it off. A foot mangled, off it comes. Better to lose a limb than die of septic shock." He reseated his hat. "Your eye was obliterated, Mr. Shughrue—yes, I know who you are. The bullet glanced off your ocular ridge—the bone, I mean to say—and dodged around inside the socket. A lucky break; otherwise it would have passed through into your brain. Then all you'd be good for is drooling."

"How did you remove it?"

"You really want to know?"

"Tell me."

"A tool called a curette," the doctor said. "A sharpened spoon, pretty much. I scooped it out, snipped the nerve. The eye was smashed fruit. Useless even as a decoration."

The doctor possessed little in the way of bedside manner, but Micah was grateful for his candor.

"You could be fitted for a fake one, Mr. Shughrue. Or a patch."

"Maybe I will keep it the way it is," said Micah, filled with momentary despair. "Or have a flagpole jut out of it with a little flag at the end, the Stars and Stripes like the kids wave at parades."

"It would be patriotic of you," the doctor said dryly.

Micah pulled his knees to his chest. He was sore but otherwise unhurt. "The black fellow?"

The doctor said, "He'll pull through. He was shot through the hip and shoulder. No organ damage."

"Where is he?"

The doctor gestured to the other side of the curtains. Micah craned his head toward the bedpost, where he always hung his pistols—

"They've been confiscated," the doctor said, sensing the intent. "The other fella's, too. Now, you could get up and try choking him to death, but I'd tell the deputy stationed outside and he'd shoot you dead."

"I will stay here, then."

"That's a good boy."

"The woman?"

"She's here also," the doctor told him. "She's hurt. She won't be bothering anyone."

"Who is she?"

"A bounty hunter, I'm told." A chuckle. "Not worth a damn at her job, though, is she?"

Micah leaned back in bed. "So?"

"You'll all live. You will all go to jail. You and the black man for the rest of your natural lives. The woman might get out just in time to start collecting Social Security. From what I gather, you have dodged the law a long time, Mr. Shughrue. Now you're going to have to pay the ferryman." He shrugged. "I hear tell you might even get the electric chair."

"So why recommend a fake eye for me? It will just melt out of my head!" Micah laughed until a tear came out of his good eye. Something might have squirted out of his empty socket, too, but he couldn't tell. "Hell of a thing, Doc. Healing me up so I can be fried."

The doctor allowed himself a small smile in acknowledgment of how ludicrous his task must seem. He then drew liquid morphine into a syringe. "I'll give you this so you can sleep."

"But Doctor, is it habit-forming?"

The sawbones chortled at this. He administered the shot and squared his hat to Micah. "Get some rest."

6

MICAH AWOKE THAT NIGHT to the Englishman's voice.

"Ho! You awake over there?"

Micah waited until his eyes—his *eye*—adjusted to the darkness. "I am up. What the hell do you want?"

"Are you mobile?" the Englishman asked.

"I can get around."

"*Wunderbar.* I, however, am confined to bed rest."

Micah sat up. A needle was jabbed into his forearm, feeding some manner of medical mixture into his veins. The needle ran to a tube, which in turn ran to a glass bottle hooked to an IV pole on casters.

Micah shuffled through the curtains; the casters squeaked as the pole rolled along. The world felt strange with only one eye. It was as if Micah's body had already accepted that the eye was gone and was in the process of reorganizing itself to account for its loss.

The Englishman lay in a hospital bed, his head slightly raised, his long dark tresses fanned over the pillow—the ends were frizzing, reverting to their natural state.

"You got me," he said.

"I apologized for that already," said Micah.

"Really? I can't recall. In any case, you shouldn't. Pistols were drawn, yes? I would have done the same to you were it not for that madwoman."

"You did her wrong?"

The Englishman frowned. "I've never laid eyes on that batty witch."

Micah said, "You do the things men like us do, you are bound to have enemies you have never set eyes on."

Micah could get a better sense of their location from here. They were in a makeshift ward. The woman was behind another set of curtains to the left; he could hear her deep, sleep-thick breathing. A small window gave a view of Mogollon's main drag. He saw the brim of a man's behatted head at the lowest edge of the window frame. The hat of a New Mexico police officer, who he assumed was standing watch. When he and the Englishman and the woman had sufficiently healed, he imagined they would be transported to a more secure location.

The Englishman wriggled his head into the pillow. "What did that doctor shoot into me? Lovely stuff."

"The doc has cooked you on it."

He nodded dopily. "Oh yes, I am well pickled."

"You seem okay."

"A few gobbets of flesh missing here and there, but I feel jim . . . *dandy*." The Englishman hummed the refrain to "Polly Wolly Doodle," then stopped. "You were very cool in the heat of it. Your hand did not tremble."

"I have been there before" was all Micah could say.

"Korea?" Off Micah's nod, the Englishman said, "Me as well. Royal Marines. The 1181st. First boots on the ground. Silent as death."

"You must have been young."

"Oh yes. A wee stripling. But I found I had an aptitude for it. Killing, I mean. It didn't trouble me. I woke up screaming in the trenches sometimes, yes, but not half so much as the other lads. It is horrible to have a talent for something so dreadful, but there you have it."

Micah nodded. They were both good at the same damned thing.

"They gave me a dishonorable discharge for knobbing my CO and breaking his nose," the Englishman continued. "He deserved it, I assure you. After that, I came here. There was nothing for me back home. The marines turned me into an agent of chaos, yes? A piranha set loose in a goldfish tank. I was not fit for polite society. But here I found a heightened need for a man with my particular skills. The land of the free and the home of the brave. Your country is still so . . . *unformed*. Even now. And that lack of form creates pockets for me to ply my trade."

"You were cool in the cut, too," said Micah. He did not exactly mean it as a compliment.

"Hm."

The men kept their peace. In time, the Englishman spoke. "The doctor took your eye?"

"He took it."

"Well then, I am sorry."

Micah said, "They will put us in prison. Give us the electric chair."

"Hmmmm."

"They took our pistols."

"Hmmmm."

Faintly, the woman's breathing carried over the curtain.

"We are still in Mogollon," Micah said. "On the main strip."

"Near the stable?"

"Near enough."

"We could take those horses," said the Englishman. "Light out."

Micah frowned. "Horses?"

The Englishman grinned. "It's a few minutes' hard gallop to the woods. They run deep and thick in this part of the state. We could melt right into them."

"Can you ride?"

"Capably, yes."

Micah had some experience with horses. He was no expert, but he could ride.

He said, "You and I?"

"Why not?"

"I do not know if I can ride with the man who stole my eye," said Micah.

"I'm humbly sorry again about your eye. We had reason to kill each other before. Money was our sole motivator, yes? Without it, there's no reason to kill anyone or do much of anything, truth be told."

Micah didn't see the line being so clear-cut. There were reasons outside of money why some men needed to get themselves dead. "What about Appleton?"

"Oh, I imagine he's well pleased by this turn of events. The prisons will eat us all up, and he won't owe anyone a cent."

"I still aim to kill him."

The Englishman grinned. "What chutzpah."

"The woman?" Micah said.

"Piss on her head. She tried to kill us."

Micah could see the Englishman's point of view . . . still, part of him rebelled at leaving her. He was curious. Clearly her attack had been planned, which meant she knew who they were—and how dangerous, too. Knowing so, why did she act so recklessly?

"I will think on it," he said, and shuffled back toward his bed.

"Micah."

Micah started. It had been years since anyone had addressed him by his Christian name.

"It will have to be tomorrow," the Englishman said.

"Can you manage?"

The Englishman coughed weakly. "With some more of that doctor's magical cocktail."

"You know my name. I do not know yours."

The Englishman seemed reluctant, but ultimately he spoke. "Ebenezer."

Micah had not known that a black man could visibly blush, but Ebenezer appeared to be doing so now.

"Ebenezer Elkins. My parents were sadists," he said with a slight shrug. "It is the only explanation. You may call me Eb, if it suits."

"Eb. That is good."

"Hm. So be it."

7

THE DOCTOR RETURNED the next day. He saturated a ball of cotton in rubbing alcohol and poked it into Micah's socket. This caused him considerable pain, as the doctor averred it would. He offered Micah another shot of morphine.

"I do not need it."

The doctor nodded. "The US Marshals are coming to get you, is what I hear."

"When?" Micah asked.

"Tomorrow or the day after."

"Just me?"

"And the other fella. The woman goes someplace else."

The doctor passed back through the curtain. Micah heard him offer Ebenezer a shot, which the Englishman happily accepted. After the doctor had left, and once Micah could hear Eb's morphine-thickened snores, he got up and went to look in on the woman.

She lay in bed with a sheet draped over her legs up to her hips and another folded across her breasts. Her stomach was bare. An ulcerated hole lay to the right of her belly button, oozing at its edges.

Her eyelids fluttered. She saw him. Her pupils constricted.

"Come to kill me?" she croaked.

Micah was not angry at her for trying to assassinate him. He had no leg to stand on, morally speaking, having done the same thing himself. He poured water from the bedside jug and held the glass to her lips. Gratefully, she drank.

"What is your name?" he asked.

"Minerva Atwater."

"You one of the Atwater clan out of Tuscaloosa?"

"I have no family in that part of the world." She drank some more. "So they took your eye?"

"It is gone."

She uttered a note of sympathy. "Was it my round that—?"

Micah shook his head. "The other man. With a little derringer, concealed."

The sun shone through a window overlooking the main street. Micah could see the back of the deputy's head where he stood guard.

"He hired me to get you," Minerva said. "Appleton."

"That was my figuring." Micah gestured to where the Englishman lay behind the curtain. "Appleton hired him, too. But it seemed you were more intent on him than me."

She shifted her body and winced. "Goddamn Christly hell, don't that hurt. But the doctor says no vitals were hit."

"Will you ever dance again?"

"What makes you think I'm a dancer?"

"You should try. You are not cut out for this."

Minerva sneered. "You figure I should be tending home fires?"

Micah offered her another drink. She snatched the glass from him. "I'm not a spit-bubbling infant." She drank and coughed, water dribbling down her chin. "I just only started collecting bounties. I'll get better."

"You will not."

"The hell I won't."

"You will not, because you are finished. The Feds get here tomorrow."

She dwelled on this. "I guess that's fair enough."

"It is for me and the English fellow. I do not know what you have done."

Micah was certain that she hadn't done much. This could very well be her first transgression. They would put her away for a long time all the same.

"Maybe they'll hang me," she said.

"It is doubtful," said Micah.

"They hanged a woman named Ellen Watson up in Natrona County for cattle rustling. And Lizzie Potts in California, on account of stoving her husband's head in with a shovel. That all went down a century ago, but still."

"You appear to have studied these matters."

"So what, then?" she said. "We just gonna let them take us, I guess?"

"That," said Micah, "or we slip our necks from the noose."

Minerva stared at him a long time.

"Take me," she said.

"Well, I do not know."

"I won't be a burden. I can move as fast as greased goose shit when I have to. How would we do it?"

"Can you ride a horse?"

"I helped out at a local stable when I was a girl. To earn some pin money. Used to canter the horses around the paddock—y'know, exercise them. Most of them were nags or glue-footers, but I can ride any horse you put in front of me."

Micah said, "Okay."

"And him?" Minerva said, meaning the Englishman.

"Oh yes." The Englishman's druggy voice floated over the curtain. "I shall be along. I was hoping to leave you for the crows, but Mr. Shughrue's veins run thick with the milk of human kindness. But be aware, milady—if you so much as look at me funny, I will snap your neck like a hen's."

8

THEY MADE THEIR ATTEMPT the following evening. The sunlight was paling over the ridges. Chain lightning flared soundlessly to the east. The day had been spent in nervous anticipation—they expected to catch the rumble of the marshals' trucks down the main road. But the rumble had not come.

Their clothes had been confiscated. Their boots, too. But otherwise their wardship was surprisingly lax. They had not been handcuffed or re-strained in any way. A deputy checked on them every few hours. In all, they had been treated more like convalescing patients—which they were—than ruthless and calculating mercenaries. This gave them ample opportunity to plan their escape.

The three of them grunted in pain as they wound bedsheets around their bodies. When they were done, they resembled Socratic disciples on their way to the agora. The deputy guarding them was an easy matter. Micah ethered him with the contents of a brown bottle the doctor had carelessly left in a supply cupboard—it was almost as if these gormless deputy dawgs *wanted* them to escape.

Micah arranged the deputy's body in the chair, tipping his head back so he would not choke on his tongue. He took the deputy's sidearm and walkie-talkie.

They crossed the street barefoot in the deepening night, bedsheets fluttering. A few solitary squares of light burned in the odd house window, but the street was empty. Nobody saw them make their way to the stable, looking like a trio of half-fleshed Halloween ghosts.

The stable was deserted, the horses penned. They found saddles in the tack room. It was a chore strapping them to the horses: the light was thin and they were badly hurt, and only Minerva was a true horse-woman. The horses whinnied softly, but to Micah's ears they might as well have been shrieking. The seconds snipped off a clock inside his head, counting down to the moment when their escape would be dis-covered.

Micah assayed his companions. The woman was clearly nauseated with pain. The doctor had stitched her wounds with catgut, but a goodly number must have popped already, because her bedsheets were bloody—only a pinpricking so far, but the more she moved, the faster the blood would flow. The Englishman was not much better. Micah re-solved to abandon them if they couldn't keep up—perhaps they could kill each other before the authorities slapped handcuffs on them, if that was their wish.

The walkie-talkie crackled. "Wylie, come in. Edie's off to the Sip N' Dip for bear claws and coffee. I get you some?"

Micah pictured the town sheriff—fat and beery the way only southern lawmen could be, a barrel-shaped gut straining against the buttons of his mule-colored shirt.

"Wylie, come on back now." Silence. Then, with a wary edge: "Wy?"

"Mount up, goddamn it," Micah said.

Minerva and Eb struggled into their saddles. Micah knotted the deputy's pistol to his saddle with a length of rawhide. The horses shied beneath them—Minerva's steed was an especially twitchy specimen. Micah shouldered the stable doors open. They galloped onto the main road, cracking the stirrups into the horses' ribs.

A few townsfolk occurred in lit windows and on the porches of the houses along the main street. They watched the criminals ride into the deep black of the mountainsides—half naked, bloody, ungainly atop animals that dearly wished to buck them off, without food or flint or medicine. What an odd sight they must have made: three pasty phantoms on horseback stampeding into the wild, like a fever dream of the Old West.

"God will see them dead," one man said to his wife once the trio had ridden from sight. "His holy eye will seek them out and cut them down."

9

MICAH'S EYELID FLUTTERED over his empty socket as he flogged his horse into the foothills. The slack flesh, no longer bulwarked by an eyeball, flapped in the wind that blew into his face. The eyelid made a tender sucking sound, the wet edges of each lid gumming shut before blowing open again, as he imagined wet curtains might do. The sensation was not entirely disagreeable—the wind washed into the empty socket, cooling the inflamed tissues. It felt as if it had been swabbed out with lidocaine, or essence of spearmint.

They halted after half an hour of hard riding. White froth foamed at the edges of the horses' mouths. They had reached a split in the path.

Micah examined his companions. The woman was slumped over the saddle, her head lolling against the horse's neck. The Englishman sat favoring his wounded hip; his sheet was red with blood, the excess running down his leg to drip steadily off his toes. His arm swayed limply from his ruined shoulder, and yet he was grinning like an idiot.

Micah considered which way to go while his companions waited patiently and bled.

"We could ride up and off the path until the ridge plateaus," he said.

"Ride, then," said Eb. "I will follow."

"And if I fall," Minerva said, her voice muffled by the horse's mane, "leave me where I lie."

Micah said, "I will."

The *whop-whop* of helicopter blades carried over the hillsides. They sallied their horses under an oak tree; the horses' hooves crackled on a carpet of rotted acorns. Once the whirlybird had passed on, Micah gussied his horse along the steep incline. The beast stirred up clouds of dust, which drifted into his empty socket. He probed inside it with his finger and touched an exposed nerve—a jolt of pain drove straight back into his skull.

The hillside carried up over bear grass and fescue and through a copse of gnarled desert willows. Micah's breath exited his mouth in plosive pops as he leaned hard into the horse. Every so often, he hazarded a glance back. The other two appeared to be held atop their horses less by gravity than by some unholy magic. Their heads sagging, their bodies rocking so it seemed they would pitch into the hawthorn on the horses' very next step. Yet they kept following Micah, a pair of ghostly effigies.

He topped the plateau. A bone-searching wind rattled the scorpion weeds. The other two caught up. Their sheets were now more blood than white. Micah gussied his horse alongside Minerva and checked to see that she was still alive. Her breath came thin and raspy.

"We must sleep together," said Micah. "Any other way, we freeze to death."

They led their horses to a dip in the earth bulwarked by a flat-topped chunk of shale. The limbs of a cottonwood tree fanned overhead to provide cover. Micah dismounted and corralled Minerva's horse. He popped her feet from the stirrups and braced her across his shoulders.

". . . goddamn hands to yourself," she mumbled. She was in a dream state, trapped someplace between waking and sleeping, alive and dead.

Micah lashed the horses to a nearby tree. They nickered unhappily, hungry after the long ride. The three escapees bedded down on the hard ground. Micah wrapped his arms around Minerva. Her spine touched his chest. He twined his thick legs with hers. There was nothing sexual in this—they were too exhausted for carnalities. Micah did not find her comely in any case; he preferred a woman with breasts and hips, some brisket on her bones. The Englishman curled up behind Micah; an oily, carbolic smell leached out of his skin from the powerful narcotics he had been given.

The wind shivered empty seedpods. It churned up dust devils that spun through the gloom like mad tops. If the woman made it through the coming hours, it would count as some manner of miracle. The Englishman was a mess, too; Micah felt the blood trickling from Ebenezer's wounds and soaking his own sheet.

If they died, he would not bury them. He had no shovel, and no time for the observance. If one of their horses was superior to his own, he would take it. He would hide out a few weeks, recuperate, then resume his pursuit of Seaborn Appleton.

He closed his eye and fell into a dreamless sleep.

10

MICAH AWOKE to spy the woman on her knees, hefting a rock the size of a stag's head, readying to bring it down on the Englishman's skull.

It was dawn. New sunlight ribboned through the trees. Minerva was a vision straight out of hell: her face a mask of dried blood. Her eyes bulged, wide and full of hate. Her arms quivered with the weight of the huge stone she bore above her head.

Micah rolled away, believing the blow was destined for him. He reached inside his sheet and came up with the deputy's pistol. He pointed it at Minerva, then looked at the Englishman. The sand under his head was soaked with blood, leading Micah to the false conclusion that she'd brained him already; a closer inspection made it clear that he was merely unconscious.

Neither Micah nor Minerva spoke. Her arms trembled under the weight of the rock. Micah gestured with the gun that she should drop it. She hesitated. He then leveled the barrel dead between her eyes. She set it down softly.

Micah shook his head—his skull was quite literally buzzing. He probed inside his ruined socket with his thumb; a winged insect clambered out of it and flew away before he could identify the damned thing.

Micah flicked the gun barrel toward a stand of pines and mouthed, *Move.* Minerva managed to stand. Her sheet crackled with blood. The bottom of it was heavy with caked crimson and dust. She walked resolutely to the trees. Micah followed.

"That marks the second time in three days you have tried to kill the Englishman," he said.

Minerva held a hand to her side. Blood sponged through the sheet and leaked over her fingers. She frowned as though it were coming from a spigot she'd forgotten to shut off. There was something to be admired about a person who could bleed with such a total lack of concern.

"I cannot travel with anyone who wishes to crush a sleeping man's skull with a stone," said Micah. "Tell me why."

"It doesn't concern you."

"It does now. Until you are dead, or him."

"It could be him that's dead," she pleaded. "Let me make it him."

"No."

"Why do you care?"

"If I am given good reason, I may be inclined to take your side in this."

Minerva scrutinized him with hooded eyes. Her stare was calculating. The odds must have toted in his favor, because, at a breathless clip, she told him everything.

11

IT HAPPENED in the springtime. Minerva Atwater was eleven years old at the time. She lived in Grass Valley, California, with her father, Charles, and younger brother, Cortland. Their mother had died in labor with Cort, whose skull was evidently too wide for her birthing chute. The loss destroyed Minerva's father, yet he continued on for the sake of his children, finding work in the silver mines.

They lived in an isolated shotgun shack skirting the Yuba Reservoir. In the summer months, Minerva and Cort explored the grasslands while their father toiled underground.

The day it happened was much like any other. Cort and Minny—as her father and brother called her back then—romped through the tall grass to a sandy wash, where the water rolled out blue and clean in the afternoon light. Cort was six. He was thin, his hair prone to cowlicks, and he wore wire-rimmed spectacles patched with cellulose tape. He wanted to hold Minny's hand while they walked—sometimes she refused, finding it babyish, but Cort's bottom lip would tremble as his eyes brimmed behind his thick glasses. He adored his big sister and was hurt when she denied him these small kindnesses. So she would take his hand, which was often sticky and moist the way only small boys' hands can be. They would wade into the water with their trousers rolled to the knees to catch mudskippers and narrow-mouth toads.

In the late afternoon, they made their way closer to home; their father would arrive soon and call them in for supper. They lazed under the trees in a shady grove, sunlight hitting the leaves and giving their bare skin a faint green tint.

"Minny?"

"Yes, Cort, what is it?"

"Why can't we have nice things?"

"What do you mean?"

Cort sucked on his knuckle. He'd skinned it scaling a rock.

"The Safeway has Granny Smith apples. I never seen a green like them. Different than grass green or leaf green or . . ."

"Or grasshopper green?"

Cort smiled. "They's so *perfectly* green. But we never get none. We hafta eat the crab apples that grow around here. They give my tummy the crummies."

"Apples are apples," said Minny. "Don't grumble."

"And buttons, too. Minny, my shirt's got two bust buttons, and Dad never gets new buttons to sew on."

Cort held his shirt out as proof. Minny knew about Cort's buttons. Her shirts were missing buttons, too, and her big toes had worn through her socks.

"We eat potatoes every night," said Cort. "Boiled and baked and mashed without butter. I believe my tongue will fall off if I have one more bite of spuds."

Charles Atwater was a fine father and a hard worker, but his one failing was at the card table. He was a gambler, and a poor one. And so, his children's clothes had busted buttons. And so, his children ate potatoes and crab apples.

"We will eat high-class apples one day," said Minny.

"Promise?"

"Of course."

There came a rustling from the feather grass. Minny faced it, ears pricked. An arrow-shaped head appeared. It was green, too. Different from the grass green or leaf green or the green of a Granny Smith apple.

The green of a snake's head. The largest snake Minny had ever seen.

She had dealings with snakes, as did any child growing up in the wilds. Harmless blackneck garters were most common, but she had startled coachwhips and Chihuhuan hognoses, even an old massasauga rattler coiled in placid contentment under the porch. But she had never seen the likes of this one.

It glided forward inch by nightmarish inch, its movements so silken it was as if its belly were lined with ball bearings. To Minerva, it was not unlike watching a train of inconceivable size steam out of a tunnel. Its scales had the shimmer of hammered copper gone green in the rain. It made its way toward them with a sickening but somehow dreamy speed, the grass whispering against its dry body.

Minerva grabbed Cort's arm, jerking him up. He uttered a yelp of pain and confusion. The grove spilled down to the water; their only escape route was blocked by the advancing snake. Minny had half a mind to hurdle the thing. Jesus, it was *thick*, as stout around as a quarter horse's leg—but she had jumped over bigger logs. But logs didn't move the way the snake did, with those lazy yet threatening undulations. And she didn't think the water was any way out: she was pretty sure the snake was as nimble in water, or nimbler, than on land. They would be at a disadvantage if it followed them into the reservoir.

So they had to go *up*. They would have to climb a tree.

Cort had seen the snake by then, too. He actually adjusted his spectacles, as if under the assumption they were deceiving him.

"That's a *biiiig* one," he said, his voice set at a high-pitch whinny.

"Go," said Minny, shoving him toward the nearest hackberry tree.

The snake . . . sweet Christ, that *snake*. It was fourteen, sixteen, eigh-teen feet long. It did not have an end.

Minny did not know then that the serpent was a green anaconda, the largest of its kind. She did not know—in fact, would never know—that it had hatched in the Orinoco basin in Venezuela and was netted by an indig-enous tribesman while it was still an adolescent. The tribesman sold it to an exotic animal merchant. It twice escaped containment and ate that mer-chant's more valued specimens, a scarlet macaw and a spider monkey. The merchant then sold the snake to a Mr. Edwin P. Popplewell, operator of the Popplewell Traveling Menagerie. For some years, the snake had circuited the southwestern states, gawped at by rubes in Bullhead City and Las Cru-ces. One night, while the menagerie was camped on the banks of the Yuba, the snake escaped. When Popplewell noticed that its cage was empty, he did not search for it or report it missing. The snake was a menace, having consumed both his gnu and a tiger cub, offering nothing in return save its sullen lethargy. *Let it be someone else's problem*, Popplewell figured.

Minny and Cort were halfway up the tree when Cort's footing slipped. His heel slid on a branch with a frictionless sound, as if the bark had been oiled. Next, he was falling. He uttered a fearful squawk, but that was all. It happened quickly—so quick that Minny didn't know he'd fallen at first. There was just this terrible *absence* below her, as if the ghostly outline of her brother were still there.

Cort fell fifteen yards straight down. He landed on his feet, the way cats always do. The lower bones of his left leg snapped with the sound of lake ice cracking in a spring thaw. He fell over then and struck his head on an exposed rock and began to jitter as if in a terrible seizure.

The snake rushed at him. Minerva's lungs unlocked and she screamed.

"Daddy! Daddy, come quick!"

They were within shouting distance of their shack. Their father was almost always home by this time. A punctual man, was Charles Atwater.

"Daddy, please hurry, a snake's got Cort!"

A snake's got Cort. It sounded so silly. Something you might cry out in a dream. But this was happening. Terribly, it was happening.

The snake could have climbed up the tree. Minerva and Cort were no safer there than on the ground, as Minerva would later realize. But that was not necessary now, seeing as its meal had fallen right in front of it. It wrapped the boy in the greasy rope of its body, which flexed and thinned as the huge muscles worked beneath its skin.

"Oh no!" was all Minerva could say, watching the snake coil lovingly around her baby brother—for she still thought of him that way sometimes, as a baby, despite the fact that he could talk and count his fingers and toes. His little feet stuck out one end of the snake's coils, one boot off, his baby toe poking out of his sock. His head on the other end, his spectacles askew with the right lens shattered, the pressure purpling his face. Blood squeezed through the pores of his cheeks and ran from the edges of his eyes. There came a series of shuddery snaps as his ribs broke.

Minerva couldn't stop screaming. She wasn't screaming for her father—it was too late for that. Not for God or some divine intercession. She just screamed at the horror of it all, at the dark, sucking hole that had opened so suddenly in her life.

The snake unwound itself. Cort's body tumbled limply from its embrace. The snake's jaw unhinged and it began to consume the boy, starting at his skull. He might still have been breathing.

Minerva screamed until she went temporarily blind with the effort. She screamed over the hot hum of the cicadas. This did not startle the red-tailed hawk circling the sky above. From that bird's vantage, what was happening below was simply nature taking its course in the way nature sometimes did. Something splintered deep inside Minny's head. Perhaps she went just a little insane on that hazy sunlit afternoon. Who could blame her?

Time passed. The snake slithered back into the feather grass. Its belly was swollen with the outline of Cort's body, stretched so that its scales separated to show the silky silverskin beneath, so sheer you could almost make out the boy's features.

Where was her father? Why hadn't he come with an axe, a butcher knife, with only his two hands and the fatherly madness that must come when he sees his youngest in such peril? But he never came. He'd turned his back on her and Cort.

It was night by the time Minerva's legs unlocked and she could move again. She shimmied down the tree—her body had detached from her mind, which was totally blank. Cort's spectacles lay on the ground. The moon glossed the one unbroken lens.

She slipped across the night-lit field to their shack. She found her father sitting dead in a chair with a bullet hole in his forehead.

Minerva was too shocked to believe it possible. It wasn't a hole at all. No, it was just a blot of raspberry jam on his forehead. Or a flash burn he'd gotten at the mine. Never mind that his eyes were wide open and his last thoughts were splattered over the wall behind him.

She touched her finger to the hole. She would wipe away the jam, was what she'd do, then tell her father what had happened to Cort. Then they would get the axe and the cudgel and find and kill that horrible snake.

Her finger slipped into the hole. Into her father's skull. It was cold in there.

12

"MY FATHER WAS SHOT by a black man with an English accent. A hired killer."

Minerva trembled as she spoke. She had begun to shake, though that could be the blood loss. Her eyes remained hard on Micah throughout. "My father owed debts. To a bookie, mainly. Thelonious Skell was the bookie's name."

"Thel . . . Skell?"

She nodded. "It was Skell who hired the Englishman to claim the debt. My father—" She gritted her teeth as a wave of pain flooded through her. "My father owed him five thousand dollars. I don't entirely blame Skell. My father owed him. But what did Cort owe? Debts should not carry forward that way." She paused, spat a sac of blood. "It was the Englishman who did it. He stole Cort's life by stealing my father's . . . He would have saved us. If he was still alive, my father . . . he would have. But the Englishman killed him, and wrecked my life in the bargain. And that is the which of why I aim to kill him."

Micah nodded. "You are sure it was him?"

Minerva said, "You figure there's a bunch of British Negro assassins out there?"

Micah had only ever heard of the one. "You have been chasing him a long time."

"Until that man is dead, I cannot rest. So. Will you let me end it?"

"No."

Minerva bared her teeth. "Piss on you."

"We are hurt," Micah told her. "Our best chance is to band together. Once we have made our way clear, go ahead and finish matters with the Englishman."

Minerva said, "I don't need your goddamn permission." Then, betraying some worry: "If I don't kill him, he'll kill me."

Micah shook his head. "He will not."

"How do you figure? I tried to kill both of you. But I tried to kill him a lot deader than you."

Micah knew men just like the Englishman—he himself *was* a lot like the Englishman. Ebenezer killed because he was good at it, and because the killing didn't trouble his soul. But he did not kill without reason or without a clear threat against him. Unless Minerva made a move, he'd bear no grudge against her for trying to flatline him back at the stables. That was just business.

"He kills for money," Micah said simply, "and you are not worth anything."

She silently digested this. Micah laughed real soft.

"Did you ever consider the sweetness of the moment? If you were to draw him in, gain his confidence, and then . . ."

Minerva bit her tongue. But Micah could tell she was pondering it.

13

THE ENGLISHMAN LURCHED into wakefulness like a ghoul shuddering from its casket. His neck wore a plated collar of blood. Micah was uncertain whether Minerva would get her chance to end his life—Ebenezer appeared to be knocking on death's door with some urgency already.

They set off again. They were dehydrated—their horses, too—their stomachs empty and their wounds festering. Simply getting mounted required a massive outlay of will. The Englishman was sinking into a delirium; he rambled on about last night's nightmare, where rats—the galling black-eyed bastards infesting the sewers in his hometown of Stretford— were packed into his chest cavity, squirming contentedly in the fuming stew of his guts, their ropy pink tails curled around his ribs—

"Their fur tickles." He tittered. "So *tickly*."

The sun crested the hills and beat down wrathfully. Horseflies alighted on their shoulders and heels, carrying away tasty morsels of flesh. They came to a pool of brackish, sulfur-smelling water. They drank and retched most of it back up, then drank some more. Their horses drank and exhibited a mild rejuvenation. They rode on. The sun turned the blood on their bodies to a dark crackling. The Englishman rode naked to the waist, the sheet wadded clumsily around his hips. His flesh was a heavy, beautiful black with an undernote of blue.

A rough path bled down through the swale to a swift-running river. They followed it in the direction of its flow, their shadows lengthening across still pools where the river ran into slackwater hollows. Micah spotted a pin of smoke rising some ways off. They crossed at a shallow meander, tracking the smoke. Micah drew the deputy's pistol.

A fire. Three men sat ringing it. Naked as jaybirds, drying themselves after bathing in the river. Their clothes hung from a line knotted between two trees.

"Stand up," Micah said.

They did. Two of them covered their privates. The third did not.

"What are you doing here?" Micah asked them.

"We're hunting for burl," the shameless man told him.

"Do you have a vehicle nearby?"

"A pickup," the second man told Micah, gesturing with a nod. "Five hundred yards thataway."

"We will need clothes," said Micah.

"So will we," said the man who had until then not uttered a word.

Micah said, "Do you have extra pairs?"

The same man said, "We do not."

A pause.

Micah said, "We need clothes."

14

SEABORN APPLETON was a happy man. Delighted, in fact.

Business was *booming*. He had experienced an unprecedented run of prosperity ever since Micah Shughrue had fallen off his scent.

That situation could not have resolved itself any more pleasantly. Shughrue was dead, or assumedly so. The English assassin and the woman had been cut out of the picture, too. He owed not a nickel for their services. Saints be praised!

Of course, he had felt some concern upon discovering they had escaped before the US Marshals had arrived in Mogollon. But those who witnessed their flight claimed that the trio was bedraggled, bloody, and without supplies—and on *horseback*, the idiots. They could not have lasted long in the unforgiving wilds. Their bones were surely yellowing inside a wolf den by now. Savages, the three of them. Appleton found no joy in his dealings with such individuals. He was a businessman. He preferred not to traffic with unsavories, other than the ones buying his merchandise.

His VW was parked in a field skirting the mining town of Chloride, New Mexico. This place had fallen upon hard times. Its citizenry was primed for the sort of succor Appleton could provide. It had gotten so that he could see the dread and anxiety hanging in a pall above such burgs. It resembled a thick gray cowl. It was an exquisite sight. It looked like money.

His men were sleeping in a car fifty yards off, in the shelter of the willows. The night was still, only the chirruping of crickets. Appleton poured a stiff belt of rum and reflected on how good things happened to good people—to enterprising people such as himself.

A sound carried across the wind-scrubbed earth, from the direction of the willow trees. A strangled scream that became a hissing whistle . . . the sound a man might make as his throat was cut. It was joined by a rising adagio of pain and bewilderment that ended abruptly, replaced by a wet hiccuping sound. That went on awhile, too, before being ushered into the softer notes of night.

Appleton adjusted the flame on his oil lamp, washing the VW's interior with its shifting light. The sliding door was open. He could barely discern the flat fall of the earth, the rich soil dark as grave dirt—

"Eugene?" he called. "Danny?"

The imbeciles. They drank without measure. They played childish games and hooted laughter well into the night, only to act petulant the following morning, their heads rotten with the ache. He really should find new men, ones whose wits challenged his own.

He held the lantern out, squinting against its greasy glow. A figure coalesced from the darkness. It was joined by another.

"You dolts," said Appleton. "If you're looking for liquor, I have none for you. Go back to the goddamn car."

A third figure joined. Appleton's breath came out in a sharp hiss.

"Mr. Appleton."

The voice seemed to come from a great distance away, deep within the guts of the earth . . . and yet it was close, too, so terribly close, nestled right up to his ear.

"I have come home to roost," Micah Shughrue said.

Hearing his voice, Seaborn Appleton began to scream.

He would scream for some time before all was said and done.

PART THREE

THE

CIRCLING

1980

1

PETTY SHUGHRUE did not know what this creature might be, but she was positive it was not a man.

It looked human. Two arms. Two legs. A head.

But that was the problem—it only *looked* that way. For one, it was far taller than any man on earth; the dairyman, Mr. Bickner, was the tallest man Petty had ever seen, and this thing was at least two feet taller than him. Its arms were long and its joints were set in weird places, making its arms bend in odd ways. Its legs were also too long and did not hinge at the knees so much as pivot in all directions, a bit like a spider's legs. It wore dark pants and a duster of black lizard skin. The coat rippled out from its body, stinking like the dead gopher she'd found under the porch two springs ago.

Its face . . . Petty didn't ever want to look at its face again. Its head was big and bulgy and hairless. It had no nose, only a pair of moist holes. Its mouth was so wide it nearly split its head apart—and its lips were plump, fleshy, somehow succulent, which was a word Petty had recently learned in grammar class. *The summer strawberry was succulent.* You almost wanted to kiss those lips—not really, in fact you'd rather kiss anything else, a bowl of razor blades or a starving piranha or any other thing at all . . . What Petty felt was an ungodly compulsion, a revolting *desire* to kiss those lips. Even though she knew they would taste like death.

Even worse than its mouth were its eyes. Two chunks of coal screwed into its head. The moonlight reflected off them in terrible ways, showing their broiling inner cores—Petty swore she could see things squirming behind its eyes like leeches in a jam jar.

It moved at a swift clip without effort. Its legs hurdled logs and snarled deadfalls in great, unhurried strides. She was carried along with it, her hand swallowed in its own. Her feet were still bare and she wore nothing but her nightdress, but she wasn't cold or sore, even though they had covered many miles. Her feet rarely touched the earth—she seemed to ghost along it on a ribbon of air.

The Long Walker. That was what she would call this thing. It was her habit to name everything: her dolls, Jenny and Josephine; her wooden trains, Honey and Tugger and Pip; even the little brown mouse that lived in a hole in the kitchen, Mr. Squeaks.

She had been with the Long Walker for . . . Petty could not say how long. Her mind was foggy like it was after the doctor took out her tonsils. Time didn't seem important. She could tell some hours had passed, maybe even a day. She was thirsty.

Soon, my dear. We both have thirsts to slake.

She had not uttered a word. Could this thing read her thoughts? It must have. It had slid into her head somehow. This worried her, but what could she do about it?

"Where are we going?" she asked.

Your father owes my father, the Long Walker thought-spoke in her mind.

The trees petered out. They came to an empty field. An encampment of some kind was set up not far away. Petty could see lights winking—brightly colored ones, blinking and circling . . .

They skimmed across the grass. A traveling carnival came into view. Shaky old rides, a midway, caravans where the workers slept. They circled the carnival's perimeter where the light was weak, a pair of wolves scoping things out. They passed a caravan; Petty caught a snatch of a familiar jingle playing on a transistor radio hanging from its open window on a strap:

"We're gonna make a . . . hot cereal lover outta you! With ready-to-serve Quaker Oatmeal—you did it!"

Cars were parked on a strip of beaten earth not far from the ticket taker's booth. There were Monte Carlos and Dodges and pickup trucks with bales of hay in their beds. Beyond the cars Petty saw a string of shotgun shacks lining a paved road; they must be near one of the little towns ringing her home, places with names like Mescalero and Pecos and Elephant Butte. *Elephant Butte attracts flies*, her mother used to joke, even though it was pronounced *beaut*, not *butt*. Petty was sure the people of Elephant Butte were nice—people generally were around here: they worked and scraped their knuckles raw and drank too much and prayed away their sins every Sunday at church.

They skirted the midway, where grizzled-looking hucksters called out "One play, one win!" and "Test your luck for half a buck!" Rain dripped from the awnings of the ring toss and whack-a-mole booths. The Long Walker pulled her toward a striped tent. Light spilled from under its canopy and shone through eyelets where no ropes had been strung. They stopped a ways from the open flaps at the back, getting a view of its insides. Thirty or forty people were seated on folding chairs, facing away from Petty. Most of them were dressed simply, in sun-bleached frocks or overalls. A lot of the men had pipe holsters threaded through their hand-tooled leather belts, with their smoking pipes looped through them.

Everyone was focused on the man who stood on a raised stage in front. A preacher. It was not uncommon to find lay preachers peddling old-time religion from town to town around here—some people just couldn't get enough. If there was a midweek opportunity for a top-up, they jumped at it. Strange to find a preacher at a carnival, but maybe some of these folk felt the urge to atone after too much cotton candy and spins on the Tilt-A-Whirl.

The preacher was tall and bony and what Petty's mom would have called onion-eyed—meaning they bulged from his sockets like pearl onions—but he spoke with great conviction.

". . . and many of them that sleep in the dust of the earth shall awake, some to everlasting life, and some to shame and never-ending contempt!" he thundered as he strode across the stage. "*Hell!* That's right, that eternal place of damnation where you *will* go if you are not right with God when you perish. That's right—Hell is a real place! And you will be sent there, sure as shooting, if you do not obey the Lord's commandments!"

The congregants swayed in their seats. Rain pattered on the tent and dripped to the earth in ragged streamers.

"What of God's promise of eternal life? There are conditions of that promise! *Whosoever believeth in him should not perish, but have everlasting life*, the Good Book says. So we must believe in Him. *As Moses lifted up the serpent in the wilderness, even so must the Son of man be lifted up!*" The preacher stabbed an accusing finger at his audience. "My question to you, my good Christian neighbors, is this: Are you lifting the Son of man up as Moses lifted the serpent, or are you wandering around the wilderness?"

The Long Walker pulled a flute from the folds of its duster. It looked as if it was made out of a bone—perhaps a human one. It held it to its lips. The notes the flute made weren't harmonious . . . but they were compelling. Petty turned toward the Long Walker instinctively, the same way a moth was drawn to a bug zapper.

The children in the tent turned, too. There were only five or six, but they all looked back. The adults didn't take the slightest notice. A child seated in the back row—a girl of four or five—stood. She had been sitting on the aisle beside her mother. Nobody saw her walk out of the tent into the spitting rain.

The little girl strode right up to the Long Walker. A shy smile touched the edges of her heart-shaped mouth. But her eyes were huge with fear and her shoulders were set way back, as if every part of her was repulsed. The Long Walker whispered to her. Petty imagined how its voice would feel sliding into her ear—she pictured a thin, unbreakable icicle. The girl giggled. The Long Walker reached out and touched the girl on the tip of her upturned nose. She covered her mouth as if the Long Walker had said a dirty word. The flesh of her nose was beginning to blister already; after the ensuing chaos had ebbed, her mother would pale when she noticed the very tip of her daughter's nose had gone the cracked gray of an old, unwrapped piece of liver forgotten in a freezer for months. The girl walked back into the tent.

"Now, what the *Loooooord* wants," the preacher thundered on, "is for you to pay the tariff! The wages of sin, ladies and gents, is a high price indeed—"

"He touched me."

The preacher stopped midsentence. The little girl's voice cut through his sermon. She stood in the middle of the center aisle with her finger pointed at the holy man.

"The preacher. He touched me in my dirty spot." Her finger dipped down and down until it pointed between her legs.

The congregation rumbled. The men—most of them with thick, sunburned necks and brush-cut hair—began to redden as their jaws went tense.

"I did no such—" A low moan escaped the preacher, who had turned pale as cottage cheese. "Oh God! Lies, lies!"

The Long Walker made a noise that could have been laughter. The men had begun to rise, their fists balling at their hips. The preacher was frantic, rung by all those blood-hungry faces.

"No! No, I . . . Where is this girl's mother? Her father?" he said desperately. "They will tell you I did no such—"

"She was lost from my sight for five minutes," a woman in the back row said hollowly. "I have never lost track of her before, not once until tonight . . ."

"Let's draw and quarter the turd," a voice called out from the rear of the tent.

The Long Walker's face was fixed in an expression Petty could not read. It might even have been sadness.

The men advanced on the preacher, who raised his hands skyward in silent plea. The first man who reached him threw a fist with pure venom; the preacher's nose exploded. He fell. The men and more than a few women then fell upon him, kicking and stomping.

"Enough," the Long Walker said, sounding bored.

He took Petty's hand and led her away from the pandemonium.

2

THE GREYHOUND PULLED OVER on the side of the road at a quarter past five in the afternoon. Micah exited under a sun hazed with the grit lifting off the breakdown lane.

"Town's a mile or so thataway," the driver said, pointing.

Micah shouldered his bag. He had to stop himself from running. After that encounter in the woods, his first instinct had been to set off on foot after the thing that had snatched his daughter. But the creature would outdistance him easily, or back-flank him and kill him . . . or do something much worse.

Micah knew Petty would not be killed. She had been taken to establish Micah's purpose, his end goal. Aside from his wife, his daughter was the only person capable of compelling Micah to retrace his steps back . . . there. And the black thing knew Micah's heart as well as Micah did himself—better, just maybe.

He had hired a caretaker for Ellen, his wife. He had done so before on occasions when he needed to be away. Ellen's sister, Sherri, was usually available, but was out of town at present. When Sherri returned, she would take over the caregiver role. Ellen posed only the smallest of burdens. She lay in bed. Occasionally she would rise, eyes open but seeing nothing, lips trembling with words Micah couldn't quite understand, and pace the bedroom, vanity to door to nightstand. Her comatose state was unaffected. The doctors said this was uncommon behavior, but not unique. Her bedsores often burst during these episodes. Micah would trail her as she walked, dabbing ointment on her sores. The bedroom door was always locked at these times. There was no need for Petty to see her mother that way. Better to remember her as she'd been.

He hired a man to feed and water the animals. By all rights, his crops should die in his absence. But they would thrive. It had made Micah a wealthy man, the envy of those who eked a living out of the same inhospitable soil. But he was no crop whisperer. His fields produced simply because that was part of the deal—and that deal carried terrible penalties, too.

The town of Old Ditch seemed comatose. The industry had moved on, and with it went the hope, and with that went the incentive for the citizenry to improve. The buildings were stooped and tumbledown, as though affected with a case of architectural leprosy. A fine layer of dust had settled over the shop windows. A piebald dog dashed across the main street, through an intersection where the stoplights had gone dead.

Micah stopped in at a diner devoid of customers. The revolving pastry case displayed its unappealing wares: a lemon meringue pie so old the whipped eggs had cracked like the mud in a dry riverbed. A flyswatter lay on the countertop; below the swatter lay the smashed remains of the insects it had squashed.

A man's face appeared in the kitchen pass. Old, fatigued, a grease-spotted fry hat cocked on his head at a defeated angle.

"What'll you have?"

Micah set a dubious eye on the deformed pie, the coffee gone bitter on the burner.

"I am looking for a man."

"We don't traffic in that kind of business around here."

"He is English. Black. Speaks with an accent."

"There's only one man in town has one of those."

"Where can I find him?"

The man wiped his nose. "Sure you don't want something? Hash is the specialty of the house."

Salmonella is the specialty of this house, Micah thought.

"Just the man and where I can find him."

Half an hour later, Micah had walked to the end of a narrow street lined with derelict dwellings. He spotted a blank, sun-challenged face peering at him from an upper-story window. The piebald dog moped along after him, flinching whenever Micah turned to face it. He rooted half of a 7-Eleven sticky bun out of his pack and dropped it. The dog ate it with that same flinching fear, as if under the suspicion that the treat was poisoned—as if it had witnessed its fellow pooches die that very way, in moaning paroxysms on the street.

The house he arrived at was small, but in better condition than the others. Micah knocked. Footsteps shuffled to the door.

"Who's calling?"

"It is me, Ebenezer."

A pause. A considerable one. The door opened. Ebenezer Elkins stood in a housecoat knotted chastely at the waist. His right hand was bandaged. He was drinking. He appeared to have been doing so for some time.

He bowed and stepped aside. "Come in."

The main room was unadorned. The walls were bare save for the crucifixes hung at every corner. A small bookshelf with books that appeared to have been well read. *Demons in America*—that title jumped out at Micah.

Eb gestured to one of two chairs before taking a seat in the other. His bottle sat by the chair leg. He poured himself a splash.

"Where are my manners?" he said, gesturing with the bottle.

Micah consented. Eb limped into the kitchen and returned with a glass. He poured for Micah.

"How long have you lived here?"

"Years," said Eb.

"Looks like you just moved in."

"It does, doesn't it." Eb blearily stared around. His eyes were bloodshot, but he did not seem especially drunk. "I suppose I never expected to be here this long."

"Are you well?"

"Not especially. Thank you for asking. You?"

"Not really. What did you do to your hand?"

Eb waved the question away. They sat for a spell, drinking in silence.

"Have you come to kill me?" Eb asked.

Micah shook his head.

"I didn't think so," said Ebenezer. "I thought you would be coming soon. I . . . Believe it or not, I *dreamt* it. Which may sound ridiculous—or it would have at one point in our lives. Superstitious drivel."

He refilled their glasses. The hooch was strong, cheap, with a wicked burn.

"Lot of crucifixes," Micah remarked.

"I got a deal on them. Cheaper by the dozen."

"The Ebenezer I knew did not have much use for them."

Ebenezer looked at his feet. Each of them had spent the past fifteen years trying to unbecome the man the other had once known.

"It took my daughter," Micah said.

Eb looked up sharply. "You have a daughter?"

"By Ellen, yes. Petty. Ellen's naming. Pet is her common name."

"Ellen. How is she?"

Micah said, "She is at home and untroubled."

Eb's brows knitted. "Her daughter is gone and she is untroubled?"

"She is unaware of the loss."

The Englishman pursued it no further. "You have a daughter," he said again, disbelievingly. "Jesus Christ."

Micah said, "It took her two nights ago, in the woods edging my home. I encountered one of the handmaids. But the other one, the more dangerous one . . ."

"The Flute Player."

Micah nodded. "If you wish to call it that. It took my Pet."

"How do you know?"

"I heard its song on the wind," said Micah. "It wanted me to hear."

"And it's taking her back to . . . ?"

"Where else?"

Eb dropped his head again. His body appeared to deflate. His breath came heavy, as a man's does just before he's about to heave up his guts.

"Bloody fucking hell. I thought we ended all that," he rasped. "It almost killed us all, and it certainly wrecked the three of us going forward, but . . . I thought we put that to bed for good and all."

Micah did not fault the Englishman his belief. But was the thing they encountered in the woods ringing Little Heaven—the *real* terror, lurking within the black rock . . . Could such a thing truly be mastered by the hand of man? Or had they shackled it for only a brief while—years for them, for itself the mere blink of an eye—and given it time to heal, to plot, and to nurse its rage?

"I need your help," Micah said quietly. "I would never ask, except . . ."

Ebenezer did not stir for quite some time. When at last he looked up, his eyes were still bloodshot, but there was only a slight quaver in his gaze. "I'll need to pack some things."

Ebenezer got up. He went into the bedroom. He shut the door and closed his eyes. He didn't want Micah to see the way he slept. His bed was a single mattress on the floor. One sheet, no pillow. Micah didn't need to see Ebenezer's crucifix collection, either. Dozens of them. On every wall. Hung from the ceiling on loops of fishing line. Ebenezer himself had drawn crude crosses with charcoal pencils, scratching them onto the walls between the nailed-up crucifixes. Even though he did not believe in God—even though the god he saw when he closed his eyes was a leering idiot—the crosses comforted him in some odd fashion.

Ebenezer tried to sleep during the day; he found it easier to surrender consciousness with sunlight streaming into the room. But he was a hair-trigger sleeper; the sound of an ant pissing on cotton batting was enough to wake him up these days. He hadn't slept—really *slept*—in fifteen years.

At night, he paced the house and stared out at the street, or surveyed the empty fields from his kitchen window. In the deepest hours of night he saw, or believed he could see, undefined shapes cavorting where the night was thinnest—just beyond the glow of the streetlights, or at the edges of the moonlight where it played over the barren grassland.

Things waiting. Things watching. Hungering.

Sometimes at night, Ebenezer slipped into a fitful doze. His system would just crap out like an old radiator. Then the dreams would come. Not just the one where he saw God's face. That one was bad enough. This other dream was even worse.

In that dream he was trapped beneath the earth in a place where no light ever shone. He had been there before. In that darkness—so absolute he felt it attaching to his skin, pulling the blood out of his veins and the very sight out of his eyes—he could hear things. Terrible things. Sucking sounds. And other, subtler tones made worse by how delicate they were. That of flesh being pulled apart, maybe . . . which is not a very loud noise at all, though one might think it ought to be. Rending flesh carries its own note, which sounds like no other—a little like silk sheets slit apart with a scalpel.

In the dream, he stood in that clotted darkness, surrounded by the moist sucking, ripping, and the high breathless inhales a person makes when ice water is poured down the back of their necks. Taken together, they were almost sexual. The ecstatic, groveling noises of sexual climax.

Wending through these sounds, riding an alternate sonic register, was a note composed of many tiny voices threaded together . . .

. . . and it sounded like the laughter of children.

Ebenezer stood in his room surrounded by flea market crucifixes and began to shake, his body wracked with uncontrollable shivers. He hugged himself and bit his lip until blood squirted. His knees went out, and he collapsed to the floor silently, not wanting Micah to come in and see him this way. He laid his head on the floor.

You have no choice, he told himself. *You have to go. Pull yourself together, for the love of Christendom.*

He got the shakes under control. He stood, jelly-legged. He wiped away the blood. It was all right to be scared. Any man would be.

He pushed the mattress aside and prized up two floorboards. He pulled up a familiar beechwood box.

"Hello again, ladies."

His Mauser pistols. A few loose bullets rolled around in the bottom of the box. The guns would need oiling, and he would need more ammunition. A great deal of it.

He dressed in faded jeans and a white V-neck T-shirt. He packed a bag with underwear, socks, shirts, and some trousers. The pistols went in the bag, too.

He took a crucifix off the wall. A four-inch Jesus with a tarnished copper face was nailed to the crossbeams.

"In you go, sport," Ebenezer said, slipping it into his bag.

He stepped into the hall and shut the door behind him. Micah was still in the chair right where Ebenezer had left him.

Micah said, "You coming, then?"

"You think I got all dressed up just to stay here?"

"You probably will not come back, Eb. Neither you or me."

Eb nodded. "It is probable."

"Well. Thanks."

"Oh well. I've lived long enough."

They went outside. Ebenezer left the front door wide open.

"Need to say your good-byes to anybody before we go?" said Micah.

Ebenezer shook his head. "My creditors can seek redress with my next of kin, if they can be found. Now, how did you get here?"

"Took the bus."

"Ah. I don't have a car."

"We can rent one."

"Not in this town we can't."

They walked down the street. Micah walked slowly to allow his limping companion to keep stride. The sunshine imparted a pleasant tickle on their skin. The piebald dog resumed its pursuit.

"We could steal a car," said Ebenezer. "That could be fun."

"Either way."

Eb sighed. "I imagine we're off to find Minerva?"

"Yes."

"Do you imagine she's expecting us?"

"Were you expecting me?"

"Yes."

"Then yes."

Eb sighed again. "I don't imagine she'll be terrifically pleased to see us."

"Pleased or not, we are coming."

3

MINERVA FIGURED it was high time to try and hang herself again.

She couldn't remember when or where the last time had been—the attempts all blended together after a while. Anyway, why not? She had no other plans for the afternoon.

Another town, another ratbag motel room. The Double Diamond Inn, this time. New Mexico was littered with shitholes just like it. The mattress was thirty years old and probably saturated with a thousand dreary cumshots milked from the nutsacks of basset-faced johns by one dead-eyed whore or another. And here Minny was, sitting on the mattress. Buoyed up on a cushion of grim, dried-up old sperm.

Minerva tended to get moody before a suicide attempt. It was tough to see the rosy side of life. But perhaps there had been happiness in this room, too. A young couple could have passed a night in this dump on their way to another city, a better life. Maybe their first child had been conceived in this very bed and had gone on to invent the floppy disk or star in an off-Broadway play or some shit. Who could say?

The noose was fashioned out of stout nautical rope. She had pulled a ceiling panel loose and knotted the rope around an exposed pipe. She sat on the bed, staring up at it.

She had a forty-ouncer of rye. Bathtub-grade shit, just slightly more pure than Sterno. She would drink as much as she could, then clamber up on the chair and stuff her head through the noose. Kick the chair away, la-di-da, carefree as a bird. Say good night, Gracie.

But there was a chance—a perfectly good one—that she'd come to a few minutes later, her pants heavy after her bowels had involuntarily loosened and the whites of her eyes gone red with hemorrhaging. If so, she'd cut herself down and get on with her day.

She had drunk the neck out of the bottle when someone knocked on the door.

Shit. Fucking hellfire.

It wasn't the cops. It never was. She had killed three men in a bar, two days and five hundred miles ago. Afterward, she had driven away. Nobody had pursued her. Nobody ever did.

It wasn't the fact that the men she had killed in that bar were themselves killers and, as such, didn't exactly inspire the police to discover who had ended their lives. When a mad dog kills another mad dog, the dogcatcher still pursues the murderous hound under the suspicion that it might kill an innocent creature next. And it was not that Minerva had left no trace. She had shot the men with witnesses present.

No, the cops did not give chase because that was part of the deal. She had made one discrete wish, but with it came all manner of consequence, unknown to her at the time. It wasn't just that she had to live with the killing she'd done—it was the lack of comeuppance for having done it.

She had killed . . . Jesus, how many? Twenty? Twenty men over the past fifteen years. Twenty souls gone to heaven or hell or just vaporized, blown to some other part of the continuum on the cosmic winds. The people she had killed were bad in a basic sense, pollutants whose dismissal off the food chain was mourned by a precious few, but still. No-body ever came sniffing after her. She went wherever she wanted and left whenever she desired. Her life was free of consequence or reprisal. She had spent not a single day in jail. She had been called in for questioning on occasion, spent a few hours in the stir, but inevitably a detective would tell her that she was free to go.

"What if I did it?" she'd asked one of them once.

"You didn't do it," the detective had said, as if reciting some boring middle-school fact, his face blank as a test pattern.

The knock came again. Insistently. Minerva set the bottle down. Her pistols lay on the bed. She reached for one.

"Who calls?" she said in a falsetto.

"It is Micah Shughrue, Minerva."

A profound coldness invaded her chest. Minny gritted her teeth and waited for it to pass.

"You standing in front of the door?" she asked.

"No."

"Why? You think I'd try to shoot you through it?"

Silence.

She put the gun down and got up. She opened the door a crack. Then she sat back on the bed. The door opened a few more inches. Micah slid his head through the gap.

"Do come in," Minerva said primly. "Splendiferous beauty awaits you."

His gaze made a quick circuit of the room; then he twigged on the noose.

"Am I interrupting something?"

"How did you find me?" she said, ignoring the question.

"Caught your scent on the wind."

Micah didn't need to explain. Although she hadn't exactly *known* he was coming, Minerva wasn't surprised. She always had a sense of where he'd been these past years—and the black sonofabitch, too, who had to be nearby. She never knew their precise coordinates, but all she had to do was close her eyes and concentrate. Little by little, their presence would start to ping. Seems they now each had the same ability, thanks to what had happened. All any of them needed to do was track those pings to their source.

"Hey!" she said. "You out there?"

"I am," Ebenezer called out.

"You scared of me?"

"A smidge."

Minerva sighed inwardly. When she considered the damage she had done over the last fifteen years to her fellow human beings—to those who deserved it, and some who had not quite been deserving—well, it would be disingenuous to say she and Ebenezer were not now peas from the same pod.

"Get your ass in here."

Eb's head poked around the door frame. He limped inside.

"Minny," he said.

"Shithead," she said flatly.

Ebenezer said, "Charmed, I'm sure."

He, too, scoped the noose. His eyebrow ticked up. Minny swallowed more rye whiskey. What the fuck did she care what they thought?

"You boys made it in time for the show. Which one of you wants to kick the chair out from under me?"

The men hung their heads, unwilling to meet her eyes. Were they actually *embarrassed* for her? Well, screw them both. And the horses they rode in on.

"Okay, then. Get the fuck out of here if you're not going to be useful."

Micah turned his cold eye on her. A point of light sparked in the center of his remaining pupil. "You think I showed up to watch you hang yourself?"

"I don't know why you showed up," Minerva said sullenly. "You followed the wrong Bat Signal, Boy Wonders."

Micah went into the bathroom. She heard him unwrap a plastic cup from its wax paper cover. Next, running water. When Micah came back, his glass eye was missing. He crossed to the dresser. A crumpled Burger

King bag sat beside the portable TV. A few salt packets were scattered beside the bag.

"You need these?" Micah asked.

Minerva shook her head. Micah ripped the packets open and spilled salt into the water. He gave it a stir with his finger to dissolve the crystals.

He leaned forward until the rim of the cup encircled his empty socket. He tipped his head back, holding the cup in place. He shook his head and hissed as the salt water cured the flesh inside his empty socket. Then he brought his head down and took the cup away. Water dripped out of his socket onto the grimy motel shag. He dabbed away the excess water with a napkin.

He then pulled the glass eye from his duster pocket and dropped it into the cup. It sat in the bottom like an olive in a martini. He swirled it around, then fished it out and put it back in.

"Good?" he asked Minerva.

"A little bit to the . . ."

Micah adjusted the glass eye with his finger.

Minerva said, "Yeah, that'll do."

Micah sat on the bed beside her. Ebenezer watched from the doorway.

"I need your help."

Minerva was surprised. Micah Shughrue wasn't one to ask for anything. He was the sort of man who would track down the doctor who'd delivered him just to repay the debt.

He said, "I have a daughter."

Minerva's surprise deepened. "*You* have a daughter?"

"Isn't life a cavalcade of wonderments?" Ebenezer said.

Micah said, "By Ellen."

Ellen. The woman who'd dragged them into it. Dragged them straight to hell.

Minerva said, "So are you sore at me for not showing up to the baby shower?"

"It has taken her."

The coldness Minerva had felt earlier intensified a hundredfold—layers of ice crystalizing inside the ventricles of her heart.

"Oh, Micah . . . are you sure? She didn't run away? Young girls make a bad habit of that."

"He encountered one of them in the woods," Ebenezer said. "The handmaids. The ones stitched together out of scraps. But it was the other one who took his daughter."

The other one, Minerva thought grimly. The Piper. The Son. Whatever you wanted to call it. How could Micah be so calm?

"It will not hurt her," Micah said. "It is taking her back to act as . . ."

"Bait, right." Minerva's head nodded numbly, automatically. "Yeah. Makes sense. No way any one of us would go back willingly."

Minerva dropped her head. She closed her eyes. The room tilted on its axis.

"And you need me, why?" she said. "What can I do? Any of us? I'm so sorry for your daughter. But we barely survived last time, and that was a long time ago. I'm a damn sight worse now than I was then."

Micah said, "You look okay. Apart from the drink."

"And the noose," said Ebenezer.

She tried to smile. "I'm used up. And I'm . . . I'm scared, Shug."

"Well. So am I."

She looked up. Micah was placidly regarding her.

"You?"

He nodded. "Not so much for myself, but yes, I am scared."

"I don't know," she said quietly. "I honestly might not be any use to you."

"Cry me a river," Ebenezer said.

"What was that?" Minerva said icily.

"Are you the only one who harbors fear in your heart?" Eb mordantly chuckled. "I am as broken as ever I've been. My own shadow on the wall scares me most nights."

"So go," Minny said. "Who's stopping you?"

Ebenezer shook his head. "I pegged you as many things, my dear. But never once did I peg you for a coward."

Minerva cut her eyes at him. He met her gaze. A challenge. She dropped her head and waved a dismissive hand.

"Sell it walking." She flipped a switch inside her mind, her eyes going hard. "Take your crazy somewhere else."

Micah stood. Minerva thought he might try to press her, but that had never been his way. They would go without her. And die wretchedly in the dark. But they would go. Ebenezer might quit when the madness got too much—and it would, as sure as breathing—but Micah would wade right in until it stole everything he had to give.

"There a bar around here?" Micah said.

"There's one jutting off the ass end of this motel," she told him.

"I think he meant one where the cockroaches don't have name tags," said Ebenezer.

"It will do," said Micah.

She waved her hand again. "Go on, then. Scat."

They did. The door shut behind them. She sat in the shadow of the noose. She ran her hand over her freshly shorn scalp. She always liked to get a buzz cut before trying to snip her mortal cord. She had this weird fear that some shitty, unscrupulous undertaker would sell her hair to a wig shop. Stupid, the things people worry about. She shut her eyes—but something leapt up, a long-forgotten shape that shone a delirious bone white in the darkness behind her eyelids. She jolted, opening them.

"I can't. Christ. I can't do it again."

She dropped a dime in the box bolted onto the TV. It bought her a couple minutes of flickery black and white. She needed the distraction. Micah and Ebenezer were in the bar now, waiting for her to change her mind. She had to hold out. One drink and they would surely leave.

She tuned in to an episode of *The Waltons*. Usually this kind of saccharine shit made her teeth ache, but right now it was just what the doctor ordered.

"Good night, John-Boy, you pig-fucking little bastard," she muttered.

A commercial came on.

"*What's inside this little blue egg that keeps Barbara Eden looking slim and trim?*" asked the jovial announcer.

"Who gives a flying fuck," Mine a said.

"*Oh, there's only one answer to that—it's L'eggs control-top panty hose! L'eggs slims and trims but doesn't bind, so you get comfort and control!*"

The meter clicked. The screen blinked out. Minerva went to drop in another dime. She stopped. She swore she could see something in the smoky square of the dead TV. Something jesting and capering . . .

Human fears obeyed a hierarchy. Minerva had discovered that as a girl. She had never been as scared as on that sunny afternoon when her brother was taken by that snake. Her fear had held different layers: the helplessness, the heaving revulsion, the understanding that the world could yawn open at any time and take what was most precious. That afternoon—those few minutes within it, dominated by the sound of the snake's mouth opening to ingest her still-breathing brother, so much like the stretching of a thousand wet rubber bands . . . Minerva never thought she would know a terror to rival it.

Her belief had stood until one night in Little Heaven, when she rounded the edge of the chapel to spy a boy sitting cross-legged in the moonlight. The darkness twitched all around him, moving with a trillion sightless eyes. The boy turned, knowing she was there though unable to see her. He smiled—so sweet, so innocent—with his eyes the color of smoke. He was holding something in his hands. Beyond him lay the feasting darkness of the woods. From behind the trees had come the sound of something consuming its prey . . . but not in any natural way.

Minerva sank down on the bed. It was there again. That old squirming fear creeping up her legs like gangrene. It got inside and ate you from within, squandered and reduced you until you were helpless to fight it. That kind of fear could ruin you—you and those around you, too, because you were no use to anyone with that dread lodged in your heart.

She sat for a few minutes, thinking. Was she seriously going to do it? Was she actually contemplating hurling herself back into that horror?

She was just a sack of skin. That was how she saw it. Hell, that's all anyone was. She was a sack, and Micah was a sack, and Ebenezer—oh, he was *definitely* a sack. Billions of sacks colliding with one another every goddamn day. Sometimes two of them collided and something good came of it. Sometimes two or three or more collided and something awful happened. But that's all life was—sacks of skin bumbling around, bumping into their fellow sacks, and stuff happening.

But she had to admit that Micah Shughrue, ole Shug, he was about the best sack of skin she'd ever bumped into. That said, she owed them nothing. Not the Englishman, for damn sure. Not even Micah. The debts still due were their own.

But then, what else did she have? What was her life? She killed people. She was denied the mercy of death. She woke up screaming more nights than not. She owed, and she was paying. Maybe it was finally time to follow that line back. Pay a visit to her old benefactor. Renegotiate their deal.

Isn't my life hell anyway? Minerva thought. *Isn't that why I want to die?*

There are worse hells than this, a voice whispered softly in her ear.

4

SHE FOUND THEM in the bar.

"I'll come."

Micah said, "Okay."

"Don't go getting all dewy-eye on me, Shug."

Micah said, "Okay."

PART FOUR

LITTLE HEAVEN

1965–1966

1

AFTER THE SEABORN APPLETON matter had concluded to Micah's satisfaction—ultimately Shughrue had allowed Appleton to continue to suck breath, though it's possible Appleton would have preferred death to the state he was left in—the three outlaws hid out on a farm on the outskirts of Angel Fire, a town in Colfax County, New Mexico.

In later generations, it would be difficult for two men and one woman with a history of illegalities to disappear quite so easily. But in the sixties, when records were written out in longhand and transferred to carbons and put in files that went into filing cabinets in dank basements infested by mice and mold, it was still a possibility. You could live off the grid, in unmapped places, sheltered from the long arm of the law. If you kept to yourself and paid in cash and didn't get sick and drove at the speed limit, well, there was a chance you might never run afoul of those government agencies whose job was to track the movements and intents of its citizenry. You could just . . . vanish.

Micah had done some work for the farm's owner back when the man had made his living by rawer means. There was a mutual respect and fealty between them. Johnny Law did not come searching for them. What had they really done, anyway? Tried to kill one another, without success, then ganged up to mutilate a drug dealer. The law had more pressing matters to address.

Over the following months, their wounds healed—not perfectly, but then, wounds rarely do. Micah took to wearing a patch over his squandered eye. Ebenezer's unrelaxed hair mushroomed into a massive Afro. Minerva kept her own hair razored tight to her skull. They slept in the hayloft above the horses. During the day, they walked the fields alone, testing their strength against some unknown eventuality. The scent of cut garlic leached out of the earth, perfuming their skin. They were happy. As happy as people like them could be. They had no family. Many of their old friends had been eaten by the war.

At night they slept fitfully, like wolves from separate packs forced to share a den. One night, Ebenezer awoke to find Minerva staring at him. Her eyes were a peculiar blue in the drowsy light of the barn.

"See anything you fancy?" he asked.

"Can't sleep."

"Try thinking pleasant thoughts."

"That's hard, looking at you."

Ebenezer laughed softly. "Oh, you are truly an incorrigible flirt."

Minerva would kill him eventually. She was as certain of that fact as she was that the sun would rise in the east—even more sure, in fact, because if the sun failed to rise one day she would still kill Ebenezer in the dark. Ebenezer believed her actions had been motivated by monetary concerns. He did not fear or suspect her. And Micah was right—it would taste all the sweeter for the wait. Minerva had read that people who had the ability to delay gratification were the most successful people on God's green earth.

ONE DAY, the farm's owner summoned Micah to his kitchen.

"There's a job needs doing."

Micah said, "I thought you were quit of all that."

The man said, "It ain't mine. Still needs doing. I figured your crew might be up for it."

My crew? Micah thought. *They are just a couple of strays.*

"Payroll job," the man said. "Hungarian gang operating out of Albuquerque." He snorted. "How they ended up there, you got me. Good payday. But it's not a one-man job."

Micah nodded. "I owe you."

"Don't owe me much. Just reckoned it would get you back on your feet, is all."

Micah floated the idea to the other two. He was surprised when they both readily agreed. Ebenezer was a mercenary at heart, happy to join any cohort so long as a payday was involved. Minerva was the real surprise—

but she was sick of bounty hunting, and her old outfit was unlikely to take her back now anyway. They were all poor as church mice, too.

She said, "Even splits?"

"Even splits," said Micah.

"Then I'll do it."

THEY TOOK A GREYHOUND to Albuquerque. Micah bought a Dodge Dart at a used-car lot, signing the ownership papers under an assumed name and paying cash—the last three hundred dollars in his wallet.

Micah drove to the payroll swap site. A hardware store on Euclid Avenue. When the delivery van showed up, Micah strapped a hockey helmet on his head and gunned the Dart's engine and charged out of a blind alleyway, slamming into the van, T-boning it, and rocking it up over the curb. His head slammed the dash, blood leaping out his nose. He gazed out the busted windshield and saw Ebenezer and Minerva—who had been sitting at a bus stop directly across the road—hauling open the van's rear doors and dragging out a pair of stunned deliverymen.

Micah staggered out of the Dart. A Hungarian mama with a corrugated dust-bowl face ran out of the hardware store with a machete. Still woozy, helmet on, he leveled his pistol at her. She got the point and dropped the blade. Ebenezer retrieved the cash bag. They dashed down the blind alley and onto another street. Sirens, distant but closing in.

They walked into a pet store. Micah still had the hockey helmet. He took it off, left it on the stacked sacks of dog kibble. They breezed past caged puppies and lizards and twittering birds, exiting out the back door. They walked down another alley to a park where kids were playing baseball. Minerva bought a lemon Italian ice from the ice cream truck. They were sweating, but so was everyone else.

Ebenezer tried to hail a cab, but nobody stopped. One did for Micah, but only once Ebenezer had hidden behind a bus bench. When Eb hopped in, the driver made a face like he'd sniffed something rank, but he kept his lip zipped. He took them to a bar on the outskirts. The cash bag sat under their table. Ebenezer played the pinball machine. Minerva played "Sugar Shack" and "Blue Velvet" on the jukebox. Micah pretty much stared at the wall.

After a few hours, another cab dropped them at the bus station. They caught the 6:30 Greyhound to Angel Fire. Back at the farm, the farmer counted their take. There was also a pound of heroin in the bag. The farmer claimed it was "primo stuff." Micah didn't care. He'd had his fill of drugs.

The job had gone off without a snag. They worked well together. The farmer said there were other jobs. The three of them didn't have much else better to do.

2

AND SO THEY FORMED a loose association. They had no obligations, no taxes on their time. It was not a natural fellowship. Each of them preferred the sound of one hand clapping. Plus one of them nursed a blood grudge against another.

But something happened during their flight from Mogollon, their recovery at the farm, and the jobs they did under the farmer's supervision. They came together in a manner none of them could credit.

They were professional and declarative in their actions. Judgment did not enter into their thinking. As they were good at their chosen endeavor, for many months they prospered. Between jobs, they would drift apart for a week or two, leaving the farm to pursue their own amusements. Then they would return like honeybees following an old pheromone trace.

This was the nature of their existence for months. Then a woman entered and changed everything, as women often will.

Afterward, Micah Shughrue would dwell on this idyll of good months and the two people he shared it with. He would wonder at their fates. Such a strange path to chart. The heart pulls, the mind resists. The heart wins. It wins.

Nobody can chart the shape of his or her life before that shape emerges. There is hardly any rhyme to that shape and almost no reason. And that is the grandest, the most irreducible mystery of all.

3

MICAH KNEW THE WOMAN was watching him. When a man spends a lot of his life with a target on his back, that man had better develop a sixth sense if he wants to keep drawing breath.

He had driven into Angel Fire in the farmer's pickup to purchase sundries: flour, sugar, molasses, a new button for his duster. Also ammunition. He'd been practicing on the farm, pegging cans off the corral fence. His aim was screwy with only the one eye—even though he used to squeeze that eye shut when he fired. He had never been a crack shot, anyway. It was more that he never flinched in the cut.

He exited the gun shop with three boxes of 7.62 mm cartridges. He crossed the road to a small groceteria. It was cool inside, an old Westinghouse wall-mounted A/C pumping, the tinselly ribbons tied to its grate fluttering. He walked the aisles. A sack of sugar. A five-pound bag of Gold Medal flour. A box of Sugar Sparkled Rice Krinkles—all men had their vices. He passed a cooler and grabbed a six-pack of Blatz. He felt like blowing the foam off a few. He picked up a church key, too.

He had spotted her by then. First, when he came out of the gun shop. She was lingering across the road, pretending to be absorbed by the display window of the hardware store: a heap of men's work gloves. Why would she be so interested in those? She wasn't. She was watching him in the reflection of the glass.

She was tall. Not stork-like, the way Minerva was put together. A hint of power down through those legs. Her dark hair was cut in a bob. She wore dun-colored Carhartts and a T-shirt of palest blue.

She had followed him into the grocery store. Maybe she was craving a Hershey's bar or a pack of Now and Laters. She didn't seem threatening. He caught her reflection in the fish-eye mirror at the head of each aisle.

A bag boy put Micah's items in a brown paper sack. The woman idled behind him. She didn't have a thing in her basket. She seemed to realize this, and tossed a pack of chewing gum into it.

His truck was parked around the side of the store in the shade of a bur oak. He dropped the tailgate and dug a can of Blatz out of the bag.

He punched two holes in the lid with the church key and took a deep drink.

The woman rounded the store. Her face was startling. Her eyes were a peculiar blue—the blue of the water in an Arctic lake—and her hair was so black it reflected the sunlight. But neither of those details was jarring. No, it was the skin on the left side of her face, trailing under her ear and along her jaw, on down her throat. The flesh was mottled and runneled like wax that pooled around a lit candle.

She stopped. She put her hands in her pockets and rocked forward at the hips. Micah was not worried about her—but he scanned behind her, waiting for someone else to show.

"Micah Shughrue?"

She took a step toward him. It was one of the worst facial burns Micah had ever seen. He couldn't imagine how it had happened or who might have done it to her. She would have been beautiful without it. Micah could not say that she wasn't, even with it.

"Sherri Bellhaven told me I might find you here," she said. "In Angel Fire, I mean. Not the grocery store."

Micah knew Sherri Bellhaven. He'd done a few jobs with her fellow, Leroy Huggins. Bellhaven had been a bank clerk. A square john with a taste for rough customers. Micah had liked Sherri, but believed those tastes would get her in trouble eventually.

He said, "I used to know her."

"She's my sister. I'm Ellen Bellhaven."

Ellen pulled a pack of Doublemint from her pocket and unwrapped a stick. Micah hitched his foot up on the tailgate, balancing his elbow on his knee. Glugged some beer.

"How is she?"

"In jail." She balled up the foil and flicked it off her thumb. "Up in Tacoma."

Micah just drank his beer.

"She trusted the wrong people," Ellen Bellhaven said when it became clear he wasn't going to speak. "Same old story, huh?"

Micah finished his beer and dropped the empty into the bag. He dug out another can. The woman, Ellen, watched him. Did she expect him to offer her one? He'd give her one if she asked.

"She heard you were out here. Jailhouse intel," she said.

Eight months ago, Micah had sent Leroy an envelope with the ten dollars he owed. He forgot what Leroy had loaned him the money for, but he never forgot a debt. The letter's postmark had been Angel Fire. Perhaps that was the how as to why this woman was facing him now.

Ellen laughed. "Like I know a thing about jail! I hardly even got grounded as a kid. The good girl, that was me. Sherri, on the other hand, got grounded so often that her windowsill had grooves in it, she had to sneak out so much."

Ellen was babbling a little. Micah understood. Normal people tended to do that in his presence.

"Listen," she said, "are you . . . ah, for hire?"

Why did some people think he was available for scut work? You want someone to pull your kitty out of a tree? Call a fireman.

"No."

Her throat flushed; the blush carried up to enflame her unburned cheek. "Oh. Okay. It's just that my sister said maybe you could—"

"You in trouble?"

"Me?" She shook her head. "No, no, it's my sister. Her son, actually. Nate. He's been abducted, I guess you could say."

"So call the police."

"No can do. He was taken by his father."

"You call that an abduction? Your sister is in the clink."

Ellen nodded. "Sure. Where else is the kid going to go, right? It's not that Reggie—that's his father—it's not that he's taken Nate so much as where he's taken him."

Micah raised an eyebrow.

"Little Heaven," Ellen said. "You heard of it?"

Micah shook his head.

"It's some kind of a compound," Ellen went on. "Survivalist? Really, I don't know the who or why of it. Religious nuts. Reggie nearly died two years ago, yeah? He was a mailman. Heart attack on his route. The doctors hit him with those shock paddles to kick-start his heart. He woke up blubbering in tongues. A real come-to-Jesus moment. Sherri says he started going on and on about taking his faith to the next level."

"When I knew Sherri, she was with Leroy Huggins."

"I remember Leroy," said Ellen. "Decent guy. Good for my sister, apart from the criminal tendencies."

Micah drank his beer.

"So anyway, Reggie's the new guy. Sherri gave up dating badasses. Total one-eighty. She and Reggie started dating after Leroy; it lasted a few years, and Nate was the fruit of it. I met Reggie once, at Nate's christening. A prissy bald-headed guy with spectacles, his back all stooped from delivering the weekly *Pennysaver*."

"Only the one time?"

She started. "Pardon?"

"Only the one time you met him?"

She nodded. "I haven't seen Nate since he was a tot, either." Ellen probably expected Micah to ask why. When he didn't, she told him anyway. "I had some issues of my own during those years. Sherri took the straight and narrow. I strayed, then came back to heel. Then Sherri went off the reservation entirely."

"So your nephew . . ."

"Is at Little Heaven. With Reggie. Living with a bunch of snake handlers, for all I know." She dipped her chin. "You a religious sort?"

Micah shook his head.

"Me neither. I mean, okay, Unitarian, Methodist, those vanilla faiths—fill your boots. But some camp in the forest, people dressed in robes praying eight hours a day . . ."

She threw her arms up in evident frustration. Micah noted the burn scar carried down her left arm and peeked from the sleeve of her T-shirt.

"Sorry. I'm probably boring the piss out of you."

"My piss remains in my bladder," he told her. "I find this interesting."

That was not one hundred percent true. Micah had heard stories like this a dozen times. But those stories had not been told by Ms. Ellen Bell-haven, from Parts Unknown.

He said, "You try the cops at all?"

"Sherri barked up that tree already. Like I said, custody of Nate fell to Reggie after my sister went to jail. He's a mailman, for Christ's sake. Police hear that—stable job, money in the bank—okay, they figure the kid's fine."

Could be he is *fine*, Micah thought. *Sure, he is getting a bellyful of scripture, but there are worse things. He is with his father, not huffing diesel fuel out of a jam jar.*

"What is your stake in it?"

Ellen looked at him funny. The sunlight fell through the oak leaves and settled on her arresting face.

"You said you hardly even know your nephew," Micah went on.

"And that matters?"

Micah squinted at the sky. He felt itchy all over. Ah, fuck it. "Beer?"

He punched holes in a can and left it on the tailgate. Ellen came closer to pick it up. She ran the cold can across her forehead. She took the gum out of her mouth and stuck it on the top and took a sip.

"Thanks."

She pulled a dollar bill from her pocket and dropped it into the grocery sack. Micah took it out and put it into his pocket.

"My sister said you would do it for money."

"You got much?"

"Our father was pretty good at making money."

"Why not go on your own?"

She said, "I thought about it. The truth? It freaks me out. The place where they are, this Little Heaven? *Really* isolated. A bunch of Bible bashers stewing out in the middle of the woods. Hell, I might turn into a pillar of salt."

"They are harmless, I am sure. Why not hire a wilderness guide?"

She drank deeply. The muscles of her throat flexed. She did not answer his question. But Micah knew that if the boy was in a rough spot, she would want him removed. Any guides would be out of their depth in that circumstance.

"I'd go if you go," she said.

"You cannot walk out with the kid."

She set her jaw. "I'll pay you to try. No, forget I said that—just to get me there, okay? I want to see the place. Peace of mind, yeah?"

Micah shut his eye. The sun warmed the eyelid not covered by the patch.

"No."

"No, you can't do it?"

"Cannot is not so much part of it."

Ellen Bellhaven put the can down. She unwrapped another stick of gum and folded it into her mouth. "Why not?"

Micah got up and shut the tailgate. Ellen took a few steps back. He opened the door and slung his body behind the wheel.

"Hey," she said. "*Hey.*"

He started the truck and set it in gear.

"I'm staying at the Budget Inn," she called as he drove away. "Just think about it, for Christ's sake!"

4

MICAH HAD NO INTENTION of thinking about it. But he did.

Which is to say, he thought about Ellen Bellhaven. Which forced him to think about her offer.

My sister said you would do it for money.

Which was true. Micah had done much more ignoble things for the coin of the realm. He wasn't picky, as a rule. But the idea of shepherding a woman into the woods so she could check up on her nephew struck him as a chapter ripped out of a Hardy Boys book. *The Legend of Little Heaven's Gold.*

But then, considering he did do pretty much anything for money, and providing Ms. Bellhaven had the means to pay . . .

He was trying to talk himself into it. Idiotically, he found that he wanted to spend more time with Ellen. Still, wasn't it easy money? Guide her to this Little Heaven and let her get a peek at the kid. So long as the boy's arms weren't covered in fang bites from handling cobras and he didn't have a crucifix branded on his forehead . . . well, they could just toddle off again, right? How hard could it be?

Micah dwelled on it for a day. Then he brought it up with the other two. He shouldn't need them on this job. But there was that old chestnut: *Better to bring a gun and not need it than to need a gun and not have one.*

"So what—this guy and his kid are shacked up with a bunch of Freedomites?" Minerva said once Micah had outlined the situation.

"Something like that," said Micah.

Ebenezer spanked his hands together and high-kneed around in a little circle. "*Hare Krishna, Hare Krishna, Krishna-Krishna-Hare-Hare!*"

"How much we talking?" Minerva said.

Micah said, "I am given to understand her family has money."

Minerva said, "So why not just rob *her?*"

Micah frowned. "It will only take a few days."

"We can have a wienie roast," said Eb, warming to the idea. "And tell spook stories. Isn't that what you Yanks do on campouts?"

The two of them were game. Micah left it at that. Ellen Bellhaven had probably left by now, anyway. Packed up and returned to wherever she had come from.

She was gone. Micah was sure of it.

5

MICAH PULLED into the graveled lot of the Budget Inn. One car was parked in the lot. He noted its out-of-state plates.

He was heading inside to check with the clerk when he heard his name.

"Micah! Hey, Micah!"

Ellen stood on the second-floor balcony. Dressed in the same Carhartts but a different shirt. The sun glossed her hair and made it shine like a mirror—which was a stupid, dainty detail to take note of. Micah chided himself for it.

He said, "How much to take you?"

She gave him a number. It was quite a high one, with more than two zeroes.

Wouldn't anything be high enough? an arch voice whispered in his head. *Wouldn't her giving you the time of day be enough?*

"We leave tomorrow. My partners will come."

She slapped the balcony railing and hooted. "Goddamn it, Micah. I was just about to give up on you."

You are making a fool of yourself, said that arch voice.

Well. Maybe so. He liked to think he never made the same mistake twice. He didn't have much experience with women—one mistake was within his rights, wasn't it?

6

IT WAS PAST MIDNIGHT. Little Heaven lay in darkness.

The Reverend Amos Flesher slept with a purple-headed erection.

Someone was touching him in his dream. Small, soft fingers running up and down the shaft of his penis. Unsexed fingers, not identifiably male or female, boy or girl. But they were very knowing, those fingers. Oh yes. Playing over the crown so teasingly, coaxing him toward climax—*oh please, pretty pretty please!*—only to slow their rhythm the instant before release.

Next the fingernails dug into the sensitive tip, pinching the slit where some semen was just starting to leak out—

Amos shrieked up out of his slumber. *My Lord!* He was clasping his cock in a vise grip. The tip was speckled with angry dots: blood vessels that had burst from the throttling pressure.

You have been thinking impure thoughts, boy.

Amos's chest was clammy with sweat. His pajamas were stuck to him. Three oscillating fans wired to an outdoor generator stirred the room's muggy air around.

He sat up in bed. A king-sized mattress—everyone else at Little

Heaven slept on cots, but Amos needed his sleep. It was when he communed with God and received His guidance.

But God had not come to him tonight. Only those knowing fingers.

Dirty stick. That's what Sister Muriel, one of the nuns at the San Francisco Catholic Orphanage, used to call the male penis. She always made that distinction—the *male* penis, as if it was necessary.

Don't fiddle with it! she would say, adding emphasis with a hard lash of her pointer. *That's what the devil wants—for you to put your hands all over your dirty sticks. Do you want your fingers to rot off, boys? They will. You can count on it.*

Amos Flesher went to the window. His compound sprawled out before him. The mess hall, the study hall, the square, and the supply shacks. The hum of gas generators. Security lamps shining around the perimeter.

Little Heaven. His own small slice of perfection.

His gaze fell on the chapel, topped with an enormous crucifix. He'd had it shipped here in pieces and nailed together. The three points of the cross were glossed by the moon—seeing this, he felt a deep tranquility settle within him. It was soon broken.

You were milking your dirty stick, weren't you? Milking it in your sleep.

Amos tried to ignore Sister Muriel's voice. His eyes wandered past the cross to the high fence ringing Little Heaven. The woods fanned out in every direction, thick and impenetrable. They offered solitude and isolation, which were necessary for his ambitions. No telephones, no mailing address. The civilized world was full of degradations that forever sought to lead a pious man into licentiousness and vice.

It was here, so far from the machinations of man, that Amos could hear God's voice clearly. He had awoken one day to hear Him calling—the true, unquestioned voice.

Come to me, my lamb.

These were the only words at first.

Amos had left his ministry in San Francisco to follow that voice. By car, by bus, on foot. He traveled many miles. The voice grew stronger. He did not eat and scarcely slept. The pull of the voice obliterated those needs. There were times during his pilgrimage when he thought he'd go mad or collapse. But the voice guided him through despair.

Come to me, my lamb.

Amos followed the voice to this spot—it was easy, like scanning a radio dial until you tuned in to a powerful frequency. He was exhausted by the time he arrived, his sandals nearly disintegrated from the thirteen-mile hike through the woods. At some point, everything went black. A fugue state. And when the darkness cleared, he was where he was meant to be.

Nothing about the spot screamed out, *Behold, the seat of the Divine!* Just trees and scrub. Had he been a bit more aware, Amos might have noticed how the sounds of nature had bled into a relative silence the closer he drew to the site. The chirping of the birds died away, as did the rustle of animals in the underbrush.

But the voice overpowered all of that. Once he had tuned in to this unearthly transmission, a direct conduit to the Lord, Amos beckoned his flock. They came, as he had known they would—they would follow their prophet. They helped build Little Heaven to Amos's exact specifications.

Not all of them had come. He had ministered to some two hundred souls in San Francisco. Only a quarter of them made the trek into the wilds of New Mexico. Still, Amos was satisfied. Most importantly, they were families. Mothers and fathers, sons and daughters. They were so much better than fifty directionless souls who could lose faith at any moment. Families stayed together. Bloodlines ran thick, oh yes.

They had been here nearly six months. Things were not perfect, but then, things never were. A few outbuildings had collapsed in a freak windstorm. Two worshippers were bitten by snakes. Greta Hughes, the children's teacher, had broken her leg in a construction mishap. The limb had become gangrenous. Neither the ministrations of Colby Lewis, a onetime medic in the Vietnam War, or the flock's upbeat prayers had much effect. The Hughes woman wept wretchedly as she was shipped back to the devil's den of society.

God must test the pure of heart in order to cull the wicked and slothful from their number, Amos had counseled his flock at that evening's sermon.

There had been one or two other . . . events. Isolated incidents. Nothing worth dwelling on. A few of the elect had claimed to see things. Shapes in the woods at night. Sounds that could not be accounted for by natural means. Amos had dealt with those complaints harshly. Such hysterics had no place at Little Heaven.

The children, too. Some of them were having trouble adjusting. Their behavior was perhaps a little *off* from time to time. But that, too, was to be expected. Everyone had to adjust. The poisonous teat of civilization, with its televisions and pinball machines and McDonald's hamburgers: you had to wean yourself from that vile nipple. The children struggled with this more than the rest of Amos's worshippers, but—

You were fiddling with yourself, weren't you? Milking your dirty stick so it would spurt. It is what syphilitic perverts do to themselves. It stains the soul, boy—and yours is stained already, isn't it?

"Hush'm, hush'm, hush'm!"

Amos spoke in a reedy singsong, the tone of voice you might use to head off an argument. It was a tone his worshippers would find quite different from the rich baritone that issued from his chest during sermons.

Smutty little fiddler fiddling with his dirty filthy stick—

Amos ground his teeth. It sounded like cement blocks rubbing together inside his head. He stared over the trees at the rock formation looming against the sky. It was darker than the night, as though carved out of a different kind of blackness altogether.

The Devil's Rock. That was its name, according to some mountaineering guide Brother Fairweather had showed him. No matter. It was not for mankind to name the works of the Creator. *We must humble ourselves before Him.*

Big Heaven. *Not* the Devil's Rock. That was Amos's self-given name for the skyscraping formation that rose pillar-like from the forest floor. He had built Little Heaven, which stood in the shadow of Big Heaven, which itself stood in the shadow of God Himself. He pictured Big Heaven as a massive antenna broadcasting the Lord's voice to his ears alone . . .

. . . although he had to admit that sometimes the voice did not sound as though it belonged to God. Just the odd blip where . . . Well, it was like when you were on a road trip and you lost the radio signal. That was the only analogy Amos could come up with—the sort of obvious comparison he worked into his sermons so that the more squirrel-headed members of his flock could grasp it. When you were driving and lost one radio station but started to pull in another at almost the same time. That brief span where the frequencies got crossed.

This was how it felt. God's voice—the calm, uplifting one—would bleed away the tiniest bit and another voice would interfere for just a moment. And this other voice was different.

It wasn't even a voice, precisely. Amos could call it that only insofar as it spoke to him, though not so much in words. Amos Flesher envisioned an immense dark space teeming with flies, their wings and legs producing a hum that rose and fell in sonorous waves to fill the void with the sound of their mindless industry.

Flies, and something else. A silky constriction that pinged on a fainter sonic register—a rhythmic coiling and tightening that called to mind a sightless worm of endless length braiding over and around itself in knots of terrifying complexity. The rub of its flesh produced a delicate hiss that was somehow staticky, like the sound on a vinyl record between songs.

This voice—*was* it a voice?—this *presence* would occasionally intrude upon the voice of God. Amos would flinch from it, shaking his head to fling it out of his mind.

Just a blip. Then it was gone again.

Amos Flesher stared over his fiefdom, shrouded in midnight dark. He heard no voice now. He heard nothing at all. Only the jumpy beat of his own heart.

7

THE ROAD RIBBONED EASTWARD, flat and gray in the morning sunlight. They had been driving for hours: Micah, Minerva, and Ellen in Ellen's '57 Oldsmobile. Ebenezer followed on a Honda CB77 motorcycle he had bought from a pawn agent in Albuquerque. Evidently he wasn't entirely sold on the idea and wanted to be able to skedaddle if things went hinky.

They had stopped in Albuquerque for the motorcycle, gasoline, and camping gear. They bought backpacks, boots, tents, and sleeping bags. Lost hikers—that would be their angle. They would hike it to Little Heaven. Ellen knew its whereabouts; her sister had demanded that Reggie tell her, going so far as to make him draw a map and mail it to her in jail. If they needed a closer look, they would claim to be lost and appeal upon the Little Heavenites' Christian decency for a night's sanctuary. Once they knew the boy was well cared for, they would thank the Bible bashers for their hospitality and leave them to their woodland rites.

According to Ellen, the settlement nearest to Little Heaven was Grinder's Switch. A village of less than three hundred souls situated in a valley, with the wilderness unfolding to the north and east. They drove down a single-lane blacktop banded by vast sweeps of sorghum. They passed the odd billboard for Dash laundry soap or Lestoil or Winston Super Kings, but most of the billboards were of a religious nature.

Satan tries to limit your prayers, one billboard proclaimed, *because he knows your prayers will limit him!*

"Well, he's doing a hell of a job," Minerva said. "I don't pray at all. So good for you, Satan."

Ellen tried the radio. They pulled in a few old episodes of *Yours Truly, Johnny Dollar*.

"*The transcribed adventures of the man with the action-packed expense account!*" the announcer intoned. "*America's fabulous freelance insurance investigator!*" When the station bled out of range, Ellen manipulated the knob with great delicacy to pull in Dr. Don Rose, broadcasting on AM 610, KFRC, all the way from San Francisco. They listened to "One Grain of Sand," by Eddy Arnold, which segued into "Roll Over Beethoven" and "Pocket Full of Rainbows." This was followed by commercials for Bubble Up gum, Roi-Tan cigars, and Ken-L Ration dog food, which Ellen sang along to lustily in a little boy's voice.

My dog's better than your dog;
My dog's better than yours—

They lost the signal in the hills. Ellen fiddled with the dial until—

"*Pestilence!*"

A great fulmination filled the car. A man's warbly, southern-fried voice.

"*The four horsemen are saddled, payy-poll! Their spurs are sharp to goad their flame-eyed steeds up from the bowels of the infernal pit to spread pain and suffering amongst the unbelievers, the heretical, the unwed muuuthers, the adulterers and the idolaters and fornicators and awwwll the ho-MA-sex-shals, the tax chayyyts, the nig- . . . -gardly of spirit, the interbreeders, the faithless, the impure, the—*"

Ellen snapped the radio off.

"Holy shit, buddy," she said. "Take a pill."

They pulled into a gun shop that sat off the freeway. Jimmy's Gun Rack. A squat, flat-topped building that resembled a bomb shelter. Barred windows, smoked glass. They needed ammunition. Micah had his Russian Tokarevs. Minerva, her US Colts. Ebenezer had borrowed the farmer's English-made Tarpley carbine, a .52-caliber single-shot rifle. He hadn't hunted wild game—a gentleman's diversion, if ever there was—in years. This trip might offer the chance to sportingly plug a deer or feral hog.

Micah wasn't sure they would even need guns. He hoped not. But then, he couldn't be certain there weren't a few rogue survivalists at the compound—if so, there was a chance those men would have guns. Better to be safe.

A bell chimed as they walked into the shop. Rifles lined the walls, with heavy-gauge chains threaded through their trigger guards. The man who was assumedly Jimmy stood behind a glass display cabinet. A stuffed boar's head was mounted on the wall above him. Some joker had put a pair of Buddy Holly glasses over the boar's snout and stuffed one of those trick cigars—already exploded—in its mouth. The boar's eyes were wide and shocked-looking, as if the cigar had just blown up in its face.

Jimmy was himself boarish in appearance. Squat and round with stiff hairs sprouting from the vee of his camouflage shirt. His eyes were loose and eggy behind a pair of thick bifocals.

"What can I do you fine folks for?" he said.

"Unusual request, my fine fellow," said Ebenezer. "I've got an old hunting rifle, .52 caliber."

Jimmy hooted. "Jesus, son—you steal it off a dead Boer?"

Micah and Minerva gave Jimmy their orders.

"Those I can do," said Jimmy. "And I'll take a look for some .52 loads. Not promising nothing."

Jimmy opened a door leading to the stockroom. Ebenezer spotted an unusual weapon just inside that door: two huge canisters and a long-nozzled gun with an attached asbestos-wrapped hose. A flamethrower. He tapped Micah on the shoulder and pointed.

"You ever use one of those in the war?"

Micah shook his head. "No flame unit in our detachment."

Jimmy returned some minutes later. His forehead was caked with dust. He slapped down a box of shells on the counter.

"Sonofabitch, boy. You're in luck," he told Eb.

The box was ancient, the colors bleached out. Jimmy opened it and checked the loads. "They look fine. Found it *waaaay* in the back, where I lay down poison for the rats. But they'll fire. I wouldn't sell them to you if they didn't."

"You are a prince amongst men," Eb said, peeling a few bills out of his wallet.

THEY REACHED GRINDER'S SWITCH just past one o'clock that afternoon. The village had a single paved road. The surrounding land was peppered with shotgun shacks. A sundry store with a gas pump out front composed the entirety of the Grinder's Switch commercial district.

Minerva pulled the Olds up beside the Sky Chief pump. She had been behind the wheel the last few hours, as Micah's depth perception tended to drift on long car trips.

Micah popped the hood. The radiator was boiling over. The rad cap was blisteringly hot. He pulled his sleeve over his hand and unscrewed it. Oily steam hissed up.

A man came out of the sundry store. The skin of his face was as thin as a bat's wing and stretched tight over his skull. He wore overalls with an oil-spotted rag poking out of the chest pocket.

"You let 'er boil dry." The man spoke in the tone one might use to address the feeble-minded.

Ebenezer pulled in on his bike. He took off his helmet. His hair stuck up in comical sprigs.

"Petrol, garçon."

The man just looked at him.

"Gas, please," Ebenezer said. "Fill it up."

The man hesitated, as if deciding whether he wanted to fulfill the order of a fellow with Ebenezer's coloration. Then he uncapped the motorcycle's tank and carefully filled it. The pump dinged at every half gallon. The man wiped a few drops of spilled gas off the tank and said, "Sixty-three cents. Pay inside."

Micah said, "Do you have a water hose?"

The man shook his head. His mouth was sucked inward, and Micah wondered if he had a tooth left in his head. It looked as if something had been feasting on him from the inside. A parasite of some kind.

"Got a pump round back," the man said.

The pump was old and rusted; a pail hung off the spout. Micah worked the handle until red-tinged water splashed into the pail. He filled it and went back to the car. The water hit the scorching radiator; steam boiled up. Micah waited for it to clear, then tipped the rest in.

The others were inside. The shop's shelves were modestly stocked. Micah picked up a tin of Spam, a can of Hunt's pudding, some wooden matches, and Tootsie Rolls. He added a quart bottle of Nehi grape soda from the ice chest, brushing past Ebenezer, who was picking up two bottles of Yoo-hoo.

"Elixir of the gods," Ebenezer said.

"The gods of diabetes," said Minerva. "Drink up."

Micah took his goods to the cash register. "Nine dollars thirty-five with the gas," the shopkeeper told him.

Micah informed the man that he needed a receipt. "Business purposes."

The man scratched one out on a bit of scrap. His fingers trembled.

"We are looking for an encampment," Micah said to him.

"It's called Little Heaven," said Ellen.

"The religious crazies?" the man said. "The hell you want with them?"

Eb said, "We are true believers who seek to walk in harmony with Christ Almighty."

The man flatly scrutinized Ebenezer. "No, you ain't."

"So you've met them?" Minerva asked.

"They came in droves, what, going on half a year ago now?" the man said. "Them, their slick-talking leader, and all their earthly possessions. They hired a track machine—a flatbed on a tank chassis, yeah?—to haul everything up. It's rough sledding through those hillside passes. Since then, I'll see the odd one pass through on their way up."

"Any of them ever come out?" Ellen asked.

"Not that I ever saw." The man flitted his tongue on the tip of his left canine tooth, one of the precious few teeth he had left. "Naw, there was the one. Had to leave on account of a bust leg."

Micah said, "They seem dangerous to you?"

"Not so much that," the man said. "They seem stupid. Whole idea of it. Who needs to slog into a forest to commune with God? There are perfectly good churches with *roads* leading to their front doors. It's damn dangerous out there. Floods, forest fires, wild animals . . . all sorts of things." An apathetic shrug. "Ain't my job to talk folks out of being stupid."

"What about the guy in charge?" Ellen asked. "You met him?"

"Not myself, no. Arnie Copps, local guy who owns the track machine, had dealings with him. Short-assed little fella. Wears his hair in a greased-up duck's ass kept in place with about a pound of pomade. The horseflies got to love him, walking around with that grease trap on top of his head. But his people bend over backward for him. Gobble up every word that falls off his lips, I hear."

"What's the best way to get there?" Ellen asked.

"Why in the hell would you want to do that?"

When nobody answered, the man came around the counter and toed the screen door open.

"Follow this road," he said, pointing. "Three miles you'll hit a cut. Walk the dry wash a ways and you hit a trailhead. I don't know the exact spot. I wouldn't go on a bet."

Ebenezer peeled the foil off a roll of cherry Life Savers and popped one into his mouth. "You prefer to worship in a civilized setting, I take it?"

"Something like that," said the man. "You talk queer."

"I speak the Queen's English. I can't imagine you hear it often."

They stowed their supplies in the trunk and made ready their departure.

"You got something to shoot with?" the man asked. "A rifle? Scatter-gun?"

Micah said, "We might."

"Yeah, you seem the type. Don't know it'll be much use against what-ever's up there, but better to have than not."

Ellen said, "What do you mean by that?"

But the man had already turned his back on them. The screen door shut behind him. Flies—dozens of them suddenly—battered their bodies against the wire mesh. The din of their wings was disquieting.

THEY DROVE TO THE CUT. Gravel popped under the tires. Road grit drifted through the windows and clung to their skin. The townsfolk watched them from sagging front stoops or from behind dust-clad windows. Their faces were uniformly ravaged, jaundiced, and cored out just as the man's at the shop had been.

It was only later that Micah would realize that he had not seen any boys or girls—no kids, and none of their harbingers. No playgrounds. No tricycles or kiddie pools in any of the weed-tangled yards.

Grinder's Switch was a village of premature ancients. Not a single child.

8

THEY REACHED the cut the shopkeeper had spoken of. They parked the Olds and stretched their road-stiff limbs. They pulled on their Danner boots and organized their packs. They tightened the straps and made their way to the trailhead. Ellen walked in front. She had a bouncy stride. Micah followed Ellen with his eye—then he caught Minerva watching. Minny shook her head with a wry smile. Micah pressed his lips together and focused on the trees. They were scraggly at the base of the valley, clinging to the ribs of rock, but they got taller and shaggier as the valley rose into the hills.

"Pitter patter, tenderfeet," said Ellen.

A trail was grooved through the dirt. It steadily ascended. They would have no trouble following it. They walked under a canopy of knit branches. The sunlight fell through the leaves and touched their skin, making it look as though their flesh had been dipped in a faint green dye.

"Didn't that guy say something about a tank delivering supplies?" Minerva said. "Why not just follow this trail?"

"It could get a lot tougher," said Ellen. "It might cross creeks and mudholes as it winds up into the hills—steep grades, rockslides, that kind of stuff."

They hiked a few hours. The day grew warm under the trees.

"Hey," said Minerva to Ellen. "What do you think would be the worst radioactive animal to get bitten by?"

"What?" said Ellen.

"You ever read *Spider-Man*?" Minerva said. "Peter Parker got bit by a radioactive spider. He got all the powers of a spider. He can spin webs, climb buildings, he's got a 'spider sense.' All in all, pretty good. But I got to thinking, what if he'd got bit by a dung beetle?"

"That doesn't sound so hot," Ellen said, laughing.

"You bet," said Minerva. "Dung-Beetle-Man. He can roll boulder-sized rocks of shit up small hills! He can leap a pile of manure in a single bound!"

Ellen was laughing harder. "What about, I don't know . . . Platypus-Man?"

"One day, on a research trip," Minerva intoned, "a humble scientist, Peter Pancake, was bitten by a radioactive platypus. That day he became Platypus-Man! What can he do? Oh, he can open all sorts of tin cans with his bill! And . . ."

"Lay eggs?" said Ellen.

"Lay eggs in the soft sand! The world needs a hero, and now they have one—Platypus-Man!"

The women were laughing so hard now that they were having a tough time staying on the trail. Micah and Ebenezer bemusedly watched them.

"What about Tree-Sloth-Man?" Ebenezer ventured. "One day a radioactive sloth fell out of its tree and bit mild-mannered podiatrist Peter Porkchop and—"

"That's stupid," Minerva snapped acidly. "Why don't you shut up? Nobody asked you."

"This is what happens when you hire professional mercenaries to take you on a hiking junket," Eb said to Ellen in a mild tone. "They are uncouth. They make things uncomfortable."

Minerva said, "Go piss up a rope."

"Example A," Eb went on pleasantly. "Vulgar, yes? Barbaric, you might even say."

From that point on, they hiked in silence. The land was dry—the crumbly, baked-earth aridness that would make firefighters pray for rain. Ebenezer aimed his rifle and obliterated a tumorlike toadstool growing on the trunk of a saw palmetto at two hundred yards. The crack of the gun pushed every other sound away, ushering in a thudding stillness.

"Simply checking the aim," he said, reloading the rifle. "Every gun shoots a little different, as you know."

Ebenezer and Micah were now breathing hard. The women fared better. Minerva's strides carried her over gnarled roots and fallen logs. Ellen moved with preternatural grace. The men plodded behind them. A fungoid smell rose from the earth, which was spongy beneath a carpet of browned pine needles.

Minerva said, "What is that?"

She was looking at a hackberry tree. Something had been carved in its trunk. A symbol, a rune. It had been gouged deep into the wood.

Micah ran his fingers over the marking. The bark had not grown back; the pale heartwood was smooth as scar tissue. He had seen things like this in Korea. The enemy would score them on trees or rocks as warnings to passing soldiers. Sometimes an army translator had been able to decipher them and gain Micah's unit a crucial advantage; other times not.

"A trail marker?" said Ellen. "Maybe someone hung their bear bag in the tree."

"There's one over here, too," said Eb.

They discovered seven of these markings hacked into the surrounding trees. There might have been others farther back, only they hadn't noticed. The markings were all roughly the same: a cross with a shorter line underneath the horizontal beam. It looked somewhat like a telephone pole. But what struck home was the intensity with which they had been laid into the wood: crude thudding chops that had torn out chunks of wood.

"It was some boys with their daddy's axe," ventured Eb. "Or a crazy fool who wanted to remember which tree he buried his jar of pennies under."

There being no more logical explanation, they silently accepted Ebenezer's reasoning. But the markings lingered in their minds. The violence with which those marks had been laid.

The path gradually rose. They wended over the foothills into the deeper passes. The land plateaued but never dipped. The trees thickened until the woods became impenetrable in some spots.

A deerfly settled on the nape of Ebenezer's neck. It bit him and flew away before Eb could slap the bugger. *Cocksucking bugs!* he thought. *Cocksucking trees! Cocksucking dirt!* Ebenezer hated everything about the wilderness. Rather inconveniently, he had forgotten this fact. He was not built for this. His was a delicate constitution. As a boy, he'd been forever coming down with the sniffles. His humors were perpetually in arrears, as his grandmother used to say. His iron was probably low. He should shoot something that hopped or skulked through this godforsaken purgatory, put it out of its misery, and eat it raw. That would surely jack the life back into him.

But there was nothing to draw a bead on. He became aware of this quite suddenly. Where before there had been the industry of animals ferreting through the brush and birds wheeling in blue sky, now there was almost nothing. An odd serenity. Just the sound of their boots and Ebenezer's own breath whistling in his ears.

We're trapped with the Monster from Green Hell.

Ebenezer flinched visibly. Where had that thought come from? Then it dawned. *Monster from Green Hell* was a B-movie he had watched, along with *The Brain From Planet Arous*, at a creature-feature matinee many years ago. In . . . where had it been? Barstow, Illinois? Bar Harbor, Maine? He'd been on a job. He watched both films at a second-run movie house where the popcorn was stale and the floors sticky. The movie's plot involved a rocket ship of mutant bees that crash-landed in an African jungle. The queen bee found sanctuary in a dormant volcano. Her progeny set about killing the local tribesmen. Then a delegation of blow-dried American scientists arrived. They tossed grenades into the volcano and triggered an eruption that incinerated the vile bugs. *Fin.*

The film was forgettable dreck—except there had been this one shot. Only a few frames of stock footage the cinematographer had jammed in to establish the setting. A panoramic view of the jungle. A riot of creeping vegetation and trees that had witnessed generations wither and die under the wide sweep of their limbs. A place where things never stopped growing, implacably and endlessly and insidiously so, pushing up through the ground and twining around whatever was closest to them, strangling it. A lunatic vista of inhospitable, brooding, vengeful green.

"*Yet his soul was mad,*" Ebenezer whispered. "*Being alone in the wilderness, it had looked within itself and, by heavens I tell you, it had gone mad.*"

Joseph Conrad. As a boy Ebenezer had been forced to study that malarial old moper. Those lines from Conrad's *Heart of Darkness* had leapt into his head unbidden. But Eb wasn't in a jungle, was he? He was in a forest . . . and yet. The green was of a different shade. But it was everywhere.

"Did you say something?" Ellen asked him.

"Nothing of importance, my dear."

THEY CRESTED the back of a ridge. The sun hung above the treetops.

"We've put eight or nine miles under us," Minerva said. "We should find a place to camp for the night."

They made their way across the ridge, scanning for a sheltered spot. The daylight was guttering, and they still had to pitch their tents and gather firewood. Minerva saw the Englishman staggering toward her, cursing. She did not want him to collapse—he might fall down the steep slope and break his loathsome neck, robbing her of the opportunity to slit it later on and dance a happy jig in his fountaining blood like a child skipping around an opened fire hydrant. She was half considering retreating to help him, when her thoughts were derailed by something that sat high up in a tree.

She stopped short. Ellen, who had been following tight on her heels, slammed into her back.

"What's the—?"

Minerva heard Ellen's breath escape in a whinny. She must have seen it, too. When Micah and Eb caught up, they also saw it.

It was seventy feet up, near the top of a ponderosa pine that had shed most of its needles. Dangling at the end of a branch. It wasn't that big. It could have been many things. Twilight prevented accurate identification.

It seemed to have been skinned, whatever it was. It glimmered wetly. If it was a body, it could only be that of a small woodland animal. A rabbit, a kit fox. It hung from the branch on a thin strip of something-or-other like a Christmas ornament suspended on a line of filament. What predator would do that? Steal the skin of its prey and hang the body way up there?

The wind spun it in a slow circle. Spinning, spinning. Rags of flesh swayed from its limbs, as though it had perished thrashing and shrieking. The longer a person gazed at it, the more familiar its outline became . . .

"Let's go," Micah said.

9

THEY CAME UPON a tiny meadow carved from the trees and hunkered down. It was too dark to hike any farther.

The tents were made of heavy canvas. The poles were packed in eight-inch sections that had to be slotted together. They snapped on their flashlights and got to work. It took the women twenty minutes to set theirs up. The men muttered and griped as they struggled with their own.

"I'll sleep outside!" Eb yelled, hurling a pole into the trees. "Bugger it all! I'll sleep outside like a dog!"

Ellen helped the men get their tent up. She worked quickly but deftly, shooing the men aside so she could work unencumbered.

"A million thank-yous." Ebenezer offered a bow. "I am afraid I'm all thumbs, my dear."

Ellen curtsied. "Think nothing of it."

Their exchanges were exaggeratedly comical—a distraction from the dread they had felt earlier while watching that small thing spin at the top of the tree.

They gathered wood and soon had a fire. The forest closed in, isolating them in that trembling pocket of firelight. Minerva pulled a Hebrew National salami from her pack; she cut it with her pocketknife and ate the thick wedges. Ebenezer drank his warm Yoo-hoos and stared at the can of beans he had brought.

"A can opener," he said. "Ebenezer, you horse's ass."

Micah said, "Give it here." He stabbed the lid with his dirk knife and levered it open.

"I am not built for such rough living," Eb said, accepting the can back.

Knots popped in the fire. Minerva produced a flask and drank from it. She passed it to Ellen, who took a nip.

"Is it even legal?" Minerva asked. "An isolated society way out here? No laws, nobody to answer to?"

"They're adults, is how you have to look at it," said Ellen, passing the flask back. "It's their right. Nobody's forcing them."

"Unless they've been brainwashed," said Minerva.

"Yeah, unless. It's not that uncommon," Ellen said. "You've got little, what, enclaves like this all over the country. Utah, Montana, California. I went to the library and looked into it. It's not that the authorities don't know where they are; it's that they don't give a rat's ass."

Minny said, "But you got kids there, too."

Ellen nodded. She had thought about that part of it quite a lot. It was—apart from her nephew's general safety—why Ellen felt compelled to make arrangements with Micah. Nate had no choice but to go with his dad. And if Reggie wanted to devote himself to God in some remote encampment, okay. But Nate was being forced down a line, was how Ellen saw it. He was being pushed, bullied for all she knew, to accept this new life. That didn't sit well with her. If he chose to walk that same line as an adult, fine. But to have that crucial element of choice taken away just because he was too young to make up his own mind seemed totally unfair.

"What about this Grand Poobah?" Eb said.

Ellen said, "I don't know a thing about him."

"We know he's fussy about his hair," said Minerva.

"Sherri and I weren't raised religious," Ellen went on. "So the idea of following someone—*one person*—devoting your whole life to him, it just doesn't add up. What if he's wrong? What if he's nuts?"

Ebenezer said, "O ye of little faith."

Eb said it with a smile. He thought this Bellhaven woman was a fool but a good-hearted one, and those were the best sorts of fools. He would gladly take her money. She would get a gander at this rug-rat nephew of hers. On the way back, he would pay a visit to Ruby at the cathouse in Albuquerque. Ruby did this most delightful thing with her hips.

Micah said, "You will not get him back."

He peered across the fire at Ellen. His face was grave.

"You should not harbor that hope."

Ellen stared back at him. "All I'm asking is to see him. He doesn't even know who I am. He won't remember me. I am—" She casually encircled her face with one finger. "I look different than I did then. Nate was just a baby anyway. Reggie couldn't pick me out of a lineup, either. I just want to make sure he's okay."

Micah said, "Okay by whose estimation?"

Ellen's shoulders drew tight. Her head dipped.

"You know what my sister said to me once? She said that maybe the best thing about having a child, especially a young one, was that you could love that child shamelessly. She said that you could put everything into that kid, love crazily, give everything in your heart and mind and soul over to that other person. You can't do that for a husband or a wife, not really. The only other entity you could love that way would be God, if you're a believer."

She looked up again. Directly at Micah.

"You and me—we don't understand that kind of love, do we."

Micah blinked his eye. He said, "We should turn in."

10

THUMP.

The first one landed softly. Micah stirred.

Thu-thump.

He cracked his eyelid. He was inside the tent. The Englishman was snoring somewhere to his left.

Thump.

Something collided with the tent. Micah heard it roll down the canvas.

He grabbed one of his pistols and crawled past Ebenezer.

"Whuzza?" Eb mumbled.

Micah pushed the flap aside. The clearing was washed in pale moonlight.

Thump. Thump.

"What the bloody hell?" Ebenezer said. He sounded like a man who had been kicked violently awake.

Thump.

That soft pattering all around them. Something else struck the tent and rolled off. Things were landing on the ground with muted *whumphs.*

"Shug?" Minerva called out. "You okay over there?"

He didn't answer. No sense in disclosing their position. He had no idea what manner of assault they were under.

Thump.

This one landed eight inches away, on the grass in front of the tent.

A bird. He did not know what kind. He wasn't a birder. It was small, its body no bigger than a plum. Its wings were folded tight to its body.

Micah reached out and touched it. Cold. Stone dead.

Thump. Thump.

They continued to fall, the oddest downpour Micah had ever encountered. Ebenezer crawled up next to him. His hair was in disarray, but his eyes were sharp to the task.

"Arm yourself," Micah whispered.

Ebenezer retrieved the Tarpley carbine. "What is it?" he said.

"Birds."

"*Birds?*"

Micah pointed at the ground. Ebenezer's fingers crept along the grass; he picked the bird up. It must have felt so light, Micah figured, seemingly hollow, but then, birds were built that way to help them fly. Its feathers were brown except the tips, which were shock white. Its beak was open as though it had died midchirp.

Its eyes were white, too. Not black, as a bird's eyes should be. The white of mother-of-pearl or of concentrated smoke.

There came a final snapping impact—the sound of something much heavier plummeting to earth. The rain of bodies slackened, then stopped.

Micah and Ebenezer crawled from the tent. Ellen and Minerva were already out. Minerva had one Colt stashed behind her waistband, the other Colt in her right hand, and a flashlight in her left hand. Her flashlight beam swept the meadow. They were everywhere. Two dozen birds, maybe more. Most of them were the small brown-winged ones, but there was at least one large bird—a hawk, could be a falcon. None of them were struggling. No wings flapped. It was as if they had died midflight and tumbled gracelessly from the sky.

"It's like that goddamn Hitchcock movie," Minerva said.

"They're kites," Ellen said softly. "Most of these birds, I mean. They're called kites. Their coloring's a bit different from the ones back home, but it's the same bird."

"Tippi Hedren," Minerva went on. "That broad's got a scream to wake the dead."

Micah scanned the trees beyond the clearing. Nothing moved.

"I've heard about such a thing," said Ebenezer. "In Dunchurch, a village in Warwickshire not far from my hometown. Birds fell from the sky there one day. Hundreds, they say. Their hearts had burst. Every damned one of them."

Micah knelt before the largest bird. Its wings were tucked tight to its body, as if it had curled into a protective ball. He tried to pull a wing back to see if it had been shot, but the flesh and bone were locked in place. That was strange in itself. All bodies were softest in the minutes after death, after the muscle and nerve spasms and before rigor mortis set in. But he could not peel the bird's wing back.

A sharp inhale. Ellen was staring at the woods to the east of the meadow. The blood had drained from her face.

"What is it?" Micah said.

"There's something there," she said.

Minerva trained her flashlight. The trees fringing the meadow shone whitely in the glare, the woods impenetrable beyond. They all looked, waiting. Nothing materialized.

"I swear I . . . ," Ellen said.

"What?" Minerva asked.

"I don't know." She shook her head as if to dispel a bad thought. "Just movement. Something . . . *Hey!*" she called out. "Who's there?"

Micah clapped a hand over her mouth. Her eyes were wide and shocked above his hard-knuckled fingers. Micah held a finger to his lips. Ellen got the message. She nodded.

"Give him one of your Colts," Micah told Minerva, nodding at Eb.

"He's already got the rifle."

"He is the best shot amongst us. You know it. Best he be armed."

Reluctantly, Minerva handed Ebenezer one of her pistols; he stashed the Tarpley back in the tent and accepted the sidearm. Minerva pulled the second Colt from her waistband and thumbed the safety off. They faced the woods.

There. A flash. A pale flickering. It trembled through the flashlight's beam, impossible to categorize.

Micah took a step back. He needed to widen his perspective. He couldn't make sense of what he'd seen or was still seeing.

But he *felt* something out there. He suspected they all did. Watching them from the blackness past the trees. Its presence was unmistakable. It galvanized their blood and rashed their necks in gooseflesh. It seethed at them with a hunger they could feel squirming in their own stomachs—hunger, and a malignancy of purpose none of them could even guess at.

It's nothing, Micah thought, his mind rioting just a little.

"It is nothing," he said. "Not a damn—"

11

A FLASH. Nothing definite.

It wasn't that it was too fast for the eye to chart—it was more that the eye *rebelled*, defaulting on its own optics and reducing whatever was out there to an indefinite smudge. Maybe their brains did this as an instinctive protective measure, to spare them the true contours of the thing.

What they did see was long and gleaming, like an enormous length of bone.

That was all they could make out. It was enough.

Ebenezer raised the Colt and fired. Three quick shots. Flame leapt from the barrel. Minerva's Colt tore the night apart, making four concussive booms as she squeezed the trigger.

The gunshots trailed away. They squinted through a haze of cordite smoke. Nothing. It had left. They could feel it. That squirming insistence in their stomachs was gone.

But then . . .

Sounds to the left of the clearing—wait, the right? No, *both* sides. Twigs and pinecones snapped underfoot. With those came another kind of sound, more difficult to grasp. Snortings, gruntings, these weird high whistles . . . scrapings and whickerings and noises that might have made sense in isolation but taken together created a lunatic symphony.

Micah ducked into the tent and grabbed his pack. Minerva followed suit. Micah stepped into his boots; Eb blundered inside the tent to yank his own boots on.

They had one obvious escape: the trail that continued onward to Little Heaven. The one they had traveled was on the far side of the meadow, where the noises were coming from. And the meadow felt constricted now—a killing jar.

Ebenezer laced his boots with fingers that shook—just a little, but still. It took a lot to rattle him. He had seen things, done things. Once a man has witnessed a certain kind of human pestilence and seen some of it reflected in his own soul, well, that man turned hard. The last time Eb had been scared, really *scared*, was during the Suez crisis. But that had been a vital fear, one shared by every soldier in his regiment: of being blown to bits by an enemy mortar, his body scattered in wet chunks over the canal banks . . . of dying far from everything he knew and could draw comfort from.

But this fear—no, this *worry*, just a gnawing worry right now—was airy and dreamlike, because it was unanchored from any clear threat. Just noises in the dark. They could be anything. An overweight raccoon, for Christ's sake!

But it really wasn't that, was it? No. Ebenezer could not say how he knew that, but it was a fact. The thing (things?) in the woods was danger-ous. So what he felt was, if anything, the terror of a boy who knows that something is lurking underneath his bed, even though he has never given that monster a name.

Minerva shone her flashlight on Eb. She saw the pinched worry on his face. Her breath rattled in her lungs. She wanted to run. More than anything on earth. She finished with her boots and picked up the flash-light and her Colt. The gun dangled limply at the end of her arm. It had never felt so useless. A mere toy.

The trees shook. Sixty-foot pines trembled as this thing, whatever it was, grazed their trunks. A smell wafted to her nose—decay and a sour-ness that reminded Minerva of something her father once said.

You ought to kill an animal with one shot, Minny. It should never die in fear, for two reasons. For one, no creature should have to die that way. And two, when a creature dies terrified, its meat tastes sour. One shot, one kill. Make sure the poor thing never knows what hit it—

She turned to Micah in time to see him raise his Tokarev and fire. Six shots in a tight grouping. He lowered his pistol and then, sensing move-ment, raised it again and emptied the clip. He ejected the mag and slammed a fresh one in. He was already backing toward the trail. He hissed at the others. They began to retreat, too.

A shape broke through the trees on the far side of the clearing. The night was too thick to make out its exact definitions, but it was enormous. Shaggy and lumpy and stinking of death.

A bear. It could only be.

Minerva fired while backing away. Ebenezer squeezed off a few shots. The thing kept coming.

Something broached the trees on the opposite side of the clearing. The moonlight glossed its contours. Another bear? Micah's head swiveled. Events occurred more slowly, the way they always did when his adrenaline started to flow.

It wasn't a bear. This creature was slightly smaller. One of its legs stepped between the pines. Long and clad in coarse fur.

Was that a . . . wolf?

It made no sense. A wolf and a bear stalking them together? Different species didn't team up to form a hunting party. It wasn't natural.

Micah watched the wolf-thing creep forward. Its paw came down near one of the larger birds on the grass. Micah squinted, his head cocked at the inconceivability of what he was seeing—

What he saw was—no, *no*. The thing's paw and the dead bird seemed to . . . to merge. The bird's body broke apart, liquefying somehow, passing into the other thing's body. It was *absorbed*. The thing's flesh rippled as the bird became a part of it. But that couldn't be. The starlight bent at weird angles, refracted unnaturally so that it merely seemed this was what had happened.

A growl rippled out of the blackness. Cold, furious, infused with a silvery note of menace.

"Go," Micah said.

They ran. They left everything. Ebenezer's rifle, Micah's second Tokarev, the food. The trail scaled up into the hillsides. It was darker under the trees. The beams of their flashlights—Minerva and Ellen were both carrying one—skipped over the earth, over roots cresting from the soil like fingers. They tripped and stumbled and kept motoring.

Crash and thunder from behind. Micah had hoped the creatures would have been satisfied ransacking the tents. No dice. They were giving chase. Goddamn it all.

Micah whistled sharply. The others turned to him. He slung his pack off.

"Give me some light!"

Ellen trained the flashlight on his pack as he rummaged through it. They were in there somewhere, he knew it. Three waxy cylinders. He had bought them back at the camping store. An impulse buy.

The things were scrambling up the incline toward them. There was nothing stealthy about their pursuit—he could hear them snapping tree limbs and scraping against their trunks. The sound was enormous, out of scale with any animal Micah had ever known. It was as if a blue whale had grown legs and started blundering after them.

They were closing in. Sixty yards, now fifty, now forty—

Ebenezer flanked behind Micah. He squeezed off four shots. The muzzle flash lit the trees, illuminating the shocked face of an owl perched on a low branch. He pulled the trigger again and got only a dry click.

"Give me another magazine," he said to Minerva.

"I've only got the one."

The things kept coming. If the slugs had hit, they had done nothing to deter them. The sounds intensified—eager squeals like a hog snuffling for truffles.

"Better me than you." Eb spoke with an eerie calm. "The clip. *Now*."

Tight-jawed, Minerva handed it over. Micah was still rooting through his pack.

"Jesus, man," Ebenezer said, tugging Micah's arm.

Thirty yards, twenty—

Micah couldn't find them. They started to run again, putting distance between themselves and their relentless pursuers. They hit a straight stretch. The trees opened up. The moon shone against the clouds to provide a weak welter of light.

Minerva spun, waiting for Ebenezer and Micah to ramble past before she unloaded her Colt. Bullets ripped into the darkness. There was no way a few of her slugs couldn't have hit their mark—providing the things were using the path, which they might not be.

For a drawn-out moment, silence. The softer sounds of night enveloped them.

Then the thud of pursuit amped up again. Harder now, more intense. The night bristled with screeches and yowls and hisses.

What in Christ's name are these things? thought Micah.

They ran hard, their lungs shuddering. Ellen tripped and fell, skidding a few feet across the dirt. Her chin was cut, blood cascading down her neck. But she got up and ran on pure adrenaline. The path dipped through a dry creek bed. Micah slung off his pack. He tore stuff out, clothes and other vital supplies, not caring anymore. How would he eat with his jaw torn off? What use were socks when his feet had been gnawed to the bone?

"Shug!" Minerva called out.

He ignored her. The beasts were closing in. Blood-hungry bastards.

They will be in for a rare fucking disappointment if they catch up and sink their teeth in, he thought. *They will find our kind to be stringy, all tendon and cartilage. Not good eating, are human beings.*

His hand closed on what he'd been searching for. He pulled out an emergency flare and tore the strip. Bright red phosphorus fanned from its tip. He tossed it into the creek bed. He scampered up the other side and thumbed the safety off his pistol.

"Go," he told the others. "I will meet you directly."

They obeyed him, scampering farther up the trail. Micah stood rooted. He had to see what he was dealing with.

They came. There were two of them, Micah was almost certain. The sounds of their chase indicated they were coming from both left and right: a scissoring maneuver, the way pack animals hunted, flanking their quarry from each side, cutting off the escape angles, and then—*snik!*—snapping shut.

The flare shed bloody light over a ten-foot radius. He had shot animals moving at a good clip before. Animals and other creatures, too. It was a matter of putting the bullet where they *would* be, not where they were at present. He listened. They might try to skirt the flare instead. But the quickest path, the one leading directly to their prey, would carry them through its—

A shape fled through the light. Micah's mind flinched—though not his body, which remained motionless. The shape was unlike anything in nature. It was composed of too many parts. A seething mass of hysterical dimension, a ball of limbs and tails and teeth, so goddamn many teeth.

It flashed across the riverbed at terrific speed. Micah tracked it with his pistol and fired three times. The thing screeched and withdrew into the trees on the far side of the creek.

The second one was coming now. The big sonofabitch. There was something terrible about its approach—the blundering, crashing awkwardness of its body. It sounded like a creature in almost unspeakable pain.

Micah saw it. Not everything, but an outline. It was huge. It rose up before the light could engulf it and stood there, as a grizzly might on its hind legs. The dry earth of the creek bed cracked beneath it. The rotten stink of its body was overwhelming. Micah had smelled its equal only once before, when he had stumbled across a mass grave in a small village in Korea. The creature made the softest noises imaginable. Little clucks and pips and peeps, gentle exhalations that sounded like a baby drawing breaths in its sleep.

It is a bear, Micah thought, shutting his mind to other possibilities. *A rabid bear.*

He emptied a clip into the bear, center of mass. He did not feel good doing it, but the creature was ill and it would die by his hand now or days later, crazed with brain fever and foaming at the mouth. At close range, he could hear the slugs smacking into its meat. If that did not kill it, it ought to at least flatten its tires a little.

The bear dropped. A rag of snot or bloody meat hit the flare and made it sputter . . .

Then it began to advance on Micah again.

Why don't you just die? he thought tiredly.

He retreated up the trail to find the others. The bear was still chasing them—and he could hear the other one, too, farther down and to the left of the path.

"Go!" he shouted.

They fled again. Slower this time, as they were exhausted and banged up. *Just keep moving*, Micah reasoned. Both animals had been hit. All they needed to do was keep hustling until their pursuers bled out.

The path switched back up a steep hillside. All four of them scanned the bottomlands for some trace of the beasts. Their faces were shiny with sweat by the time they hit the summit. The land beneath was black and unknowable. They couldn't hear anything.

"Stay close," said Micah.

They moved down the trail in a tight knot. The path hit a bottleneck. The trees pinched in on either side—

Minerva heard it before her brain was able to grip what was happening. A sly cracking under her boots—

The ground broke apart under her feet. She plunged into darkness. She caught sight of Ebenezer scrabbling at the lip of the earth, bellowing madly, before his purchase slipped and he was falling with the rest of them.

There came a strange weightlessness, that feeling in the pit of the stomach when a plane takes off. *Oh*, Minerva thought giddily. *I'm falling*. It lasted no more than half a second. Minerva hit the earth so hard that the breath was knocked out of her. Pain needled across her chest as her spine bowed—then something slammed into her skull with terrific force.

12

MINERVA'S EYES cracked open. She was squinting up at a box of daylight.

"She's coming to."

Where was she? She rolled over, moaning. She could feel an enormous lump on her forehead—as if a hard-boiled egg had been sewn under her skin.

"Minerva?" A woman's voice. "How do you feel?"

She opened her eyes fully. The sky was breathtakingly blue. Why couldn't she see more of it? Why only that box? It was as if she were staring up from the bottom of an open elevator shaft.

A face loomed over her. Micah's. Blood lay gluey on his neck. Minerva swallowed. Her throat was as dry as chalk. Micah tipped his canteen to her lips. She drank and coughed.

Ellen said, "Can you get up?"

Minerva managed to sit up. Her skull thudded. She dropped her head between her knees and breathed deeply.

"Where are we?" she said.

"Trapped," said Micah.

"Trapped how?"

"In a trap," he answered her.

She lifted her head. Jesus, that hurt—her skull felt like it was full of pissed-off hornets.

They were in a pit. Clay bottom. The walls were sheer and went up fifteen feet. Severed roots poked through the dirt. Must have taken days to dig.

"Was someone looking for a fucking brontosaurus?" she said.

Micah picked up one of the snapped sticks littering the bottom of the pit. Minerva could see it had been sawed partway through. Her father had dug a similar pit trap on the west side of their shack to catch the foxes that had been killing their Buckeye chickens.

"What's that smell?"

Ellen pointed behind Minerva. She craned her neck to spy a heap of spoiled meat in the corner, squirming with maggots.

"Bait," Ellen said.

"How long have I been out?"

"Four hours or so," said Ellen.

What a mad galloping donkeyfuck this had turned into, Minerva thought. Stuck in a pit with their dicks hanging out. And as the cherry on top of this particular shit sundae, she had a knot the size of a goddamn golf ball on her head—she could see its shadow hanging above her left eye like some overripe fruit set to burst.

"Can we get out?"

"I tried already, standing on Micah's shoulders," said Ellen. "No such luck."

"Why didn't you help them out?" Minerva growled at Ebenezer. "You got two broken legs?"

"Not quite," he said, pointing at his left ankle. His boot was off. His flesh was swollen at his ankle, the sock stretched out like a gruesome balloon.

"You bust it?" she asked.

"I don't believe so," Eb said. "Just a bad sprain."

Minerva said, "Lucky you. I'd have left you in here otherwise."

Ebenezer's smile was as gruesome as his ankle. "You're a peach."

Minerva stood. The blood rushed to her head. She swooned, steadying herself against the pit wall. It was then that they all heard a voice from somewhere above.

"Who's in there?"

A man's voice. Gruff and a little worried, but not threatening.

Minerva still had one of her Colts. Micah had his pistol, too. But what were they going to do—shoot at the only person who might be able to get them out?

"Hikers," Micah called up. "Four of us."

"I see a gun on the ground up here."

"That would be mine," said Eb. "I dropped it when the ground opened up and ate me. I'm sure you understand."

"The rest of you armed?" the same voice asked.

"Pistols," Micah said.

"Why are you hiking with pistols?"

"The same reason you must have dug this pit," Minerva called back.

The man said, "Toss them out."

Micah launched his Tokarev over the edge of the pit. Someone approached above. A shadow fell over the lip of the pit; then it withdrew.

"Never seen a gun like this before," the man called out. "You do some work to it?"

"It is stock," Micah lied.

The man said, "I don't know about that."

Minerva heaved her gun out next. "You going to help us or what?" she said.

"Considering it," the man said.

Minerva clenched her teeth. Her head hived with pain. That she would be left at the mercy of these Bible suckers—who else could they be?—was infuriating. She wanted to quote scripture at them, something about the milk of human kindness or whatever, but she had never memorized a single verse.

In time a rope was lowered over the side of the pit.

"Mind your p's and q's. We *are* armed," the man said.

13

THE COMPOUND known as Little Heaven was carved back against the encircling trees. The perimeter fence bowed under the menacing weight of the woods. The fence was fifteen feet tall and topped with coils of razor wire. Each supporting rib had been fashioned from a delimbed pine tree, with chain-link fence strung between them. It gave the place the look of a backwoods prison. Upon her approach, Minerva could see the roof of a long, warehouse-like structure, and the smaller peaks of the outbuildings scattered around it. She was half shocked to not spot guard towers manned by shotgun-toting Jesus freaks.

It had been a two-mile hike from the pit to Little Heaven. By the time they arrived, they had learned the names of the men who had hauled them out: Otis Langtree and Charlie Fairweather. They seemed the same age, mid- to late-thirties. Otis was the bigger of the two, but both looked like they could use a good meal. Their faces were drawn, their eyes tunneled too far into their skulls.

Minerva learned a bit more about the men besides their names, as they were both happy to talk. Charlie had been a member of the flock for about three years; Otis, much longer. Otis was single; Charlie had a wife and a son, Ben. Charlie had worked at a box factory before coming here. Otis did not speak much of his history. They had both made the decision to join their leader, giving their life savings over to the erection and continuance of Little Heaven.

They both carried .30-30 rifles. Charlie had a Ruger pistol in a holster, too.

"Sorry you fell in," Otis said. "We dug the pit for animals."

Ebenezer was slung between Micah and Ellen; he limped painfully along. Minerva refused to help him.

"What did you dig it to catch, pray tell?" Eb asked.

"Bear?" said Otis. "Wolves? Something's been carrying off our dogs. We used to have five or six. Then a month or so back they started to go missing. Squirmed under gaps in the fence, never came back. Got eaten, we figured."

"Or ran into something bigger and hungrier than they were," Charlie said.

"You do see the odd thing out there at night," Otis said. "Just shapes in the trees. A flash and flicker. What's born wild stays wild despite us being here, you know? All God's creatures."

Charlie had spat in the dirt when he heard that. Minerva noticed he had a way of spitting that conveyed total disdain.

"Dogs are one thing," Otis went on, "but we got kids about, too. Not that they're foolish enough to scramble under the fence, especially come nightfall, but . . ."

"We dug the pit ten feet deep." Charlie hitched up his pants, which were swimming around his hips. "We hit a seam of caliche at eight feet. After that it was hard slogging. Busted a few shovels. Our hands had blisters on top of blisters."

Otis said, "Ten feet—what's going to get out of that?"

Charlie said, "Well, something did. We come back one morning to find the top brush all busted. But the pit was empty."

"Maybe it didn't fall in," Minerva said. "What if it just kind of carried over the top, like over thin ice as it's breaking?"

Otis said, "No, it was in there."

"The bottom of the pit was all torn up," Charlie told her. "Claw marks dug deep into the clay. A lot of them, too. Like they were put there by an animal made *entirely* of claws."

"And teeth," said Otis.

"Yeah, teeth, too," Charlie said.

"Bear?" said Micah.

Charlie shrugged. "Could only be. But they aren't supposed to be that size in this state. You got browns, blacks. They can be ornery, yeah, but not too big."

"Could be a Kodiak roamed over from California," Otis hazarded. "A rogue."

"Anyway, we dug the pit deeper." Charlie spat again. "Another five feet."

Otis said, "And covered it over same as before. A few days later we check and see the cover's broken again." Otis shook his head. "We creep up and—"

"Empty as a politician's smile," said Charlie.

Otis said, "At *fifteen feet*. And we spotted something else strange, too."

"What was that?" said Minerva.

Otis swallowed heavily. "There were sticks jammed into the side of the pit. The sticks we'd laid across the top, yeah? Stabbed into the dirt all the way up. It was like whatever had been inside used them as handholds, right? To climb out."

"What animal would have the sense to do that?" Ellen asked. "Or the dexterity?"

"No animal on earth," Minerva said.

UPON THEIR ARRIVAL at Little Heaven, Otis and Charlie led them past a few pickups and dirt bikes to the wrought iron gate. Each half of the gate was ten feet wide and nearly twenty feet high. What a hassle it would've been, hauling that damn thing out into the sticks. A golden letter *L* was inset on one side. On the other side, *H*.

It was unlocked by a woman in overalls. She did not introduce herself or speak to Otis and Charlie. Her face had the same winnowed aspect as the men's. Minerva found it unnerving. She pictured carnivorous roots anchored to the pads of everyone's feet, slowly sucking the life out of them.

The grounds of the compound were uncluttered. A parade square sat in the center. There were bunkhouses and storage sheds. A tiny playground. Minerva spotted a strip of flypaper dangling from a strut of an open toolshed. Not a single insect—fly or spider or midge—was gummed to the sticky coil.

A row of outhouses sat behind the fence on the easternmost edge of the compound. They sat quite close to the woods. Minerva wondered how many of these people would risk a late-night piss, what with their dogs going missing left and right.

The chapel was the focal point. The eye was drawn to the massive cross rising above it. The horizontal beam was almost as wide as the chapel roof. Looking westward, beyond the chapel and above the trees, Minerva could see a towering rock formation. The rock looked black, not the rust red of most of the igneous rock around there.

Charlie and Otis led them across the square. Minerva saw Ellen's eyes zipping about in search of her sister's kid. But the grounds were empty. They walked to a small, well-maintained lodge. Flower boxes were hung on the windowsills. The door was made of heavy oak with an ornate knocker.

The door opened as if in anticipation of their arrival. A man stepped out. He spotted the six of them—two familiar faces, four new ones. His skull rocked back in mild surprise. He recovered quickly and spread his arms.

"We have guests." A beatific smile. "Welcome to our home under God's eye."

14

FUSSY.

That was the first word that popped into Minerva's head.

Dickhole.

That was the second.

What a fussy fuckin' dickhole.

There was nothing about the man that screamed *dickhole!* precisely. The fussiness, absolutely. His hair was oiled up in an elaborate pompadour—who the hell would do that out here, with the horseflies and tree sap? She suspected he cultivated the hairdo to make up for his diminutive stature; she wouldn't be surprised if he had lifts in his shoes, too.

But a dickhole? Or a rat-assed bastard, as her father might have said? There was no definitive proof that he was, not yet. Just a marrow-deep sense.

The man wore a button-down shirt with wide lapels and cowboy boots of blue-dyed leather. Mirrored aviator sunglasses hooded his eyes. Minerva hated those—they were the sort of shades policemen wore, and you could never tell where a person's eyes were looking.

He strode purposefully toward them. "Little Heaven welcomes you."

Minerva said, "Little Heaven?" as if this was the first time she'd heard the name. They had roles to play now—the naïve hikers—and she hopped right to it.

"Our perfect slice of it, yes," the man said. "I am Reverend Amos Flesher."

He did not shake their hands—rather, he lifted his fingers limply toward them as if offering the blithest of benedictions.

"We found them in the pit, Reverend," Otis said with a small bow. "They had fallen in." A nod at Ebenezer. "This man's hurt."

Minerva caught the trace of an apology in Otis's voice: *One of them is hurt, Rev, or else we wouldn't have brought them.*

"Oh, boys. You and that pit of yours." Reverend Amos tsked. "How did you poor folks stumble into Charlie and Otis's pet project?"

"We heard it was a nice hike around here," Minerva said.

The Reverend's eyebrows lifted—a *please, do go on* gesture.

"We came up from the lowlands and across the Winding Stair pass ten miles north of here," said Micah. "My grandfather made the trek. Said it was hard going, but worth it."

"Your grandfather?"

Micah said, "Years back."

"Before you folks were here," Ebenezer said. "Or your pit."

The Reverend scrutinized Eb. "You're hurt."

"I'll be all right." Ebenezer smiled warmly. "I'm not going to sue, if you're worried."

"You're not dressed like any hikers I've ever seen." The Reverend nodded at Otis. "I see a gun tucked in Otis's waistband. Since I know he doesn't carry one and it's unlikely he found it under a rock, I take it that it belongs to one of you."

Minerva thought: *This guy might wear his hair like some discount Liberace, but he's no dummy.*

"It's mine," Minerva said. "Lots of animals out here."

"There are," the Reverend agreed. "Most hunters use rifles."

Minerva lip-farted. "Wasn't hunting. Just wanted to scare them if I had to."

"Where are your tents?" Flesher said, flinching slightly at Minerva's raspberry. "Your sleeping bags?"

"We had to abandon them last night," Ellen said, speaking for the first time. "There was something in the woods. Some animal—*animals*. They chased us."

The Reverend sighted her down his nose. "You sound like Otis. To hear him speak, the woods are full of man-eating bears and pixies and leprechauns, no doubt. Any animals in these woods are more petrified of us than we could ever be of them. That is how the Lord decreed it. My dear child, don't you know that we are the highest order of life?"

My dear child. Did he just call Ellen that? Minerva tried to swallow her anger, but it lodged in her throat like a peach stone.

"Then why dig the damn pit in the first place?" she said hotly.

The Reverend's gaze pinned her. She felt his eyes on her body, even if they were covered by those aviator shades—his eyes boring into her not in a sexual manner, but invasive in a different way: the feeling of sightless bugs crawling over her skin.

"Well." He spread his hands again, signaling their conversation had come to an end. "I must prepare for the afternoon sermon. The Lord has brought you to our bower and it is our duty to shelter you. Charlie, Otis, they may stay in Greta Hughes's old quarters. Have Dr. Lewis attend to this fellow's ankle."

He cocked his head at his visitors. Their faces were warped in the silver convex of his sunglasses.

"I would invite you to the sermon, but that is only for the elect here at Little Heaven. You will amuse yourselves, though, I'm sure."

He hadn't even bothered to ask their names. It was all *this fellow* and *my dear child*.

He really is *a dickhole*, Minerva thought, happy to have her first impressions confirmed.

Otis and Charlie led them to a cramped bunkhouse with two cots. They said they would send for Dr. Lewis. Their guns were not returned to them.

15

ONCE THEY WERE SETTLED, Ellen Bellhaven decided to take a tour of the compound.

"I'm going for a walk," she announced.

"We've been walking for twenty-four hours," said Minerva.

Ellen expected Micah to object. But he simply nodded. "I'll stay close by," Ellen promised.

The sky was scudded with clouds. A cool wind skated across the earth. The parade square remained empty. Apart from the Reverend and the woman who had opened the gate, Ellen hadn't seen anybody since she'd gotten there.

She crossed the square. The tinkle of a piano drifted across from the chapel. The pianist must have been warming up for the service.

She didn't want to hear the damn sermon anyway—Amos Flesher struck her as many men of the cloth had done over the years: a bully who had learned to fight with scripture rather than his fists. A wise choice on his part, as he didn't look like he could punch his way out of a wet grocery bag. Still, her exclusion reminded her of the Catholic services she had attended with her childhood friend Susie Horton; she had to sit in the pews with the other heretics while everyone else enjoyed their tasteless wafers and watery wine.

The perimeter fence followed the northern edge of the forest. The light between the first cut of trees was thin, almost drowsy, like a summer twilight that falls through a girl's bedroom window as she slips off to sleep. But beyond that point it grew gradually darker until nothing could be seen at all.

Ellen walked the fence line, trailing her fingers along the links. She noticed that the trees were green and healthy except for a stretch, maybe ten yards wide, where they were uniformly sick and dying. Their bark was the gray of dead fingernails, flaking away from the yellowed wood underneath. No needles clung to their branches. The ground beneath was ashen. Ellen could see no cause for it—unless someone had soaked the soil with gallons of tree killer, and who in their right mind would do such a thing?

She peered through the maze of dead limbs, leaning forward until her nose nearly touched the fence . . . She recoiled.

The light moved differently the deeper into the woods she looked. It shifted and churned and took on a life of its own. Ellen got the unpleasant sense that it was staring right back at her. Which was utter foolishness. It was the middle of the afternoon, and neither light nor shadow had its own animus.

Her eyes lifted over the wasted trees to the rock formation looming to the west. It was massive and boxy, less a mountain than some kind of obelisk—a boxy tusk—pushed up from the earth. It rested against the horizon in solitary abandonment.

She continued past a string of bunkhouses where the Little Heavenites must spend their nights. The windows were transparent sheet plastic stapled to the frames—it would be hard to transport glass up here, Ellen guessed. But all the windows on the Reverend's dwelling were made of glass, weren't they? What had these people left to come here? Surely homes more impressive than these. But that was part of faith, wasn't it? Suffering. Ellen had never cottoned to that thinking. Life was too damn tough on its own terms to go depriving yourself further.

She hoped she'd see her nephew, Nate, gazing through one of the plastic windows or chasing a ball across the square. Even seeing mailman Reggie would be fine, as it would mean Nate was nearby. They couldn't have left, could they? Well, better if so. Better Reggie was back delivering letters and Nate back in school.

The living quarters gave way to a warehouse strung with wooden doors. All were closed except one. She peered through it into an area containing an array of familiar equipment: an open-faced furnace, metal blowpipes, and buckets of decorative glass beads. A glassblowing setup. Ellen had taken a course on it years ago—she was going through a bohemian phase while dating a modern primitive who played the pan flute in the Tenderloin district. Folly of youth.

She passed around the edge of the warehouse and found herself facing the playground.

A gaggle of children was immersed in some distraction beside the teeter-totter. Curious, Ellen wandered over. It was good to finally see some life at Little Heaven.

Three girls, one boy. The boy was not Nate—he was too old, and a redhead. Nate had brown hair, or was it black? Their laughter frothed over Ellen. They were hunched in a circle, working intently at something.

She drew closer. They all wore the same shoes—Buster Browns. The soles were cracked and scuffed. Maybe they were brother and sisters, or maybe all the children at Little Heaven had to wear the same clothes the way the Amish do? She could hear their animated whispers.

"Stir them around," one girl said. "That will make them bite."

The boy did something with a stick. A stirring motion followed by a series of quick jabs.

"Yes, oh yes," a girl with plaited blond hair said, "that's working. Do it some more."

Ellen was five feet away. None of them had noticed her. A powerful dread built inside of her. Why was she so worried? It was just some kids playing.

"Hello," she said.

They turned, all at once. Ellen's breath hitched. She took a step back. *There's something the matter with these kids.*

That was her first, purely instinctive thought. They weren't sick in an obvious way. No boils on their arms or open sores on their faces. They were not palsied, their mouths hanging open and leaking drool. And yet there was something—absolutely, *fundamentally*—wrong with them.

"What are you doing?" she asked.

"Who are you?" asked one of the girls. She wore a yellow dress that had faded to the color of old parchment. Her voice made it sound less of a question than an accusation. "You scared us."

Their faces were caved in the same way Charlie's and Otis's had been, but worse—or perhaps it only seemed worse because they were young?

Their flesh appeared to be slumping into their skulls, the way the earth sags before a sinkhole opens up in it. There were fine wrinkles around their mouths and eyes and even the knobs of their ears. They looked as if they had stepped from a terrible compression chamber that had added years to them.

Ellen stared past them to their industry—she couldn't look at their too-old faces for another second. She saw a small ring of sticks jabbed into the dirt, with twine banded round to keep them in place.

Things were moving inside the ring of sticks. Quite a lot of things—

Something was thrashing around in there, too. Thrashing and squealing.

"I'm . . ." Ellen said slowly. "We were lost in the woods. Some of your people found us and brought us here."

The boy smiled at her. It was not a pretty smile. His skin seemed too hard and white, more bone than flesh. "Little Heaven welcomes you," he said.

Ellen stepped closer. The children moved aside so she could see. They exhibited no shame—in fact, they seemed eager to show her.

A hairless shrew was staked inside the ring. A loop of wire was knotted around its tail, the trailing end wound round a stick sunk into the dirt in the center of the ring. The shrew was covered in red ants. They surged over its body in a thick carpet, four deep in spots. The shrew shrieked as the ants mercilessly stung it.

"There are no animals left," the boy said. "But if we're good, he gives us one."

He who? Ellen wondered.

"Why are you doing this?"

One of the girls said: "For everything there is a season."

The bone-faced boy waved the stick he'd used to stir the ants like a conductor urging his orchestra toward a crescendo. He hummed a tuneless ditty. "Hmmm-hm-hmm-mmmm, ha-hum-hmmmm . . ."

The girls giggled. The boy's fingertips were bloody from shrew bites and swollen from ant stings. He seemed to neither notice nor care.

Ellen said, "Where are your parents?"

"You talk too much," said the girl in the faded dress. They all giggled some more.

The shrew's struggles were slackening. Its black eyes stared out from the massing ants, dull and expressionless. A terrible soft hiss rose up, the sound of the ants' bustling bodies. Ellen wanted to kick the ring apart. But she was worried about what these children might do to her if she stopped their barbarous game.

She knelt and pushed the children aside. She did so roughly, mildly revolted by the soapy feel of their skin. They parted willingly, brushing past her, leaving the playground. Ellen thought they had merely grown bored, or were going to tattle on her for pushing them, but they were moving toward the chapel, whose bell had now begun to toll.

The girl with plaited golden hair spun nimbly on her heel.

"You're going to love it here," she said. "You won't ever want to leave."

Ellen pulled the ring of sticks apart. She saw it had been built around the ants' hill—they were only defending their home.

The shrew wasn't moving anymore.

16

"A SHREW?"

Minerva forked chunky, tasteless stew into her mouth. They were sitting in the mess: Minerva, Ellen, Micah. Ebenezer was back in the bunkhouse, waiting for the doctor to look at his ankle.

Ellen had found them here shortly after her encounter with the children. She could only manage a bite of stew. Her appetite was gone. She had buried the poor shrew in a patch of dirt along the fence. Its body was swollen to double its size from the ant venom, so much that its skin had split open.

"They pinned it on top of an anthill," she said. "They tortured it."

Minerva picked mystery meat from her teeth. "Little shits. Well. Who am I to criticize? I had a magnifying glass as a kid. You think I used it to look at stamps? I must've fried a small city's worth of ants."

Ellen nodded. She, too, understood how kids could be. But it was one thing to allow nature to take its course—to watch a spider consume a fly in its web, say—versus actively pushing a horrible outcome. There was something sadistic about it. Not to mention there had been four of them. One child engaging in solitary sadism, okay. You put that kid on a watch list. But to see four of those children celebrating an animal's suffering . . .

The mess was empty apart from the cook who had served them the stew. When they had asked the cook where they should sit, he just flapped his hand toward the back of the mess.

"They didn't look well," Ellen said. "The kids. They looked . . . . malnourished. I've never seen anyone with scurvy—could that be it?"

"They could be underfed," said Minerva. "Who knows what they eat out here, or how often. Could be some lean days."

"Yeah, but isn't that abusive?"

Minerva shrugged. "Not if they signed up for it. Not if they stay."

"This place," Ellen said. "I don't like it. I don't like *him*. The Reverend."

"We will soon depart," said Micah.

They might—the hired guns. Ellen realized they had been tasked with getting her here, nothing more. They had lost their guns the other night, and it was not shocking that they would want to leave, seeing as the denizens of Little Heaven were quite unwelcoming. But could she go? After seeing those kids and catching a sense of the sickness that appeared to infect this place—and after encountering those things in the woods last night, the creatures that had chased them relentlessly—could she leave without her nephew? What could she tell her sister? *Sorry, Sherri, the place creeped me out. I had to hightail it.* Even if Nate seemed okay now, who was to say he wouldn't soon be infected by whatever was spreading around here?

But *was* anything happening? Or was she just spooked by Little Heaven's weird vibe and its pompadoured head honcho? It wasn't like they were sacrificing virgins or dancing naked in the light of the moon.

Not that you know, anyway, said a wary voice in her head.

"I don't like not having our guns," Minerva said.

Micah nodded his agreement. "Our weapons are a ways off," he said. "We do not want to return to the campsite. Not yet." He lowered his voice. "We will keep an eye out. Perhaps there is a way to get our hands on something."

The chapel bell tolled as the service ended. People began to file into the mess. They had a glaze-eyed expression that made them look like sleepers roused from a pleasant dream. They filed in silently, shoes whispering on the floorboards. Most of them wore field clothes, overalls and dungarees, even the women. They took notice of the new arrivals, but nobody stopped to say hello. There were about forty in all. Ellen counted fifteen children, including the four who had tormented the shrew. The oldest could have been thirteen, the youngest a toddler.

Reggie and Nate came in last. Ellen's heart lifted, then sank.

She had not seen her nephew in years. But she recalled a ruddy-cheeked and, well, *robust* little fella. A stout bowling pin of a boy who had careened recklessly around her sister's front room, shrieking merrily as Sherri chased him and tickled him under the armpits. The Nate she spied now was pallid and drained, as if there were leeches at work under his clothes. He had the look of a future telethon case: a boy propped up in a bed with tubes poking out of his arms while dewy-eyed viewers called in their pledges.

His father didn't look a hell of a lot better as he shuffled into the mess behind his son. The skin hung slack off Reggie's neck, and the flesh under his eyes was the yellow of an old bruise.

Reggie and Nate got in the chow line. Neither of them glanced in Ellen's direction.

Micah raised his eyebrows. *That them?* Ellen nodded.

The Reverend Amos Flesher came in last. The sermon had evidently revivified him—it was as if he had stolen vitality from his worshippers and taken it for himself. He passed down the queue, offering that limp-fingered blessing until he reached the head of it.

Great way to cut in line, Ellen thought sourly.

He took his meal—it was served on a fine china plate, Ellen noted, while everyone else's stew was plopped into green plastic bowls—to his table at the head of the mess. There was only one chair at it.

When everyone was seated, the Reverend stood. The congregation followed suit.

"Mighty Lord," the Reverend intoned, "thank You for this bounty You have placed before us. Thank You for this bread, this meat, this wine."

"What's he talking about?" Minerva whispered so low that only Ellen could hear. "I don't see any wine."

"Your beneficence, dear Lord, is unending. Without You we are nothing. You nourish and sustain all things. You provide food for all Thy creatures. Blessed art Thou, Lord, who feeds and waters His children here at Little Heaven. And blessed is Your mouthpiece, who carries Your divine word to the ears of Your flock."

"Nifty," said Minerva.

"Amen," said Reverend Amos Flesher.

"Amen," said the congregation.

"Amen," said Ellen, uncomfortably.

Absolutely nothing, said Micah and Minerva.

A strained silence prevailed during the meal. Few people spoke, and if so, they did so in whispers. Even fewer hazarded glances in the newcomers' direction.

Ellen watched the Reverend. He had an aggressive manner of eating: he held a slice of bread a few inches away from his face, and instead of bringing it to his mouth, he would dart forward like a predatory bird, snapping off bits of crust.

"We have guests tonight," said the Reverend once he'd finished pecking at his food.

The congregation turned to them now, as if given permission. It was not unlike a single organism with a hundred eyes turning its concentrated gaze upon Ellen and her companions all at once.

"The Lord has brought them to our doorstep," the Reverend said. "They fell into the pit dug by Brother Langtree and Brother Fairweather."

He clapped his hands, a dry sound like wood planks spanked together. "Finally! They managed to catch something!"

Laughter from the congregation. Ellen cast a sidelong glance at her nephew, Nate, sitting with Reggie. She caught no spark of recognition in their eyes. Good.

"They will stay with us only as long as it takes the fourth member of their party to heal," he said. "If that is more than a few days, we will arrange for transport to the outside. The Lord has put this hurdle before us and we must abide."

He's speaking like we're *poison*, Ellen thought. *As though our presence is tainting his perfect utopia.*

Dessert was passed around next. Tapioca pudding, as tasteless as the stew. Perhaps the Reverend viewed flavor as a sin? They ate in silence as before.

"Well, whoop-de-doo, what a fun bunch," Minerva muttered. "What do they do on wild nights, watch paint dry?"

Twilight gathered against the mess hall's plastic-sheet windows. Wind hissed through gaps in the walls with a zippery note.

Two men entered the mess. They had the look of brothers: the same sharp cheekbones and ferret-thin frames. One had a scoped rifle slung over his shoulder. The other had a revolver holstered at his hip like a Wild West gunslinger.

They moved briskly to the Reverend. All three inclined their heads in conversation. The two men spoke animatedly yet in hushed tones; the gunslinger made a few wild flourishes with his hands. The Reverend nodded and signaled for them to depart.

For a minute, the Reverend sat very still with his eyes closed. He opened one eye once, briefly, and his gaze was trained on Ellen's table. His jaw worked side to side and his lips moved as if in silent prayer.

In time, he stood. His eyes remained closed. His body trembled slightly. The congregation sat riveted. Ellen caught sight of Reggie out of the corner of her eye. His face was cheese white and twitchy as he stared at Amos Flesher, enrapt.

"There come a test," the Reverend said in a stagey kind of whisper. "In the life of every man there come a test . . ."

Nods from the congregation. *Yes, oh yes*, Ellen could picture them all thinking. *The Lord tests the faithful.*

"The son of Brother and Sister Rathbone has wandered into the woods."

A shocked group inhale from the congregation—it was as though they had taken a breath as a single unit.

"Eli?" said a woman in a paisley frock. "Eli Rathbone's missing?"

The Reverend paused, as if unsure of the boy's name.

"He is safe," Reverend Flesher said sharply. He cast a baleful eye upon the woman until she sat down again. "The Lord assures me of this. Brother Swicker and Brother Neeps have been looking for him, along with his parents. But now we all must gather. The light draws thin. The poor boy shall not spend the night outdoors."

Everybody rose. People were animated now—their bodies moved with the jerky-limbed mania that grips a group of people on the cusp of mass hysteria. The Reverend's chin was tilted upward, his face set in a mask of forbearance—Ellen wondered: Did he envision the boy's disappearance as a test for *himself*?

Ellen, Minerva, and Micah filtered into the square, where the adults were gathering. The children had been sent off to the bunkhouses. A few people had flashlights. Ellen spotted Reggie carrying a lantern that gave off a weak glow, its glass blackened with kerosene smudges. Rags were tied to the tips of scrap two-by-twos and dipped into a bucket of creosote. The jury-rigged torches were lit with a Zippo passed from person to person. This all happened quickly and silently. The two-by-twos, rags, and creosote were all at the ready, as if waiting for this very eventuality.

The armed men who looked like brothers addressed the throng.

"Eli's folks is out thataway," the one with the rifle said, pointing at a general area past the fence. "They ain't seen the boy in a few hours. They thought he was with the others in the play area."

The man with the holstered gun was smoking a home-rolled cigarette.

He flicked the butt into the weeds and said, "A mother ought to keep mind of her kids." He cast an eye on the group, picking out the mothers in its midst. "Ain't that a pure fact?"

Nobody spoke against him. The torches crackled, sending up plumes of stinking smoke. The flames flickered on the worshippers' pale pinched faces.

"We'll fan out," said the rifleman. "East, west, south, north. No telling whichaway the boy went, or how far afield."

"Better not be too far," his partner said. "The woods are a dangerous place to be at night."

The rifleman grinned. "Lovely, dark and deep."

Ellen did not care for these two. They seemed to be taking delight in this. The rifleman then pointed at the outsiders.

"You stay here. This is not your calling."

Minerva and Micah were already holding torches. Micah levered his torch back on his shoulder until his face grew dark. "Your call," he said.

"It is," said the rifleman, and spat. His partner rested the heel of his palm against the butt of his revolver. "And I say *sit*."

The group exited through the main gate. The monolithic expanse of the woods dwarfed them; the flimsy light of their torches quickly dwindled under the brooding darkness of those trees. The worshippers paired off and began to sweep the woods. Voices called out from every direction.

"Eli?"

"Eli!"

"*Eli!*"

"Child, come home! God wants you to come home!"

The light of their torches was swallowed by the night. Soon their voices were gone, too. Ellen, Minerva, and Micah stood in the parade square. There was not much else to do. It wasn't like there was a horseshoe pit or a bingo game they were missing.

A lone figure rounded back into the compound. Charlie Fairweather.

"I don't care what Cyril or Virgil says," he said. "That boy needs all the help he can get."

"Okay," said Micah.

17

DURING THE WAR, Micah used to drive trucks full of the dead.

Between ten and fifteen bodies piled into the back of an old GMC Deuce-and-a-Half. The bodies of GIs and medics and radiomen and the odd noncombat pogue who had found himself in the wrong place at the wrong time. The bodies were intact, by and large, though sometimes the stray parts had to be zipped into canvas sacks. They were usually frozen—not strategically, just because the icy temperatures ensured that most of them were rock hard for transport.

Micah and another marine, Eldon Tibbs, would drive them from the front line to Hamhung, a port town under US occupation. It was suspected that the Chinese would strip, loot, and debase the corpses otherwise.

There was one night, winter of 1952. Micah was at the wheel for that haul. He was nineteen years old. The road wound through the pines, which were cottony-looking, with bluish moss hanging from their branches like seaweed. Tibbs didn't talk much. He and Micah got on just fine. Tibbs smoked a pipe packed with cherry tobacco. He received it every month in a thick waxed envelope. One of his brothers sent it. He was smoking when it happened.

Micah did not see or hear the shot that killed Tibbs. It was either perfect or just plain lucky—bad luck for Tibbs. A hole appeared in the passenger window, and the side of Micah's face was plastered with wet warmth.

Tibbs's lit pipe fell into Micah's lap. The road hit a bend. Tibbs's body slumped heavily against Micah. A flap of skin from his blown-apart face slapped against Micah's neck. He smelled the thick iron of Tibbs's blood.

Wind shrieked through the window hole as the truck veered into the trees. Micah tried to correct the fishtail, but the front end dipped over the edge of the road into a gully. Micah was thrown into the windshield, which splintered when he struck it.

He grabbed the pistol from Tibbs's holster and heaved himself from the cab. Blood flowed freely from his forehead. Whoever shot Tibbs couldn't be far away.

He staggered around the side of the truck, keeping low on the gully side. The truck's rear doors had popped open. Bodies lay scattered over the road. Corpses rested at horrible broken-backed angles. A few of the zippered sacks had burst, spraying remains. The ragged edges of frozen flesh had a crystalized look, crusty red like freezer-burned steak.

Micah crept to the bumper. Ice had formed to a webbing between the black bones of the trees across the road. A figure was approaching down the ditch across the road. Micah fired. The slug missed wide. The figure dropped out of sight.

Next, a round struck the truck a few inches above Micah's head. He spun away; his heels skidded out from under him and he went down hard on his ass. He pivoted onto his stomach, watching the road from under the truck chassis.

A single Chinese soldier crept out of the ditch. What was he doing so far behind enemy lines? Either crazy or overconfident. He must have thought he'd hit Micah, that he was dead. The man drew nearer. His face was smeared in lampblack. Micah waited until he was so close that all he could see was his legs, then squeezed the trigger.

The slug went through the man's shin. The man cried out and awkwardly fell. Micah put another round into his head. The man's flyaway corn-silk hair puffed up as the bullet drilled into his brain.

Micah spent the next twenty minutes loading bodies into the truck. Some had spilled into the earth under the trees, which was weirdly spongy despite the night's chill, carpeted by a strain of moss he had never encountered. It was hard work—dead bodies possessed an ornery, uncooperative weight. He put the dead Chinaman in with them.

He backed out of the gully and drove on to Hamhung. He left Tibbs in the cab. His body was going stiff . . .

This was the memory that blitzed through Micah's mind—collecting frozen bodies under the pines—as he now entered the woods encircling Little Heaven with Charlie, Minerva, and Ellen. This earth had the same soft, rich, obliging, somehow cake-like quality. But there was no moss here. The ground simply felt mushy underfoot, as if it had been saturated with thick and fatty oil.

It feels like flesh was Micah's thought. *The waterlogged flesh of a corpse coughed up from the bottom of a lake.*

What a stupid thought. But the inkling remained: they were walking on a huge carcass. If they were to dig, their fingernails would scrape its wormy skin. And if they dug into its hide, its black blood would surely gush out, syrupy as crude oil.

They tried to chart a straight path, but the trees and blowdowns made it hard. Micah spotted the light of a torch burning to the east, a paling pinprick. Shouts rang out—"Eli! *ELI!*"—but those, too, began to soften as the searchers fanned out in ever-widening orbits.

The light of Micah's own torch illuminated a ten-foot radius; there was barely enough to navigate by, much less spot the boy. A night in these woods would feel like an eternity to a child. Why would he have taken off? Any number of reasons, Micah supposed. He'd chased an animal. Or his parents had scolded him and he had run away.

Or else something lured him in.

"Needle in a haystack," Charlie said with a defeated grimace. "I can barely see the fingers at the end of my hand."

Micah said, "Tell me about those two."

"What two?" said Charlie.

"The men giving orders."

Charlie cocked his torch on his shoulder and rubbed his elbow nervously. "The one's Cyril Neeps. With the longish hair?"

They both had long hair. They were practically identical.

Micah said, "The one with the rifle?"

"That's the one," Charlie confirmed. "The other fella is Virgil Swicker."

"So they're not brothers?" Ellen said.

"They look it, don't they? But no. They weren't part of the congregation back in San Francisco. To be honest, they don't seem to have much faith at all. I haven't ever seen their heads bent in prayer."

"What are they doing here?" said Micah.

Charlie scratched his elbow in a nervous way, like a child called to the front of the class to finish an equation on the chalkboard.

"The Reverend, he brought them on. Guess he figured with the camp being so isolated, and not too many of us having real survival skills, it would be good to have them."

"I thought the Lord would be your shepherd," Minerva said.

Charlie gave her a look. "The Reverend had his reasons. He is guided by the Lord."

Micah noticed that Charlie hadn't referred to the men as Brother Neeps or Brother Swicker. They had the unmistakable whiff of hired guns. Why take on those two? Maybe, as Charlie said, simply to keep the flock safe . . . or else to keep the flock in line?

The lights of Little Heaven were no longer visible. Micah's eye swept the woods for any sign of the missing boy. The darkness rebounded at him, empty and dead.

"We should split up," he said.

They had already drifted into two distinct parties. Micah and Ellen on one side. On the other, Charlie and Minerva.

"Boy, girl, boy, girl—is that what you're thinking, Shug?" Minerva said archly. "How orderly."

Minerva and Charlie moved off in a westerly direction. Micah and Ellen continued straight on.

"Eli!" Ellen shouted. Then, lowering her voice: "Poor little guy."

They walked beside each other. Micah could have reached out and taken Ellen's hand. He could smell her: campfire smoke and sweat and something sweet, too, that smelled a little like field berries.

"Are you well?" he asked, just to say something. It was not like him at all.

"I'm okay, considering. Nate and Reggie are here, at least. But they don't look well, Micah. Nobody looks well. Is that just me thinking it?"

"It is not just you."

"Right? Everyone looks . . . sick. The guts vacuumed out of them— the vim, the vitality. A bunch of shambling undead."

It wasn't just the people in Little Heaven that set off Micah's alarm bells. It was the thing or things that had chased them the night before, too. Things Micah assumed must have been bears or wolves. But they hadn't moved like that, and when he caught a glimpse of their bodies in the flare's sputtering light—that heart-stopping flicker of movement—in that split second he thought: *These are like no creatures I have ever encountered.* Those creatures, and the shower of dead birds, and the denizens of Little Heaven, and the soft give of the ground underfoot, and the way the darkness melted unpleasantly into his bones . . . everything was a bit skewed, a degree off center. None of it seemed odd enough to raise a panic over—you could convince yourself that it was just the weak-nelly dread that domesticated humans felt nowadays, after spending most of their lives in well-lit cities. This was life in the woods. It was dangerous, full of threats. And his experiences in Korea and afterward had enabled Micah to operate calmly under threat. He did not rattle, even when he should. But maybe that was the true danger: you were lulled into a false acceptance as what had once seemed odd came to feel perfectly natural, and by the time things really started to go south it was too late. You were trapped.

"I don't know if I can leave without Nate," Ellen said. She was looking directly at Micah. "I'm not expecting anything from you. I just wanted to say."

Micah said nothing. But he knew he would not leave Ellen. If he was not exactly a good man, he had always been a loyal one. If he took a job, he finished it. Unless something happened to him that prevented it.

They traced a path through the trees. No sounds filtered out of the darkness: none of the little clicks and whistles and snapping twigs that should be there in a forest teeming with life. But the woods felt arid and lifeless—they could have been walking on the moon.

The ground underfoot went from dark to light. The white of pulverized bone. Micah's boots kicked through drifts of ash . . . except it wasn't that. Nothing had been burned.

"I know where we are," said Ellen. "I saw it this afternoon."

Dead. Every tree and bush, every tuft of grass. The vegetation was decimated in a manner Micah had never seen: the bark peeled off trees in brittle shreds, the underlying wood gone a sick bile yellow. He saw no termite bore holes, no blight of any kind. It was as though they had died of old age—they had the look of wretchedly ill seniors at a cut-rate old folks' home, wasted away with cancers that had rotted their bodies from the inside out.

"It's only right here," said Ellen. "Ten, fifteen yards wide."

She reached out tremblingly. Her fingertips brushed a tree. She recoiled as though she had touched a dead body.

"Do you think Eli would have come this way?"

Micah scanned the route they had just walked. He felt something for just an instant. A presence—a delicate, quick-stepping movement he sensed not with his eye but rather a center of perception buried deep in his lizard brain, wed tightly to the fight-or-flight instinct the human species had developed back when we were as often prey as predator.

Yet he saw nothing with his eye. Just the liquid shiftings of the night.

Or—

Fifty yards down the path. Peeking slyly between the ruined trees.

Peekaboo, I see you.

A face. It hovered ten feet off the ground, a tiny earthbound moon. Not a human face. It wasn't round at all. More long and curved and vulpine. It was as pale as the moon, too—the jarring white of flesh that had never tasted daylight.

Its eyes—were they eyes? was any of this *real?*—were black as buttons. It opened its mouth. Its face split in half, pulling its head apart; the top of its skull levered back like a Pez dispenser. Inkiness bled out of that slash, a blackness more profound than Micah had ever known.

Ellen grabbed his hand. She had seen it, too.

"*Run,*" she said.

They sprinted through the woods, their feet flashing over the ground. Ellen veered sharply left, off the path of death. Micah spun around to see if the face—and the body it was attached to—was in pursuit. He tripped and dropped the torch. It fell sputtering into a patch of dry earth. He abandoned it. They followed Ellen's flashlight. It bobbed against the trees, the beam occasionally skipping skyward when she stumbled. Micah wasn't sure where they were going, but Ellen ran with a purpose. Already the image of what he had seen—that bloodless face staring at them amid the tree limbs—seemed absurd. What creature could be that tall?

Unless it was up in the tree, he thought. *Hugging it like a spider.*

He pictured a terrible arachnid-like thing hooked to the spine of a dead pine, its thick furred legs throttling the trunk . . .

He grabbed her hand. "Stop."

She checked up. They stood panting.

"We will get lost," he said.

She pointed to her left. "The compound is that way. I see the light of torches."

She shot a look behind him.

"Micah, you did *see*—?"

He nodded. "An animal. An owl."

He could tell she wanted to believe him. He wanted her to, too.

They walked toward Little Heaven. Whatever the thing was, Micah could hear no breath of its pursuit. Had it even given chase? He wasn't at all certain. He was becoming less certain of many things.

Those creatures from last night, this one now—what if something unnatural was at play? In the army, some of his more superstitious barrack mates would talk about seeing things while out on patrol. Unearthly lights, distant figures that seemed to float above the earth. Spooks. Ghosties. Another man, a sniper named Groggins, used to claim Korean scientists were creating half-human, half-animal hybrids in underground labs. Super soldiers, ape-men and snake-men, which was what Groggins kept glimpsing through his scope during night watch: lab mutants who had escaped containment roaming no-man's-land, feasting on rotting corpses sunk in the mud, too skittish to attack—yet.

Micah never put any stock in it. Men's minds went to strange places when put under pressure. And he knew that even if something strange was happening around Little Heaven, the worst thing to do would be to run half-cocked into the woods. No. They had a home base. Not a very hospitable one, but it would do. They were being fed and sheltered. There were weapons, even if they weren't yet in Micah's hands. He could get a gun, if push came to shove. So their best bet was to sit tight, assess the situation, and act only once all the information had come to light.

They walked quickly. Ellen swept the fringing bushes with her flash-light. No sign of the boy. They spotted torchlight. Soon they encountered two searchers trudging back to the compound. Their clothes were dusty, their spirits low. The boy had not been found and it was nearing midnight.

Virgil Swicker and Cyril Neeps idled at the front gates. They had not done much to look for the boy, as evidenced by their clean trousers. Neeps's jaw tightened at the sight of them.

"What'd I tell you?" he said to Micah.

Neeps grabbed Micah's sleeve. Micah swung round until they were facing. Neeps's breath washed over him, hot and electric. Neeps waited until the Little Heavenites had passed from earshot before speaking.

"The fuck are you up to, sonny boy? Told you to stay out of this."

Neeps's fingers clawed into Micah's forearm. If he wanted Micah to wince, he would be disappointed.

"There's a missing child," said Ellen. "How could we not—?"

"Wasn't talking to you, bitch," Neeps said casually. Swicker, who had been standing a ways off, pinched in at Ellen's side. He could reach out and grab her if he wanted to.

"You being a clever Clyde?" Neeps's eyes drilled into Micah's un-patched eye. "Lost hikers, uh? Nah, I'm thinking not. You're gonna want to hit the dusty ole trail real soon. Skedaddle your asses."

Neeps picked a shred of boiled gray meat from between his teeth and flicked it at Micah's chest. It stuck.

"We are a long way from anything, son," said Neeps. "Ain't no rules, except what the good Reverend says." A chuckle. "And even then . . . well, Virg and me ain't never been much for godly matters. I get a sense you ain't, neither. So go. Take your show on the road, Pontiac."

Neeps shoved him. Micah stumbled back, then calmly straightened the lapels on his duster. "You bet" was all he said in reply.

He and Ellen walked back to the bunkhouse. Cyril said something to Virgil, which was followed by a donkey bray of laughter.

Micah could tell Ellen was unnerved. Whether it was by the face in the woods or the confrontation with the hired guns, he could not tell. He wondered if he would have to kill Swicker and Neeps. He hoped to avoid it. It would be ideal if they were able to leave soon, just like Neeps wanted. As soon as Ebenezer was well enough to walk. But sometimes men like Neeps pushed a collision. And Micah always made a point of hitting first, and hitting harder.

18

EBENEZER AWOKE from a dreamless sleep. It was dawn. Frail sunlight leaked through the bunkhouse window.

He sat up. The others were asleep on the spare cots that had been brought in last night. Sleeping, or playing at it. Ebenezer wasn't sure Micah ever really slept—he got the sense the man merely closed his eyes and faked it for a few hours a night.

Ebenezer put his feet down and tested his injured ankle. Dr. Lewis, the compound's de facto sawbones—an old army meatball medic—had fashioned a splint to take the pressure off. He had given Ebenezer a few pills to help him rest. Ebenezer had taken them and dozed. When he had awoken for the first time, he'd noticed Minerva and Ellen bustling about, searching for a flashlight.

"What's happening?" he'd asked

"Shut up." Minerva tossed the pill bottle at him. "Take another pill, Phil."

Ebenezer thought that a fine idea; he took another one. He slept for hours and swam out of unconsciousness in the early hours of morning. Perhaps it was the effects of the medication or a dream he couldn't shake off, but he swore he had seen something at the window. The face of a child. But it was bleached white apart from the eyes, which were black, as if the pupils had been pricked like the yolk of an egg, the darkness spreading across each eyeball—

He had slept again and woken up only minutes ago. He stood. The pain was definitely there, a sharp spike radiating up his shin, but it was manageable. He was starving. He was always hungriest after he had been hurt—his body worked so hard at repairing itself that it drained its energy reserves.

He limped out of the bunkhouse. Dawn was streaming through the trees. He saw lights moving in the woods and heard the occasional cry of a boy's name. *Eli*. It made him think of the boy he might have spotted at the window last night—the boy who had been nothing but a figment of his pill-addled mind.

He spied a man clocking his progress. A fellow with straggly white-boy hair—the hair belonging to a particular breed of man you'd call a reb—and a pistol holstered at his waist. This man watched him limp across the square with a flat, jeering expression on his face.

"Bit early for your kind to be up, ain't it?" he called over.

Ebenezer stopped and stared at the man. "Early for a nigger—is that what you mean, my good man?"

"Nope," the man said chummily. "I meant early for a faggot. You ain't gonna find a hairdresser for that flowsy hair out here, boy."

Ebenezer nodded impassively. "Good to know."

"Get better quick," the man said dismissively. "Then get your ass out of Dodge."

Ebenezer found the encounter quaint yet crass. *Faggot*? The bastard should be so lucky. Eb vowed to slit the hayseed goober's throat if the opportunity ever presented itself.

He limped into the mess. Begrudgingly, the cook gave him a bowl of porridge. Ebenezer dumped brown sugar on the porridge and ate it and asked for more. The cook groused.

"It's for the kids' breakfasts, and the people out looking for poor Eli."

The cook was about fifty, with a potbelly and a nose that begged for a punch. Ebenezer would have happily kicked him down a flight of stairs, but there were none of those around, and anyway his ankle hurt too much.

"Whensoever you come across a man in need, you shall freely open your arms to him, and shall generously lend him sufficient for his need in what-

ever he lacks." Ebenezer showed the cook his outspread palms. "Book of Ephesians, my friend . . . my friend in *Christ*."

The cook gave him another bowl. Ebenezer was delighted. He had just made that shit up! When he was finished, he burped and said, "My compliments to you, chef; I'll be sure to mention you in my review for *Bon Appétit* magazine."

He departed on the chef's scowl. Fah, to the devil with him. To the devil with this whole miserable encampment. If he were healthy, he would leave this minute with only the clothes on his back. The others could come or not; he wouldn't care.

Ebenezer could not say what bothered him about Little Heaven, aside from the obvious—that it was a dismal enclave run by a short-assed Bible thumper with a discount Elvis haircut. It was more the smaller details, like how the sunlight seemed shabbier over the compound, leeched of its heat and vibrancy. Or how everyone was stooped like trees struggling to survive on a windswept mountain peak.

He stood in the parade square, watching people come in from the woods. They were exhausted and dirty, carrying torches that had burnt down like enormous wooden matches. What had the cook said? *Out looking for poor Eli . . .* Had a boy run off? If so, a missing child was Little Heaven's concern, not his own. Concern was not and had never been a quality of Ebenezer's nature. While that counted as a failing in him as a human being, it held many benefits in respect to his chosen profession.

THE MORNING WORE ON. The search continued. Ebenezer overheard Minerva and Micah strategizing while Ellen was out of earshot. Minerva spoke loud enough for Ebenezer to hear—she wanted him to hear, Eb figured. Why couldn't they just leave? she reasoned. Let Ellen keep her money. If Ebenezer couldn't make it on his bum ankle, tough shit. Micah shook his head. Ebenezer didn't hear what he had to say, but it probably had something to do with not wishing to leave Eb behind. Micah was a dutiful fool, though there was a strong possibility that he wished to linger on Ellen's behalf. He was sweet on her, as even Helen Keller could've sniffed out.

"What about the guns back at the camp?" Minerva said. "We could use those."

"Yes," Micah admitted, but their conversation stopped there.

The midmorning sermon was short, only fifteen minutes. His holiness Reverend Flesher was committed to organizing the search for Eli Rathbone, but he refrained from setting foot in the woods. Probably didn't want a bird to shit on his head, Ebenezer figured.

Someone should tell him bird shit makes an A-1 hair conditioner, he thought. *That would get him out to shake a few trees.*

Ebenezer and the rest of them had been banned from the search, according to Micah. The Reverend's hired men made the decree. Big deal. Hobbled as he was, Eb would be useless in any search even if he wanted to take part—which he did not. The four of them passed the afternoon watching the Little Heavenites come in from the woods. The worshippers would eat, pray, head out again. The Reverend beseeched God for the safe return of young Eli, who was without sin.

Ebenezer did not spot the missing boy's parents. Evidently they had been in the woods since yesterday afternoon, when they first suspected their child had run away. They could be ten or fifteen miles from the compound by now—together, though maybe separate—delusional with grief, wandering aimlessly, calling out for their lost son.

The Reverend prayed for Eli's parents, too. Helluva guy, that Reverend.

Flesher's hired goons, the rifleman and the other one with a stupid bovine face—Ellen gave their names as Cyril and Virgil, respectively—supervised. They did so with a bored and vaguely hostile air, like ranch hands herding cattle. Ebenezer assumed they were overjoyed at the work: they got to keep the flock in line, following the orders the Reverend doled out, and at such time as Little Heaven came apart—and it would, as the cracks were already showing—they could take what they wanted and escape while the place went to hell.

At six o'clock, dinner was served. The mess was sparsely occupied. Those who were there spoke in whispers.

Should we head to the outside, talk to the police, and organize a proper search party? . . .

The Reverend, sensing the winds of dissent, stood and addressed the gathering.

"It is at times such as these, when we are at our greatest need, that we must band more closely together," he said. "Did I not bring you here so that you could hear the word of God more clearly? And now, at the first sign of trial, you talk of fleeing back to the godless heathens who compelled our departure?"

The Reverend's hands tightened on the table, twisting into claws.

"Do you want to be cast out of the Eden we have made? Do you? The boy will be found. God will bring him back. God is merciful until His works are questioned. Eli must wander the desert as Moses did until God brings him back, and He will. He *will*."

Silence from the congregation—until a tremulous voice spoke up from the back.

"Are you sure this was the first sign, Reverend?"

Amos Flesher scoured the room until his gaze fell on a woman dressed in a plain smock. She sat with a man, equally plain, obviously her husband.

"What did you say, Sister Conkwright?"

"The first sign of trial." The woman struggled to hold the Reverend's gaze. "Because Sister Hughes broke her leg, remember? And . . . yes, a few other things."

"Such as?"

Sister Conkwright's hands knotted in her lap. Her husband set his hands over her own. She put her head down.

"Nothing," she mumbled. "God is good."

The Reverend let a few seconds tick past. His gaze settled on Ebenezer and the others for a moment—the flat, dead gaze of a viper—before flicking away.

"Sister Conkwright, if you or anyone here so gathered wishes to leave Little Heaven, you may. With my blessings."

But the way the Reverend spoke, it was like he was inviting her to step off a cliff.

"Cyril and Virgil will escort you out. But once you are gone—just as it was with Adam and Eve from Eden—you are . . . *gone*."

The congregation filed out. Sister Conkwright required her husband's assistance, as she was shaking badly. The men and women of Little Heaven returned to the square to fashion more torches. The search continued.

19

THE CONKWRIGHT BITCH. She would ruin everything.

Amos Flesher paced his quarters. His heart bappity-bapped in his chest. Every so often, he slammed his fist into his palm. The meaty slap of skin was soothing.

To hurt is to love.

Who had said that? One of the nuns at the San Francisco Catholic Orphanage? He had been left on its steps as a toddler. It happened a lot in that city. A city of whores. Amos barely remembered his mother. His father was unknown—but Amos knew he must have been a great man. A man of God who had been called away to follow the same voice that Amos himself could hear.

Amos had lived at the orphanage for sixteen years. His was the longest residency in its history. The goal was to have every child adopted into a God-fearing family. But Amos never was. He would spend a few weeks with a family, but they always sent him back. One time, he had overheard his prospective mother and father whispering with the nuns.

Peculiar boy. Strange tendencies.

All the other boys and girls got adopted. Even the dwarfs and the ones with harelips and the ugly specimens with IQs no bigger than their belt size. They were shipped off to families who lived in sparkling houses overlooking the bay. Amos stayed at the orphanage with the nuns and the pea green floor tiles.

The nuns became his surrogate mothers. None of them took a shine to Amos—they treated him as a burden once it became clear he would never get adopted. But one of them, Sister Muriel, saw it as her duty to teach him the wages of sin. And the wage was high, oh yes. Your immortal soul.

Prurient desires are the devil rapping at the door to your soul, she said to him. *If you give in, boy, you let Satan trip-trap in on his cloven hooves.*

She meted out discipline for lustful behavior. It happened a lot with the older boys and girls. If Sister Muriel found out that a boy had been fiddling with his dirty stick or a girl with her pink button—and Sister Muriel had an unerring way of knowing this—those transgressions would be met with lashes.

Sister Muriel's discipline did not extend to the encephalitic or soft-brained orphans—*God's children*, as they were known—who were kept in a separate ward. Those unlucky souls should be allowed to act on the impulses other boys and girls must stifle, she reasoned. Amos had not seen it that way at all. All vice was an affront to the Lord, was it not? And if those imbecilic simpletons could not check their acts of self-gratification, why should they escape punishment? It wasn't fair.

Once he turned twelve, the nuns began to assign duties to Amos so he could make himself useful. One of those duties was to preside over God's children during naptime. Many of them had to be strapped down so they didn't hurt themselves—some of them shook so badly that the bonds actually helped them sleep: they would struggle uselessly for a few minutes, then fall into an exhausted slumber.

Amos would walk the rows of cots in his crepe-soled slippers, same as the nuns wore. They made no noise on the tiles. Sunlight streamed into the ward, honey gold on all those terrible misshapen bodies.

One of God's children, a boy named Finn, rarely slept. He had a head like a pumpkin, his features stretched across that bulging canvas. He was thirteen or fourteen, nobody knew for sure, and nearly blind. During naptime, he would work at his wrist straps until he popped one hand loose. That hand would immediately go to his crotch. He masturbated furiously. His erection was a permanent fixture. All day, that fleshy spike in his drawers. Sometimes he would orgasm without even touching himself. He could bring himself to climax with the workings of his mushy mind alone.

Amos wondered what Finn thought about. Girls? Boys? Maybe just the pressure of his hand on his penis? Finn only produced guttural groans and blabbers, so it was impossible to say. But Amos didn't like it. Finn strained against his straps so diligently that his wrists were forever scabbed. The nuns had to change the bloody linens every day. Finn ought to be taught a lesson.

Amos knew every crevice of the orphanage, and stole a pin from the nuns' sewing room. He didn't consider it stealing, though, because he was doing the Lord's work.

That afternoon during naptime, he crouched beside Finn's bed.

"Stop your fiddling, Finn," he whispered, liking the way the order rolled off his tongue. His voice had already developed a rich tenor. "Or else."

Finn just grunted and continued to work at his straps. His erection tented the soft material of his sleeping gown.

Amos pulled the pin out of his sock, where he'd put it for safekeeping. It was three inches long. He pushed it through Finn's gown until the tip dimpled Finn's skin. Finn grunted quizzically. Amos pushed harder. The pin broke Finn's flesh, skewering a half-inch into his thigh. Finn moaned. He seemed to enjoy it. Interested, Amos pushed harder. Finn made a noise that could only be interpreted as one of ecstasy. He never stopped trying to get out of his restraints. How very odd.

For the next few days, Amos stuck Finn with that pin during naptime. He stuck a few of the other children, too—none of the ones who could talk, however. Their reactions were more in line with Amos's assumptions: inarticulate screeches of pain. But Finn *liked* it. He loved the pain. It made him feel more alive, maybe, or it deepened the pleasure he was already experiencing. That, too, was a sin. And Amos was participating in it. But he was learning some very important things.

Before that week was out, the nuns noticed the bloody pricks up and down Finn's torso. Bedbugs were suspected. The mattresses had to be fumigated. But Sister Muriel gave Amos the stink eye, and he was taken off naptime duty. Sensing he would be questioned, he dropped the pin down the playground storm drain.

The experience taught Amos this: he enjoyed being in charge. He had never had that agency in his life. And it stood to reason that people *liked* to be dominated. Not just morons like Finn—regular everyday folks. They needed to be told what to do and how to act. But you couldn't just stride up and start bossing them around. You needed to get ahold of the whip hand somehow. People *knew* that they were sinful and licentious. Finn showed it plainly, but most people wore a mask. Under that mask were all the depraved, malignant elements of their souls. They wanted to be punished, because after punishment comes forgiveness.

And if Amos were to punish those people as he saw fit, well, it was a punishment that God would surely smile upon.

To hurt is to love, he now thought as he restlessly paced his quarters. The Conkwright bitch. *Bitch, BITCH.* Speaking out against him. She wanted to flee like a chicken-gutted weakling, shrieking for help. It would ruin everything. He didn't want his flock to think about the outside world; it should not be acknowledged except as the seat of sin. He had placed blinders over their eyes and now one of them was trying to rip those blinders off.

Eli. Stupid child. Run off into the woods. He would come back; he would be fine; why wouldn't he be? Children had run away from the orphanage all the time. Hopped the fence and vamoosed. If they never returned, it wasn't necessarily because calamity had befallen them. It was because they didn't want to come back. But Eli had no choice. His family was at Little Heaven. His God was here.

Amos would set everything to rights tomorrow. He would call the flock in from the woods whether or not the boy had been found. He would speechify to them until he saw that stunned, goatlike gloss touch their eyes again—a look he first became familiar with years ago, preaching atop a soapbox in Haight-Ashbury, amassing a small throng of worshippers. He'd soon gathered enough to start his own ministry. He understood the keys that opened the locks to human nature better than any headshrinker. Those keys were labeled *Vice, Punishment, Forgiveness*. That last key was the crucial one. If you withheld it, banishing unbelievers from not only the Kingdom of Heaven but also the earthbound circle of fellowship they had come to know . . . that was the worst thing they could possibly imagine. It kept them at heel.

Amos stopped before the window. Night had drawn down on Little Heaven, but the security lamps burned. He stared at his church, topped with that mighty crucifix.

He stood, transfixed, listening to the Voice.

It came to Amos every night. God's Voice—whom else could it belong to? He let it settle into his bones, soothing him. The Voice had already warned there would come a dissent. Amos had known this before the first fence post went up at Little Heaven. It was why he had hired Cyril and Virgil, whose acquaintance had been made through unsavory but needful methods.

Any flock could stray, despite the best efforts of its shepherd. That was why a smart shepherd trained a few ill-tempered dogs to keep the sheep in line.

He would weather this storm. He would cast out the irritants and prevail. He *must*. God had a plan for him. He felt it gathering in the deepest recesses of his mind: that other voice whispering to him, using words he could not make out. A low continuous drone like the massing of flies over rotted offal. The Lord works in mysterious ways.

He retreated to his bed, where he lay stiff as a rod. Without being aware of it, he began to knead his groin. He opened the night table and pulled out the long sharp pin that lay beside his Bible.

Release, he thought. *By God, release.*

20

EBENEZER COULD NOT SLEEP his second night at Little Heaven. His blankets itched, as did his ankle while it healed. He rolled off the cot and pulled on his trousers and one boot. The others were still sleeping. He hobbled out the door.

The night was cool. Combers of ground fog rolled across the square. It flooded over his legs, so thick he could barely see his own feet. A flashlight snapped on behind him.

"What are you doing?"

He turned. Minerva was pointing the light directly at his face. "Lower it," he said.

She snapped it off. Folded her arms against the chill. She beheld him the way she always did—as if picturing how his head might look on the end of a sharp stick.

He was fairly certain she hated him. That was not so odd in itself—Eb had repulsed plenty of women over his lifetime—but there was no legitimacy to her loathing. On their first encounter she had tried to kill him as a matter of business. That he could understand and even approve. Why, then, throughout their acquaintanceship, had her hatred not slackened? It wasn't the color of his skin. Eb could sniff a racist at twenty yards. It wasn't his Englishness, either. So what, then?

"I was going to pick posies for you," he said. "On account of you being so peachy keen."

"Oh yeah?" She spat in the dirt. "Drop dead in a shed, Fred."

"Dive off a cliff, Biff," he shot right back.

Little Heaven was silent. The only light came from the security lamps strung round the perimeter. The fog hung thickly between the first cut of pines. It swirled in odd patterns, as if at the beck of forces Ebenezer was not attuned to.

They heard it then. Ringing, singsong. The laughter of a child.

They moved toward it, Minerva walking and Eb limping. Ebenezer didn't want to take another step—the laughter had developed a throaty undertone he didn't much care for—but his feet would not obey him. He kept gimping on, vaguely horrified at his inability to stop. Minerva's flashlight shone on the ground in front of them. Nobody else was awake. The compound was at rest. It was just them, alone.

The sound was coming from behind the chapel. The shadows were heaviest there, as the chapel lay at the edge of the compound facing the trees. The flashlight illuminated its rough boards, the paint beginning to flake. The laughter hummed against Ebenezer's ears like the beat of tiny wings.

"Hello?" Minerva said.

The laughter stopped. In its place was a dry crackly noise that made Ebenezer picture wet seashells, thousands of them, tumbling over one another.

They rounded the side of the chapel that faced the woods. A shape hunched under the silhouette of the crucifix. The fog was hugged tight to it.

"Who's there?" Ebenezer said.

The flashlight beam jittered toward the shape; Eb got the sense Minerva was reluctant to illuminate this thing, whatever it was. The light crept over the chapel wall and down, falling on the head of the figure sitting there. The fog peeled back, divulging more and more of its body—

A boy. He sat facing away from them. The mist still clung to his lower half. He was doing something with his hands. The dry, chittery sound was quite powerful now. Ebenezer had no clue what was making it, but the noise itself was enough to sour the spit in his mouth.

They approached the boy, who seemed to have taken no note of them. Fifteen feet, ten feet . . . the boy turned. He was naked from the waist up. His ribs protruded. His clavicles jutted like beaks. His flesh was white as soap. His eyes were gray. The color of a slug.

Minerva stumbled back and bumped into Ebenezer. He felt the beat of her heart through her clothes—it was hammering hard enough to rattle her entire frame.

The boy smiled. He was bucktoothed—teeth like elephant toes. His slug eyes seemed to pin them both, though lacking pupils it was hard to tell for sure.

The shucking, chittery sounds intensified . . .

The boy held a dead bird in his hands. The bird's eyes were the same as the boy's. He stroked it tenderly. His demeanor was quiet and content, as if he had been found playing with his Matchbox cars in his bedroom.

There was something the matter with one of his hands. The skin seemed to have melted or calcified or fused, the fingers welded into a solid scoop of flesh. He stroked the bird with it, lovingly so. Later, Ebenezer wouldn't be sure he had seen any of this—there was a vacancy in his memory, a dark sucking hole where something dirty had been buried.

The mist rolled away from the boy's lower half, the white wisps trailing off to reveal a bristling carpet of perpetual industry.

Bugs. Bark beetles and cockroaches and God knew what else. Millions of bugs covered the boy to his waist. They surged around his hips, antennae waving, crawling over and around one another the way insects do—a way that humans never could, because that mindless proximity of bodies would drive any person mad. They flooded around the boy's legs, fanning out in a ten-foot circle. Most of their bodies were the brown of a blood blister, but some were a larval albino white. They massed in a pattern that seemed random, but if you looked closely, their movements appeared to have some spirit of organization.

Minerva turned to Ebenezer, her eyes bulging in horror. Ebenezer was barely able to stifle a scream himself—when was the last time he'd screamed in abject fright? As a child, surely, at the prospect of the boogeyman lurking under his bed.

The boy beheld them with those horrid, soul-shriveling eyes and said, "I am so happy to be back home."

21

THE NEXT MORNING, Brother Charlie Fairweather showed up at their bunkhouse.

"Mind if I come in?"

Micah was still trying to piece together the events of the past night. He'd heard Eb get up, and Minny after him. He hadn't made much of it when they both stepped outside—Minny wouldn't make her move now, he knew, so the most she'd do was jaw at him a little.

Minutes later, there was a big commotion. Had Micah misjudged it— had she tried to flatline Ebenezer? It would have to count as strange timing, but Minerva was an odd woman. But then he'd heard the Reverend yelling: "Cyril! *CYRIL!*"

Turns out that the boy, Eli, had been found behind the chapel. It was Eb and Minny who found him. But by the time Micah made it to the square, the Reverend had already hustled the boy off to a private bunkhouse. Nobody had seen him since.

Afterward, Ebenezer and Minerva sat on the same cot. Minerva's face was white as clotted cream, Eb's a bloodless gray. They said they had come upon the boy covered in bugs. The boy had pupil-less eyes. Something fucked to do with his hand, too.

Following this revelation, serious consideration was given to just up and leaving. What if they were to kidnap Nate? Knock him out—did that Doc Lewis have any ether? If Reggie raised a stink, Micah was willing to knock him out, too, either with ether or his fists. But the plan was imperfect. Eb was still hobbled, for one. And chances were they'd be spotted. While Neeps, Swicker, and the Reverend would be happy to see the ass end of them, they weren't likely to permit Micah to cart one of their lambs away over his shoulder like a sack of oats. Neeps and his partner had guns, too, and things had soured to the point where Micah was pretty sure they would use them. After that, it would be him, Eb, and Minny flung into shallow graves with quicklime eating their eyes. Maybe Ellen, too. Still, snatching the boy could be their best shot. Do it quiet, cause a distraction, leave in the pandemonium. Let Little Heaven go to hell in a handbasket and read all about it in the papers a few months later.

They were discussing this when Charlie knocked. Micah opened the door and ushered him inside. Charlie cleared his throat and said, "A few of us been talking. Me and Otis, Nell and Jack Conkwright. Plus my own wife. We think . . . well, we might like to take a break from Little Heaven."

He spoke as though the words gave him physical pain. He peeked out the window to make sure nobody was poking around outside. "We figured you could help us," he said.

"We're hikers," said Micah.

"You aren't no hikers. And why wouldn't you want to leave?" said Charlie. "Why not we all go? Safety in numbers."

"We cannot all go." Micah nodded at Ebenezer, laid up on his bunk. "Not with him in his shape." He eyed Charlie cagily. "Why now, Charlie? What is prodding you?"

Charlie shifted foot to foot like a man with a bladderful of piss. "Was there something wrong with Eli's eyes?" he asked Minerva. "Dr. Lewis says it isn't anything. A milky glaze . . . an *occlusion*, he called it. Just a coating, like pulp or something. He wiped it away and Eli's eyes were just fine underneath."

Minerva rolled her own eyes. "I think Lewis wouldn't say shit if he had a mouthful. He'd hold it until your Rev gave him permission to spit."

"Eli's off limits," Charlie said. "Nobody's seeing him 'cept the doc and the Rev. His folks haven't come back yet. Two full days they've been gone."

"Your utopia is blowing up," Ebenezer said.

Charlie stuffed his hands into his pockets. "The Lord sets trials for us all. And I'm not one to scurry from them. But I got a kid, right? My son, Ben. And to be honest, he's not been himself lately."

"What do you mean?" Ellen said, leaning forward on her cot.

"I don't know, just off. Kind of, well . . . cruel. The other day my wife found him out back of our bunkhouse watching a big ole green grasshopper die in a jar of gasoline. When she asked what he was doing, Ben said that grasshoppers breathe through their sides—like, imagine if we had little mouths all down our ribs, sucking in air. He had a book of matches, too. My guess was that he was gonna wait until the bug was nearly drowned before fishing it out and lighting it up."

Charlie shook his head. "That isn't my boy. He'll collect bugs, sure, and toads and snakes and what all. But he puts them in a shoe box with cotton batting so they're good and comfy. He makes sure to poke holes in the lid. He likes the idea of owning them, I guess, and studying them, but he lets them go when he gets bored. Ben's never purposefully killed them. And it's one thing to thoughtlessly squash a bug to see the yellow of their guts squirt out—boys do that, and the Lord forgives them. It's another thing to torture them, then light them on fire. That takes real consideration. Takes *planning*."

Charlie shook his head again. "I gave Ben a proper hiding when I heard. Bent him over my knee and beat the white off his ass. Wasn't right, Lord knows. I think I was more scared than him, because it's like waking up to find something that isn't quite your son sleeping in your son's bed. Ben didn't cry out or anything. He kept looking up as I spanked him like to say, *That all you got, Pops?*"

"A lot of people acting weird in Little Heaven," Ellen said softly.

"It's not always been so," said Charlie. "The first bunch of months were great, just like the Rev said they would be. But lately, with the animals in the woods and the dogs going missing and the kids acting out of turn and now this with Eli . . ."

Micah said, "Do you think the Reverend will let you go?"

Charlie's hands balled into fists. "We came willingly."

Micah said, "Even still."

"I worry about Cyril and Virgil," Charlie admitted. "What they might do."

Micah stared at Charlie. "Our other guns are back at the campsite."

Charlie nodded. "I had your pistols, but Cyril, he took 'em."

"You really think we'll have to blast our way out of here?" said Ellen. "Have things gotten that nuts?"

Things can get nuts pretty fast, Micah thought. He knew it. He'd seen it.

Minerva said, "There's something else in these woods."

Everyone looked at her. A flush crept up her throat.

"Just something hostile," she went on, undeterred. "I felt it the other night, searching for the boy. A million eyes scuttling over my skin. I don't care if that sounds stupid. Maybe I'm going a little nuts myself." She stared at them, her jaw fixed tight. "This fucking place."

Nobody disputed her sense of things.

22

THEY DEPARTED MIDAFTERNOON. Micah, Minerva, Charlie, and Otis. As it turned out, it was an easy matter to slip away. The Reverend and his hired men were currently taken up with Eli. Not long before they left, Micah had spotted Cyril exiting the windowless bunkhouse where Eli was being kept. The man looked green around the gills.

Ellen agreed to stay back with Ebenezer. If anyone noticed they were missing, she would tell them the God's honest truth—they had gone to recover their belongings from the campsite and would soon return for their injured friend.

"Be careful," she told Micah. "We need you back here."

Micah wondered: Was she worried they wouldn't come back? Did she think they might get the guns and continue to the car, pedal to the metal, tear-assing eighty miles an hour away from Little Heaven?

They set off under an overcast sky. They walked through a forest drained of life. Not a peep, not a rustle. Charlie had his rifle and pistol. Otis had a compound bow and a quiver of hunting arrows.

"I don't think you'll find much to shoot at," Minerva told him.

Otis nodded. "I haven't spotted so much as a sparrow."

They chatted to pass the time. Minerva asked Otis how he had come to know the Reverend.

"I've been with him going on fifteen years now," he told her. "Long before Charlie came along. I was a pill head when Reverend Flesher found me. Staggering around the Tenderloin chock-full of drugs. I'm ashamed to tell you how I laid my hands on them, but that's the way of that particular devil—you'll do anything to please it." He hung his head, humiliated at the memory of the man he'd been. "The Rev took me in. I was one of his first. I just looked at him and knew. The Lord speaks through this man. My folks raised me serious southern Baptist, but I fell away from the path. The Rev dragged me back on it. I helped stain and sand the floor in his new chapel, and I slept there at night. It gave me something to do with my hands. Helped keep the devil at bay. That, and the Reverend's sermons. Then later, when he said he's taking his flock into the unspoiled wilderness, away from all the wickedness and vice—I said, sign me up!"

"And it was good," Charlie said. "Real good for a stretch here."

"That's a fact," said Otis. "Little Heaven was just that. Heaven on earth. And now the clouds have rolled in. But the devil tests us, and he tests the Reverend most of all—because Satan knows if he can break the Rev's resolve, he can snatch our souls. But the Reverend won't let it happen." Otis's voice rose to the pitch of a true believer. "No, sir. He's gonna walk Satan down and stomp a mudhole in his ass, pardon my French—"

"Ah, we're all friends here," said Minerva.

"The Reverend's going to send Old Splitfoot back down to the pit," Otis went on. "We just got to stay the course in our hearts and spirits. If we have to leave for a spell while the Reverend wages this battle, well . . . dark days, sure, but we've been through them before. Reverend Flesher has always guided us out."

Charlie said, "Amen to that."

They walked in silence until they came upon the pit. It was empty, the bottom filled with groundwater. They continued on, glimpsing few signs of the things that had pursued them nights ago. The odd snapped branch, ripped bark torn off trees, even a few pines torn out at the roots— but the damage seemed random, following no particular path.

Darkness was coming on by the time they reached the campsite. Their tents were undisturbed. Nothing had been torn apart or scattered. Micah crawled inside his tent and retrieved his second Tokarev pistol and several boxes of ammunition. He also found the long-bore Tarpley rifle. He felt reassured by its sturdiness. Heavy as a blunderbuss.

Minerva retrieved several boxes of ammunition for her own guns, currently in Cyril's possession. She exited the tent with a small revolver.

"I found it in Ellen's pack," she said. ".38 police special." She laughed. "Who would have figured Little Miss Bellhaven was packing heat? What a hellcat, uh?"

Maybe Ellen had brought it thinking she could take her nephew from Little Heaven by force. A desperate move, in Micah's opinion. One that could have gotten her killed. He didn't like to picture Ellen dead—and yet he did. Just for a flash.

They sat round the fire pit as dusk settled between the trees. A cool wind howled over the grass, making each blade sing like a tiny instrument.

"We have no choice but to make camp here," said Micah. "Return tomorrow morning."

Micah caught Minerva's unspoken worry: *What if those things are still hanging around?* He had no assurance they weren't, but it seemed wiser to batten down in a spot with clean sight lines and establish a watch rather than hike back through the unlit woods.

"Reverend's gonna know we've been gone for sure now," said Otis.

Charlie nodded. "Got to accept it. We'll make our amends if it comes to that."

They got a fire going. They ate the food Micah and the others had bought back in Grinder's Switch—it was completely untouched, even the bread. They skewered bits of Spam on sharpened sticks and grilled it over the fire. It tasted bad, and not just because it was Spam: some bitterness in the wood imparted a foul essence into the meat. Being ravenous, they ate it anyway.

One of them would have to keep watch. Micah volunteered to take the first shift. Minerva took one tent. Charlie and Otis bedded down in the other.

Micah fed the fire. Acrid smoke spiraled up. The flames warped the woods beyond, creating shapes where there were none.

He would sit that way, nearly unblinking, for many hours.

23

THE NIGHT AFTER he returned to Little Heaven, Eli Rathbone paid a visit to Nate.

They weren't even friends, not as Nate saw it. Eli had always been kinda mean—and he'd gotten a lot meaner the past few weeks, right up until he vanished into the woods.

Eli was a tall, skinny redhead with a wiry frame and bony hands. He liked to hold the smaller kids down and give them the Rooster Peck: sitting on their chests and jabbing his fingers into their breastbone while they struggled to name ten chocolate bars, which was the only way to get him to stop.

Milky Way . . . uh, ah, AH—Hershey bar, aaaaah! Payday! Milky Way!
You said that one already, dummy. Start again!

He'd done it to Nate, too. Elton and Billy Redhill laughed when Nate had gotten hung up on nine. His brain froze. He could think of any number of candies and gums and soda pops—*Flipsticks, Lemonheads, Black Bart, SweeTarts, Frostie Root Beer!*—but not one stupid chocolate bar. Eli's fingers punched into his breastbone so hard that Nate had been sure his chest would cave in.

"Scooter Pie!" he had screamed.

Eli said, "Judges?"

Elton and Billy shook their heads. "Nah, that's a cookie," said Elton.

Eli grinned. "Start over!"

Eli could be mean as rattlesnake venom, as Nate's grandmother might say. But he was sweet as pie when the Reverend came around. A real honey-dripper—a suck-up. Eli knew the Bible well. His ability to recite catechism made him one of the Reverend's favorites, although it seemed to Nate that the Reverend looked at kids the way Nate looked at the monkeys at the zoo.

And it was Eli's voice Nate heard now. He could swear it, even though that would be crazy. Eli's voice, coming from the darkness just beyond his bunkhouse window.

Nate . . . wake up, Nate . . .

When Nate first showed up, Eli hadn't been bullying anybody. Back then they were supervised by Missus Hughes, a foreboding woman who didn't take any sass. But then Missus Hughes broke her leg and had to leave. The kids had been left to do whatever they wanted, pretty much; their only obligation was to attend the sermons. Eli used this newfound freedom to torment his chosen targets.

Eli hadn't always been quite so nasty. Rooster Pecks, sure, but that was the same sort of treatment Nate had received from bullies back home. Everyone had to deal with bullies, Nate reasoned, until you became an adult, at which point everyone stopped acting so mean . . . except that his dad's old boss, Postmaster Jim, was a bully, too—a grown-up version of Eli. He used to make fun of his father to his face, even when Nate was right there. "Sunny" Jim would slap his father between the shoulder blades so hard that his dad would stagger, and laugh and say something like, *You'd be better off in a flower shop, wouldn't you, Reg, pruning pansies.* And the other mailmen would laugh, which was what kids did, too—laughed along with the bully so they didn't get picked on themselves.

It was times like that when Nate wished his mom was still around. She would have slapped Sunny Jim in front of everyone for speaking that way—which was sad when you thought about it, because Nate's father wouldn't even defend himself. Nate often wondered *why* his mother even loved his father, or vice versa; they were so unalike it was as if they were different species. But if Sunny Jim were to say, *You need your wife to defend you, Reg?* his mother would slap him again. And if Sunny Jim ever raised his hand to her in return, she'd find something sharp to stick him with. And if ole Sunny Jim did the same to her, well, Nate was sure his mom would get a gun next. Her temper wasn't just hot; it was lava. She went supernova.

Which was why she was in jail. Society frowned on people who couldn't keep their rage in check—even if they were defending someone they loved. But his mom wasn't in jail for that reason. She broke the law trying to make money. And even though she had cried and told Nate she only did it for him, he couldn't fully forgive her—because her crimes meant he had to move with his father to Little Heaven.

Nate rolled over in bed. The cot springs squealed. It was dark inside the bunkhouse. His father snored a few feet away. They used to live in a house. A teensy three-bedroom with a postage stamp lawn, but still. Now they lived in something a hunter might squat in while trapping minks in the winter. There was no indoor plumbing, so Nate had to use the outhouse. Sometimes he had to pee at night, which meant he had to cross the square to the jakes, as they were called, and squat over a pool of dark, smelly waste. As he tried to force his pee out, something would *scratch-scratch* on the outhouse. Just the branches of a tree, he knew, but at three o'clock he couldn't help picturing a witch, all dried up and pruney with teeth like busted periwinkle shells, raking her nails on the boards behind his head. His piss tube would clamp shut in fear. Some nights he lay in bed in abject agony, his bladder bursting, cursing himself for having that second glass of water at dinner. Better his bladder burst, better he soak the mattress with pee, than he have to crouch in that outhouse with those witch's nails scraping at him.

Nate got out of bed. The bunkhouse was cold. His bare legs broke out in gooseflesh.

The phosphorescent hands on the alarm clock read 2:55 a.m. He screwed his knuckles into his eyes and stared blearily at the window. Nothing there . . .

. . . but he could feel something out in the dark. Just a few feet away from the window. Waiting.

Little Heaven hadn't been quite so bad when they first showed up, but Nate had never felt at home here. His mom didn't put much stock in religion—*People can eat whatever they want,* she'd said, *but they better not show up on my doorstep asking if I want a bite of their apple*—so Nate was at a disadvantage from the start, seeing as he didn't know the Bible. He had to wear thick wool pants to every service; now his legs itched like fire whenever the Reverend even opened his mouth—this was called a Pavlovian response. Nate had learned that back at his old school, where they studied things like science and the human brain. Such things weren't talked about at Little Heaven. *Science gets in the way of our communion with the Lord,* Nate was told. He missed his old school. He missed other things, too. TV and comic books and the smell of the dime-store vanilla perfume the girls in his class used to wear and even the smell of car exhaust and of cigarettes in movie theaters—even though, if you'd asked him, he would have told you he'd never miss tailpipe fumes and throat-itching Marlboro smoke, not in a million years. What Nate really missed was going places in cars. Just like he missed watching movies at the theater. But that all got mixed up in his head with the bad smells associated with those joys—and he couldn't give voice to those more sophisticated thoughts. He was a boy. He just *felt*.

The Reverend didn't pay much mind to Nate or his father; they were late joiners, low on the totem pole. It didn't seem to bother his dad, but it bugged Nate a whole bunch. And things had been going downhill for a while. Everyone looked different. Skinnier and wasted away. Even Nate. He hated looking at himself in the mirror now. It was hard to put a finger on it. There was no cause for it, which was why nobody talked about that stuff. This was where the Lord had led them. Why would He lead them into sorrow?

But Nate could feel it. Something working all around him. As if the air were filled with a trillion invisible mouths, each mouth studded with microscopic teeth, all those mouths gnawing at you all day long. Or—an even worse imagining—those same tiny mouths all over the ground, every inch, but instead of teeth, each mouth had a needle tongue that jabbed into everybody's feet, sucking the way a mosquito sucks, funneling everyone's energy into a pale bloated sack like a stomach deep under the earth. A single tube led from that stomach even deeper underground, where it nourished something much larger and more terrible—

Nate was now walking toward the bunkhouse window. He didn't want to. He was exquisitely aware of this. More than anything he wanted to slip back into bed and pull the covers over his head and . . . pray. He hardly ever prayed for *real*. Yes, he could recite the words and cross himself and all that paint-by-numbers stuff, but he wasn't asking for anything or talking to God man to man. In his life, he had really prayed only a few times. When his mother got put in jail, he prayed that God would keep her safe because he used to watch *Dragnet* and some of the people Joe Friday put in the clink were tough tickets and he wanted his mom to be safe if she got a cell mate named Big Bertha or Hellcat Hettie. He had prayed for his dad a few times, too, because even though he was a wimp—and it was horrible that a boy would already understand this about his father—Nate thought his dad was essentially a good man.

But Nate wanted to pray now. Oh yes. He wanted to hear God's voice and be reassured. But he couldn't because his feet kept guiding him toward the window. Toward Eli's voice—which didn't sound much like Eli's normal voice. It sounded clogged. As if Eli's throat were packed with potting soil or rotted sewage, so that what came out of his mouth was a choked gargle.

Nate . . . don't be a pussy like your daddy the mailman. Come see me. No Rooster Pecks, honest Injun . . .

His father snorted in his sleep. Nate tried to call out—*Dad, wake up!*—but his throat was so dry that nothing came out, like trying to whistle with a mouthful of soda crackers.

It wasn't just how everyone at Little Heaven had started to look lately, either. It was how they acted. In the beginning, the kids had all been normal. More religious than Nate was used to, sure, but pretty much like everyone else he knew from his old school. He would join them after breakfast and Missus Hughes would have them read their Bible and do Christian crossword puzzles and stuff like that. After the midday sermon, they had supervised playtime. The kids welcomed Nate outwardly, it being the right thing to do.

But after Missus Hughes left, the playtime sessions turned strange. The older kids, led by Eli and the Redhill brothers, started playing nasty games. One was called Doctor Psycho. They would chase someone around until they caught him; then they pinned that poor kid down. Eli would pretend to put on rubber gloves and say, "This operation is in session." He would slice his captive's belly open with an imaginary scalpel and start pulling out the insides. Each would be examined for a second before he said, "Nope, not good enough," and threw it over his shoulder and reached in for more. If the captive knew what was good for him, he would scream and gasp, "No! No, *please!*" Eli took it easier on you if you played along instead of sitting there like a dead fish.

Nate . . . you are starting to piss me off. You don't want to piss me off . . .

Nate was only a few feet from the window now. The wind fluttered the plastic in the frame. There was nothing at the window. Maybe there was nothing at all. Was he dreaming? Nate's fists clenched, nails digging into his palms. Maybe he would wake up and this would all be—

He saw it then. At the outer limits of his sight, past the edge of the window on the right-hand side. Standing there silently, tucked tight to the bunkhouse wall.

Eli's playtime games had become more and more nasty. Little Heaven used to have an ant problem. There were five or six big hills scattered around the compound. The ants were of the stinging variety. One afternoon, not too long ago, Nate had come upon Eli, one of the Redhill boys, Jane Weagel, and Betsy Whitt crouched around one of the hills. Eli had a bottle of lemon juice. He was squeezing juice down the ant hole. Drip, drip, drip. The ants scurried around crazily. The other kids held the busted bottoms of Coke bottles. They focused the sun through them, sizzling the ants as they rushed about. *Zzzzsssssstap!*

"The acid in the juice screws with their brains," Eli told Nate with a vacant smile. "They don't know up from down."

The other kids barely noticed Nate. Betsy Whitt's eyes were glazed and moony. She was the sort of person the phrase *wouldn't hurt a fly* was coined to describe. Nate had actually seen her open a door and shoo a fly outside so it wouldn't get swatted.

"Move," she said, shoving Nate. "You're blocking the sunlight."

Later that same day Nate had found Betsy behind the warehouse. She was crying. Tears streaked her cheeks.

"I didn't want to hurt those ants," she sobbed. "I don't want to hurt *anything*. If you hurt another living thing, God sees it. He judges. But I couldn't help myself." Her face scrunched up. "Do you ever feel that way, Nate?"

Nate hadn't known what to say. But yes, he felt it. The feeling was getting stronger each day. Sometimes he wanted to hurt things, too. Anything would do. Whatever was weakest, and easiest, and nearest at hand . . . He'd never felt that way back home.

It wasn't just the kids, either. One night Nate awoke to find his father standing in the corner. He was naked and sweaty and muttering, "Kill you kill you fucking kill you." Nate had never heard his father swear. His hands were clenched as though he was choking someone. He was sound asleep. But he rose happily the next morning, claiming to be hungry as a horse.

Nate . . . ole buddy ole pal-o-mine . . .

Nate was only a foot from the window now. He could make out the shape in profile. Thin and grisly white, hunching next to the bunkhouse. He caught a mad buzz, a sound like flies bouncing around inside an empty jar of Gerber baby food.

"Eli?" he said tremblingly.

The figure swung round to the window like a door blown closed by a stiff wind.

Thwap! A face hit the plastic.

Nate took a step back. A great big one.

It was Eli Rathbone. And Eli looked . . . not good.

Eli was white as tallow, white as the flame in the deepest part of a fire. His hair, clown-red before, was now old man's hair. It was bone white, as if some follicular vampire had sucked all the color out of it. He was thinner than Nate ever could have conceived a person should be—his ribs poked out, his nipples stretched and elongated, his flesh threadbare.

Eli's face was the worst. A leering Hollywood idol, pure plastic. His eyes bulged, and his teeth pushed past his lips like blunt discolored tusks. He looked unspeakably lonely and lost . . . but also very, very hungry. His face and frame radiated a yearning that pinned Nate where he stood, a moth skewered in a specimen case.

Oh, hello, Nate. May I come in? Mother, may I?

A drowsy terror settled upon Nate—it wasn't a heart spiker, the kind of fear that shot adrenaline through your body; no, this was a lazy and drifting fright that bobbed like a kite on a string, dipping and ascending without ever settling.

"I don't think so," Nate whispered. "You look sick, Eli."

The buzz grew louder. Nate noticed an emptiness under Eli's armpit. Things were moving in there. Nate could see stuff crawling and stuttering about.

Oh no, Nate thought. *Oh no no no no no—*

Nate's eyes were riveted to the spot under Eli's armpit. Things were coming out of it. *Flies.* Or things that looked like flies—

Eli lifted his arm. A deep hole was sunk into his flesh, all pulpy and black. Things squirmed in it. White things. Darker things.

"Go away, Eli." Nate was amazed at how calm he sounded.

Eli leaned forward until his nose touched the window again. The plastic dimpled with the pressure. Eli's eyes switched back and forth like a metronome set to a hi-hat beat. *Tick-tock-tick-tock,* back and forth, *tick-tock.*

He gave Nate a chummy wave. His hand was misshapen, the fingers fused into a mangled hook. Flies now boiled out of his armpit and pelted the plastic. *Puk! Puk! Puk!* They were larger than common bluebottles, with gas mask faces. A few tried to squirm through the plastic at the window's edges; they buzzed frantically, a gleeful note.

Eli smiled. His lips peeled back from his dirty yellow teeth, the buckteeth of a rat. Flies crawled between them—they were coming from inside Eli's mouth, their bodies wet with saliva. They flew at the window and hit, leaving moist blots on the plastic.

You will come with us, Eli said. His lips were not moving, but Nate heard his voice all the same. *All the sweet boys and girls. You are good meat.*

His teeth clicked animatedly, the sound of bone castanets. Nate lunged forward, moaning, and yanked the flimsy curtains shut. Eli Rathbone stood in front of the window for a few moments before his shape drifted away.

Shivering, Nate retreated to bed. He pulled the covers over himself and shook until he was sure his body would rattle to pieces.

24

MINERVA JOLTED AWAKE. Firelight played through the gap between the tent's canvas flaps. Micah was supposed to be keeping watch outside.

She got up. Grabbed Ellen's gun. Crawled to the flap.

Micah stood outside with his back to her. He was staring at something across the fire. He held the Tarpley rifle at port arms.

"Shug?"

He glanced over his shoulder. Saw her. Turned to face the woods again.

Minny's eyes were adjusting. Inky darkness pooled past the glow of the fire. She couldn't tell what Micah was looking at.

"Get Otis's bow," he said carefully.

Otis's compound bow lay outside the other tent. Neither Charlie nor Otis had stirred. Minerva crossed to the tent quickly and brought the bow and the arrows to Micah.

"What the hell?" she whispered.

Micah chucked his chin toward something lurking in the first cut of trees. Minerva couldn't see anything. Her vision was all staticky as her eyes adjusted.

"There is a flare in my pack," Micah said. "And tape. Tape the flare to an arrow. Quickly."

Minerva located the flare and a roll of duct tape. She peeled a strip of gray tape and paused. "Near the arrowhead or further back?"

"A few inches from the head," Micah said calmly.

"We could burn the whole forest down," said Minny.

After a moment, Micah replied with: "Good."

Minerva became aware of a series of sounds coming from not far away: clicks and wheezes and peeps and other animal noises. It was like listening to a disjointed sound loop from David Attenborough's *Zoo Quest*, the voices of a dozen beasts all blurred together.

"What *is* that?" she said.

But she knew. It was one of those things that had chased them the other night. The things Otis and Charlie had tried to capture in the pit that had caught them instead.

She taped the flare to the shaft of an arrow. "Can you shoot a bow?"

Micah indicated his eye patch. "Not so well."

Otis poked his head out of the tent. "What is it?"

"Come here," Micah told him.

Otis came over at a low crouch. "It a bear?" he whispered.

"Or something," said Micah.

Minerva could see it now. Its shape seemed impossible. She had seen bears before—not in the wild, but in photographs. This did not echo her understanding of a bear. It stood fifty yards away, motionless between the trees. Its body pooled upward from a wide base like a bell laid on the ground. It did not have legs, or if it did, they were stubby and deformed— or else it had a multitude of them and moved in the scuttling manner of a crab. Minerva could perceive a host of strange protrusions all over its body. Shortened limbs, bulbous growths. It looked to be covered in huge, throbbing lesions.

Otis saw it, too. "That's no bear," he said in a voice full of dread.

The sounds it was making were equally senseless. Syrupy exhalations, ticks and whirrs and chirps and growls and hoots. A cacophony of noise as if an entire menagerie were speaking through a single organism.

"Can you hit it?" Micah said.

Otis nodded shakily. "If it stays put."

Micah said, "It has not moved since I saw it."

Otis took the bow from Minerva and notched the flare-weighted arrow on the bowstring. Minerva pulled the strike strip. The flare popped alight.

Otis drew back the arrow and let it fly. It arced through the night, the flare fraying in the wind, and struck the thing. It did not move.

The glow of the flare spread, bringing the shape into sharper relief. It made no sense. It was not one identifiable thing. It was many, or parts of many.

"What am I seeing?" Minerva said.

The thing was never at rest. It twitched and jerked. Parts of it opened; other parts closed. A stew of parts. Heads, snouts, tails, limbs. It was enormous. A seething hillock of flesh. It was nothing God's light had ever shone upon.

At last it shambled forward. Micah shouldered the Tarpley. Minerva cocked Ellen's .38. Her hands shook.

A random strip of fur ignited down the thing's side. The hair went up like a fuse. The thing shuffled toward them. It undulated, seemingly legless, hovercrafting across the ground. It shrieked and gibbered and emitted phlegmy dog-panting sounds. Watching it, Minerva was reminded of

Play-Doh. Little shreds of Play-Doh, red and blue and yellow and green, scattered on a table after arts and crafts class. She imagined rolling all those bits into a ball. Squashing everything into a solid mass while still being able to see the individual components: streaks of yellow, blots of red, veins of blue. But instead of Play-Doh, this thing was made of animals, all compressed and crushed together—

Micah fired. The bullet tore a chunk off. The thing squealed in a half dozen pitches with as many mouths. It continued toward them, faster now.

"Oh God," said Otis. "Let's go go oh no oh no let's *goooo*—"

Minerva aimed and fired. Four shots, each one finding its mark. Gouts of blood—or whatever the thing was full of—spurted wildly. It did not stop. She could smell it now. The reek of spoiled meat and fricasseed hair.

The fire licked downward to spread around the belled shape of its body. It looked like the grass skirt of a hula dancer that had leapt up in flame.

Micah picked up the lantern and tossed it thirty feet ahead of them, directly in the thing's path. "Shoot it," he told Minerva. "The kerosene tank."

Minerva steadied herself and fired. The bullet raised a burr of dirt six inches left of the lantern.

The thing neared the lantern. Eight yards, seven, six . . .

She fired again. The slug struck a half-buried rock and whined off target.

She fired again. A dry click. The gun was empty. She glanced at Micah, stricken.

He unloaded with the Tarpley, firing from the hip. The carbine boomed. The lantern flipped end over end, spraying kerosene onto the thing. It went up with a roar. Flames rose along the tortured slag heap of its body as flesh melted off in thick gobbets. It made noises that should be heard only in hell. Its many mouths screamed and bleated as its limbs swung spastically.

Charlie clambered out of the tent. He watched with numb horror as the thing toppled onto its side and lay there, squealing and hissing. Nobody could tell if the noises it made were the product of its mouths or the sound of its untold organs rupturing and popping from the heat. In time, it stopped moving.

Micah approached the creature. Minerva clenched her jaw and followed him. She couldn't believe she had missed the lantern . . . *twice.* She had made shots like that a thousand times. She could pick tin cans off a fence post at forty yards. But it's different when your back's up against it. Your cool crumbles. You fuck-up.

The body still smoked. It was already softening into the earth. Its configuration was lunatic. It was made out of different animals, a mishmash of species. Fish, fowl, insects, beasts of the woods. All melted together. Every one of its faces—fox and deer and pheasant and coyote and otter—was wrenched into an expression of tortured despair. Everywhere Minerva looked, some awful horror greeted her. Here, a clutch of bats' heads sprouting from the mouth of a gray wolf. There, a naked rib cage housing the flayed remains of a squirrel, its innards studded with a half dozen eyeballs that had burst in the flame. A blackened ball of ants compressed to the density of a baseball hanging on a strip of organ meat.

Minerva saw the melted remains of what looked to be a dog collar. Had this thing eaten one of Little Heaven's dogs?

Micah lifted the flap of skin that shielded its means of locomotion. Minerva gagged. How could he stand to touch the thing? The stinking flap rose to reveal dozens of legs. This was how it moved, trundling about with its limbs hidden as though beneath a hoop skirt.

Micah let the flap fall. There came a rude farting noise as a bladder let go inside the thing. The shock was so profound that nobody could speak for some time.

"This is the devil's work," Otis finally said. His arms wouldn't stop shaking.

Minerva checked her watch. It was coming up on five o'clock. The light of dawn was flirting through the trees.

"We have to go back to Little Heaven," said Otis. "Warn the others."

Micah and Minerva shared a look. *Do we?* But they did. She cared nothing for the Englishman, but Ellen and the others did not deserve to be abandoned.

She gazed down the path that led to their car. It looked wide and safe—a hop, skip, and a jump and they would be back at the main road.

But then something stirred. Her breath grated in her lungs.

She pointed. "Look."

They were out there. Strung all through the woods. Shapes. Some big, others more compact. Some shaggy, others sleek. All unmoving as sentinels.

Micah said, "Grab what you can. Quickly."

25

EARLY IN THE MORNING, before anyone else was up, Reverend Amos Flesher crossed the square to the bunkhouse where the boy was being kept.

Virgil was asleep on a chair outside. Both he and Cyril refused to be inside the windowless bunkhouse with the boy—not together, and certainly not alone.

Amos kicked Virgil's foot. The man cracked one eyelid open.

"Yeah?"

"Did you hear anything out of him?"

Virgil licked his lips, which were cracked because he sucked air through his mouth when he slept. *Mouth-breathers* was what Sister Muriel called the children who did that.

"He must have slept like a baby," said Virgil. "I didn't hear a peep."

Amos nodded. "Wait here."

"You're fucking-A right. I sure as hell ain't going in there."

Virgil spoke flippantly, but the whites of his eyes quivered like undercooked eggs. Amos set his hand on the doorknob and took a breath.

The Lord love me, save me, and preserve me. Amen.

The bunkhouse was a single room. Eli Rathbone lay in bed. Uncovered in only his underwear. He looked to have not shifted an inch since Amos had last seen him. But his feet were filthy. Covered in dirt and pine needles. They had been clean the last time Amos had seen them—the Reverend was positive of that.

Amos moved cautiously, not wanting to wake the boy. Eli's chest barely moved. Had he died in his sleep? Perhaps that would be for the best. Yes, all things considered, it just might be. The Lord's will be done.

Eli's chest hitched and fell. A ghost of a smile graced his lips.

Amos's jaw clenched. Adrenaline flared in him. He did not like being near this boy. There was something unseemly about his wasted frame and ashen hair.

Dr. Lewis refused to tend to him any more than he already had. It was all Amos could do to prevent the simpering boob from fleeing into the square in fright after . . . the earlier unpleasantness. The man was supposed to be a doctor, wasn't he? A healer of men. He couldn't even hack the sight of a sick boy.

Granted, the boy was sick in a peculiar way. And granted, Amos wasn't entirely comfortable around him, either.

There was a stain on the floor a few feet from the bed. Amos gave it a wide berth. Silly. It was only the boy's blood. The same blood that pumped through the veins of every man, woman, and child at Little Heaven. Except it hadn't looked like blood when it had come out of the boy the other night. At that time, it had been black and thick as ichor.

It was Lewis who had made the incision. Amos had been the sole witness to it. He had banished everyone from the bunkhouse—he didn't want anyone else seeing the boy. It would cause alarm. Two of the outsiders had found Eli behind the chapel. The black fairy and the bald-headed lezbo. Amos had actually watched them cross the square in the dead of night; he had been up at the time, listening to the Voice. It had bothered him—nobody should be out at such an hour—but they would all be gone as soon as the black one's ankle healed. Minutes later, Amos witnessed them stumble around the chapel, their eyes wide with horror.

What the Reverend had then found behind the chapel nearly unhinged him. Pewter-eyed Eli Rathbone immersed in a sea of squirming insects, cradling a dead bird. Glimpsing the boy's young-old face as his ears had filled with the quarrelsome hiss of the bugs—it conjured within Amos a fear that infested him like a sickness: the sight infected his soul, shriveling it like a slug doused with salt.

"Hello, Reverend," Eli had said. "Did you miss me?"

Amos had been dismayed to discover how much Eli's voice mimicked the one that came to him every night.

For Amos, only one fact was certain: if the residents of Little Heaven saw Eli right then, everything he had been building would crumble. Fear would lead to disharmony, which would encourage desertion. *The devil has come to Little Heaven*, they would say. They would flee with the clothes on their backs, every last cowardly one of them, rats leaping from a flaming barge.

This is a test, he thought. *The sternest one I have ever faced.*

Swallowing his disgust, Amos had reached for the boy. Bugs crunched under his boots. Amos's revulsion swelled when Eli reached for *him*, with a mangled hook of skin that had replaced one of his hands. Amos dodged it and grabbed Eli by the elbow; the boy's flesh was clammy, that of a corpse in a vault. Amos pulled him up, his strength buoyed by a cresting wave of fear. His scalp was hot and itchy, melting the Dapper Dan pomade in his hair, which trickled down his face in gooey strings. Eli laughed at him. Amos might have been laughing, too, though he couldn't properly remember—if so, it was the manic laugher of a man whose sanity was under threat.

"Cyril!" he had screamed. "*CYRIL!*"

Amos managed to drag Eli to the bunkhouse with no windows; the Reverend had had it built specially, thinking there might be a need for a place nobody could see inside. He flung the boy through the door and wiped his hand on his trousers. The boy staggered forward—his legs were wretched sticks—and collapsed. The roaches clinging to his legs let go and scuttled through cracks in the floor. The boy was still laughing.

"Shut up," Amos hissed. "Shut your rotten mouth."

Cyril came in. His mouth fell open and a thin moan came out.

"Hello, Cyril," the boy said, waving his hook.

"Get the doctor," Amos said. "And not a word of the boy's state to anyone. If anyone asks you, say that he is back and he is perfectly fine."

Brother Lewis soon arrived with his black bag. The boy was in the cot by then, covered in a sheet. Lewis took one look at Eli and blanched.

"Is this Eli?" he whispered, stunned. "Little Eli with the red hair . . . ?"

Eli stared at Lewis with those calculating gray eyes. He licked his lips. His tongue was brown and pebbled with waxy lesions.

"Do something," Amos said. "Fix him."

"This child is broken," Lewis said remotely. "Unfixable."

"Fix me, fix me, then you have to kiss me," the boy warbled.

The sheet slipped down Eli's chest. The men saw a bulge under the boy's armpit. A swollen ball like a fleshy balloon set to burst.

It . . . pulsed. The entirety of it. Throbbing like a misplaced heart.

Amos watched it, revolted—but also entranced.

"Cut it," he said mildly.

"I'm sorry?" said Lewis.

"Cut it open. See what's inside."

Lewis gave the Reverend a look of open horror. "I couldn't possibly—"

"You will," Amos said deathly soft. "If a poison is festering in this child, we must release it."

Lewis unzipped his bag and produced a scalpel. The man did not question the Reverend any further. Flesher was adept at spotting the most spineless specimens of humanity, and Lewis had always been one of the most obedient lambs in his flock.

Lewis held the tip to the boy's flesh. The swollen ball shuddered. Eli's skin opened up under the blade as if it had been begging to do just that. The blood, what there was of it, was black and clotted. The boy tittered. A terrible reek bloomed up. Things squirmed in the spongy red meat inside the scalpel-slit—the red of a blood orange.

"Never seen anything the likes of . . ." Lewis trailed off.

The slit widened under the pressure of whatever pushed back from inside the bloated ball; the cut opened up like a smile until—

Maggots. A wriggling fall of them. They pushed through the boy's sundered flesh, writhing animatedly, their fat ribbed bodies making greasy sounds. Amos struggled to conceive of the flies these enormous flabby things would turn into when they assumed their final, revolting shape—a crude image formed: flies as big as cockroaches, inconceivable bloatflies laying their bean-shaped eggs in old cratered meat. The maggots pattered to the ground, where they began to squirm and shudder toward the darkened corners of the room.

Amos stood stunned, trapped in a bubble of disgust. That bubble popped—a wet *thop!* inside his head—and he set about stomping the foul things to paste under his boots. He relished the soft give of their bodies as they burst moistly, like skinned grapes.

"Hah!" Amos screamed. "Hah! Hah! *Hah!*"

Something else crawled out of the boy's wound. A fly. A *massive* one. It picked its way out of Eli's ruined flesh and fanned its wings. It took flight, zinging straight at Amos. It hit his chin—it almost flew into his *mouth*, oh God!—and bounced away, producing a whine like a bullet.

More followed. The room was suddenly teeming with flies. Their buzz was monolithic. The boy's laughter climbed through several octaves to marry itself to that buzz. The sound drilled into Amos's ears and beat against his brain.

Dr. Lewis bolted for the door and was out before Amos could lay hands on him.

Amos rushed outside in pursuit. "Stay here," he told Cyril, who stood watch at the door. "Don't let anyone in."

Amos chased Lewis across the square. Nobody had seen a thing except for the outsiders, who would stay out of this if they knew what was good for them. He caught up with the doctor behind the storehouse, where he had collapsed in a sobbing heap.

"No no no no no . . .," he said, hiccuping each *no* between sobs.

Amos knelt and ran his hand through Lewis's sweaty hair.

"Sh-sh-sh-sh-sh," he said. "You will wake the children. We can't have that."

Lewis stared up at him. His face was pink as a boiled ham. "We have to leave, Reverend. That boy . . . this place is cancerous. It's making us all sick."

"Nonsense. You have had a shock."

"The devil is here," Lewis said. "I can feel him. The devil took that poor boy and sent him back to us as something vile."

Amos's hand clenched in Lewis's hair. Gently but firmly, he cranked

Lewis's head upward until the simpering imbecile was forced to gaze directly into the Reverend's eyes.

"The devil was with you in that movie theater in the Tenderloin all those years ago, wasn't he?" Amos said softly. "There in the dark, wasn't he? Watching you. And he must have slipped inside of you for a spell, too. Isn't that right, Brother Lewis? How else could you explain what you did with that boy in that dark theater with the sticky floors? And he *was* a boy, wasn't he? No more than sixteen, wasn't that what you said? A runaway, no doubt. Blond and fair with ruby lips."

Lewis began to shake. His eyes welled with fresh tears.

"It was the devil who made you ache for that boy. It was the devil who brought you there. It was the devil who unzipped your pants and guided that boy's mouth onto your—"

"Stop," Lewis sobbed. "Please, Reverend, please stop."

"It was the devil who did that, but it was the Lord who brought you to my doorstep. And haven't I always done right by you? Haven't I always kept your confessions and occasional indiscretions a matter between myself and the Lord?"

"Yes."

"The devil is not in Little Heaven," Amos said firmly. "I won't allow him in. If there is a sickness, then we must stand together under Christ's good guidance and expunge it. Do you understand, Brother Lewis?"

"Yes."

"We must not lose our heads."

"I can't," Lewis said. "Reverend, I can't go back in there."

Amos petted Lewis's scalp. "Very well. But if anyone should ask, you will tell them that Eli is recovering nicely."

"Yes."

"His parents have yet to return. Nobody else needs to see him. Am I right?"

"Yes."

"That is your official medical opinion?"

"Yes."

Such were the ways in which a flock must be kept in line, Amos mused. An observant shepherd must not spare the rod.

But now, a day after that hellish experience, the Reverend faced yet another challenge. A fork in the road, you could say. What to do about the boy? This was the question the Reverend had been debating. The question was simple—was Little Heaven better off with the boy alive or dead?

There was a very good chance the boy would die anyway. The Reverend was no doctor, but Eli's health could not be good when insects were actively birthing inside of him. But then, children were known to have amazing recuperative powers.

Or . . . the Reverend could take matters into his own hands.

He had never killed anyone. Much less a child. But Brother Lewis had been correct in one way: Eli did not seem so childlike anymore. A corruption of spirit had occurred. And Amos had never been one to advocate exorcisms.

It could be no easy thing, killing a person. Amos harbored no illusions about that. Humans were tough. They didn't want to die—even the devout, who would be ushered directly to the gilded gates of heaven. But couldn't it be seen as a public service in this case? The boy was sick. He was suffering. Was murder a sin? Absolutely. But what of mercy killings? Shouldn't God turn a blind eye to those, so long as it went toward the greater good?

So then, let's suppose Eli expired. The Reverend could simply announce that the boy had slipped away painlessly. God retrieved one of His little angels. They could hold a funeral. A closed coffin. Bury the body in the woods. All the proper observances. His parents could grieve if and when they returned. Then things could go back to normal. The flock would calm. Amos would implement a tighter policy of supervision for the children. Yes. He saw the shape of his plan. But it required something of him as well.

He sat on the cot. The boy breathed thinly. Amos's heart fluttered. A chill washed through his veins. He wasn't sure what he was feeling, exactly—this was strange for Amos, as he was highly aware of his motivations. But now he was struck with a question of an existential nature.

Did he need to kill the boy as a matter of expedience in order to maintain order at Little Heaven . . .

. . . or did he *want* to kill him, just to see how it felt?

The first was bad enough. The second was positively monstrous.

Why don't you just do it, you filthy little monster?

It was Sister Muriel's voice in his head. Muriel with her viperish mean streak.

Amos slid the pillow out from under Eli's head. He bounced it in his hands as if testing it for his purposes. It had an agreeable density. The boy's eyes were shut, his lips pursed in a queer Mona Lisa smile.

"You horrid abomination," the Reverend whispered.

He realized that the cold wash through his veins was anticipation. It was the same way he'd felt back at the orphanage, before sticking one of God's children with a pin. He wanted to do this. Not just because the boy disgusted him. Not simply because it would make his life a whole lot easier. Amos wanted to kill the boy because, in some recessed chamber of his heart, he had always wanted to kill a member of his species. The instinct had been there a long time; Amos had simply never turned his mind to reflect upon this facet of his nature, but now that he had, it was clear and bright, like the sun slanting off a mirror that had been angled to catch its rays. This was the first time when Amos was in a position to profit from murder, too. Before this, the act might have satisfied that predatory side of him, yes, but that wasn't reason enough to abandon his general prudence and take such a drastic step—but now it was essential. It would salvage everything he'd worked so hard to build.

Kill the boy. Save himself.

A sick child was the perfect start, wasn't it? He would not have to worry about being overmastered by Eli's strength. It would be as simple as drowning a rat.

"Amen," he said, and stuffed the pillow over Eli's face.

The boy's arms and legs remained motionless for a few heartbeats. Then he came alive. His hips bucked. He thrashed. A feeble buzz emanated from his armpit. Amos bore down on the pillow. Greasy balls of sweat popped on his forehead.

Eli's hands rose to touch the Reverend's face—gently, the caress of a lover. The melted hook tugged at the skin just below his eye, snagging on the socket bone. *You little bastard!* The fingers of Eli's other hand hooked into claws that tore shallow cuts into the Reverend's cheeks.

"Hell spawn!" Amos hissed.

The Reverend pushed down so hard that he could see the distorted features of the boy's face through the pillow. A nest of snakes thrashed somewhere behind his abdominal cavity, just above his groin—a fluttery squirming sensation. He was doing it, by thunder! He was actually *doing it!*

More flies buzzed out of Eli's armpit, sluggishly as if drunk, bumping into Amos's face. Amos was much bigger than the boy, who was nothing but a wasted shell; Eli soon began to flag. His arms waved about weakly. His heels drummed on the cot. Then the electricity went out of his body. Amos felt it, no different from pulling the plug on a blender.

Amos exhaled. His arms relaxed. The boy sank down into the mattress; with the life sucked out of it, his body seemed to deflate like a leaky balloon. Amos took in a shuddering inhale and let it go. His breath came out as a series of whimpery giggles.

"Hee-aah-*heeeeee*-hee-heee . . ."

He wiped the blood off his face. He would have to come up with an excuse for the cuts on his cheeks. He could say he'd been scratched by a critter from the woods, but he couldn't recall seeing an animal for some time now. No matter. He was adroit with lies. Already that feeling of elation was ebbing; the seltzer effervescence that had percolated through him during the act of killing Eli was going flat. In its place was a leaden heaviness, as if his veins were full of molasses.

He removed the pillow from Eli's face. The boy's eyes were closed, his features reposed in death.

"Ashes to ashes, dust to du—"

Eli's eyes popped open. They were black—the irises blown out, a thin band of bloodshot gray at the edges. His mouth split in a grin, an expression that sat horribly upon the face of someone so young: the come-hither leer of an ancient fairground carnie.

"Was that fun?" Eli asked teasingly. "Did you enjoy that, Reverend?"

The boy shivered in obvious delight. His breath was indescribably foul, bathing the Reverend's face with its noxious vapors. His grin stretched wider and wider. He began to titter. The sound hacksawed across Amos's nerve endings. His initial sense of shock and soul-deep revulsion gave way to a terror that coated his brain in a tar-like layer of blackness, choking out every rational thought.

I sent you to hell, the Reverend thought helplessly.

"I came back," the boy said.

Eli reached for him with the witchy, gnarled fingers of one hand. The nails were as black as if blood had burst beneath them. The Reverend reared and fell off the cot; his ass struck the floor as a shock wave juddered up his tailbone.

Flies escaped from the hole in Eli's armpit. They massed in the high corners of the bunkhouse. A thick, pendulous blanket of flies—a thousand starving spiders wouldn't be able to eat them all. The air teemed with the maddening purr of their wings.

Eli sat up. His chest quivered with industry—the Reverend couldn't help but think that his entire body was full of flies, his insides cored out and replaced by a dark colony of insects.

Eli began to issue full-throated, booming laughs that shook his entire body.

The Reverend finally found his feet. He began to back toward the door on benumbed feet.

"Come back," Eli pleaded, mock-coy. "I have so much to share with you."

The Reverend reached for the doorknob. He opened the door, staggered outside, and slammed it. Cyril was eying him warily.

"I heard something," Cyril said.

"It was nothing," the Reverend said. "Lock the door. Nobody goes in there." He swallowed with difficulty. "Not one goddamn person."

Cyril padlocked the door. Then he moved his chair a few feet away from it.

"Just so you're not totally in the dark, two of your flock lit out with the one-eyed prick and the scarecrow chick," Cyril said. "They left sometime yesterday."

"Who? Which two?"

"Charlie Fairweather and Otis Whats-his-face. The nigger and the other woman are still here. So's Charlie's wife and kid."

"Then they'll be coming back," Amos said, regaining a measure of composure.

He staggered back to his dwelling. The boy's mocking laughter continued to echo in his ears. He was on the verge of hysteria. The dread boiled up from the soles of his feet, spanning through his veins and nerve endings like a poisonous flower coming into bloom.

He collapsed on his bed, burrowed his face into his lilac-scented pillow, and screamed. In the darkness behind his shut eyelids, he kept seeing the boy opening his eyes, the cancerous black of them peering into his lacerated, penitent inner self.

Did you enjoy that, Reverend?

He screamed so hard that his vocal cords frayed. He was only mildly aware when the timbre of it changed—when it came to sound a little bit like unhinged, slightly deranged laughter.

26

THE THINGS IN THE WOODS did not follow them. Or if they did, then at a distance too great for Micah to sense.

They had set off from the meadow at a hurried clip as soon as it became clear that retreat was their sole option. They had taken only what they could easily carry. Dawn washed over the woods, creating trembling pockets of light between the trees. Nothing moved. The forest was drained of natural life—or that life had been repurposed into something infinitely more grotesque.

Micah could not shake the sight of the thing from the previous night. Alive it had been fearsome. Dead, more pitiful. Its slack, flame-eaten pelt, thick as a radial tire. Its many heads and eyes and limbs. Most of all, Micah could not forget the sense of agony that radiated off of it. A thing that would like nothing more than to die, yet was kept alive by infernal mechanics Micah couldn't possibly understand.

Initially they had run from the meadow, their metal cups and utensils rattling from the riggings of their packs. They had sprinted until their breath came in heaves. But when it became clear that they were not being pursued, their pace had slackened.

"So what the hell was that?" Minerva said.

Nobody could answer. It was nothing that should exist in this world.

"Whatever they are, they are purposeful," Micah said. "They would prefer we not leave."

Otis said, "What, do you think they're . . . ?"

"Funneling us back to Little Heaven?" said Minerva. "I think that's exactly what Shug means. Isn't it?"

Micah offered the faintest of nods. He wasn't sure the creatures themselves were knowingly directing them back the way they had come—perhaps whatever had minted them was doing that.

"Satan," Charlie said. "Instruments of the devil."

"*Be sober, be vigilant,*" Otis quoted tremblingly, "*because your adversary the devil, as a roaring lion, walketh about, seeking whom he may devour.*"

Hours later they walked into the midmorning sun. They were tired and dirty and fearful. Even Micah was scared—Micah Shughrue, a man who some said was so cool that he drank boiling water and pissed ice cubes. He was afraid of no man. He had glimpsed the blackness of the human heart. Yet somehow they had now passed from that known realm of evil—one he could sense in the Reverend especially, and to a lesser degree in the Reverend's hired men—to a new and uncharted one, populated by forces Micah had never encountered. It unlocked a thirsty horror within him. One so dark he couldn't see any light in it.

They came to a dip where the path bellied out to a cut between the trees. The land fell away in layers of shale and red dirt into a narrow valley. Micah stared through that cut and saw something he had not seen either time he had passed this spot before.

A squat shape was visible several hillsides over. A structure of some sort. It looked much bigger than a hunting shack.

Micah said, "What is that?"

"I never keyed on it until just now," Otis admitted.

"You figure somebody's living out there?" said Minerva.

Micah clocked the distance, judging it at six or seven miles. He could make out a narrow path winding across the valley floor.

"You're not thinking . . .," Otis started.

"We should take a look," Micah said.

"That's a good hike," said Otis. "The daylight will be gone by the time we get there."

"Do you want to spend another night in the woods?" Charlie asked Micah.

"There is evil at Little Heaven, too," Micah reasoned.

"My wife and kid are there," said Charlie.

Micah nodded. "I will go. You need not."

"You do that," said Otis, his face reddening. "You go right ahead and fill your boots to the brim with *that*. See how it works out for you."

Charlie and Otis took a few steps down the path leading back to the compound. They looked miserable but resigned.

"I wish you would reconsider," said Otis, abruptly penitent.

Minerva hung between them. "Ah jeez, Shug. Really?"

Micah said nothing.

"Ah, fuck it. What's that old expression?"

Micah said, "You only live once."

Minerva shook her head. "That's not the one I was thinking of. It's more along the lines of *A stubborn bastard and his head are soon parted, unless I go with him.*"

Micah said, "I am unfamiliar with that one."

"Yeah, well, something like that. Let's go, you pigheaded sonofabitch."

Otis and Charlie watched them skid down the incline to the base of the valley, their heels kicking up puffs of red dust.

"We will return tomorrow," Micah called up.

"Go with God!" Charlie called back.

"I'll go with the crisp, refreshing taste of Shasta instead!" Minerva shouted. "It *hasta* be Shasta!"

Minerva gave Charlie a cheery wave, but she didn't feel that way. She felt lost and freaked out. She wished she could see this situation the way Micah surely did. He wasn't inclined to consider how things came to be. His mind was tuned toward dealing with things the way they were. To him, the creatures in the woods existed, somehow, and had to be reckoned with. Which was the best way of seeing it right now, trapped in the heart of it. Minerva knew Micah was scared—the man was tough, but he wasn't insane—but his fear inspired a direct levelheadedness. Those awful things were an equation to be solved. Micah didn't need to explain or understand them. He only had to act. She wished she had that particular nerve, or bone, or part of her brain that allowed her to do the same.

THEY PRESSED THROUGH the valley in the midday heat. The land was deadly quiet. They, too, walked in silence, to conserve energy and because Micah rarely had much to say. They came to a stream. The water was clear but foul, burdened with an aftertaste that slipped down the backs of their throats like toxic oil. But they drank and gagged and drank some more, as they were parched and there was no telling when the chance would come again.

Gray clouds massed against the horizon, ushering in an early twilight. Minerva's feet ached. Blisters had swollen and burst on her heels; she could feel the warm blister broth soaking into her socks. She had not eaten since yesterday, but her appetite had deserted her, replaced in her stomach by a restless fear.

The valley bellied into a basin studded with cottonwoods. They moved through the waist-high grass, pushing the dry thatches aside with their hands. Not one cricket clung to a single blade. *So terrible*, Minerva thought, *to be the only living things here*. A person forgets how she is surrounded by life all day long. Spiders making webs, mice scurrying behind walls, raccoons feasting in your garbage cans, fruit flies colonizing your bananas. And while it could be annoying to rebag your torn trash sacks or sweep up mouse shit, at least it was normal. Otherwise, it felt like you were living on the desolate surface of an uninhabited planet.

"There," said Micah.

Minerva followed his finger up the spine of a hill. Tracking that rise, about a mile distant, sat the dark outline of what was clearly a homestead.

"Quickly," Micah said. "Before it rains."

27

ELLEN BELLHAVEN SPENT the morning at Little Heaven's glassworks. She melted the borosilicate beads, added tints, rolled and snipped it and worked the molten glass into shapes of her liking. Nobody troubled her; the Little Heavenites had bigger concerns than unauthorized use of the glassworks. The busywork kept one part of Ellen's mind occupied while the other parts spun off on crazed orbits. She put her hands in service of small tasks to dull the riot inside her head.

Everyone here was so damn . . . odd. Ellen had known Bible bashers; they could be grating, those sideways looks confirming their belief that Ellen already had one foot in the eternal flames of hell. There was also this sense—implicit, but as yet never stated—that they believed she and the other "outsiders" had brought an indefinable sickness to Little Heaven. A curse. But the thing was, Little Heaven had been ill before they had shown up. And it was only getting worse.

First there was that incident with the kids and the shrew. Then the thing in the woods she and Micah had seen. Within the compound, all sense of oversight seemed to have vanished. Parents barely minded their children, who were free to run amok so long as they didn't go into the woods. Nobody had gone in there unaccompanied since Eli's disappearance. It was as if the threat—and there *was* a threat at Little Heaven, though Ellen couldn't pinpoint what it was—had not registered. The Little Heavenites continued on in their own obedient way. Narcotized, as if a powerful gas were being pumped up from the ground that made them accept whatever terribleness was coming.

She glanced up to see Cyril Neeps stepping into the glassworks. Tall and ferret-like, with a canine tooth that jagged down to divot his lower lip.

"Well now," he said breezily. "What do we have here?"

She felt momentarily reduced under his predatory gaze, no bigger than a grasshopper or some other bug. Then she set her jaw. Fuck this guy.

"Just keeping busy. Nobody seems to be using this place."

Neeps nodded cheerily, but she'd seen this kind of thing—false sunniness hiding the glint of a blade.

"Sure, yep . . . that's about the size of it." He smiled. "Still, shouldn't you have asked permission first? I mean, you didn't buy all this stuff, did you?"

He waited for an answer. When she didn't say anything, he dismissively waved his hand. "Enjoying yourself, are you?" He laughed in a way that encouraged her to join in, although nothing he said had been remotely funny.

"Like I said," Ellen told him, "just filling time."

Neeps cocked his head. Assaying the steel in her spine. She stared back equitably. She wasn't scared. It had been a long time since a man looked at her that way. She'd be damned if she would ever be scared of the Cyril Neepses of this world again.

"Filling time, huh?" His smile turned wolfish. "I can think of better ways to fill it. I'm kind of an expert at filling . . . time."

Unflinchingly, she returned his smile. "That so?

He hitched his thumbs in his belt. "Oh, that's a fact."

"What about your friend? He an expert in anything?"

"Who, Virg? He's an expert at sticking his thumb up his rear end. That, and following me around like a lost puppy. You could say I'm the brains of our particular operation."

"Then Lord help you."

Cyril's smile faded. Something dark and hungry passed over his face.

Ellen said, "I can fill my own time, but thanks a bunch."

Neeps's fingers diddled along the hilt of a knife sheathed on his belt.

"Yeah, well, here's the thing about women I've learned. Sometimes they need a good filling . . . of their time. So it's just a matter of filling it for them until they come round to the sport of it."

Ellen withdrew the glassblowing pole from the kiln and balanced it on the anvil. Its tip glowed white-hot. It was pointed at Neeps, right around crotch level.

"Glassblowing is my little getaway," she said, not breaking eye contact. "Do you understand, Cyril?" She spun the pole on the anvil. Around and around. "Solitude is important for any of us, wouldn't you say?"

Neeps stared at the glowing tip as if mesmerized—

"So why don't you make like a tree and get the fuck outta here, Cy?"

Neeps's eyes snapped up to her. His lips curled in a sneer. He seemed to be debating taking matters to the next level, the physical one, but something in Ellen's face—or the searing metal pointed at his balls—prevented it.

He lip-farted. "I was trying to throw you a bone. A pity poke, plain and simple. To tell it straight, you don't merit a good fuckin'," he said with sunny good cheer. "I take one look at that burn all down your face and my pecker just wilts. Christ, what a sight! Face all messed up like that." He shoved his palms toward her like a toddler pushing away a plate of peas. "Your head looks like a marshmallow someone dropped in a fire."

"You sure do know how to charm a lady," Ellen said.

"Maybe you got something going with that one-eyed mute you chum around with. Or the skinny bitch? You're a slit slurper, that it? You're as frigid as one, that's for damn certain."

"If that helps you sleep better."

Cyril screwed the toe of his boot into the dirt. "I've been watching you. If you take one step out of line, any of you, I will happily . . ." He checked his threat. "You're trespassing. So mind your p's and q's, *hmm?*"

"Good-bye, Cyril."

"Good-fucking-*bye*, Melto," he called over his shoulder as the door shut behind him.

NATE RAN ACROSS the woman down by the cistern outside the dry goods shed. One of the outsiders. The one with the burn on her face.

Nate had not slept again after Eli Rathbone's visit. The night had stretched out like taffy, seconds becoming minutes becoming hours. An eternity trapped under the covers with his dad zonked out a few feet away. He felt no safety in his father's presence. His dad wasn't strong or especially smart. If Nate had gone with Eli—or if Eli had come into the bunkhouse and taken him by force—Nate couldn't picture his father doing much more than crying out in horror. He didn't picture him tackling Eli in order to rescue him. Sure, his father would search for Nate once he was gone, and he'd be weeping sorrowfully and hunting harder than anyone else. But he wouldn't have done anything when it really mattered.

This was why Nate hadn't bothered to tell his father about Eli's visit. His dad wouldn't believe him. He'd say Nate dreamed it all. And who knows? Maybe he had. When Nate inspected the bunkhouse that morning, he found no trace of Eli's presence: no footprints in the dirt, not even the smudge of his nose on the plastic window. Nate desperately wished he *had* dreamed it. But the memory was full of too many perfect details—Eli's bone-white hair, the flies with gas mask faces—to believe he'd imagined it.

He bumped into the burned woman just before noon. She was up to something in the glassworks. She emerged with her shirt dark with sweat. Nate was filling his canteen from the cistern. He had been digging marble pits out behind the dry goods shed. He used to have a sack of marbles, cat's-eyes and oilies and king cobs, but the sack had gone missing. Nate suspected Elton Redhill, but it was un-Christian to accuse anyone of theft. Nate made the pits anyway, stabbing the heel of his boot into the dirt until he'd made a groove, then scooping out dirt with his hands. The patch of earth behind the shed looked like some crazy old coot had been digging for buried treasure without a map.

"How are you?" the woman asked.

Nate shrugged. His father had told him not to talk to the outsiders. Their thoughts were almost certainly impure.

The woman filled a cup from the cistern and drank. "Thirsty work," she said.

She somehow reminded him of his mother, even though she did not look like her. It was just Nate's loneliness that made her seem that way. When she smiled, the scarred skin down her face and neck stretched alarmingly, as if it might tear open. But Nate remembered hearing that scar tissue was actually stronger than normal skin, kind of like how cardboard is stronger than foolscap. It was skin that had been hurt and healed into something more durable than it had been—still, it looked pretty gross. Nate apologized inside his head for thinking that.

"I saw you doing something out behind the shed. I wasn't spying," she said a little too quickly, the way someone would if she really had been spying. "*Qué pasa?*"

"Pardon?"

"What are you doing back there?"

He shouldn't be talking to her. But his father was cleaning up in the chapel and nobody was watching, and anyway, it would be rude to stand there like a lump.

"Digging marble pits."

The woman's eyebrows went up. "Oh? Marbles. What kinds do you have?"

Nate twisted the toe of his shoe into the dirt like he was crushing out a cigarette. "I used to have a sack. But I . . . I must have lost it."

"Well, you're not going to believe this, Nate—" She turned her head away, muttering something that sounded like a curse word. "Is that your name? Nate?"

Nate nodded.

"Lucky guess! You look like a Nate. I've been working on something that you just might like," the woman said. "Why don't I meet you back here?"

She returned a few minutes later. She reached into her pocket and pulled out six polished glass balls. Their insides were shot with blues and blacks and whites. They looked a lot like marbles but weren't exactly.

"Will they do in a pinch?"

Nate took one from her palm and rolled it toward the nearest pit. It wasn't perfectly round but close enough. They were more beautiful, more *unique*, than any marbles he had ever seen.

"They're swell," he said, picking the almost-marble up and handing it back to her.

"Keep them," she said.

"Seriously?"

"I used the glass your father and everyone else paid for, right? They're more yours than mine, when you think about it."

"Yeah, but you made them."

"It's okay. They're my bloopers, anyway. So take them."

She pulled open Nate's hip pocket and rolled them into it. They clinked against one another in a satisfying way. He could feel them in his pocket, six hard bulges against his thigh.

"Thank you." It was the nicest thing anybody had done for him in a while.

"*De nada.*"

"Pardon?"

"No problem."

The woman hung around while he shot marbles. It was nice to hold things that were his own. Back home, he'd had a few things. His bike, a shelf of books. But at Little Heaven, everyone owned everything and nothing—except the Reverend, who had permission from God to have his own special stuff. But for the rest of them, it was only their Bibles and a few personal items. Nate's marbles had been about the only things that were his alone. Which was why they were stolen, probably. He would have to hide these new ones. There was no way he would be allowed to keep a gift from an outsider.

"You like it here?" the woman asked. She was looking somewhere else, as if it didn't matter much to her what Nate said.

"It's okay," he said. "It's what God wants."

She faced him. "And you feel . . . safe? I mean, I know you feel safe with God watching over you. That's great. But here in Little Heaven?"

Nate nodded, but it took a while. "Sometimes I miss my old home. Miss my mom."

"It's natural to miss home," she said.

"I think some of the other kids miss their homes, too."

"Oh yeah?"

Nate swallowed. Was he actually going to talk about this to a total stranger? Sure, she gave him some marbles, but Nate and his father could get exiled for this sort of thing.

"I think . . . I don't know. Just that everything feels a little weird lately. People aren't acting like themselves."

The woman nodded as if she understood. Maybe she did. She'd been here long enough to feel it.

"And then last night I think I saw Eli Rathbone, the kid who went missing, walking around with no shirt on in the middle of the night."

Nate clamped his hand over his mouth. The words had spilled out crazily, without his even thinking about them. He realized just how badly he needed to tell someone, even if it was a woman he'd never met before and wasn't sure he could trust. But maybe that was it—she *was* a stranger, so she would understand better than somebody who was stuck in the same monstrous machine.

She leaned forward, prompting him to speak. "What . . . ?"

"He didn't look too good," said Nate. "He . . . uh, looked like he was almost dead. Or like he *was* dead, which is stupid. This one time my mom took me to the drive-in. We watched *To Kill a Mockingbird*. Mom gave me a dime for a Zero bar. Coming back from the concession stand, I saw the movie playing one screen over. It was called *Premature Burial*." Nate shook his head. "I shouldn't have watched it. There was this dead guy, all white and hungry, crawling out of a casket. Grave dust was puffing off his shoulders. I had nightmares for a week. Anyway, that's kind of how . . . ."

"How Eli looked?"

Nate swallowed. "Yeah."

"Did you tell anyone about this?"

"Only you."

"Why not your dad?"

"He wouldn't believe me. He'd say I have an overactive imagination. That it's the devil burrowing into my brain."

"Are you going to tell anyone?"

"Maybe I dreamed it," said Nate hopefully, but the look on the woman's face said she wasn't so sure about that. "Nobody has seen Eli since he got back," Nate went on. "Maybe he's okay."

"My friends saw him," the woman said. "Before the Reverend took him away. The way they tell it, Eli didn't look so hot at all."

"Oh" was all Nate could say.

"Enjoy the marbles, okay?" She glanced over her shoulder as though she'd felt eyeballs tiptoeing up her spine. "And if you see anything else weird or scary, will you promise to come tell me?"

He hesitated, unsure.

"Nate," she said, "*I* believe you."

Relief washed over him. "Okay," he said. "But I hope I don't see anything."

"Me, too."

She returned to the glassworks. A frigid wind screamed around the edge of the shed and brought up goose pimples on Nate's calves.

28

THE PRESTON SCHOOL FOR BOYS.

These five words were stamped on a strip of tin that arched over the entry path. But the wooden poles that had once held the sign aloft had rotted; the sign hung from the second pole on a rusted spike, the tin eaten through by rain and wind.

The path itself was just a ghost, two narrow strips grown over with weeds and bracken. A set of pitted concrete steps—only two of them, like a staircase that had been abandoned in midbuild—sat beside the path, just past the sign. These were wagon step-downs: a driver would pull a horse-drawn cart beside them to allow passengers to dismount without spraining an ankle.

"*Greeeen Acres is the place to be,*" Minerva sang. "*Faaaarm livin' is the life for me.*" Off a look from Micah: "What, you don't watch TV? What the hell do you do at night, Shug—stare at the hands on the clock?"

They walked toward the buildings. Minerva tried to whistle the *Green Acres* theme—anything to drive the stony silence away—but a scouring wind wicked the spit off her lips.

"Old private school, you figure?" she said. "Rich folk sending their Chads and Coopers and Athertons out to the sticks to put some bark on their satiny skin?"

Micah shook his head. "Reform school. Juvenile delinquents."

"So you've heard about this place?"

"No. Just ones like it."

The Preston School for Boys appeared to be made up of three primary buildings. Two large outbuildings and one house. They approached the larger of the outbuildings. Its door hung cockeyed on rotted hinges. Inside were two rows of bunk beds, five to a side, enough to sleep twenty kids. Ashen light filtered through the dirt-caked windows. The bed frames were remarkably well preserved. The mattresses had a few rips and tears where the horsehair was leaking out. Shingles had blown free of the roof in spots, creating gaps where the sun had bleached the floorboards. But overall, there was an oddly hermetic, museum-quality air to the interior.

Words had been scratched into the far wall. Each letter gouged into the wood—frenzied-looking strokes with a penknife or other sharp object.

Why is 6 afraid of 7?
789! 789!

"A riddle," Micah said. "Six is afraid of seven because seven ate nine."

They walked between the bunks. Old footlockers with cracked leather hasps lay at the foot of each bunk. Minerva opened one. Inside sat a tin toy. A stork wearing a top hat. When she wound a key on the stork's back, the thing chittered to life. First it tipped its hat. Then its long beak opened to reveal a tiny swaddled infant lying on its tongue. Most of the baby's face was eaten away by rust. The key revolved. The stork's beak snapped shut on the baby. The gears wound down.

Minerva turned the toy over. Stamped on its bottom was: *GELY TOYS 1870*. A ripple of discomfort raced up her spine. She put it back in the footlocker, disliking the feel of the metal on her fingertips: warm and greasy, as if it had just recently sat in a child's clammy hands.

Micah inspected some of the other footlockers. More than a few were empty. Those that weren't held scant possessions: moldering Bibles, crucifixes, a glass jar half full of marbles, a doll made of braided hair. Items the boys who'd once slept in these beds had been allowed to bring, or else had smuggled in.

Minerva said, "How many boys were here, do you figure?"

"Hard to know," said Micah. "Ten. A dozen."

"It's a long way from anywhere."

"Better than jail."

"If you say so."

They went back outside. The land past the sleeping quarters lay flat in the afternoon sun. A metal plow, the kind hauled by oxen, stood not far from a boarded-over well. Fifty yards from the well, Minerva sighted two squat metal boxes in a nest of weeds. They weren't much bigger than coffins. They had also rusted through in spots, though the metal was quite thick.

"What the hell are those?"

Minerva walked across the field until she drew near to the boxes. Each had a door on the side. She lifted the latch, knelt, and opened one. Micah followed her. He watched, saying nothing. Minerva caught the smell of rain-rinsed steel and something else, more primal, still traceable after all these years. She got down on her hands and knees and stuck her head and shoulders inside one box. Words had been scratched on the metal. Fanatical and somehow helpless ones, etched with sharp field rocks.

HELP and OUT and SORRY and PLEASE.

A lot of PLEASEs.

All that, plus two alternating words, scratched with terrible precision on the lower left side.

FLESH. BEAST. FLESH. BEAST. FLESH. BEAST.

She squirmed out of the horrible box. Jesus, that couldn't possibly be legal. But this place was in the middle of nowhere. Who would have been watching?

Micah took in her shocked pallor. "It was a different time," he said.

"Bullshit," Minerva spat back, trembling with rage. "Basic humanity is timeless, isn't it? These were boys."

They carried on to the other large building, which turned out to be the mess. Like the sleeping quarters, it was intact. The chairs and tables, immaculate. Jars of preserves lined the kitchen cupboards. The seals had burst and many jars had broken, but this had happened so long ago that the stink was gone. The food, whatever it had been, was no more than a crusted stain. No animals had been at the jars. No insects, even. The damage was simply the result of the decades passing by.

"Bizarre," Minerva said. "It's as if this whole place has been . . ."

"Curated," said Micah.

They exited the mess and made their way toward the house. The front of the house, the porch and veranda, was black from fire. It had not engulfed the entire structure, but it had blown out the front windows and charred the veranda roof, the wooden ribs of which sagged down in fire-thinned quills. Minerva noted the effigy of a rocking chair heat-welded to the porch. She imagined the owner of this house sitting on that rocker in the high heat of a summer afternoon, watching his young charges till the fields. From this distance, he would have heard the boys screaming in the hot boxes, too.

The porch creaked ominously but bore their weight. They walked through the gutted door frame into the house. The fire had made no inroads here. A thick layer of dust had settled over everything. The furniture was still in good enough shape to fetch a fair sum at an antiques show. There wasn't much of it, however, as the house's occupant seemed to prefer a spartan living style.

A rack of rifles lined a cabinet in the front room. Micah swung the glass front open and inspected them.

"Civil War era," he said. "That is a Lindsay model. A Whitworth, there. These guns are over a hundred years old."

They went upstairs. The walls were papered with a pattern of cabbage roses faded to dim blots. The front bedroom overlooked the mess and sleeping quarters. A pair of field binoculars rested on a tripod before the window. Minerva peered through them. She could see across the fields to the woods fringing the basin that they had climbed earlier.

The room had a desk. The home's sole photo sat upon it. A sepia shot of a man whose large round head sat atop a thick neck. A walrus mustache. Fat fleshy lips. He stared forward with a certain imperiousness, as if challenging the viewer to contradict his view of the world.

Augustus C. Preston was written on a brass nameplate below the photo.

"The lord of the manor?" said Minerva.

"I reckon."

"He kept a framed, labeled photo of hissown self on his desk?" Minerva spat on the floor. "Maybe he had Alzheimer's. Needed to remind himself of who the hell he was."

Micah opened the desk drawers. Receipts and logbooks, all dated the years 1873 and 1874. The papers were yellowed and dry; a few slips crumbled apart in his fingers. Minerva saw receipts for shipping notices, sums paid, debits owing. Another notebook was labeled *ENROLLMENT*. Ten boys were listed, between the ages of nine and fifteen. Walter Albee. Percy Snell. Horace Fudge. Cornelius Benn. Wilfred Tens. Five more. *Orphan* was marked beside eight of the ten names, and *Ward of the State* beside the remaining two. *Recidivist* was jotted beside six of the ten—even Merle Pugg, the nine-year-old.

Micah found a sheaf of letters in another drawer, all sent from one Conrad Preston. He teased the first letter out of its envelope. It was dated August 17, 1874. He looked it over and then passed it to Minerva.

"Read it."

Dearest Auggie,

LEAVE THAT PLACE. I BEG YOU.

My brother, you must. That godforsaken wilderness has clambered into both you and your misbegotten charges. I fear something dreadful shall befall you.

You speak of a voice. A shadowy herald calling to you from the trees. But do you not recall it was a voice that called you into that blasted wilderness in the first? The voice of God, as you told me? Perchance it was, Auggie dear. And so you set about building your refuge, where you only wished to educate young striplings under the watchful eye of the Lord—while never sparing the lash, as it must be.

But now you write to me of such grim tidings. The Devil walks those woods. You speak of hearing the lonesome notes of a flute coming from the forest. Boys wandering away never to return—or if so, horribly altered. I am not one to jump at spooks, but there is much of this world we do not comprehend. That land is known only to the Red Indian, and perchance he possesses a savage means to cope with such deviltry. You do not. You are a white man, and civilized.

Come home! Your ambitions are noble, but having already used up your inheritance on the erection of the School, you have, I fear, left yourself in a position of keen vulnerability. I would come myself, but my tubercular state has rendered me inert. Only heroic doses of laudanum keep the agonies at bay.

Do not be so pigheaded, Auggie! If the boys will not come with you, leave them. They are runaways. That is their nature! Whether it be through cobbled side streets or into the dim woods, they run! I admire a streak of iron as much as any man, but there comes a time when that iron turns poisonous in the blood.

Your latest missive . . . Auggie, do not take this wrongly, but if I had not recognized your handwriting I might have thought it had been misposted from the nuthatch up in Courtney Hills. You find yourself in a dark place—darkness of the spirit, a darkening of the heart. Why put your soul at peril? Leave, please. Take those charges who will come, abandon the rest. They are society's leavings. Nobody shall place blame on you or mourn their passing. They have no kin.

YOU have kin, Auggie. Me. Your loving brother. Come back to me. I beg of you. From the bottom of my heart I beg.

Yrs as ever,
Connie

That was the final letter. The ones below bore postmarks from earlier dates. Minerva skimmed them, reading the odd snippet. The initial excitement and productivity at the Preston School appeared to have given way to creeping signs that became increasingly menacing. Sounds from the forest. The haunting trill of a flute.

According to the letters, boys at the Preston School had started to disappear—or this was Minerva's understanding based on Connie Preston's one-sided narrative.

The boys disappeared, but they came back. Just like Eli Rathbone? With his white hair and gray eyes and blanket of hissing bugs?

In the second-to-last letter, Conrad Preston mentioned the desertion of the school's guards, leaving Augustus as the lone authority. Minerva tried to picture Augustus and his delinquent boys stranded on this solitary outcropping. Yet throughout it all—to judge by Conrad's increasingly desperate letters—Augustus maintained a fervent belief, even as events spiraled into madness. He was Ahab pursuing his white whale.

"Jesus, Shug," Minerva said. "Do you think . . . Is it possible that what's happening at Little Heaven now has happened before? Nearly a hundred years ago?"

Micah said, "I cannot say what is happening now."

"But if it did happen, how could nobody know about it?"

"People go missing. Whole groups."

"But this many? Ten boys, maybe more, and their batshit-crazy warden?"

"There are a million ways it could have happened."

"But I don't think it happened any of those ways, Shug. I think it happened the way it's happening at Little Heaven. And I think you do, too."

Night had begun to fold over the Preston School. Micah said, "Make a fire."

THEY FOUND A POTBELLIED STOVE in the kitchen. Micah hurled the mattress off Augustus Preston's bed. He put his boots to the bed frame. The wood was hard oak. Micah was sweating by the time it started to splinter. He ripped the shattered wood from the joists. When he had enough, he slit the mattress and ripped out handfuls of stuffing.

He filled the stove with that cottony fluff, then tossed in bits of the bed frame. Before long, a fire was roaring. Micah seemed pleased. He must have found it cathartic to torch the bed of a blue-blooded sadist who had locked up little boys in boxes.

Minerva hunted through the cupboards. Just crockery. A ringbolt was set in the kitchen floor. Pulling on it opened a trapdoor leading to the cold cellar.

"Flashlight, Shug."

Micah handed it to her. She went down the worn steps. The cellar swept out under the flashlight's glow. Ancient dust swirled in the flashlight beam.

The shelves were stocked with preserves that had long gone off. Some of the mason jars had burst, their contents hanging off the edge of the shelf in stalactites—as if the shelves had grown fangs. The liquid had gone thin in other jars, the color of formaldehyde. Things sat suspended inside the liquid. Bulging shapes like beets or blackened turnips or . . .

something. A jar of pickled eggs with some kind of weird flagellate tails attached to them . . .

She swept the beam away from the jars. It fell upon something that puzzled her. Bars. Crosshatched iron bars. A square of them set into the center of the wall.

It was a cage. A cell dug into the cellar clay. Four feet deep, maybe a foot and a half high. There were three of them, side by side, each fronted by a barred door. They were too small to admit a full-grown person.

Minerva backed away. Her ass hit something. She spun to see a chair. A Chippendale? Brass rivets. Leather cracked over the years. It was then she realized that the cells had been dug at eye level, like . . . like pictures on a wall. Their occupants would have had to climb up into them—or, worse, they would have needed a boost.

And someone must have sat in this very chair. Smoking a pipe, maybe sipping a brandy. Watching whoever was inside.

What in God's name had happened in this place?

Nothing that happened here was in God's name, came a whisper in her head.

She went back up the stairs. She had found a bottle. Whiskey, the cork still waxed. She set it in front of Micah. Her fingers trembled.

"Don't go down there" was all Minerva said.

"Okay."

Micah slit the wax with his thumbnail and pulled the cork.

"Drink," he told her.

The liquor scorched her throat. But Minerva swallowed it and drank some more and handed the bottle to Micah. He drank in turn and then disappeared upstairs and came down with the binoculars. It was nearly dark. He scanned the mess and sleeping quarters through the binoculars. He then went through the rifle cabinet. He inspected each one and threw it aside.

"Cap and ball. Useless."

He found a bayonet and slid that into his sack. Minerva watched him make minute improvements to their lot, working with the situation as he found it. She wouldn't want to face this with anyone but him.

She grabbed stacks of plates from the cupboards and smashed them on the porch. The broken shards gritted under her boots as she walked back inside.

"Anything comes, we'll hear it."

They retired to the stove and drank. The whiskey kicked like a mule. Soon Minerva's head was swimmy.

"Your legs," said Micah.

"What about them?" Minerva said.

"Squeezed pretty tight."

"Old habit," she said. "I grew up in a religious area. In school, all the girls had to squeeze an aspirin between our knees for two hours a day. Y'know, to teach us to keep our legs shut until marriage."

Micah gave her a look.

"I'm fucking with you, Shug. I got to piss like a racehorse." Switching to a southern belle voice: "Mah eyeballs are plum doin' the flutter kick, Ah do declare."

"Piss on his bed."

Micah did not seem to be joking. Okey dokey, then.

She went up to Preston's bedroom. A coldness wept from its walls and sent a wire of fear through her—the curdled presence of Augustus Preston. The mattress lay on the floor with its guts slashed open. She yanked down her pants and squatted over it. A stupid desecration, like a child pissing on a hated schoolmaster's shoes. Her water was locked up inside her. She shut her eyes and exhaled. It began as a trickle and built to a stream that the mattress soaked up hungrily.

She stepped off the mattress before a rill of piss hit her boots. Thunderheads gathered over the hills. Lightning forked down to illuminate the trees—

She saw them then. Three shapes. Shaggy lumpen things. Staggered fifty yards apart in the field facing the house, two hundred yards away.

She hurried downstairs. Micah was at the window with the binoculars.

"You see them?" she asked.

Micah nodded.

"They coming closer?"

Micah shook his head. "Just there. Waiting."

"For what?"

Micah looked at her. How should he know?

They retrieved their packs from the kitchen. The stove kicked warmth into the front room, where they sat watching the shapes in the field. Micah took another glug of whiskey.

"You can never know the shape of the world, Minny," he said. It always tickled her when he used the name her father used to call her by. "When you think you have it compassed, something breaks from that geometry to bedevil you."

It was not like Shug to make such pronouncements. Was he drunk?

"What about Ebenezer?" he said, looking at her.

"I'm still going to kill him, if that's what you're wondering. I would have done it earlier, but it's been a busy stretch."

She rooted through her bag until her fingers closed around something. She pulled it out and tossed it to him. Micah turned it over in the finger of firelight falling from the kitchen. His gaze reflected puzzlement . . . until it clicked.

It might have been the first honest-to-God smile she'd ever seen from him.

He said, "You went back."

"Bet your ass I did. I was fourteen. Climbed the same tree and waited. Knife—two knives, actually. No gun. Wanted it to be a fair fight. It came the next day. It almost killed me. Got my one arm coiled up and squeezed. Busted that arm, crushed the air out of me. But I still had the other arm. I'd lashed the knives to my hands with baling twine so I couldn't let go. Its skin was real durable—imagine trying to cut through a bike tire. But I hacked its head clean off. Didn't come easy. Most creatures have got plenty of fight in them even when the battle's long lost."

She watched Micah turn the snake's head over. It was a foot long. Its eyes were dried-up peas in its sockets. Minerva had lost its lower jaw somewhere. The head would become drier and more brittle until all that remained was a fang or whatnot. She'd put that fang in a locket and string it round her neck.

"You are certain this was the one?"

She said, "How many fifteen-foot snakes you think there are? As soon as it was dead, I felt at peace. Like I'd set my brother's soul free."

Micah handed it back. "You are a wonder."

She stuffed the snake's head back into her pack. "There's still room in here."

"For?"

"The Englishman's head."

"He will not go easily, Minny. He is good at what he does."

She sighed. "I was a bounty hunter. You and him are mercenaries. You've killed people. There's a difference between us. I know that. But I want it more."

"He will want to live."

The storm had reached them. Rain began to pelt the windows.

"Do you still dwell on them?" Micah asked her.

"My brother and father? Not so much as I used to . . . You know, as time goes on they become less people in my memory and more, I don't know, *motivations*. I don't like that. Thinking of them that way. When the Englishman's dead, they'll come back to me the way they were."

"You think so?"

"I have to think so."

Micah nodded. "You sleep. I will keep watch."

"You sure?"

When he didn't answer, Minerva went into the kitchen and sat with her back to the wall. The warmth was narcotic. She fell into an uneasy doze.

MICAH STAYED UP and watched the fields. Lightning cleaved the sky. He could still see them out there. Three unmoving shapes in the lashing rain.

They wouldn't attack. He was pretty sure of that. It was the same in

Korea: the enemy would harass you, nipping at your flanks, funneling you to a choke point where they could kill you more easily. In this case, the choke point was Little Heaven. Except Micah wasn't sure these things had killing in mind. What was going on at Little Heaven was a different sort of thing. Nobody was dead, not yet. They were all just sick. And it was either that none of them had the good sense to leave, or the Reverend and his men were preventing it—or something else, some terrible specific gravity, kept them all locked in place. That being the case, those shapes out there in the field were more like ranchers squiring cattle back to the feed pen, which lay in the shadow of the slaughterhouse.

Micah had been thinking about it lately. Souls ascending. It wasn't Little Heaven that turned his thoughts in that direction; the Reverend's compound seemed about as divine as the Preston School. No, just the feeling a man gets when he senses the chain of his own life drawing tight around his throat. Micah felt the links of that chain cutting into his neck. And he wondered, idly but with as much feeling as he could summon, how thin a cut it was between a man like Augustus Preston and the man he himself had been at some earlier, rottener time in his existence.

He had killed men for money, and less than money. There were times when an evil had invaded his soul. He felt it drop over him, black and suffocating. That same mantle seemed to hang over the Reverend's shoulders, too—Micah sensed it to a certainty. And so the question was: If you let a man like that indulge his nature and didn't do anything about it, are you any better than him? A crazy dog bites, that being its nature. But if you let that dog go on biting, servicing its own ill-bred temperament—knowingly, and with an agency to stop it—then are you not whelps from the same litter? No, you are worse even. That dog cannot help but bite. You know better. Your inaction encouraged that evil to flourish. The blood was on your hands.

Micah thought about things like that. All the time he thought.

29

CY . . . OOOHHH, Cy baby, I need you . . .

Cyril Neeps started up from his sleep. He was kicked back in his chair against the side of the bunkhouse that housed Eli Rathbone. He snapped forward, the front feet of the chair stabbing into the dirt.

Jesus. He'd fallen asleep with his *head* touching the *wall* of the *bunk-house* with that *thing* shambling around inside. That fucking—

—abomination—

Yeah, okay, fucking-A right, that was the word. A bigger word than Cy was used to throwing around, but sure. A fucking abomination. Those curdled gray eyes and the grubs twisting around in his cored-out armpit. The *bugs.* Hard as he tried, Cy couldn't drive that image out of his mind. The boy was just covered in bugs right up to his chest, the little fuckers scuttling all over while the boy stroked that dead fucking pigeon with his disgusting melted hand—*Kee*-rist, all the liquor in the world couldn't wash that picture out of a man's head.

Not that Cy wouldn't give that a go. Hey! The good ole college try. But the Reverend, the slant-heeled killjoy prick, ran a dry compound. Hell, he and Virg had even tried whipping up a batch of home brew out of spud peels, a bag of sugar, and a few weird-smelling herbs Virg hunted out of the woods—the same woods they had steered clear of lately. But the finished batch smelled of grim death, and when Virg took the tiniest sip, his tongue turned toad green. They agreed it would probably drive them both blind, and then they'd never find their way out of Little Heaven—and their departure was fixing to be sooner rather than later, if anyone wanted the God's honest truth. Time to blow this pop stand, was Cy's professional opinion.

And the Reverend—that rat-assed, greasy snake oil salesman! Cyril kinda hated him. He couldn't understand why all these bozos followed him out here, hanging off his every goddamn word—that was, until he'd seen him in action behind the pulpit. Oh, he changed then. Grew two feet taller, that big voice rumbling out of his pudgy body like a rainbow arching out of a dung pile. Cyril wasn't a churchgoing man, but he could appreciate the power the Reverend had, and so far as Cy could tell, he'd earned it. The fucker paid good, too. He vacuumed every nickel out of his cow-eyed worshippers' pockets and gave some of it to him and Virg.

But in Cy's not-so-humble opinion, no amount of cashola was enough for *this*. Nope. No way, no how. What good was money when you couldn't buy the finest things in life: liquor off the top shelf, a pack of Colts wine-tipped cigarillos, and, after a drink and a smoke, maybe a nice slice of pussy? In fact, it didn't have to be that nice a slice. Just willing. Or, if not willing, at least present. All the women around here had a broomstick up their asses, or else rode one. And they had prick-shot husbands and kids, too, and everyone knew that once a woman had a kid, her cooze flapped like a wind sock at the airport. Cy liked a tight fit. This one clam-faced bitch he'd nailed had told Cy that no fit would be tight enough for his Phillips-head screwdriver of a dick unless he took to fucking electrical sockets—but she had only said that *once*.

Cy-by . . . where's my handsome Cyyyyy-by . . .

Cyril's head snapped toward the voice. A blast from the past. An honest-to-Christ mind melter.

"Carlene . . . ?"

Jesus, didn't that name feel weird in his mouth? Carlene Herlihy from Carbine, Alabama—the glue-trap town Cy had grown up in. Couldn't be her, of course. But there it was, her voice calling from the heart of the woods just as sugary sweet as he remembered.

My baby, my handsome honey-bunny . . .

Carlene. Juicy Carlene. A box as sweet as canned peaches. Only you had to wrench the damned lid off her jar. Women! They learned or they got taught, and either way worked fine by Cy. Hell, the fight was half the fun.

Honey-bunny, though? Carlene had never called him that. She wasn't one for gooey phrasings—as a cashier at the Carbine Pinch N Save, she could scarcely be bothered to make eye contact, and had a way of snapping her gum that made a man feel about an inch tall. Christ, she had no clue Cy even existed until he made his move—which it must be said was a bit . . . what's the shit-eatin' word? *Forward.*

He was twenty-five. Carlene, eighteen. Body tight as a snare drum.

Dewy was the word to race through Cy's mind looking at her. Just as slick and wet as the earth after a rainstorm. He wasn't on her radar, so he made damn good and sure to put himself there.

He'd been ready to roll out of town at the time, no forwarding address. But before he left, he had matters to attend to. He caught up with Carlene one night at a bush party. He shouldn't have been there—he was too old, and with that jittery look he used to get when he was up to something. His eyes were hard these days, no matter what he was doing. He almost missed that old feeling.

Anyway, Cy let Carlene know he'd come into some acid. That bug-fuck weirdo Leary had hipped him to it, Cy said. As if one soul in that scratch-ass town *really* had acid. But Carlene went with him, bold as a bull. He took her into the woods. She was pissed to the gills; he figured she wouldn't be able to bat so much as a butterfly off her arm. But she had fight in her. Ooo-eee, what a hellion! Scratching and biting, all but clawing Cyril's eyes out. She wore fake nails or some shit, took a nice chunk out of his cheek. But when she gave over to him, it was with a sigh. Her legs could have been oiled, the way they spread. Wide open, smooth as creamery butter—

Cy . . . Cyril . . . Come over here, Cyril . . .

Cyril was up off his chair without really thinking—as if he'd grown a second brain in his ass that was controlling his legs. *Hey, ass brain, hold your horses!* He almost laughed at how fucking silly it was . . . except the spit had gone sour in his mouth. He took a few hesitant steps away from his post by the bunkhouse door. Sweat trickled down his spine to soak his underwear. His rear end was clammy, and it itched in a place he was helpless to scratch.

The fence shielding Little Heaven from the woods was twenty yards off. He lurched toward it.

Stop.

This was his conscious, direct thought.

Stop moving, feet.

It was strange to address a part of your body as if it had its own will, no different from telling your asshole not to let fly with a fart in a crowded elevator. But he was asking now—*begging*. His arms and legs had been disconnected, their controls rerouted.

"Stop." His breath came out in a harsh pop. "Goddamn it, *stop*."

But he kept on. Staggering more than walking, part of him putting on the brakes while the other part, the more powerful one now, continued to grind his body forward. You'd think the earth was lined with fucking ball bearings, the way he kept slip-sliding ahead.

Oh, Cy . . . come on, baby, we're gonna have us a time. A real screamer.

He'd seen Carlene a few years ago, back in Carbine. Sitting outside the dairy bar with a couple of her runny-nosed, scabby-elbowed kids still shitting in diapers. A human trash pit, it must be said. Oh, how the mighty, y'know? Big flappetty tits hanging off the front of her like two gunnysacks kicked down a bad stretch of road. She didn't look dewy then, not one bit. More like *doody*.

He wasn't surprised. She was nothing special. He remembered her ass had been dimpled with cellulite when he had finally seen it in the woodland moonlight. Like the cratered surface of the fucking moon! It had been like opening a really pretty box to find a dog turd inside. But the way she wore her jeans back then, you'd never know. Well, Cy knew. There had never been a damn thing special about her, which is what pissed Cy off the most—she'd sold him a bill of goods, which had put him on the hunt in the first place. But she was the same ignorant, ditchwater-dull bitch that you'd find anyplace. She hadn't been worth his time or interest, and he held his old obsession against her.

He had sat down beside her kids, who were clearly the sort who would spend the rest of their bitter, useless lives in that tar pit town. Carlene's eyes went wide with that old fear at the sight of him.

You're a shell of your former self, he'd said to her, then got up and sauntered off.

It hadn't even felt that good. Not like how he'd wanted. Life had already ripped the spine out of every dream she'd ever had. How much could the truth really hurt?

"Virgil," he moaned now as his feet propelled him helplessly toward the fence, hoping his partner might hear. But it was the dead of night and

Virgil was probably asleep, the pudding brain. Cyril felt a little sorry for Virgil. Dumb as a box of hammers, that one. He'd be lost without Cyril. Then he had to ask himself: *Where am I going?*

At the fence now. It ran fifteen feet up to the razor wire. Cy hooked his hands into the chain link. The sensation of his fingers clawing through that rough industrial metal washed a dry taste of horror through his mouth, as if he'd taken a big gulp of shitty wine.

Come on now, baby. We're gonna have such fun . . .

He started to climb. The terror shot through him sharply, a bone-deep electricity radiating from every nerve center. He tried to jerk himself backward, hurl himself to the ground. He didn't care if he broke a leg, or both legs plus an arm. Anything was better than being dragged toward that voice like a man chained to a winch.

He saw something in the trees. Carlene Herlihy. The pride of Carbine, Alabama. Naked as a jaybird. Jesus please us. He'd never seen a woman so goddamn lovely. Creamy-dreamy red bikini. Breasts not all droopy and sucked out, but firm and high. A nice tanglebush. Boy howdy, Cy would walk twenty miles of busted glass to lay one kiss between those legs.

Except her eyes. Yes indeedy, there was something a bit queer about those.

He was up the fence now. He'd scaled it like a blackie up a coconut tree, hadn't he? Climbed it faster than that fairy English nigger ever could. Cyril paused, his body trembling, then started to crawl through the razor wire. Oh fuck. *Stop. STOP!* The wire was studded with long sharp blades just like the ones his father used to shave with. They effortlessly slit Cy's clothes. Blood leapt out in greedy bursts.

He kept his eyes on Carlene. That traffic-stopping body. Those inhuman eyes. What would she do to him with that body—more important, what would she do with those *eyes?*

A razor raked his throat. Blood pissed out his neck, a shiny redness spritzing against the night. Fuck it all to hell. He didn't even feel it. Carlene's hands were moving between her legs, fingers feathering that space between. Her breasts were so big—way bigger than he ever remembered, though he was an ass man by trade—so big they threw round shadows down her rib cage.

There came the sound of a wet, shredding, rubbery fart—Cyril almost yelped laughter. Sweet Jesus, someone just ripped their britches! A real denim-burster. Except he knew that wasn't it. In a far-off, unreal, day-dreamy sense, he understood that some other part of his anatomy was responsible for that noise. It was the sound of something opening up, and something else slipping out. In some distant chamber of his mind—which sat beside a second chamber where something small and helpless gibbered in mindless fear—he realized that he also had a thudding erection.

A *stiffie*, as they were called. A *peg-pounder*. A *cunt-corker*. A *bon*—

He saw someone else now. Standing behind Carlene. A bigger shape. Tall. Pale. Kind of pear-shaped.

Playing some kind of musical instrument. A flute, was it?

Cyril was halfway through the razor wire. It was slicing him to ribbons. Who cared? It was good. He would go to Carlene and she would fix him. With her lips and tongue and tits and her perfect pink pussy. Her *love*. More than anything, that's what Cy needed. The love of a good woman. That's why he'd gone wayward. Followed the bad path. But he'd change all that. Him and Carlene together.

Cy jerked his leg. There was a long cold sizzle down his calf, and then that leg was free. He climbed down the other side of the fence. He felt heavy all over: the soddenness of his clothes, sopping with blood, plus a bricklike heaviness of mind. But it would be over soon. It would be fucking beautiful.

He staggered toward Carlene. The lights of Little Heaven reduced until there was no light at all. When he spun, laughing a little, he couldn't see the chapel or bunkhouses. Just that vast darkness peering back at him.

Who gave a flying fuck, anyway? He had Carlene. Jesus, he'd treated her bad, hadn't he? He'd been young. An animal. Could you fault him? Any creature is only the sum of its instincts and interests, right? But Cy could change. She could declaw him. He'd be okay to stand for that now. He'd be a kitten for her. He'd curl right up in her lap.

Dimly, so dimly now, Cyril understood that he was dead. Or he would be soon, in a way he had never imagined. The human mind lacks a capacity to embrace such oddities of fate. He was a mess, woozy as blood leaked out of him from a dozen fleshy rips. He smiled, the dopey grin of a child. But a small, helpless voice, locked in the deepest cells of his brain, continued to scream without ceasing.

And Carlene was *right fucking there*. Just . . . *bam!* Ripe as a plucked peach. The years peeled away and they were both young again. Wouldn't that be just the best? To live forever as you once were, back when you could run half a mile at a dead sprint, drink a six-pack, and then fuck like a rabbit? Yeah, that was the ticket!

She opened her arms. The flute's music rose to a weird pitch that made his ears itch.

"Carlene . . ."

Baby . . .

Carlene's face started to change. To bubble and run and worse things—

Oh, so so much worse.

Which was when Cyril Neeps began to scream for real, and for a long, long time. But of course, not one soul in Little Heaven heard a thing.

30

ELI'S BACK.

Nate awoke lathered in sweat, clutching his belly as if he'd been stabbed. These two words echoed within his mind.

Nate got up. The bunkhouse floor was icy on his bare feet. He went to the window. The moon was a ghost behind a smear of thin night clouds. A security lamp burned weakly; yesterday Nate had overheard that gasoline was running low, so the generators were running at half power.

Wind licked through paper-thin slits around the window frame. Nate shivered. He clenched his jaw. *Stop it. Don't be a baby.* He glanced at his father, who slept with a pinched look on his face.

Distantly, Nate heard the notes of a flute. Thin, high notes that held no melody—more the random, inharmonious notes the wind might make as it blew through a dry reed. Yet there was something compelling about the sound. Frighteningly so.

Nate moved toward the bunkhouse door. He was barely aware he was doing it. His arms were overtaken by the numbness he'd felt when a dentist stuck a needle in his gums before filling a cavity. His hand was wrapped around the doorknob—he looked at his fingers clasping it and thought, *Huh, isn't that weird?*

It took an enormous effort, summoned from a part of his brain he had never accessed, to activate his other hand and hook his fingers to the window frame. Grindingly, teeth set, he dragged himself back to the window. His fingers pulled away from the doorknob, which felt as warm as a penny clutched in a hot fist.

"Daddy . . . ," he whispered in a hoarse rasp. His father did not stir.

Nate stared out at the compound. Just shadows, shifting and swirling . . .

He's back.

Eli Rathbone. Nate saw him. Nate knew it was Eli, even though he didn't look much like his old self. Eli didn't really look human anymore.

The bold strokes were still there, sure. Eli had two arms, two legs. But everything else was *off.* That was one of his mom's pet words. The old man who sat in the public park watching kids play with hungry eyes was *off.* The neighborhood boy who used to walk down the sidewalk after a rainstorm eating every wriggling worm he could find was *off. You know* off *when you see it,* his mom used to say.

Eli Rathbone was naked, his skin white as the chalk dust they spread on the base paths at the ball diamond. He radiated a sick glow, like those deep-sea fish whose bodies produce their own light. He was so skinny now that Nate could see each of his ribs, even the short one at the bottom. His head was just a skull covered in onionskin. His arms were elongated, the arms of an orangutan. He did not seem to walk so much as float—

He ghosted across the compound under the sputtering light of the security lamps. Shadows pooled under his feet—shadows that seemed to bristle with a powerful intensity, like a collection of tiny individual shadows all huddled together.

That flute music zephyred through the air. Each note bristled with an intensity that quilled the hairs on Nate's neck. He wished he hadn't woken up. A helplessness rose up in him, this sense that he and everyone else in Little Heaven had been tricked. Though he could not articulate it, he felt the same way an animal in a snare must feel as the trapper's footsteps approached through the glen.

Eli's head swiveled. His eyes pinned Nate. Eli's eyes were black as tar. Nate felt totally naked, as if his body had been touched with a powerful spotlight. Eli smiled. His teeth were all gone. His skin sagged. It was the smile of a million-year-old infant.

Eli passed out of sight beyond the edge of the bunkhouse that belonged to the Rasmussen family. John and Anna and their daughter, Elsa, who had been nice to Nate when he first showed up. That ended when she started to play the games dreamed up by Eli and the Redhill brothers. All the children had slowly given themselves over to cruelty. It was like watching a sickness spread. And now everyone was infected.

He stood at the window for a span of pulseless seconds. Then he went to his father's bed.

"Dad," he said. "Get up."

He shook his father. His dad's eyes stayed closed, a clenched expression fixed on his face.

"Dad, come on, *please*."

His father mumbled and rolled over. Nate returned to the window. A squalid darkness overhung Little Heaven. Nothing moved. Not a single insect buzzed around the exterior lamps. Then—

They came around the edge of the Rasmussens' bunkhouse.

Eli Rathbone came first, followed by Elsa Rasmussen. Then the Redhill boys, Elton and Billy. Linked hand to hand to hand. Elsa wore pajamas with a pattern of umbrellas. Billy and Elton only wore their underwear, their undeveloped chests pocked in gooseflesh. They did not walk so much as skip, as if they were playing some school-yard game.

One-two, skip to my Lou—skip to my Lou, my darlin' . . .

They passed under the spotlight. They weren't just holding hands—their skin was melted together like sticks of wax heated with a Zippo, then pressed together. An ugly mess of flesh welded into a distended knot. They skipped along, Eli leading, toward a spot in the fence where the darkness collected in a narrow slit.

As one, their heads swiveled in perfect unison to Nate. His groin went tight, then seemed to splinter apart, little terror-spiders scuttling up and down through his body, turning his knees to jelly and shooting pins and needles down his fingertips.

Dreamily, in a state of near-paralyzing horror, Nate backed away from the window. He went to his father again.

"Dad!" he said, finding his voice. "Wake up! *Wake up!*"

Nate's fingers clawed into his father's neck. He shook him as hard as he could. He would sink his teeth into his father's shoulder next—anything to rouse him.

"Wuzza?" his father said, his voice thick with sleep.

"Get up! *GET UP!*"

Reggie sat up. The fear in Nate's voice must have penetrated his fogged brain.

"What, Nate?"

"Come look," he said, hauling on his father's arm. "Please. *Quick.*"

"Nate, what is the matter with you?"

His father gazed at Nate with a look of confused apathy. His father had never been the most independent thinker—after his near-death experience, he'd become fond of phrases like *The Lord's will governs all things*—but now he too often wore this deeply bewildered expression. It made Nate angry: his father had checked his brain at the gates of Little Heaven, which left Nate to make the grown-up decisions.

"Get UP!"

Obediently, Nate's father followed him to the window. Eli and the others were almost out of sight as they skipped into the widening dark.

"Look!" Nate said, pointing.

His father followed Nate's finger. Then his eyes did a funny thing.

They went kind of soapy and retracted into their sockets like a turtle's head tucking into its shell.

"Look at what?"

His voice seemed to come from the corner of the bunkhouse instead of his mouth. Nate gazed at him with a mixture of shock and disbelief.

"That's Eli, Dad. Eli and Elsa Rasmussen and the Redhills, Elton and Billy. Can't you see them, Dad? Right there?"

His father laughed—the laugh of a person desperately trying to find the humor in something that isn't funny at all: a car crash or a public execution or a yellowy old body toppling out of its casket at a funeral.

"There's nothing out there, Nate. You're imagining things."

His father wouldn't look at him. Nate's disbelief shaded into dread as a sinister realization began to dawn on him.

Either his father couldn't actually see what Nate was seeing—some protective part of his brain had switched on, erasing the four gruesome children from his sight . . .

Or else—and this possibility was unspeakably worse—they were seeing the exact same thing, only his father was either too terrified or too cowardly to acknowledge it.

"Oh, Dad. Dad, please—"

"There's nothing out there," his father said robotically. "Not a thing."

A profound desolation settled over Nate. He felt alone in a way he had never thought possible. He might as well be at the farthest reaches of the universe, at the point where all light died.

"Go back to bed, Nate. You're being silly."

His father turned—Nate got the sense of his dad's body as a tightly coiled spring on the verge of snapping. He ruffled Nate's hair. His fingers were hard and his nails too long; it was like being raked with sharp twigs. He lay down on his bed, his back to Nate.

Nate's gaze fled to the window. Eli and the others had vanished. But he could see something in that rip of darkness. Just an outline.

A figure. Far too tall to be human. Long-legged and long-armed, with a giant cask belly. It capered and jigged with evident merriment. Smaller shapes, children-sized ones, danced around it. The discordant melody of the flute cut through the night.

The shape retreated. The smaller shapes followed it into the wooded dark.

31

AMOS FLESHER AWOKE to the sounds of his empire crumbling.

He was unceremoniously hauled out of a contented sleep—a dream where the world was covered with living black oil and he had the only rowboat. The Voice bubbled up from the oil, whispering and hissing . . .

Next: hysterical shouts. Names hollered over and over.

"Elsa! Elsa!"

"Billy! Elton!"

"Oh God! Oh God, it's happened again!"

"*ELLLLLLSAAAAAA!*"

Next: rapping on his door.

"Reverend!"

He opened the door only to be confronted with the agonized faces of several worshippers. Maude and Terry Redhill, the Rasmussens, a few more.

"She's gone!" Anna Rasmussen screamed. "Our baby girl!"

Worshippers were streaming into the square by then, their faces bloated with sleep. The Reverend's mind whirled as he processed the situation, calculating the new configuration of things and finding his own angle within it.

"Calm down," he said. "Tell me what happened."

"She's gone!" Anna Rasmussen screamed, harpyishly. "Our daughter! Her bed was empty this morning!"

"And Billy and Elton's, too," said Terry Redhill.

Amos's mind clicked and ratcheted. "You're telling me—"

"Reverend! They're *gone!*" Maude Redhill spat. "They've been taken just like Eli Rathbone got took!"

Everyone watched the Reverend. Amos was struck by how sick they all looked: their bodies withered, their postures sunken. Their weakness made him ill. His gaze twigged on Reggie Longpre and his son. There was something in their faces he couldn't intuit and didn't entirely care for.

"Have the grounds been searched?" he said. "Every nook, every cranny?"

Nobody spoke. The Reverend sensed their collective uncertainty and needled through that gap.

"Search the compound!" he said. "Everyone, now! They could be hiding somewhere. A game to them."

"It's not a game!" shouted Anna. "They're gone! Taken into the woods! Gone just like Eli and Eli's parents!"

"We don't know that, Sister Rasmussen. I understand that you're—"

"We should have left—all of us! As soon as Eli went missing and then came back . . . came back . . ."

His worshippers' faces reflected a vaporous panic—now laced with a hint of resentment directed toward Amos himself. He must step nimbly here.

"Search the grounds," he said emphatically. "I must confer with the Lord our God, seeking His guidance."

The worshippers reluctantly dispersed. Anna Rasmussen glanced over her shoulder at him—a poisonous, hateful glare. Amos pictured his hands closing around her throat and tightening until her eyes filled with blood . . .

"Cyril's gone, too."

Amos turned to find Virgil Swicker standing beside him.

"What?"

"Cy." Virgil looked spooked. "Can't find him anywhere."

The Reverend's mouth filled with bitter saliva. He could barely contain the nervous energy building inside of him; he wanted to scream to let it free.

"If he's not there, then who is watching the boy?"

Off Virgil's stunned silence, Amos started across the square at a fast clip. He had to restrain himself from breaking into a run. Virgil tagged along on his heels. He reached the bunkhouse where Eli Rathbone was being held. Cyril's chair was empty. Amos took a deep breath and unfastened the padlock.

The bunkhouse was empty. Only the fetid stink of the boy's now absent body remained. Amos closed and locked the door again.

"You keep your mouth shut," he said to Virgil, who nodded in docile assent.

Amos needed a plan. Quickly. He sized up his options.

One, they could abandon Little Heaven. But if the children really were missing, nobody would agree to that with the little bastards still lost in the woods . . .

Two, they could accuse someone of taking all four children. A scapegoat, or scapegoats. By Amos's count, there were two possibilities. He cocked his head, as if to catch the strident bleating of the goats best suited to his purposes—those whose necks could be most easily slit.

"Go to the outsiders' quarters," he said. "Do not let them leave."

A FRANTIC SEARCH ENSUED. The compound was scoured. The children were not found. By the time the worshippers returned to the square, Amos was ready.

"I held palaver with the Lord," he said. "And I heard His Voice, clear and unfiltered."

The faces of the worshippers changed: they went from fearful, perhaps even slightly mistrustful, to enrapt—even that bitch Anna Rasmussen, with her hopeful red-rimmed eyes. They wanted answers. Which was all people like them ever wanted. Any answer at all, so they didn't have to think on their own.

"The evil comes from outside," he said. "From those not pure of heart or spirit. We opened our door to them, as good and God-fearing folk must, and they have repaid our kindness with malice of the deepest and most hateful nature."

He pointed at the bunkhouse shared by the English faggot and the burn-faced woman.

"*Them.* They are the evil that has come as a plague upon us."

This was the smart bet, and the shrewdest move Amos could make under the circumstances. His flock was already suspicious of the outsiders—Cyril and Virgil had overheard their whispers, and filtered them back to him. It would be an easy pill to swallow; they *wanted* to swallow it. He watched their faces. Sweat trickled down his neck and soaked his collar. He had worked hard, so hard, for years to put these people under his yoke. They trusted him . . . or they had until just lately.

One by one their faces began to reflect this. They began to believe. Yes. Of course. The evil lurked, as it always did, in the hearts of men. And the four outsiders had come from far away, bringing a terrible curse with them. They were the devil's Trojan horse. Little Heaven had accepted and sheltered them, only to be poisoned by them. The Reverend's people needed a target to channel their rage and fear into. All Amos had to do was provide one.

"Get them," he said.

EBENEZER OBSERVED the morning's proceedings with a gathering sense of doom.

He'd leapt out of bed when those agonized screams shattered the calm. He landed on both feet. His ankle was quite a bit better. He could put almost his full weight on it. He and Ellen watched people gather in front of the Reverend's place. He opened the door and listened. Ellen was at his elbow.

"Oh God," she whispered when they overheard the Little Heavenites tell the Reverend about the new missing kids. But her nephew was safe. Eb saw the boy standing beside his stoop-shouldered loaf of a father.

Ellen told Eb that she wanted to help with the search of the compound.

"You should, if only to show your empathy," he said. "But I can't go."

"Why not?"

"My ankle."

"You're fine," Ellen said. "You're walking on it now."

"Yes, but I don't want them to know that."

"Why not?"

Ebenezer thought about quoting Sun Tzu but thought better of it. Ellen said, "Fine, do whatever you want," and began to pull her boots on. But then Virgil—the more moronic of the Reverend's two lapdogs— showed up.

"You're not going anywhere," he announced.

"Why not?" said Ellen.

"Reverend's orders."

After that, the compound was searched. The kids were not found. Worshippers rounded back into the square. Ebenezer listened at the shut door, trying to catch what the Reverend was saying.

"I believe this stands to end poorly for us," he said to Ellen.

They watched out the bunkhouse window. The Reverend pointed in their direction. A group of supplicants began to stalk toward them. Next, the door swung open and the denizens of Little Heaven poured in.

A red-faced man rushed Eb. He kicked the man in the knee. The man screamed and twisted aside, but another man steamed in behind him and clocked Ebenezer spang in the face. Jesus! Wasn't very Christian, was it? Ebenezer reeled to see Ellen crushed under a weight of bodies. She was being dragged outside. The man who'd slugged Ebenezer came at him again—big, with a baleful glare in his eyes. The father of the missing girl, Eb was pretty sure. He pinned Ebenezer's arms to his sides; Eb brought a knee up into his gut. Eb felt slightly bad doing so, the man's agonies being what they were. Undeterred, the menfolk of Little Heaven hurled them- selves at him. Ebenezer tagged a few others with solid shots as they rushed him, but ultimately they got him down, hit him until he could taste his own blood, and hauled him into the harsh morning sunshine.

"You took the children," the Reverend said. "The four of you planned it, and the other two executed it. They are holding them now, aren't they? You thought that we wouldn't catch you out? The Lord has laid your plans bare."

"Why would we take them?" Eb spat blood. "That makes no sense. Can't you see that?"

What did these people think they were—a roaming quartet of kidnappers combing the woods for isolated camps so they could poach children? It wasn't logical, but Eb knew logic had a way of dissolving in circumstances like this. Fear and worry ate into reason like acid, making the most ludicrous possibilities seem plausible.

"Oh, but isn't the devil a coy liar?" The Reverend's lips fleered into a manic grin. "The father of lies! Do you think you could prey on our most innocent ones? Did you think the Lord and His humble servants would not strike you down for your vile trespasses?"

"How did nobody hear?" Eb said. "Three kids are gone—"

"*Four*," said the Reverend. "Eli Rathbone is missing again, too."

A strangled moan from somewhere in the crowd at this news.

"Snatched from his bed like the others," the Reverend plowed on. "But you knew that, didn't you?"

"Four kids gone," Eb said, swallowing the blood collecting in the back of his throat, "and nobody heard anything? How could that be?"

The Reverend said, "Satan has his ways. His minions, too."

A voice broke out of the crowd. "Where is Cyril?"

The worshippers peeled back. Otis Langtree stood there, flanked by Charlie Fairweather. They were caked in trail dust, wearing backpacks. Eb figured they had just recently rounded back into the compound.

The Reverend stood stunned, a wristwatch stopped midtick. "What?"

"Cyril," Otis repeated. "Your man."

"You two left the compound," said the Reverend with a leaden swallow. "Isn't that right? You left with the other outsiders. Where did you go?"

"They wanted to get their gear," said Otis. "From their campground. We guided them back. We would've been back sooner, but we got turned around." He bit the inside of his cheek. "Lost all track of time. Hours that neither one of us can account for. Something's gone real screwy in those woods, Reverend."

"And the first thing we noticed coming back is that Cyril, he ain't standing watch over Eli's quarters like he was the other night." Charlie squinted at Amos Flesher—a bold, assessing glance. "Is he still here, Reverend—Cyril, I mean? He anywhere about?"

Weird voltages raced under the Reverend's face. "I . . . He should be—"

Ebenezer watched the scene unfold with keen interest. It was happening fast, but then the balance, when it swung, often did so swiftly—

"Reverend?" said Otis. "If Cyril's not anywhere to be found . . ." A meaningful pause, with a nod to Eb and Ellen. "With all due respect, I think you might have chased the wrong dog here. I'm not certain these are your culprits."

The congregants murmured among themselves. Charlie and Otis were two of the most respected persons at Little Heaven.

Reverend Flesher's eyes went hard. "The Lord has spoken to me, Brother Langtree. These are His words."

Otis's head dropped . . .

No! thought Ebenezer. *Don't let him cow you! Be a man for once in your goddamn life!*

Then, slowly, Otis's head rose again.

Bloody good show! There's the iron in that spine!

"Reverend, I've been with you for many years," Otis said. "I followed you and I'm going to keep on following. But I think this one time you got your signals crossed up."

Another murmur raced through the throng, an electric one this time. Dissent, discord. Ebenezer felt a shifting of the tide—a physical, almost visual swing, like the bubble in a carpenter's level.

"We've been with those other two," said Charlie. "The outsiders. We took them back to their camp, like I said. We left them many miles shy of Little Heaven. But they ain't running away. They aim to return. I don't forecast they should arrive much before dark, if so at all tonight."

"All that's to say, they were nowhere near here last night," said Otis.

"And these two," said Charlie, with a nod at Eb and Ellen. "They been in their bunkhouse all this time, ain't that right?"

The Reverend's face shaded pig-belly pink. Eb could practically see the gears inside his skull burning out in stinking puffs of smoke.

"All things considered, I think Cyril might be your man," said Otis.

"You take that back!" Virgil said tremblingly.

Otis ignored him. "It might not have been Cyril. Snatching four kids right out of their beds, quiet as a whisper? That'd be a tough job for a whole team of men. So . . . it could have been something else."

"What else could it be?" the mother of the missing boys said despairingly.

Charlie shot Otis an angry look. "Nothing," Charlie said. "It's not worth talking about now. We have to search the woods," he went on, not looking at the Reverend.

"In *groups*," Otis stressed. "Four or five people to a search party."

"And if we don't find them by midafternoon, we send a delegation out to get a proper search team," said Charlie. "Helicopters, sniffer dogs, and whatnot."

"I second that idea, Brother Fairweather," said the missing girl's mother. "Oh please, let's do that."

The fathers of the missing children nodded to each other. One of them went over and helped Ellen up. Another man hauled Ebenezer to his feet. There were no apologies—they couldn't quite bring themselves to do that, not in front of the Reverend. That small kindness rendered, the men and their wives headed toward the gates. Otis and Charlie followed behind them.

"We'll pitch in," Ebenezer called after them.

Charlie accepted the offer with a nod. Eb and Ellen began to make their way toward the gates, too. The remaining worshippers stepped aside to let them pass.

"But you can't . . . ," Eb heard the Reverend say.

Only a few had stayed with Reverend Flesher: Doc Lewis, Nate's father, an unidentified man with the carbuncled face of a toad, and the cook.

"The Lord will punish you!" Flesher shouted. "*Take heed, brethren, lest there be in any of you an evil heart of unbelief, in departing from the living God!*" His voice rose to an impotent screech, his face knotted in rage. "The Almighty shall smite you for flouting the word of His earthbound prophet!"

"Oh, shut up, you twat," Ebenezer muttered, and kept going.

32

MICAH AND MINERVA arrived back at Little Heaven with dusk coming on. In the waning light, they could see torches burning between the trees.

"Not again," said Minerva. "Please no."

Their return had been remarkably uneventful. When the morning sun washed over the Preston School, the field lay empty. Maybe the creatures had an aversion to daylight, because they were nowhere to be seen. Micah and Minny hiked through the day, talking little, and made it back in time to hear the shouts ringing out from the woods surrounding the compound. Names being called in hoarse, frightened voices.

They walked through Little Heaven's main gates, which had been left unguarded. Was everyone out in the woods? A generator chugged sluggishly, powering the overhead spots—but Micah couldn't help noticing that the bulbs flickered, blinking out for half a second before burning again. His eye roamed over the compound under the faltering lights, settling on the windowless bunkhouse that the boy Eli had been held in. Neither Cyril nor Virgil was occupying the guard post. He walked over. A busted padlock lay near the door. He turned the knob. The door opened into a small room. The smell was foul. The bed was empty, but there was a gluey stain on the mattress.

"How bad do you figure things are?" said Minerva, joining him.

Micah said, "Bad."

They dropped their packs off at their bunkhouse. Their weapons they kept. Finding nobody about, Micah wandered to the edge of Little Heaven while Minerva changed into fresh clothes.

The children's playground sat forlorn in the dusk. Micah sat on one of the swings and watched the torches bob through the forest. The sky was the red of a blood blister, the sun's final rays pooling behind the trees. He had never been scared of nightfall. Even as a child, he'd welcomed the darkness. But bad things tended to happen at night in Little Heaven. Those same terrible things might happen in the day, too, soon enough. But at least they would be able to see them coming.

Ellen Bellhaven appeared on the other side of the fence. Her clothes were smudged with dirt and sap.

"Hey," she said to Micah.

"Hey."

She entered through the gates and sat on the swing beside him. Her eyes were encircled by dark rings like washers. A goose egg sat high on her forehead.

"Were you hit?" Micah said.

She nodded. Rage flared inside him. She put a hand on his shoulder.

"I'm fine," she said, and related the morning's events. Micah closed his eye and rocked on the swing.

"How many this time?"

"Three children. Two brothers and a little girl," Ellen said. "And Eli's gone again, too. We've been searching all day. I'm worried."

"Yes."

"I can't see things getting any better."

"No."

"This isn't about Nate anymore. We should all get out. Every person here."

"There was a chance we could have. But now . . . the kids."

Ellen nodded. "We can't leave without them. It would be . . ." She sighed. "Hate to use the word, but it would be un-Christian of us."

"The Reverend?"

"I don't know how much power his word holds anymore," Ellen said. "People are scared, Micah. Really, really scared."

Micah felt that fear seeping out of the woods, where all of Little Heaven was searching for those kids. He could almost smell it coming out of Ellen's pores, too. He had known that fear himself, years ago. It was kindling in him again now.

Fear finds a home in you. That was a lesson Micah had learned at some price. It finds the softest spots imaginable and sets up residence. That place behind your knees where the nerves bundle up, buckling them. Inside your lungs, pinching the air out of them. Within your head, spreading like fungus. Fear will make you abandon those you care for, even those you claim to love—the people you tell yourself you'd save, sacrificing your body for theirs, if it ever came to that. And hypothetically, yes, you would . . . at least in those dream scenarios we all concoct. The burning houses, the crazed gunmen. You'd risk that heat or take that bullet. In a man's fantasies, he always does the right thing.

But sometimes a man must face the absolute reality of his fear. And he'll discover that terror can chew him up and turn him into something else. A monster of wrath, or of cowardice. That man finds himself inhabiting the skin of a total stranger . . . except not really. It is the creature he becomes in the pressure cooker. Fear can warp a man. Turn him into a repellent specimen whom he never thought he could be, not in a million years.

Micah knew. He'd seen it. He'd lived it.

In the summer of 1953, a month before the war ended, Micah had found two American soldiers torturing a Korean POW. The incident was being overseen by Captain Luker Beechwood, Micah's commander. Beechwood was the classic southern dandy. The sort of man whose father drank sweet tea on the porch of the plantation manor where his forebears had had their slaves whipped in the dooryard.

The POW was a kid, eighteen. He was strapped to a chair with baling twine inside an isolated shack on the edge of their encampment. The soldiers were busily cutting pieces of skin off his chest and arms. The POW's trousers were soaked with blood, and snot was bubbling out of his nose.

"We're just letting some air into him, Private," Captain Beechwood told Micah.

The soldiers were from Micah's unit. One was Lyle Sykes. Fat, suffering from trench foot. He had a furtive and rattish air despite his girth. He was the sort of soldier whose skull you considered clandestinely putting a bullet into, out of the sense that he was somehow more dangerous than the enemy. Declan Hooper was the other man. A good egg. Micah was not surprised to see Sykes at the scene of this atrocity, but Hooper was a shock.

A sack sat at Captain Beechwood's feet. Inside, Micah caught the gleam of wire cutters, a hammer, some nails. The air was hot inside the shack, filled with the reek of blood.

Micah said: "This is not to code."

Micah was twenty. He had grown up rough, and by then had done some rough business himself. But what was happening in the shack had nothing to do with the war. Micah understood that Beechwood and the other two men could have as easily done the same to a US soldier if they thought they could get away with it.

"Private Shughrue," Beechwood said in his plummy southern twang, "this man has information of a vital nature. We are simply endeavoring to extract it."

Micah regarded them. Sykes, beefy and beady-eyed. Hooper, looking like a boy caught filching dimes from his mother's purse. But what Micah recalled powerfully was a personal dryness: his own fear leeched the moisture out of his eyes and nose and mouth, his veins running thick as if his blood had been mixed with flour.

"You cannot," he said more firmly.

Beechwood smiled. "We *are*, and we *will*."

With that, Micah hit his CO in the face. Beechwood's nose cracked and he fell back with a squawk. The Korean soldier moaned. Hooper and Sykes came on next, clouting Micah with closed fists. Micah fought back, but one of them clipped his chin and sent him crashing to the ground. Beechwood had recovered by then. They all put it to him, stomping his skull with their heavy mud-caked boots.

"Enough," Beechwood announced, panting. "We'll kill him. Can't get away with that."

They dragged Micah to the brig, where he was imprisoned for assaulting his commanding officer. One month in a lightless cell, fed bread teeming with lice. By the time he got out, Captain Beechwood and the others had shipped out. He never knew what became of the Korean soldier.

Once home, Micah nursed fantasies of hunting Beechwood down and doing to his former commander what Beechwood had done to the Korean. But Micah's tendency to square the scales was not so strong then. And anyway, some part of him understood the impulse. The three of them had been scared deep in their souls. Fear manifested in terrible ways, especially during wartime. It shows a man the face he didn't know he had. Later Sykes and Hooper might have been remorseful—Hooper especially—waking with nightmares about what they had done. Beechwood, probably not. All men are built to different tolerances. Put in identical straits, they react differently. And those who act rightly despite that crawling fear cast shame upon those who cave in to it.

Quite simply, you never really know what type of person you are. Micah understood that now. A man never can tell which side of the line he lives on. He will exist forever ignorant until that moment—ruinous and unflinching—when he is forced to confront his hidden inner self.

"Did you get everything from the camp?" Ellen asked, snapping Micah back to the present. Off Micah's nod, she said, "Any problems?"

"We saw something."

"What?"

"Some . . . creatures" was all Micah could say.

"Animals?"

"Not quite."

He could tell she was about to launch into a barrage of questions about their encounter. Tiredly, he held his hand up to stop her.

"They could be dangerous," he said. "That is the key point. They may have followed us back . . . or they have been here all along."

"Did they attack you?"

He shook his head. "Not yet."

"Not *yet*?"

How could he frame it? That those things had seemed more like prison guards than attack dogs? He didn't want to talk about it. Or about the Preston School, either—both he and Minerva felt it would sow deeper fear within a group that was already crippled with it.

Ellen said, "I made something for you."

She reached into her pocket and came out with three small glass balls.

"They're eyes," she said. "I made them in the glassworks."

"You did not have to do that."

"Nobody *has* to do anything, Micah. I did it because I wanted to. I tried to match the shade." She peered into his eye. "I think I got pretty close. Go on. Try one."

He took one from her palm. It looked like a marble, except with a credible human eye structure at its center. He reached for his eye patch . . . then hesitated.

"It is not pretty," he said.

"I don't imagine so." She feathered her burn scar with the fingers of her free hand. "At least yours can be covered up."

He took the patch off. His empty socket had some lint in it, same as what collects in a belly button. He swabbed it out and tried to pop the glass eye into his socket. It wouldn't fit.

"Wait a sec," said Ellen.

She went to the pump and returned with a bucket of water. She dipped the eye and handed it back. The wet eye still didn't fit. It was too big.

She handed him another one. "They're slightly different sizes."

He dipped the second eye in the water. This one slipped past his eyelid and into his socket. He could feel it bumping around.

"Too small."

"Aha, it's like the three bears," she said. "Porridge too hot, porridge too cold." She held up the third and last eye. "Let's hope this one's just right."

Micah winked; the second eye popped out of his socket. He tried the last one. It fit pretty well.

"Let's take a look," Ellen said. "It's . . . hmmm, it's drifting left. I'll center it."

She put her finger on the eye. Micah felt it move.

"There." She clapped. "Perfect. You look like less of a desperado now. You can get a square john job after this. A cashier, a bank teller."

Now Micah smiled. "Those would suit me fine."

He could picture it. The little house in the burbs, the white picket fence. The nine-to-five. Ellen was part of it, too. A goofy fantasy, but still, he could see it.

"Can I ask?" he said, touching his face—the spot where Ellen's was burned.

She faced away from him. Had he spoken out of turn?

"A bold ask, Mr. Shughrue," she said.

She remained silent for a spell. Then she faced him and said, "When someone can no longer scare you into doing what they want you to do . . . well, let's just say they resort to other tactics."

She pumped her legs and started to swing. Her eyes did not leave his own.

"You don't know how bad someone is sometimes," she said. "Because at first, none of that badness is evident. It's all goodness—or, if not outright goodness, then at least nothing especially cruel. That's my problem. I like guys with an edge. But there's edge and then there's *edge*, and when I was younger, I couldn't tell the difference. My sister's the same way."

She pumped her legs harder. The swing carried her up and down. The hinges squeaked.

"So when you finally see that badness, Micah, you're kind of wed to it. That badness doesn't want to let you go. And it gets angrier and angrier that you won't bend to it the way it thinks you should. It's pissed that you aren't scared of it anymore. So it tries to make you scared again. Any old way it can."

"Uhhh . . . ," said a voice behind them. "Hey."

Micah craned his neck to see Ellen's nephew, Nate. Ellen dragged her feet through the dirt, bringing the swing to a stop.

"What are you doing here?" she said. "Isn't someone watching you kids?"

"I snuck away."

Ellen said, "God, Nate. Someone has to know where you are at all times."

Nate sawed his forearm across his nose. "Sorry."

Ellen went over to him. Hugged him fiercely. The boy didn't protest.

"I'm sorry I didn't say anything this morning," he said. "When . . . when they dragged you and the other man out of your house."

"Like what?" Ellen said. "What could you have said?"

Nate breathed in and let it out in a shivering exhale. He mumbled something too garbled for Micah to understand.

"What did you say?" said Ellen.

"I said, I saw them last night. Eli and Elsa and the Redhills."

The story poured out of the boy. He told them that Eli had come back last night. Nate had seen the four children daisy-chained together, hand to hand. Something about flute music from the woods—*that* detail raised the short hairs on the back of Micah's neck. Nate's last sight of the children was of them dancing around some enormous shape that the boy could not name.

"Do I sound crazy?" Nate asked when he was done.

Ellen said, "No, you don't sound crazy. Not at all."

Micah did not know how to take Nate's story, though it was clear the boy believed it. But then the thing he had glimpsed at their old campsite the other night wasn't believable, either—and it had been real enough.

"Did you tell your father?" Micah asked.

The boy's chest hitched. "He didn't see anything. Or . . . I don't know, maybe he couldn't. He said I was imagining it. That there was nuh-nuh-*nothing*."

Ellen hugged Nate again. "We believe you, Nate. Okay?"

Nate sucked back snot. He had nearly cried, but then he hadn't.

"We're going to get out of here," Ellen said. "This place? Little Heaven? We're done with it. We'll take as many people as want to go with us. Your dad, too. Hike back, get in our car, and drive someplace for a burger and fries and a chocolate milkshake. A real pig-out. Sound like a plan?"

"Uh-huh."

"How about it, Micah? Sound like a good plan to you?"

Whether it was a good plan or not, Micah wasn't sure she should promise the boy anything.

Otis and Charlie appeared at the fence. Their faces were etched with defeat.

"Good to see you back," said Otis wearily. "No further troubles?"

"No," Micah told him.

"Glad to hear it. Like the new eye, too. It humanizes you."

"Hey," Ellen chided. "He looked plenty human before."

Otis's shrug was noncommittal. "Charlie and I are leaving tonight with Terry Redhill. Time to get the police. Get some real help. We should have done it days ago, I guess."

"We're taking the truck, Micah," said Charlie. "Fastest way. Will you come with us?"

33

FORTY-FIVE MINUTES LATER, they were set to depart.

Darkness bled over the compound. The search had been called off. Only the Rasmussens were still looking; they had broken away from their search party, moving deeper into the woods—just like the Rathbones had done. And the Rathbones had never come back.

The remaining denizens of Little Heaven assembled to see the pickup truck off. They were worn and fearful, their faces showing little hope. The Reverend was nowhere in sight.

Charlie and Otis sat in the cab of the truck, Terry Redhill in the bed. "We'll drive to the river," Otis told everybody, speaking over the idling engine. "If it's running low enough to cross, we'll take the truck over. If not, we hike the rest of the way."

Charlie spoke next. "We can make it down in three-odd hours in the truck. If we have to hike, maybe a day. We'll tell the police. They'll send helicopters and sniffer dogs. The whole shebang."

Charlie's wife and son stood beside the truck. Both looked worried. Maude Redhill hopped up on the tailgate and gave her husband a kiss. Her eyes were bloodshot and her face blotchy, as if she had been crying nonstop for hours.

"Please be careful," she said. "I've already lost enough today."

"Not lost," Terry said. "Just missing. We'll find them. God will see to it."

"Are you sure you won't come?" Charlie asked Micah.

Micah approached the truck. He spoke low so nobody could hear. "Those things. They might have followed us back."

Otis bit his lip. "You think so?"

Micah said, "There is a passing chance."

"How many?"

"I could not tell you."

"Do you think they'll attack?"

Micah met Otis's question with a shrug. Charlie and Otis conferred. The truck's diesel engine ticked along, blurring out their voices.

"Here's the thing," Otis said finally. "There may be more of those things out *there.*" He pointed down the road they would be driving. "And if we don't get past them and down the hill—well then, everyone here is in real trouble."

"What about Minerva and the black fella you came with?" Charlie asked. "That one seems a pretty icy character."

Micah glanced over his shoulder. Minerva stood fifty yards back from the group. Ebenezer leaned against the door to their bunkhouse, much farther away.

"Couldn't they do something if those things tried to get past the gates—I mean, if you go with us now?" Charlie said.

Micah figured they could, if compelled to. Minerva for sure; Ebenezer was a fifty-fifty proposition—but if those abominations invaded Little Heaven, Ebenezer would have to fight them as a matter of survival.

"We need you," Otis said simply.

Micah glanced back at Ellen. She stood beside Nate, their shoulders nearly touching. She nodded as if to give permission.

"Give me that scattergun," he said to Charlie.

Charlie handed an Ithaca pump-action through the window, along with a box of shells. Micah hopped up on the bed beside Terry Redhill. He distributed the shells between his pockets, then jammed two into his mouth, storing them in either cheek—he looked like a chipmunk hoarding nuts. He slapped his palm on the roof.

"Go."

They set off down the dirt path. Dark lay heavy between the trees. Otis flicked on the high beams. The firs shone whitely under their light, as if they were composed of bone instead of wood. Terry Redhill crouched in the bed beside Micah. A big man with a thick red beard. Pinpricks of sweat stood out on his forehead.

The truck prowled along at five miles an hour. The chassis juddered over rocks and stumps. Drool collected in Micah's mouth; he removed one shell, spat, then jammed it back in. It was a trick he'd learned during the war; the company sniper always kept one cartridge in his mouth.

It's the quickest way to get at it, he'd told Micah. *Always have one bullet in your mouth for when you really need it.*

Little Heaven receded. Otis flicked on the dome light as he nudged the truck down a steep slope; its knobby tires stuttered over the shale, differentials squealing. Micah and Terry leaned against the cab as the truck tilted downward. The headlights pointed directly at the road, throwing the fringing forest into inky blackness—

Micah saw it before anyone else, but even he caught it too late. It flared from the left-hand side, his bad side, streaking out of the trees and hammering into the truck. A huge shape rocked the truck on its axles, the driver-side wheels temporarily leaving the ground. Micah tumbled into Terry Redhill, who barely managed to stay in the bed. Charlie let out a muffled shout; Otis hit the gas as the truck slewed sideways, fishtailing toward the pines. Micah cast a glance through the cab's rear window and saw the driver-side door was dented inward. Otis's femur was punched through the fabric of his Carhartts at midthigh, a spike of bone shining deliriously white in the dome light. Otis's face was bleached and greasy with shock and—with the calm observation that always came to Micah in times like this—he could see that Otis's foot was pinned to the gas pedal.

The truck accelerated and struck a knotty pine. Micah was thrown against the cab. He ricocheted back, skidding across the bed until his head hit the tailgate. Terry Redhill fell over the side of the truck with a hoarse squawk. The engine cut out, its *tick-tick* dimming into the nothingness. Out of that enveloping silence came other sounds. Grunts and howls and brays and hisses.

Terry Redhill stood up woozily. His face was bathed in blood from a cut running slantwise across his forehead.

"Whuzzat?" he said dazedly. "Whuzz—?"

Micah didn't get a good look at the thing that killed Terry Redhill. There was some mercy in that. It darted down from the trees. Part snake, part bird or bat or some winged creature at any rate. It carried with it the ripe stink of death. Micah did catch a glimpse of eyes—a dozen or more bunched like grapes within the runneled ruin of its face, or one of its faces—all staring with bright, malignant hunger. It flapped down with a sort of breezy insouciance, not at all predatory, as if it had merely happened upon Terry Redhill by accident and decided to do what it did to him.

It . . . it *enfolded* Terry. Somehow lovingly. Terry's head, specifically. Those sheer, dark, bat-like wings wrapped around his skull in a suffocating embrace.

"Whuzz—?"

What happened next was hard to explain. The scene was chaotic, the light thin, the air swimmy with diesel fumes from the ruptured gas tank. Micah was aware of the smallest details—the oily taste of the shotgun shells in his mouth, the thin fingernail paring of the moon through the trees. He experienced the following events with senses that were super-attuned in some ways and dulled in others. Later, he would suspect his mind had done so automatically, shielding him from things that would have driven him mad on sight.

The thing that was wrapped around Terry Redhill's head began to flex. To *constrict*. The whiplike cord upon which it had unfurled from the tree thinned with tension. Terry issued terrible choking sounds that were muffled by the stinking flesh draped over his face—flesh so sheer Micah could see the man's pain-wrenched features. Those muffled chokes quickly became squeals.

The thing tensed, every part of its awful musculature quivering; then it torqued spastically—it reminded Micah of a man struggling to open a stubborn jar of strawberry jam, that moment when the seal finally gives. This was followed by a wet ripping note. A fan of blood jetted from Terry Redhill's neck with incredible pressure and painted the side of the truck.

The thing ascended into the tree again. It took Terry's head with it. The whole thing happened in a matter of seconds. Terry's body stood there for another moment, blood fountaining from the raggedly severed neck, before collapsing to its knees like a penitent Pentecostal. Headless Terry fell forward and struck the truck with a hollow *bong*.

Something rushed from the trees at Micah. He caught the briefest inkling of its shape: a trio of timber wolf heads thrust from a long and eelish body rippling with legs of all different sorts. He raised the shotgun and fired as it hurdled Terry Redhill's corpse; buckshot tore into the thing, ripping away gobbets of flesh; the impact steered it off course so that, instead of hitting Micah flush, it glancingly struck him, one of its claws or teeth tearing across his rib cage to leave a sizzling note of pain. He fell, his skull striking the tailgate and shooting stars across his vision. The thing carried over the truck bed, a horrifying freight train of legs and snouts and snapping jaws.

Micah staggered up and took aim as it retreated, pumping the Ithaca and firing three shots. The muzzle exploded with flame, illuminating the woods in brief flashes. A chunk blew off the thing's hide, splattering the side of a ponderosa pine. It squealed and reared—the sinuous segmented movement of a snake sitting up, its spinal cord popping like chained firecrackers—as it moved deeper into the forest. Much else lurked there in the trees, slavering and snapping.

"Otis! Oh God, *Otis!*"

Charlie was trying to haul his friend out of the truck. Charlie's nose must've broken when his face collided with the windshield; it was squashed off to one side, blood painting the bottom of his face. But Charlie was focused on Otis, who was trapped. The crumpling door had not only broken his leg high up—it had also pinned his foot. Otis's face was tallowy with shock. Slick balls of sweat rolled down his cheeks. The pain was such that he'd vomited; under the fritzing dome light, Micah could see chunks of that evening's hastily eaten meal on his shirt.

"Otis!" Charlie hauled on his friend's arm, too terrified to be gentle about it. "We got to get out."

Otis's eyes rolled back in his skull. A ludicrous half smile graced his face. Micah had seen it before. Pain, shock, and adrenaline can put a man into a beatific dream state.

"Come *on!*" Charlie jerked Otis, who shook like a rag doll. Blood shot from the compound fracture and spritzed the dashboard.

Something thumped off the truck's roof and bounced into the bed. Terry Redhill's head. Terry's lips had been bitten away—*such clean, straight teeth*, Micah thought with dreamy panic; *he must have had a good dentist*—and his eyeballs had been sucked out. Half his scalp had been peeled back like a stubborn toupee, from the rear of his skull to the front; gravity folded it down as Micah watched, a vein-threaded red curtain draping Redhill's ruined face.

Micah fired up into the tree from where the head had fallen. He heard a rippling shriek up there. He saw something latched around the trunk thirty feet up—a jumble of parts, long and arachnid, a sight a human mind couldn't even summon in a nightmare. Seeing its shape in the muzzle flash, Micah felt as if someone had levered the top off his skull and whispered directly into the twitching gray matter—a terrible secret that he would have to live with the rest of his life. The thing unfurled with effortless grace, its blood pattering down on the truck as it scuttled farther up the tree.

Micah spat the saliva-coated shells into his palm and plugged them into the shotgun. He hopped over the bed. He could die here. In a second, a minute, or anytime between. That fact bestowed an eerie calm within him. This was the world as he'd found it. His only option was to deal with its new parameters.

"Charlie!" Micah shouted, grabbing the man's shoulder. Charlie turned to face him; his face swam with mindless fear. "He is stuck!" Micah said. "We must free his leg."

Charlie's mouth opened and closed like a fish dying on land. But he nodded. "Okay, okay, okay, okay—"

Micah handed him the shotgun. "They are everywhere."

He climbed inside the cab through the passenger door. It was hot and tight and perfumed with blood and diesel. The windshield was spider-webbed where Charlie's head had struck. Micah glanced past Otis, out the window, where shapes were massing some twenty yards off.

"Otis, sit tight," Micah said, as if the man had any other choice. "This is going to hurt."

Otis issued a garbled note that Micah took as one of recognition. He crawled down into the foot well. Wires hung from the busted fuse box. He wormed past Otis's right foot, shoving it rudely aside; Otis screamed as the pain shot up his leg. Micah didn't apologize; there was no time. He squirmed forward until he was able to close his hand around Otis's boot, pinned under the buckled metal. He wrapped his fingers through the bootlaces and yanked as hard as he could. Otis screamed afresh. Micah couldn't summon much force with his body at a bad angle, one arm partially trapped under his chest. But he was redlined on adrenaline and this helped. Otis just kept on screaming. *Let it out, friend*, Micah thought. *Maybe it'll keep those things at bay.*

One hard wrench succeeded in popping Otis's heel out; Micah let out a small cry of delight as Otis's boot slid from the crimped metal. He just had to crawl his fingers in a little farther and yank his toes out now—

Charlie screeched. The shotgun boomed.

Something crashed through the windshield above Micah. The dome light dimmed. Next something was inside the cab with them. Micah felt its weight, heavy as several anvils, pressing down on the steering wheel. It poured itself through the shattered glass, thick and black and alive with horrifying industry. In Micah's fractured view, it resembled nothing more than a ball of parts: the most dangerous and vile bits of every beast and bird and reptile that had once inhabited these woods. Teeth and claws and fangs dripping venom—and eyes. Oh Christ, all the *eyes*. Some of those eyes spotted Micah. Parts of the thing's lunatic anatomy oriented on him, hissing and rasping, darting down. But he was under the steering wheel, which provided a barrier; he could see things squirming around the wheel, their mouths inches from his face. One of the thing's limbs hit the horn; it blatted on and on, a high curious note.

The thing was more interested in Otis. He'd stopped screaming, now face-to-face with it. Otis's lips trembled as he called out, oh so weakly, for his God.

Then the thing attacked. Otis might as well have walked into a garbage disposal. His face was shredded, legs jittering crazily as he was torn to bits. Blood burst forth and sheeted down, a veritable waterfall of the red stuff splattering Micah's face.

Micah heeled himself across the foot well toward the passenger door. He heard Charlie scream as he pumped the shotgun.

Nonononono—

BOOM.

The cab filled with noise and light and smoke. Micah's hearing cut out from the blast; his skull filled with a tinny ringing. The thing attacking Otis jerked as the buckshot riddled it, but it didn't stop. It hardly mattered. It had torn the first three inches off Otis's head, which now stopped at his ears: a clean cliff of red meat and cartilage, his jaw hanging cock-eyed on a strip of sinew.

Charlie fired again. The thing squalled and retreated, shimmying out of the hole in the windshield. Micah levered himself out of the cab and staggered back, slumping into Charlie.

The thing that had killed Otis was sprawled across the truck's hood. Twelve feet long, thick around as a trash can. It scuttled backward, its movement more insectoid than animal, claws screaming on the hood.

Micah grabbed the shotgun from Charlie and fired. The first shot blew a hole in the thing's face. The next shot went into its chest. The thing slumped off the hood, still thrashing and not even close to dead.

Micah turned and started back toward Little Heaven—then tripped over Terry Redhill's corpse where it slumped against the truck. He went down, snuffled dirt, and spotted the gun tucked in Redhill's waistband. He grabbed it and gave it to Charlie.

"Go."

Charlie was staring at Otis. At his friend's dripping carcass.

"He is dead, Charlie. *Now,* or we are dead, too."

Dazedly, Charlie followed. Micah pulled shells from his pocket and thumbed them into the shotgun. The truck's horn blared on and on. He and Charlie staggered away from the wreck. Its taillights winked in the dark. Micah noted the rip in his shirt. A five-inch slit across his ribs, the meat flayed open.

The two of them scrambled up the slope to the main road. Little Heaven was five hundred yards off. They hadn't even made it half a mile.

Charlie stumbled. Micah grabbed his hand. Charlie was in shock. Even having glimpsed those things the other night, Charlie could not wrap his head around what they had done to Terry Redhill and his dear friend Otis.

Partner, it is happening, Micah thought as he hauled Charlie on.

The road peeled away from the trees, bathed in creamy moonlight. The night bristled with sounds, but they had dimmed to a low and satisfied purr.

"Otis," Charlie mumbled. "Oh no, oh no, *Otis*—"

Something streaked out of a dogwood thicket behind them—a liquid ripple of movement. It passed behind Micah almost soundlessly, an enormous bird zipping low across the earth. He tried to look at it, but a warning klaxon went off in his brain—*Danger, Will Robinson!*—that kept his head from making the necessary revolution.

Charlie grunted like a man who'd been punched in the gut. His hand—no, his whole arm—dropped three feet. He'd fallen again.

"Come on, Charlie," Micah said.

Charlie wouldn't get up this time. Micah had to haul Charlie across the ground. Charlie's fingers tightened and cut off Micah's circulation.

"I got you."

Charlie wasn't so hard to pull now. Light as a feather, in fact. Must be the adrenaline kicking in. Little Heaven was getting closer. Micah would haul Charlie back and make new plans. A daylight run when they could see the fuckers coming.

Charlie's fingers began to relax. Micah clenched his own and pulled him another five feet before Charlie's belt got hung up on a root or some other snag.

"Jesus, Charlie. Help me."

Micah turned to look. Charlie wasn't there—the bottom half, anyway. His body had been torn apart at the hips. His legs were gone; Micah couldn't see them anywhere. Charlie's guts spilled out of his chest cavity, long ropes with a whitish-blue sheen that trailed ten yards behind him until they blended into the gloom. His face was set in an expression of awestruck shock: eyes wide open, lips peeled back from his teeth.

"Come on," Micah said stupidly. "It will be okay." He pulled until Charlie's halved body became unstuck from the snag. He kept hauling Charlie mindlessly, his brain stuck in a time warp where Charlie was still alive. Charlie's remains made a graceless burping sound as another knot of intestines drooled out and unraveled across the cracked earth.

Micah's strength was deserting him; he was now using the shotgun as a cane. "Okay . . . we are going to be okay, Charlie . . ."

Let him go, Micah. He is dead.

With a moan, Micah did. Charlie's arm flopped to the ground. Micah staggered on. Fuck the things that had killed these men. Micah would murder them all and burn their carcasses until the air went black with their smoke.

A DOZEN OR SO PEOPLE were clustered at the gates of Little Heaven. The truck's horn continued to blare. Seeing Micah alone, Maude Redhill let loose a desolate wail. She was joined by Charlie's wife; Charlie's son only stared at Micah openmouthed, not yet gripping what had happened—he was too young to understand that, yes, everything really could go to shit just this quickly.

The gates closed once Micah had shuffled through. His face was wet with blood—Otis's or Terry's or Charlie's, he had no clue. He crumpled to his knees as two dozen eyes stared at him, waiting on some kind of explanation.

"It is death out there" was all he could manage.

Maude Redhill flung herself on him. She grabbed double handfuls of hair and yanked viciously, snapping his head side to side. Micah let her do it, too tired to fight back and feeling that she deserved her wrath.

"Bastard!" she screamed. "What did you do to them? What did you do to my *Terryyyyyyyy!*"

Somebody finally pulled her off. Maude Redhill's sobs spiraled up into the night.

God did not hear her. Or if He did, He kept His peace.

The devil had come to Little Heaven.

PART FIVE

JOURNEY TO THE BLACK ROCK

1980

1

THEY PASSED THROUGH several villages unseen and unheard, skirting settlements like coyotes on the lope. The Long Walker carted Petty Shughrue swiftly over great distances. She wondered what had become of the preacher back at the carnival. How badly did the townspeople hurt him? The Long Walker hadn't even seemed all that delighted when those men started to beat the preacher down. It had actually looked bored.

The Long Walker carried them up a hillside and across the narrow spine of a ridge. Petty could not help but notice how the plants wilted wherever the thing passed. A trail of death.

The ridge fed down to a grassy valley. A faint prickling of light between the trees. They came upon an isolated shack. Smoke spindled from a flue in its roof. Firelight cut between the chinking of its logs. Skins were tacked to hide stretchers near the door.

The Long Walker's posture was loosey-goosey, shoulders rounded forward and head hanging between its shoulders. Its fingers twitched at the ends of its hands as if in search of some more spirited pursuit.

"Is someone out there?" came a man's voice from inside the shack. "I can hear you."

From inside, there came the popping of knots in the fire. After that, the unmistakable cocking back of a shotgun's hammers.

"I will ask once more. Then I must assume you mean to cause harm. Who the hell is out there?"

Finally, the Long Walker opened its mouth—its terrible, skull-spanning mouth. In the moonlight, Petty could see its insides: the soft, pulpy flesh of a toothless infant.

"*It is your mother, Cedric Finnegan Yancy!*" the Long Walker cried in a voice that could not be its own—this was the shrill tone of a woman. "*Will you not come out to greet me?*"

Silence. Then a trembling voice: "That ain't you, Ma. You're dead, God rest your soul. You been dead eight years now."

"*And whose fault is that?*" the Long Walker said, its lips spreading in a corrosive grin. "*Who left his mother when she was just getting sick? Whose departure quickened his mother's path to the grave?*"

When the man finally replied, it was in a tone of disbelief. "What devil lurks past my door?"

"*Devil?*" The Long Walker laughed. "*Devil! Ha! My own son, flesh of my flesh. Come outside, boy. Apologize to your mother. For your sins are plentiful, as we both know. The whoring we may set aside, for what man has not fallen afoul of the pleasures of the flesh? But to leave your own mother, who cradled you and kissed your scraped knees—to leave her alone to die? This, my son, is a sin most unforgivable.*"

"They sent me to 'Nam!" the man shrieked. "I was given no choice in the matter!"

"*I died in pain greater than you could imagine.*" The Long Walker spoke in a crooning singsong. "*My body rotted from the inside. The sawbones cut my tits off—the same tits you latched to as an infant to suckle and bite—yes, bite, for you were a cruel nurser. Where did the doctor toss my diseased old tits? To the dogs, for all I know. Nobody was there to speak for me. My husband dead, my ungrateful son gone and run off. I screeched and bled night after night. Nobody cared. Nobody came to help me.*"

"Please." The man's voice was choked, pleading. "Ma, *please*."

"*My cunty rotted out, Cedric,*" the Long Walker said matter-of-factly. "*Everything that had gone off inside of me came right out, slicker than snot on a doorknob. But it was slooooooow. It took months. I lay there for hours in my own shit and ruin. I died alone, all alone.*"

A thundering *BOOM!*—

A ragged hole punched through the shack door, splinters spitting in every direction. Lead shot whizzed past mere inches from Petty's ear, so close that it sent her hair fluttering.

The Long Walker advanced. The door opened without it even touching the handle, as if blown open by a mammoth gust of wind. The Long

Walker's body expanded, the flaps of its duster billowing, then shrank again to fit through the doorway. It dragged Petty inside with it.

The shack was lit by a kerosene lantern. A fire guttered in a potbellied stove. Animal skins cured on the walls. The man was big and self-sufficient by the looks of it, with a graying beard. He was jacking shells into his double-barreled shotgun as the Long Walker came in.

"Oh God," the man said, dropping the gun. "Oh no . . ."

He curled up in the corner and covered his face with his hands and shook. He had lived in these inhospitable woods with the howling of wind and wolves, yet he had been reduced to a child at the mere sight of this thing.

"Go away," he pleaded. "Please just go away."

The creature seemed even bigger within these confines, its milky skull brushing the roof. A coldness wept off its body, particular to creatures that live at the bottom of the ocean. It crossed the shack, passing the man where he sat mewling, to a tool rack on the wall. Knives and other sharp implements for the flensing, puncturing, and skinning of animal carcasses.

The Long Walker selected one seemingly at random—but Petty could tell that this thing never acted randomly. Its every gesture served some terrible purpose. The knife was fingerling thin. The blade was pitted and rusty, but its edge was sharp—and it became keener, more *glittery*, when the thing took possession of it, as though the Long Walker's touch conferred a deeper refinement of its purpose. The Long Walker ran the edge along its fingers. The blade slit its tissue cleanly, but no blood welled: its flesh was flawless porcelain clean through to whatever bone might have lurked at its core.

"Vivisection," it said. "Is this word familiar to you, my Pet?"

Petty shook her head. The Long Walker flirted the blade over its fingers.

"Oh yes," it said. "Sometimes it is the only way."

The Long Walker hunched before her with its arms hugged round its knees, the knife's tip touching the oiled dirt floor. Its posture did almost nothing to change the sweeping size of its body. Its eyes were very strange indeed. To Petty they resembled Christmas tree ornaments but darker, more secretive—and she could see things moving behind them, their shadows held by the lamp.

"To know something—to truly *know* that thing—you must open that thing up."

The man continued to moan. More than anything in the world, Petty wanted to run away, to run and keep running even if that meant she would be alone in the woods. She had an overwhelming sense that the Long Walker was going to show her things soon. Open her eyes to wonderments she could go several lifetimes without ever knowing.

"The only way to understand anything is to see what makes it tick." The Long Walker exposed its toothless gums. "Tick. Tick. Tick." It held the knife by its handle and let the blade swing side to side like the pendulum on a clock. "To see how those things fit together, yes? To expose the soft and delicate parts."

"You already know how they fit together," said Petty.

The Long Walker shook its head. "Each is subtly different, my Pet. And it is these subtleties that intrigue."

She could see that it was excited for what was to come. Its skin jumped with anticipation. Yet mixed in with that excitement was a strain of deep tiredness, as if it had done this exact thing so often that the act had long ago surrendered any enjoyment. Seeing this, Petty felt a weird pity for the thing.

Wretchedly, the man asked: "Am I in hell?"

The Long Walker hung its head between its shoulders. The knife moved from one of its hands to the other, never stopping, as if the blade was white-hot to the touch.

"Hell is a box," it said to the man. "Yes, it is. Hell is a box not much bigger than your own body. It is dark inside the box, and cold, but the encasement is thin—so thin that you can almost convince yourself that you can break out if you only tried. You cannot feel anything inside this box. But you can hear and . . . sense, to a certain extent. Outside of that box is everyone you ever loved. All the people you have cared for and who care for you. And they are in agony. You cannot touch them. They are screaming, calling for you—your name is always upon their lips. And you cannot go to them or comfort them in any way. And that is your hell, friend. Hell is a box."

The knife's handle danced along its knuckles, a neat trick. The shadows thickened and the lamp's light bled low.

"What I have for you is not hell," the Long Walker told the man. "But for a brief while, it may feel something like it."

2

THEY DROVE EAST in the lightening day. Micah had rented a Cadillac Coupe DeVille. White leather seats, mahogany dash, A/C, crimson trim, quadraphonic stereo system with an eight-track player. Its big-bore V-8 purred. It wasn't the sort of vehicle he would normally drive, but it suited his doomsday demeanor. No use saving for a rainy day when your days were numbered.

"You never moved far away, did you?" Minerva said from the backseat.

Micah said, "It is where we settled. Ellen wanted it."

"That close? Practically living in the shadow of it?"

Micah said, "Somebody had to."

They followed the road, letting it pull them back to the source. It felt almost like driving back through time: the last fifteen years washing away, putting them right where they had been . . . except they were older and more worn out and much more frightened than they had been all those years ago. They drove in silence for the most part, not listening to the radio even though the car speakers were top-of-the-line. The odometer clicked off the miles to Grinder's Switch. They arrived early in the afternoon.

They pulled into the same gas station where they had stocked up on provisions fifteen years ago.

"I'll wait here," Eb said, stretching his bum leg out in the backseat.

"Get you anything?" Micah asked.

"A few bottles of Yoo-hoo, for consistency's sake."

Micah stepped into the store with Minerva. It looked remarkably as it had, apart from the addition of two video game cabinets beside the newspaper racks: *Asteroids* and *Pac-Man*. Micah watched the little yellow character like a pie with a wedge cut out of it racing round its maze, *wakka-wakka-wakka-wakka*. What was the point? Ah God, he was old. A fogey. Petty had asked for an Atari system not long ago. Micah said he didn't want to see her wasting her time. But it was the duty of the young to waste their time, seeing as they had so much of it.

The man behind the counter was the same from years ago. He looked roughly a thousand years old. He wore dentures that pushed his lips apart, and his nose had been broken since Micah last set eyes on him. Micah bought Eb's Yoo-hoos, some wooden matches, a jar of peanut butter, and a loaf of Wonder Bread. The clerk totaled up his purchases sullenly and put them in a paper sack. Minerva bought a quart of Dr Pepper and two Milky Ways.

They returned to the car. Micah drove to the cut. The old trail was still there. Micah popped the trunk. They unloaded their gear: a rifle, sleeping gear, a lantern, and flashlights. Minerva handed Micah his backpack from the trunk. Its weight surprised her.

"What you got in there, Shug? Pet rocks?"

They shouldered their packs and made their way through the long grass to the head of the trail. They had to move slower on account of Ebenezer's limp.

The sun hung above the western hills, shining with a dull glow that cast no shadows. The air was still, but a sweet breath came from the woods rowing the hillside: a mild note of camphor. The twittering of birds, too: only a few, but at least some animals were about. The path followed a gradual rise. They could spot no signs of the old fire. Everything was thriving, in fact.

Minerva twisted the cap off her Dr Pepper. Ebenezer broke into a commercial jingle as he limped along.

"*I drink Dr Pepper, don't you see,*" he sang in a redneck twang, "*as it's the perfect taste for meeeee . . .*"

"Whatever you paid for singing lessons, it was too much," said Minerva.

The two of them needled each other simply to hear themselves talk—anything to push away the silence, which had become heavier as they forged deeper into the woods.

They stopped for a rest. The woods did not feel quite as hostile as they had fifteen years ago. Had they actually hurt the thing back then? Micah could not credit that. He wasn't sure something like that could be injured or killed because he was unsure if it was truly alive. But more than that, it just seemed so ineffably old that, whenever Micah turned his mind to it (which was not often, because even his thoughts scared him), notions of it ever dying seemed farcical. Something like that existed outside the bounds of time and scale—outside human bounds, anyway, and those were the only measurements he could apply.

"Are we ever going to talk about that part of it?" Minerva said. She must have read something in Micah's face.

"What part?" said Eb.

"Whatever happened down there in the dark."

"With the . . . ?" Eb started.

"Yeah, the . . ."

Minerva trailed off. It was hard to say what, exactly, they had been given. *Wishes?* Is that what happened? Had they been granted wishes, like the old story about the genie in its bottle?

"'The Monkey's Paw,'" Eb said.

Minerva nodded. "You read it?"

"A few times," said Eb. "Seems rather apt."

"But what . . ." Minerva grimaced, her brow beetling. "What did we ask for? I don't remember saying anything. More just something kinda bubbling up from way down inside me. Something I must have wanted real bad. And that fucking thing granted it."

"Mine's not so hard to figure," Eb said. "I wished to see the face of God."

Ebenezer wiped his nose on his sleeve and took a sip of Yoo-hoo. He stared at them imploringly, as if hoping the other two would understand—intimately, in their marrow, knowing the way he knew. Ebenezer had been so desperately scared. Those moments, in that place beneath the world, had nearly broken him . . . or *had* broken him, in a way he was unable to unravel or give voice to or properly grapple with. Like a greenstick fracture of some invisible bone—a vestigial one, the bones we all had as children that fused and changed so that, as adults, we have a different number of them in our bodies. That phantom bone went *snap*. The cleave was clean and flawless, as if a surgeon had done the work with a bone hammer. And that little bone was unhealable—it was forever broken, the jagged ends grinding together inside his mind. Looking back, Ebenezer was unsure that human minds were built to cope with any of . . . of what happened down there. He felt no shame thinking that, either, as he did not believe humans were built to come to grips with anything that existed beyond their conventional means of reckoning. When humans experience something that challenges their fundamental belief of the world—its reasonableness, its fixed parameters—well, their minds crimp just a bit. A mind folds, and in that fresh pleat lives a darkness that cannot be explained or accounted for. So they ignore that pleat as best they can—it, and the darkness it holds. But it's always there, always seeking redress.

"I wanted to see the face of God," Eb said again. "I must have. I was not a religious person, as you both know. I killed for money. But in that moment, all I wanted was to know there was something larger than myself up there—a benevolent god to protect me. If not my body, at least my immortal soul."

The men turned to Minerva. She spat into the nettles. Why even speak the words? They must know what she'd asked for: *I will never be killed by the hand of a man.* Minerva could not say that was her exact wish—she was still unsure, then as now, as to the precise compass of her desires. But look at her now. The past fifteen years. The Sharpening, that most terrible gift. She could kill and not be killed, even by her own hand, much as she might now pray for death. What worth were those prayers? She had made a deal with something as powerful, if earthbound, as any god. Perhaps it was a god of some sort. A dark one. An ancient one. But yes, she must have wished to be cleansed of the fear and anxiety she had once carried into life-or-death encounters. As Micah had said years back, she was not cool in the cut. Her hands always took fright, fluttering like startled chickadees. Minerva figured that was what the vile thing had dredged up. It found that flaw in her, one that shook her straight to her core, and whispered: *Oh, my ladylove, my dove, I will make it all better.*

And it had, hadn't it? As sure as eggs is eggs. But it had played a dirty trick, too. Well, fuck a duck. You couldn't expect a thing like that to play fair, could you?

The light was fading between the firs. An owl hooted from a low bough.

"And you, Shug?" Minerva said. "What did you get?"

"Only everything I asked for."

THEY HIKED UNTIL DUSK. Ebenezer hissed every time he set his foot down. Minerva felt no sympathy for him.

A shape broke through the trees ahead. They checked their strides, approaching cautiously. A solitary shack. Smoke spindled from its chimney. The door was ajar. Light from a potbellied stove threw flickering shadows across its interior.

From inside, there came an ominous sound. Minerva envisioned someone sitting on a whoopee cushion filled with thinned lard: a wet *spluttering*.

We don't have to look, she thought edgily. *We can walk right on by . . .*

Too late. Micah toed the door open. His eyes fell upon something inside. His knees buckled; he leaned heavily against the door frame. The spluttering sounds were much louder with the door open.

In the firelight flickering through the door, Micah's face was drawn and haunted. He drew a shuddering breath, then stepped into the shack. Ebenezer hesitantly followed, and quickly saw whatever Micah had beheld.

"I can't," Eb said, shaking his head violently. "Oh Christ, no, I can't, I *cannot*—"

Borne on a sudsy foam of dread, Minerva advanced to the door. She didn't want to see, either. But she couldn't not bear witness.

The cramped shack reeked of blood. The stove, a folding card table, pelts tacked on the walls. Something hung among those pelts—much larger than the coyote and muskrat skins, oh yes. And it was still moving. A paralyzing chill spread down her back, as if liquid nitrogen had been injected into her spinal column.

A man was tacked to the wall. His bare feet kicked weakly six inches above the ground. He had been opened up, his chest split down the middle starting at the level of his clavicles. The skin was peeled back in quivering wings that had been pinned to the log walls with pelt tacks. The silverskin and fascia and yellow adipose tissues had been flensed away with clinical skill; whoever had done it had great facility with a boning knife. The man's arms and legs had been slit down their middles, the skin peeled back to reveal the shining bone of femur and kneecap and humerus.

Humerus? Minerva thought, her mind taking a sickening lurch. *There's not a damn thing humerus here—hey-o! Gimme a rim shot, Doc Severinsen!*

The flesh was slit back from his nose in petals, the strips tacked to the wood. The musculature of his face twitched, his eyes massive without anything to cover them; they peered around with a vaudevillian shock that forced a cascade of giddy giggles to bubble up Minerva's throat. It was the only way to get rid of the chest-splintering pressure building up inside of her.

It took a moment to grasp the final horror. The source of that spluttering.

The man's neck had been slit, but he was still breathing. The man's lungs heaved, forcing breaths out, the air *blllpphhphhph*-ing from his severed windpipe. Minerva watched the erratic beat of his heart through the naked bones of his ribs; his innards still pushed stubborn shreds of food along.

What infernal sorcery was keeping him alive? Was it the same that kept her own heart beating every time she tried to off herself?

She grabbed a hatchet from the wall rack. She took two steps toward the man and brought it around in a wicked arc. It buried in the man's neck, widening the slit. His body thrashed, blood spraying. She pried the blade out of the wall and swung it again and again until the man's head was completely separated from his body: it hit the floor and rolled under the table like a lopsided bowling ball.

Minerva stared at Micah, breathing hard. Her face was flecked with blood.

"Merciful," Micah said after a span.

Noise from under the table. The man—no, the *head*—was laughing. The gibbering sounds of lunacy you might hear at a nuthatch.

That laughter unseated something in Minerva—it filled her with panic and sorrow and, yes, rage. She kicked over the table and swung the hatchet at the giggling head. The blade cleaved the skull dead center, splitting the bone; there came a hiss as pressure forced a chunk of gray matter through. Minerva threw the stove open and hurled the head inside with the hatchet still embedded in it. The head continued to howl laughter, and the pitch ascended as its lips began to melt. Minerva slammed the stove door. Fire flared behind it; there came a small explosion as the juices inside the man's head heated up, blowing out part of his skull. The giggling ceased.

They gathered outside. Ebenezer collapsed against a fallen log.

"How?" he asked helplessly.

"It's the work of that thing." Minerva was doubled over, breathing in huge gulps. "The Big Thing. The Piper. Whatever you want to call it."

The smoke rising from the chimney now had a meaty smell.

"I don't know if I can go through with this," Minerva said. "I thought I could, Shug, but . . ."

"I understand."

"I'm scared."

"I understand."

LATER, MICAH WALKED from the fire they had stoked a ways from the cursed shack. He stared through the trees in the direction of Little Heaven. They weren't far now. It would all come to an end of sorts. He was ready for that. He had one last fight in him—and if he had to, he would fight alone. Petty was his blood; in the end tally, neither Minerva nor Ebenezer owed him a debt. Their ledgers were clean with him.

But Petty—yes, he owed her. A parent always does. He stared into the formless dark, and a memory molded itself within it. Petty was young at the time, two or three years old. This was before Ellen entered her endless sleep. But that day she wasn't with them; it had been Micah and his daughter, alone. He'd been working in the paddocks when he spotted a caterpillar—a big brown one wriggling along, doing its caterpillary thing. He called Petty over and drew her attention to it.

"Touch it," he said. "It is . . . fuzzy."

Micah simply wanted her to feel the soft, bristling, undulating little carpet of fuzz that is a caterpillar. Pet put her finger on it and pressed down. She wasn't big in human terms, but to a caterpillar she was gargantuan. The caterpillar curled into a ball. He snatched Pet's hand away. "*Gentle.*" She gazed at him with no comprehension. Micah thought the caterpillar would be okay—it had just turtled up defensively. It would uncurl once the threat was gone. But the wind picked up and blew the caterpillar across the boards, light as a dried seedpod, in a way that told Micah the life had drained out of it. It happened so quickly. A thing was alive; next it was dead. Petty lost interest and ran off after her ball. Micah stared at the caterpillar a long time. It was the first thing his daughter had killed that he was aware of. Micah had guided her to the act. And yet life went on. It always did. Pet was chasing a ball. The birds were singing. The horses nickered in their stables.

You tell yourself it's just a caterpillar. The world's full of them. Which is true. But the world is full of us, too. And any of us can be lost—or taken—at any minute.

Micah thought about endings. Some were abrupt, like the way that caterpillar's life had ceased. Some took longer, and you could see them coming from miles off. In so many ways, Micah wanted it to end. He felt every one of his years. He was old and bone-weary. His body ached; his mind was plagued. Everything he loved had been ripped from him, and he deserved it. Guilt and regret were different qualities, yes, but still tightly wed. You could not outrun your past. Your history was a lonely hound pursuing you over field and fallow, never resting, always hungry, tracking you relentlessly until one night you heard its nails scratching at your door.

I am coming, Pet, he thought. *Please just hold on a little longer. If I can, you can.*

PART SIX

THE DEVIL IN THE ROCK

1966

1

NATE WAS STILL AWAKE. Everyone else was asleep.

Only a few hours had passed since the one-eyed man had come back. He and Mr. Redhill and Mr. Fairweather and Mr. Langtree had gone off in the truck to get help. They hadn't made it far. In fact, they were still within earshot when Nate heard Mr. Redhill start to scream. He thought it had been Mr. Redhill, anyway. It was too dark to see, the truck too far away by then, and anyway, when people scream—even full-grown men— they all tend to sound the same. That wasn't something Nate would have guessed, but he could say so now. Only the one-eyed man had returned to Little Heaven alive.

Now Nate was in the mess hall with his father, the three outsiders, and Ellen—she had told him her name, so she wasn't an outsider to him anymore. A bigger group was over in the supply warehouse. A few stragglers were standing watch at the gate.

After the one-eyed man came back, a lot of people tried to get into the chapel. *Sanctuary* was the word Nate had heard. But the chapel was locked. The Reverend wouldn't answer his door, either. What did it matter? Nobody cared what the Reverend had to say now. *It's about time*, Nate thought. He had never really liked Reverend Flesher. He reminded Nate of a door-to-door salesman: he spread out his wares on your living room rug, and they weren't much good, all scuffed and cheaply made, but he pressured you to buy them anyway. Nate was glad the Reverend had lost some of his control. Nate could say that now, couldn't he? Sure. He could say or think almost anything. And that was a scary thought.

Everyone had questions for the one-eyed man, too. A lot of those questions had been screamed into the one-eyed man's face, and they were less questions than accusations. He didn't answer any of them. It was as if whatever had happened out there had temporarily melted his brain. That was a scary thought, too, because the one-eyed man seemed tough. Steel-belted, his mom would say. If whatever had happened out there was bad enough to do that to him, Nate figured it had to be *really* bad.

One thing was for sure: nobody wanted to step past the gates. The only thing they could do was take cover and wait until morning. Everyone was praying that whatever was in the woods—the things that had killed Mr. Langtree and Mr. Fairweather and Billy and Elton's dad—wouldn't enter Little Heaven. It was whispered that they must be afraid of the lights—but with the gasoline dwindling, who knew how much longer the lights would stay on.

Now everyone had split up and made their way either to the warehouse or the mess. The watchers at the gate had whistles in case they saw anything. Nate's dad wanted to sleep in the warehouse with Maude Redhill and the others, but Nate wanted to stay with the outsiders. He trusted them. Plus, they had more guns. His father gave him a look but said that God would abide.

So they settled in the mess hall. The Englishman was appointed as first watch. The adults quickly fell asleep—even the Englishman. Someone might as well have slipped a knockout drop under their tongues.

But Nate couldn't sleep. Something awful was happening—had been happening for a while now. Maybe it had been happening since the moment the Reverend stumbled upon this spot in the woods, driven here by the voice of God. What if he'd followed the wrong voice? Sacrilege to think it, his dad would say. Well, maybe his dad was dead wrong, too.

Had *all* the adults been wrong? Was building Little Heaven their biggest mistake? Even the strongest adults could be misguided—guys like Mr. Fairweather and Mr. Langtree, who Nate was pretty sure were both dead. *Dead*: before tonight he had never felt the coffin nail finality of that word. He had lost two goldfish and a hamster, Mr. Pips. That was his only experience with death. His mother had flushed the fish down the toilet—a burial at sea, she called it. Mr. Pips got buried in a shoe box in the backyard of a house they had been renting outside Portsmouth. Nate felt bad at losing them, but their deaths had been quick—he woke up to find the fish floating in their bowl before his mom scooped them out with a little skimmer; Mr. Pips died over the weekend when he was away at his dad's place, so Nate only saw him inside the box, which his mom had padded with cotton batting. They hadn't screamed like the men had earlier tonight. He had never heard the fear or the wretched bewilderment that their screams had held, either—fish and hamsters just went *glub-glub* or *squeak-squeak*, and then, Nate guessed, they died. So it was different. Humans died in worse ways, or at least Mr. Fairweather and Mr. Langtree and Mr. Redhill had.

Nate wondered, if those men could walk it all back—the decision to join Reverend Flesher's congregation and come here to Little Heaven— would they do it? But it was too late. You can't relive your life. You couldn't hop into H. G. Wells's time machine and zap back to the site of your bad decisions and make a better one. If the decisions you made were stupid ones, well, it wasn't just you who suffered. No fact seemed clearer to Nate than this: adults were as often wrong as right. And what choice did their kids have but to follow along? Wasn't that your job as a kid—to tag along and not make noise? And a kid has to believe that those added years should equal added wisdom, right? H-E-double-hockey-sticks *no*! Adults could be stupid when it came down to it. When the rubber hit the road, as his mom would say—his mother, who had been stupid herself, getting locked up in jail when Nate needed her most. He hated being mad at her, and angry at his father for his weakness . . . but his parents' mistakes had led him here.

It dawned for the first time how difficult and perhaps how fearful it was to be an adult. And Nate was suddenly and selfishly afraid not only for himself now but also for what it seemed he might become.

Nate got up. The one-eyed man snored and rolled over—he actually had two eyes now, even though one of them was glass. His shirt was torn, his wounds clumsily covered with duct tape. The black man was slumped in his chair. Nate thought about shaking him for abandoning his responsibility, but he seemed the sort of person who might punch a boy in the face for waking him up. Nate walked to a window. The compound lay motionless under the security lamps. His eyes flicked left, then flicked ri—

The air soured in his lungs. He tried to back away from the window, but his legs locked up.

His old playmates. They were back. The four of them linked together, hand to hand. Their skin so pale it was nearly translucent. Could nobody else *see* them?

Eli Rathbone was at the end of the chain this time. Eli couldn't stand; the others dragged him carelessly, the way a toddler might haul a teddy bear by its arm. His body bumped over the ground. He was so thin: a collection of driftwood lashed into the shape of a boy. Nate could see his hip bones—he never knew how bones might look, really, because they were always covered in enough skin. The only skeletons he'd seen were the cardboard ones hung in the windows at Halloween. But Eli looked too much like those skeletons now.

They approached him quickly; in a heartbeat, they were at the window. Nate tried to call out, but his lips were frozen. A wire ran through his entire body from the tip of his head to his pinkie toe—and that wire tightened, paralyzing him.

Go away was all he could think. *Oh please, just go.*

Elsa was naked. They all were, but Elsa was different. Nate had never seen a naked girl. Boys, sure. A lot of boys were eager to show their penises to whoever. But girls' bodies were a riddle Nate hadn't yet solved. Elsa was wasted but with a big tummy like those starving children in *Life* magazine. Her tiny breasts were deflated like balloons found behind the sofa three months after the party was over, all wrinkly and saggy. Her . . . her *vagina* (as Missus Edwards used to say in sex-ed class) was a stiff trench between her legs, covered in delicate hairs that had gone gray to match the hair on her head. All the kids' hair had gone gray—no, *white*, the shocked white of a fright wig. That, along with their bony bodies and pruney skin, made them look ancient—these young-old things dancing to the jangly notes of a flute.

They paraded past the window one by one, grinning at him. The skin of their faces was lined and crepey around their jaws but pulled tight around their sockets so that their eyes bulged out. Their teeth were gray as tombstones. Their pupils were a shade of black that didn't exist in nature, and blown out to cover their whole eyeballs.

Eli was last. And worst. Nate could see his skull. His skin had worn through at his temples, wearing down the way your toe wears through a cheap Kresge's sock until there's only a few fiber fluffs left. His lips were gone: they hadn't fallen off or been bitten away but had thinned out to the point where they weren't really there anymore. His gums peeled back from his teeth, which were *waaay* too big; they looked like the molars the dentist had pulled out of his friend Gregory Betts's mouth—the dentist gave them to Gregory in a little glass jar and Nate was amazed how long they were with the buried roots visible, like fangs.

Eli pressed his face to the window. The other kids helped prop him up, like a lifeless puppet. The plastic stretched to flatten his features. His face projected inward, threatening to rip through. His mouth stretched into a grin. His eyes were dark and huge; they reached through the plastic somehow, horrid, swallowing, hunting for something soft inside Nate's chest.

Come out, said a voice in Nate's head. *Come out and play.*

Oh no. Nope. No way. That was the last thing on earth he wanted.

And yet . . .

His arm jerked. He had no control of it. He tried to scream, but all that came out was a wheeze. He reached toward Eli's face; Eli's grin stretched even wider, so big that Nate was sure Eli would eat his fingers through the plastic, grind up his skin and chomp his knuckles and keep on moving down his arm . . . and Nate was even more terrified he would *want* to keep feeding Eli, helplessly shoving his hand and then his wrist into Eli's mouth.

He flung his gaze away from the window. His father was sitting up on the floor, watching Nate. His face was bathed in sweat. His eyes huge wet discs.

Daddy, Nate mouthed. *Oh, Daddy, please . . .*

His father nodded curtly, as if he had just received some bad news. Then he pulled the blankets up, his eyes still bugged out and his hands trembling, lay down, and rolled over into a little ball.

Nate's fingers made contact with the plastic window. His head whipped back to see he was touching Eli's face through the plastic; Eli's skin was cold and hard, as if Nate had touched stone. He moaned and shut his eyes.

Oh please, please just don't make it hurt too much and don't make me into one of them—

Then the pressure went away. When Nate looked, Eli was gone. Nobody was at the window.

He sagged to the floor, shivering uncontrollably. The tips of his fingers were still cold—would they ever feel warm again? He glanced at his father, still rolled on his side, pretending to sleep. A wave of hatred rolled through Nate, so black it made him woozy.

Coward, he thought. *Chicken-guts FAKER.*

Rattling from the mess. Back in the kitchen.

No, Nate thought. *No-no-no-no—the cellar.*

He raced through the swinging galley door. A security lamp shone through the lone window. The kitchen countertops gleamed; the stink of rancid grease hung heavy. A trapdoor was set into the floor at the far end of the kitchen, next to the fridge. The door led down to the cold cellar, which could also be accessed through a set of doors outside. Nate had watched the cook swing those doors open and hump sacks of flour, rice, and potatoes into the storage area; he would bring them up through the trapdoor as needed. The outer doors weren't locked—only three places in Little Heaven always had locks: the chapel, the Reverend's quarters, and the windowless bunkhouse.

The trapdoor rattled again. Nate jumped; his skin felt too tight all of a sudden, as if it were about to split down a hidden seam. The trapdoor was held down under two chains lashed to the ringbolt. When it rattled, the chains rattled, too. Nobody heard it except Nate.

The trapdoor opened—just a hair. In that heart-stopping slit of darkness, Nate saw their faces. All four of them clustered under the door, peering out at him.

"You're cute," said the Elsa-thing, and giggled.

It was no longer the voice of a child. It was a choked and sewage-y gurgle, the sound that bubbles up from a clogged drainpipe.

"Come with us," said Eli. "Come and be meat."

"It will be neat," said one of the Redhill boys, laughing at the silly rhyme.

Nate could smell them: ripe and fruity, the stink that wafts through the car vents when you drove past days-old road kill. He said, "No."

Eli grinned. His mouth stretched so wide, almost ear to ear—the smile of a shark. Flies buzzed through the trapdoor, fat sluggish ones that landed on the kitchen window and blotted out the moon.

"It wants you," Eli said. "It wants you all."

Eli began to laugh. The others joined him. Cold nausea swept over Nate. He hated them. Not Eli and Elsa and the Redhills—though they had never been very friendly to him—but whatever they had become. They were disgusting and lewd, and it made his soul sick to look at them.

Before he knew what he was doing, Nate rushed at them. *Stop! STOP!* his mind chattered. But he was as mad as he'd ever been. They were bullies before and they still were. You had to stand up to bullies or you would spend your whole life in fear. You would grow up to be a man like his father.

Nate leapt and came down on top of the trapdoor. It banged down hard. He stood there a moment, seesawing his arms, fear rising in him like a fever. What was he doing? Was he crazy?

"Go away!" he shouted. "Leave me alone!"

He felt like raising his arms in victory, washed in a giddy sense of triumph—until the door popped up with a sharp bang, rattling the chains and spilling Nate onto his ass. He yelped and dug in his heels, trying to crab-walk away from the—

A withered arm shot through the trapdoor gap and snatched his ankle.

EAT KILL SWALLOW EAT EAT HURT KILL EAT CHEW KILL EAT

—schniiik!—

Nate reared back, screaming and clawing at his skull. Something had leapt into his head the moment those fingers closed around his ankle. His mind had been covered in choking oil that blotted everything out—everything except a powerful, uncontrollable urge to break and hurt other living things.

He was in the kitchen again. The trapdoor was shut. The skinny outsider woman was next to him. She held a huge butcher's cleaver. Her lips
moved, but Nate couldn't hear her. His head was fuzzy. It had felt as if . . .
as if a giant worm or leech had fixed its mouth around his brain, inhaling
it into its black guts and transmitting its alien thoughts into him. They
were the crudest, the most awful feelings imaginable: of eating and chewing and ripping and just *hurting*, hurting scared helpless creatures before
eating them.

The skinny woman stabbed down with the knife, impaling something
on the tip. A child's hand. Black blood oozed from its severed wrist. She
flung the knife and hand away. It skittered across the floor and jammed up
under the fridge.

"You okay?" she asked. He could hear her now.

There were five icy blots on Nate's bare ankle where those fingers had
touched him. Nate managed to nod. Whatever had invaded his head was
gone now, but coldness continued to seep over his scalp ten times worse
than an ice cream headache.

The one-eyed man came into the kitchen, followed by Ellen and the
Englishman.

"What happened?"

"One of them was grabbing his leg," the skinny woman answered the
one-eyed man. She stabbed a finger at the Englishman. "What the hell
happened to you?"

The Englishman wiped sleep drool off his chin. "I'm sorry. I don't
know how I—"

"You fucking moron," the woman said.

"One of who?" said Ellen. "*Who*, Minny?"

"The children," the skinny woman said in disbelief. "The boy Eli.
Jesus, I've never seen anything so awful."

The one-eyed man approached the trapdoor. Nate said, "No, please
don't open it."

The man pushed him out of the way and lifted the door a few inches.
The skinny woman pulled Nate to her chest. The man took another knife

off a magnetized rack above the sink, unhooked the chains, and went into the cellar. Nate waited for him to start screaming. Thirty seconds later, he came back.

"Empty. But the outer doors are open."

"What happened, Nate?" Ellen asked.

The experience seemed too huge and horrible to talk about. The children's dead eyes, the force taking over his mind . . .

The one-eyed man crouched beside the severed hand. He touched one finger with the tip of the knife. The other fingers jerked. Nate began to cry when he saw that. Sobs ripped out of his chest, these loon-like whoops.

We're all dead, Nate thought. *Or worse. Death might be better.*

He glanced over the skinny woman's shoulder and saw his father hovering at the kitchen door. He waved at Nate. Apologetically, or just confusedly, Nate would never know.

"Did you see anything, Reggie?" Ellen asked.

Reggie paused, then shook his head. "I was asleep like all of you. Didn't see a thing." He swallowed and said, "We need the Reverend's guidance. He will tell us—"

"We don't need shit from him," the skinny woman spat.

Nate glared at his father.

I hate you.

The fury of Nate's thought zipped through the air and slammed into his father. Nate saw his dad flinch from the psychic pain of it. He went back through the swinging door, leaving Nate in the kitchen.

2

THE REVEREND AWOKE in the chapel covered in blood.

He had been biting his hands while he slept. He'd worried divots of flesh out of his palms and wrists and woke up sucking on his own blood.

Amos was sleeping in the chapel sacristy, in the credenza. He felt safe in there, curled into a ball with the doors shut. He let his hatred collect into a hard little ball, too, nursing it on his own black bile.

His flock had abandoned him. All but a few—the stupidest and most useless ones. After all he had done for them! The bastards! Cunts! He imagined stealing into the mess hall and finding the largest knife to slit all of their Iscariot throats. Or, if not all of them, then those who had instigated the insurrection. He pictured grabbing Otis Langtree's hair, drawing the skin of his neck taut, and sawing through his treacherous windpipe. Reaching into Nell Conkwright's mouth, gripping her eelish tongue, slicing it out at the root, and laughing as the blood splashed his chest. Pinning Charlie Fairweather down and carefully slitting his eyeballs, pushing on them until the gooey centers burst through the slit like peeled grapes—

Yes! Nothing would be finer. But of course, he could not. He was physically weak, always had been. His gift was to make people do his bidding through guile and honeyed words and his command of the Good Book . . . or it had been until now. He was powerless, a declawed kitten. His most trusted lieutenants had instigated a rebellion against him. It made him boil with rage. And now, if his understanding of the situation was correct, it was too late to kill them himself. Langtree and Fairweather were dead. He'd watched the scene out of his window—the one-eyed bastard returning alone, then his assault at the hands of Maude Redhill. Good. It was perfectly fine that those traitorous scum were dead. His only sadness was that he couldn't have watched the life drain out of them personally.

He heard something out in the chapel.

Amos crawled out of the credenza. His blood sang and his skin prickled all over. He walked out of the sacristy into the chapel proper. The Voice beckoned him.

He walked between the pews. Musical notes came from all around him, but from inside of him, too. Something was there in the chapel with him. But the doors and windows were locked. It was Christ's sanctuary. Yet it was here. A presence. Something with a massive weight and gravity that sucked at the deepest part of him. His soul, just maybe.

"Hello?" he said childishly.

Up here.

His gaze ascended. Something lurked in the apse, in the shadows above the crucified Christ. It seethed in that arched vault, a dark mass that shifted and breathed and chittered.

"My God . . ."

Amos Flesher's heart fluttered. His insides went to water.

Oh no, the thing spoke in his mind. *Not God, child.*

Of course not. It never had been. That understanding arrived with a thunderclap. What he was hearing now was the same Voice he had followed to this spot all those months ago. Not the voice of God, but a different one—a Voice of chaos and blood. A Voice that hummed like flies sometimes; other times it sounded like a worm of limitless length coiling around and around its own infinite body. And . . . Amos was fine with that. Yes, he was. The fact rested easily in his head. A gear locked in place, spinning contentedly on its axis.

The thing in the rafters of the ruined, befouled chapel gibbered and giggled. Amos saw only a hint of its true shape. It was enough. It spoke to him in a familiar voice.

"You have been fiddling with your dirty stick, haven't you?"

Amos was unsurprised to find he had an erection. It tented the satiny material of his pajamas. Idly, he reached under the waistband and began to pull on his cock. It felt nice to milk it like an itsy-bitsy udder.

"Yes," he said stupidly.

"Fiddling and fiddling and fiddling . . . ," the thing crooned.

Amos pulled with greater force. He was going to make a mess. Back at the orphanage, he hated doing that; he would tease himself to the point of release, then grip it and squeeze so his seed wouldn't spill out, so hard that blood vessels burst on the head of his penis. But he wasn't worried about that now. He pulled on it real hard, just like the soft-brain Finn used to do to his own thick mongoloid dick. Amos yanked so forcefully that the skin ripped down the shaft, though it didn't hurt at all. In fact, it felt wonderful. The air touched the ripped flesh with a pleasant tingle. He wasn't thinking of anything remotely sexual; instead, he envisioned that his body had turned into an enormous mouth with teeth the size of bricks, snapping and chattering around inside the locked orphanage, chasing screaming kids and grinding them up, breaking their bones and pulping their soft flesh and cracking their skulls between his mammoth molars like walnuts and—

"What do you want?" he asked, feverishly.

"*You know what*," Sister Muriel said.

And Amos *did* know. The Voice wanted what it had always wanted. What it had brought Amos out here for. The sweetest fruit of Little Heaven.

Amos began to laugh. It started out as effervescent titters but soon became throaty, then booming. It was not entirely sane, that laughter, but then, Little Heaven was no longer a sane place.

Amos wanted to obey the Voice. More than he'd ever wanted to follow the tenets of God. The Creator was a stodgy old bore. God stifled the true nature of man. The Voice spoke directly to that nature and asked that Amos do nothing more than give vent to the brutality that had long lurked at his core.

"*Give it to me*," Sister Muriel—or the thing that was speaking in her voice—called down to him. "*Give me what I want and I'll give you what you need . . .*"

But as Amos was a physical weakling and at heart a coward, he would have to be crafty. Well, crafty he could be. A plan was already flying together in his head, the pieces slotting flush.

"Yes." His voice floated up into the poisoned chapel as Christ stared down impassively from His cross. "*Yes.*"

3

EBENEZER WAS UP AT DAWN, heading out of the mess hall and across the square. Micah called after him, but Eb didn't bother to acknowledge his hail.

Eb stopped at a shed and grabbed a red toolbox. The box rattled against his thigh as he strode across the compound to the front gates. The sun was rising over the trees to lighten the woods. A few hollow-eyed Heavenites stood watch.

"Good morning, chappies," he said to them. "Open up, daylight's wasting."

He was tired of these cornpone, Bible-bashing troglodyte shitbirds. They could go eat a bucket of elephant testicles, for all he cared. A big ole pailful, as these buffoons might say. *Hyuk, hyuk.* Crass, yes, but he had reached the end of his tether. If he was going to die, so be it. But not among these ingrate yokels, who would drag his soul into some hillbilly purgatory, where he'd be forced to listen to washboard-and-jug band jamborees for all eternity. Hell would be preferable.

When the morons didn't move, Eb lifted the latch himself and pushed the gate open. He was whistling a Cockney tune. His hair had gone frizzy and was tangled up with shreds of dead leaves and maple keys—he would kill, quite literally *kill*, for a hot shower and a bottle of Lustre-Creme shampoo. Sunlight washed the access road, touching the body of Charlie Fairweather, who lay three hundred yards off. Well, half of Charlie, by the looks of it. Poor bastard.

Two motorbikes were parked past the gates. One was an old French Metisse with a 350cc two-stroke engine. The other was a newer Japanese model.

Micah caught up with him. His posture wasn't threatening, only curious.

"What are you doing?"

"Leaving, good chum," Eb said. "Hitting the lonesome trail, in your Yank parlance."

He snapped open the toolbox, which he had stocked the day before for this very eventuality. He retrieved a can of two-in-one oil. He lubricated the chain and the suspension rig on the Metisse, straddled the seat, and bounced up and down to work the oil into the shock absorbers. Minerva hung back at the gates, watching him.

Micah said, "Think you will make it?"

"A bike is more nimble than that truck. It's perfect for this terrain."

"You think you're gonna leave us with our asses hanging out, huh?" Minerva called over.

Ebenezer spoke to her over Micah's shoulder. "I'm taking a sabbatical, milady. Much to your dismay, I can only guess. I promise to send a post-card."

Minerva pulled Ellen's pistol from her waistband, cocked it, and held it to her thigh. Ebenezer could only smile.

"Will you shoot me in the back?"

Minerva cocked her head as if to say, *Try me.* Ebenezer's smile widened.

"Your aim is suspect, my dear. I'll take my chances."

He bent over the bike to check the timing gear. Someone shouted. "Hey! What the hell you think you're doing?"

Ebenezer turned. Hooray, if it wasn't Virgil, the more dunderheaded shitkicker of the Reverend's gruesome twosome.

"Hey—black boy! That ain't your property! You ain't gonna—"

Virgil's voice drilled into Ebenezer's ears, unlocking an old memory. As a child, he and a friend had queued up for a showing of *Crossfire* starring Robert Mitchum at the Grenada Theatre. They had saved up all week. But when they reached the wicket, the ticket seller told them *No Negroes allowed.* He said it casually, almost apologetically—an existential apology for their bad luck to have been born black, a stain that would doom them the rest of their lives. So Ebenezer and his friend snuck in through the fire door and sat in the empty balcony section. But before the newsreel even finished, an usher found them. He clouted Eb on the ear with one fat fist. *Sneaky little tar babies!* he'd hissed, and chased them down the stairs. They ran out the emergency door closest to the movie screen. The sunlight hit Eb's eyes, dazzling in its intensity; he turned to see the white people in the front row rearing back at the sudden light, their faces pale and marbly as cheese—they looked like terrified vampires at the moment Van Helsing let the sunlight into their coffins. Eb and his friend dashed down the alley to the street. The usher pursued for a block or two, but he was a porker and he faded fast, heaving on the cobbles, shaking an impotent fist.

Afterward, Eb sat on the curb outside the sweetshop, nursing his swollen ear. He had a powerful urge to go back and hurt that usher. In his young mind, he pictured a very sharp, long knife. He saw himself pinning the usher's hand down by the wrist and cutting deep between the webbing of his fingers, halfway down his palm, so that when the flesh healed the man would be left with these tangly, freakish witch-fingers, long and spidery with almost no palm to speak of. But Ebenezer hadn't owned a knife and lacked the will to steal one.

Ebenezer now thought of that afternoon because Virgil looked an awful lot like that usher. He wasn't nearly as fat, but he was stalking toward Eb with the same goatish belligerence, his eyes squinted in vaporous idiocy. Ebenezer reached into the toolbox and selected a heavy wrench.

"What the fuck you think you're doing, you uppity nig—"

Ebenezer threw it. The wrench spun end over end, tomahawk-style, and poleaxed Virgil spang between the eyes. Virgil went down on one knee, looking like Al Jolson singing the crescendo of "My Mammy," then staggered up and tilted off in a new direction toward the trees. His forehead was split open, blood pissing out.

Eb curled his hand around an old spark plug lying in the toolbox and walked over to Virgil. He swung his fist in a tight arc, clouting Virgil on the back of his head. Virgil grunted and fell face-first into the dirt. Ebenezer turned him over and punched him in the face, hard. And again. And again. Virgil's eyelids fluttered, and blood leaked from both sides of his mouth.

"Eb," Micah said.

Ebenezer turned. He could feel the warmth of Virgil's blood freckling his face.

Micah said, "Lay off."

"Cheerfully!" Eb said. He rolled Virgil over, grabbed the man's gun from his waistband, then walked back to the bike and tossed the spark plug into the toolbox. Virgil lay still with blood bubbling out of his mouth.

"Those things in the woods, Eb," said Micah, taking no interest in the downed man. "They are fast."

"I saw them before, Micah. Back at the campsite."

"No. These ones are different."

Eb sighed. "What choice do we have? No phone, no telegram, no carrier pigeons, no smoke signals. Someone has to get out of here. Who does it hurt if that someone is me?"

Micah said, "You coming back?"

"No," Eb said evenly. "Why the hell would I? But I promise I'll call the authorities. I'll have Johnny Law dispatched here posthaste."

"If you make it."

"If I make it."

Micah considered this. "Give us some time. We can help."

Micah went away with Minerva. Ebenezer spent the good part of an hour tinkering with the bike. Doc Lewis and another man showed up meanwhile and dragged Virgil off; Virgil's boot heels left shallow rails in the dirt.

The sun skinned above the trees. Shapes shifted in the bad light of the woods. The electric tang of dread lay heavy in Eb's mouth. Micah returned with Ellen and two male followers. Both men carried compound bows.

"Ellen made these."

Micah held up a globe of paper-thin glass with a hole in the top. The men filled each globe with gasoline—now a precious resource—and lashed the globes to hunting arrows with duct tape.

"We will try to hit a few," Micah said. "At least you will see them coming."

Ebenezer duct-taped Virgil's gun to the motorbike's handlebars. He kick-started the engine. The motor coughed, sputtered, then buzzed to life.

"You better make that fuckin' phone call!" Minerva shouted over the engine.

"I'll miss you most of all!" he shouted back to her.

The men notched arrows in their bows. Ellen lit the gasoline in the glass bowls. Micah hefted the Tarpley rifle. Minerva had Ellen's .38 pistol.

"We'll lay down cover," she said grudgingly. "Race like your ass is on fire."

Minerva and Micah jogged fifty yards ahead. The shapes in the trees were massing now. Ebenezer gunned the engine; the bike buzzed louder—those wine-swilling Frenchies made one hell of a motorcycle.

Ah, well, Eb thought. *Who wants to live forever?*

Two arrows arced over his head. One hit a tree, whose trunk went up in a furious cone of fire. The other arrow hit one of the creatures, which shrieked as flames burst over its body. The fire clawed all over it to showcase its enormous and baffling size.

"Go!" Micah shouted.

Eb opened the throttle. The bike took off like a scalded cat. He raced between Minerva and Micah, bike screaming, tachometer in the red. The bike bottomed out in a rut, the chassis kicking up sparks. He shot past Charlie Fairweather's corpse—Charlie's eyes wide open, his dust-covered intestines resembling floured sausage links. Two more arrows arced overhead; something went up fifty yards ahead of him, a lunatic combustion that threw the woods into momentary relief. Noises from all angles, a cacophony of screeches and howls.

Something charged from his left-hand side; he cranked the bars to the right. Micah's rifle cracked; the thing skip-tumbled away, a good chunk of its anatomy obliterated by the blast—

The tires hit a rut; the bike wobbled, threatening to spill him off, but he recovered and rose up off the seat as the bike launched out of the rut on a bad line. The wheels spun, engine whining, before he slammed back down. His skull hammered the handlebars. He pulled his head up, woozy, seeing stars—he was riding straight at the trees. An abomination loomed out of the woods: the skulls of many animals smashed together, the bone humped and carbuncled like a walnut with a horrible mouth splitting its surface. Ebenezer dropped one leg down and wrenched the bars hard, spinning a tight one-eighty; he gunned the throttle, and the bike reared up as something snagged at his shirt collar, slitting the material and leaving a burning line of pain down his back. He cat-walked the bike away from the trees, shifted his weight to bring the front tire down again, and slewed onto the path. Blood was trickling down his back. He shot past the pickup truck and caught a flash of blood on its windows and a headless body slumped against the tire.

Sweat dripped into his eye; he blinked, and when his vision cleared, he saw something in the firs to his right, forty yards ahead. It kept rising and rising in a crazed mass of limbs like a living totem pole. It slumped forward, falling like a tree but much faster—more like an enormous whip being cracked. It slapped down on the path, sending up a stinking puff of dust, this terrible skinned rope studded with red-rimmed eyes and mouths full of teeth gnashing with mindless hunger—

Eb jerked the handlebars, popping the front wheel up, and hurdled the thing like a speed bump. The tires burred over its body, sending up the stink of burned rubber; for a heart-sinking moment Eb was sure the thing's teeth or claws would puncture the tire, leaving him to flee on the shredded rim, but the rubber held, thank Christ.

The path widened and ran flat; the shapes between the trees began to thin. He sensed movement from behind, things blundering and crashing through the bush, but he was moving faster than them now.

Ha-haaaaah! he thought joyously. *Run, run, just as fast as you can, you can't catch me—I'm the bloody GINGERBREAD MAN!*

A shadow fell across his shoulder. He caught the decayed smell of his pursuer. He glanced back in time to see something swooping in from above. Its plated wings were fanned out, a fearsome ten-foot span of vein-threaded blackness. He swerved to avoid its predatory strike; its wings flapped directly overhead, the air filling with rancid white dust like the powder off a moth. It latched onto his ear; its talons were blunt but incredibly powerful—it was like getting pierced with ballpoint pens. The creature flapped its enormous wings; Eb's ass lifted a few inches off the seat. He screamed as the thing tried to muscle itself skyward; it raked his head with other claws, these much sharper, slicing his scalp open.

Eb clung desperately to the handlebars as the thing rose up, clutching his ear like an angry schoolmarm. One hand was pried off the bars, his fingers barely holding on; his screams intensified as his panic hit maximum intensity. Then, with a fibrous zippering tear, part of his ear was gone, ripped right off the side of his head. He barely felt it, on account of the adrenaline washing through his system. He dropped back onto the seat; the shocks groaned as the bike bottomed out again, spraying a fan of gravel. There came a pressurized hiss as blood sprayed from the wound, flowing around his jaw and down his neck.

The thing screeched and wheeled through the air in front of him. This huge black thing, part bat and part buzzard and part snake but larger than those creatures by far, with a segmented tail that winnowed to the stinger of a scorpion.

Eb ripped the pistol off the handlebars and fired. The second bullet hit its chest; the thing was blown backward in midair, body crumpling as it crashed into the roadside nettles.

Ebenezer tossed the gun away. This was his chance, maybe his only one. He could hear them behind him, a murderous stampede. He opened the throttle. The bike whined in protest; fingers of black smoke trailed up from the transmission.

Come on, Eb thought desperately. *Just a few more miles, little pony.*

The path dropped steadily downward. He maneuvered the bike over small dirt moguls and shale slides, laying off the throttle and letting the momentum take hold. Casting a glance back, he saw nothing.

The engine was so hot that it baked the flesh of his calf, but the little Metisse didn't overheat or conk out. If he made it through this, Ebenezer would never speak ill of the French again. The side of his head throbbed where part of his ear had been wrenched off; he touched the wound and recoiled as blistering pain shot through his skull. Christ Almighty. Well, at least he already wore his hair long. Blood leaked down his forehead from the shallow cuts in his scalp, but he didn't feel faint yet.

He rode until he hit the creek. Its bottom was covered in water-polished stones as one might find in an ornamental aquarium. He gussied the bike down the banks and into the shallows. Water hissed off the engine. He gingerly nosed it forward. The rear tire stuttered over the smooth stones; the bike slid out from under him, but he was able to hold it up and goose the throttle until the tires caught again. The motor almost cut out at the deepest point, water rising up to the base of the gearbox, but Eb powered it through with a few quick punches on the throttle.

He geared up the far bank and let the bike idle. He wanted to switch it off and let it cool down, but he wasn't sure it would start again. He was not being pursued, that he could see. He swung the bike around and continued down the road.

At some point, the path bled into a clearing. The grass ran waist-high on either side. In the afternoon sunlight, he could see Ellen's car parked at the cut.

"Holy shit." He slapped the side of the bike the way a cowboy might the flanks of a trusty steed. "We made it."

He was fifty yards from Ellen's Oldsmobile when the bike's engine rose to a pained squeal. Smoke poured from the transmission compartment as the gears stripped loose. The bike sputtered once and died. Ebenezer pushed the bike to the car. He laid it down reverentially.

"Thank you," he said to it. "Thank you so much."

The car keys were still tucked under the bumper where Micah had stashed them. He slid the key into the lock and sat in the driver's seat. He gripped the steering wheel. He stared at himself in the rearview mirror. His skin was grayish, a pallor it had never held before. The top quarter of his left ear was gone, blood dried down his neck. He was not fit for human eyes. But he was alive, goddamn it. *Alive.*

He pumped the gas pedal and cranked the key. The engine caught with a magnificent roar, that eight-barrel engine rumbling. He backed into the tall grass, swung the big car around, and drove away from the cut. He unrolled the window and let the cool air play over his face.

"Free at last, free at last," he hooted, "good God almighty, free at last!"

4

"YOU FIGURE the bastard made it?"

Minerva stood at the fence with Micah. It had been hours since Ebenezer had left.

Micah said, "Think so."

Minerva was pretty sure he had, too. The devil's own luck, that prick.

Little Heaven was chilly in the late morning, skies hung with the threat of rain. The compound was quiet. The things in the woods seemed content to remain where they were so long as everyone in Little Heaven stayed put.

"We got to find them, Shug. Or try, at least."

"The children?"

"Yeah, Shug. The children."

Micah said, "We have not heard the last of the Reverend."

"What do you think he's up to?"

"Something," said Micah. "He will commune with God, or so he will tell his flock. Then he will make his move."

Minerva looked at him, sucked at her teeth, then glanced away. "It's still weird."

"What is?"

"You. With two eyes."

"One is glass."

"Really? The old one didn't grow back?" She frowned. "Sorry. I'm ill at ease."

Minerva hooked her fingers through the fence. The sun fought through a bank of clouds and shone down on the woods. They appeared empty; the things could be clustered closer to the road, disregarding the northern flank of Little Heaven. The massive rock formation loomed over the trees. Her fingers tightened.

"I think we're gonna die here, Shug."

Micah didn't reply. She hadn't expected him to. She closed her eyes. She saw the children clustered together under the kitchen trapdoor, their faces white as gaslight. She opened her eyes again, not wanting to see them anymore. "Any clue where they went?"

Micah angled his chin at the black rock that rose at a blunt angle against the sky.

The two of them walked back to their bunkhouse. The grounds were unoccupied; everyone was inside, out of sight. Ellen and Nate were inside. Nate's father was not. Minerva grabbed her backpack. She checked the loads on Ellen's pistol.

"Where are you going?" said Ellen.

"To find the kids," said Micah, arranging his own pack for travel.

"What about those things?" Ellen said.

"We're going north, toward the rock formation," Minerva told her. "They don't seem to be gathered out that way."

"But what if they are?"

Minerva gave her a grisly smile. "It'll be a short trip."

"Why?" said Nate. "I mean, I saw those kids. I don't think . . . they may not come with you. It won't let them."

"What do you mean, *it* won't let them?" Minerva asked.

"That's what Eli said when he came up through the door," the boy told her. "*It wants you*, he said. *It wants all of you.*"

A chill fled down Minerva's spine. "If we don't know what we're up against, we stand a much worse chance of surviving."

"But don't you think Ebenezer will send for—"

"I have no fucking idea," said Minerva, cutting Ellen off. "I don't trust that shithead any farther than I can throw him. Sorry for cursing, kid."

"I want to go," Ellen said.

Micah shook his head. "Someone needs to stay. Keep an eye."

"Why me?" said Ellen, pissed.

Nate clutched her hand. "Please don't go."

"Okay," Ellen said after a pause. "We'll stay."

"We won't be gone long," Minerva promised.

"Just be careful," Ellen said, looking at Micah.

THEY SET OFF in the early afternoon. Nobody saw them leave—or if so, they made no effort to stop them. What would be the use now? Micah snipped the fence at the farthest edge of Little Heaven with some bolt cutters he'd found in a supply shed. He and Minerva slid through the gap, entering the woods.

The trees were thin, with no discernable trail through them. Minerva had a pistol. Micah went unarmed. A gun felt trivial in his hand now. A useless toy.

They stumbled upon a path of sorts. A band of desolate gray stripping through the woods. Not a thing was living along it. Not a tree, a shrub, a weed. It was as if a scouring fire had burned across the ground, leaving only powdery ash behind.

The path wound toward the black rock, which Minerva could glimpse through gaps in the trees. An unsettling sight: a sheer cliff of blackness so dark it swallowed the sunlight. The woods were silent. They were not being trailed.

They kept their own counsel. Minerva could tell that Micah was exhausted. His encounter with the things that had left Otis and Charlie and the red-bearded man dead had sapped his energy. His stride was labored, but his pace was remorseless. Minerva felt weary, too. It was like living in the shadow of a dormant volcano: you never knew when it was going to erupt and spew molten lava all over you.

Clouds rolled in. Rain pattered down. A steady trickle soon grew to a sheeting downpour. They found shelter under the firs. Minerva became aware of the powerful funk of her body. How long had she gone without bathing? She thought back to her last shower in a motel bathroom a few hours' drive from Grinder's Switch. The yellowy water spraying from a calcified nozzle. The mildewed shower curtain with a pattern of bow-tied ducks. How much would she pay to take a shower right now? A thousand dollars? Ten thousand?

The downpour lasted fifteen minutes. The rain turned the ash into a slurry that clung to their boots. They walked until the sun began to fade.

They rounded a bend, and it came into view. The black rock.

The trees petered out, becoming more stunted and palsied. The surrounding landscape was as sandy as a desert. It was monolithic. A giant rotted tooth pushing up from the red sand. It was a mile distant, but Minerva could feel its forbidding magnetism gripping her already—she was a lead filing dragged toward its brooding shadow.

"You do not have to come," Micah said.

"Like hell I don't."

5

YOU'RE ONE DUMB BUNNY, *Virgil Swicker.*

Virgil's mother used to say that. His own mother, who was so damn smart she got knocked up eight times by five different daddies. So damn smart she couldn't wring a shaved nickel out of any of them in child support, so she and her brood lived in a saltbox shack on the edge of the Mojave Desert, sucking on sand. A real smarty-pants, his ma!

But she had him dead to rights. Virgil was dumb. He was just smart enough to know it. Which was a pretty sad place to pin the tail on that particular donkey. If he'd been *juuuuust* a little dumber—if he could have killed off a few measly IQ points—he probably wouldn't have been able to grasp how witless he was. And then it wouldn't have bothered him so much. What a kick in the teeth, huh?

One thing about knowing your limits is you learn how to operate within them. Virgil Swicker had learned early on that his lot in life was being a follower. He felt safest behind someone else, looking down at that man's heels. A leader needed smarts and fire and drive. All a follower ever needed to know was where to line up.

Virgil had left home at fifteen to little fanfare; his mother could barely care enough to wave good-bye from the stoop. He hitchhiked to San Francisco and lived on the streets, eating out of dumpsters behind Chinky restaurants. He was a big kid and nobody had raised him right; he started rolling drunks, and that went well for a while before this one rummy wheeled on him with a switchblade. The guy was nimble with that blade, too, even three sheets to the wind—"I'm over from Stockton, motherfucker!" he kept screaming, as if that should mean something to Virgil, as if laying your hands on a wino over from Stockton was a capital crime. That Stockton trash maniac opened a big slash under Virgil's armpit, then chased him down the street, laughing like a schoolboy, *tee-hee-hee*—if the nutzoid hadn't tripped into a gutter, he would have caught Virgil and stabbed his eyes out.

After that, Virgil mooned around the Tenderloin like a kicked dog. There were times he thought about buying a knife or maybe a gun—that bastard with the switchblade wouldn't have been so high-and-mighty if Virgil had stuck a pistol in his face, bet your ass on *that*—but he couldn't afford either of those items. It was in the depths of despair that a single ray of sunlight brightened Virgil's world. That ray had a name: Cyril Neeps.

They met on a bench in Union Square. Virgil was puffy and scabbed, his teeth loose in his gums from eating dumpster fruit. Cyril was tanned and fit and had this way about him that said, *Hey, world, get a load of me!* He seemed the kind of man who could do anything he wanted with his life, and Virgil was instantaneously awed by him.

"What's your story, fella?" Cy had asked without much interest, investigating the cracks of his teeth with a cinnamon-flavored toothpick.

Virgil had hemmed and hawed for about fifteen seconds before Cyril laughed great big, sucked a shred of meat off the tip of the toothpick, and said: "You're as dumb as a box of rocks, ain't ya?"

". . . I guess so."

Cyril clapped him on the back. "Hey, no big whoop. You probably didn't spend enough time in your mama's belly. You came out like a cake that's still mushy in the middle."

"I guess."

"Here, have a toothpick," Cy said, unwrapping a fresh one. Virgil was overcome by this small charity.

"That's right, dummy," Cyril said cheerily. "Use the pointy end."

There was nothing cruel in the way he said *dummy*—just stating a fact, which Virgil guessed was true. Cyril would call him dumb in many flavorful ways as their relationship went along. Dumb as a bag of hammers. Three bricks short of a load. Squirrel-headed. Pudding-brained. Not the sharpest pencil in the drawer. Drooling fuckin' mongoloid when he was running hot. Sometimes Virgil would go red in the face when Cyril said these things, but he never argued. He just wished Cy had the good manners not to mention his dumbness, the way you shouldn't call attention to the fact that a kid was missing his hand or was blind or something like that. It was mean, pointing out defects. But then, Cyril wasn't really a nice guy.

But he *was* smart. A whole lot smarter than Virgil—granted, that was a low bar to clear. But Cyril had command. *Presence*. When he walked into a room, people looked up. If they looked long enough, they would see Virgil trailing in on his heels. Virgil helped Cyril stick up a few gas stations and a Chinatown grocer. It was dead easy. Cyril laid his hands on a gun. They wore panty hose over their faces. They made good money, too. Fifty bucks here, thirty-seven bucks there. All in cash! *Untraceable* was the word Cyril used.

Still, they got pinched. Bad luck, was all. They both did a hitch. Two years, sentences reduced due to prison overcrowding. After they got out, they returned to the Tenderloin. Virgil tried to sell his body to the waify mincers and nine-to-five types who trolled the park for rough trade. But Virgil looking how he did, there weren't many takers. Cyril was tired of him by then, Virgil could tell. He wanted a real partner, someone to help him become the criminal big shot he knew he could be. Someone a damn sight better than shit-a-brick Virgil Swicker. But Cyril never did find that running mate—maybe because he wasn't such hot shit, Virgil secretly thought.

One day, they wandered through the doors of Amos Flesher's church. Cyril thought they might steal a chalice or something and pawn it. Instead they met the supreme-o creepster himself, ole Reverend Flesher with his greasy muskrat-pelt hair. Flesher had bumbled out of the whatever-the-fuck-you-call-it, his dressing room where he put on his goofy church clothes. He saw them skulking around.

"You looking for something, fellas?"

He had an aw-shucks way about him. But Virgil could see that was a sham. This was a guy who could spot the angle in a circle.

"Gimme all your money," Cyril said mock-jokingly, but with that ever-present flint in his eye.

The Rev cocked his head at them. Then he reached into his pocket and pulled out a flashy roll—a wad of cash. What was a man of God doing with a pimp roll? He peeled off a few twenties and handed them over.

"The Lord provides," he told them. "Why don't you come back later? I might have a job for you."

The Rev saw something in them that he could use. And so it transpired that they came here to Little Heaven, to buttfuck nowhere, to nursemaid a bunch of religious freakos. It wasn't too bad at first. The Reverend promised them plenty of dough. It was easy work. They would've been happy to keep the churchy fuckos in line, really crack the fuckin' whip, but the Rev's followers never fell *out* of line. So most of the time, he and Cy sat around with their thumbs up their asses, feeling antsy. They had plenty of ammo, so they shot their guns off in the woods. But after a while, there wasn't much to shoot at.

Virgil hated it—nothing but trees and dirt clods and people mumbling prayers. Cyril was madder than a wet hen, too. Little Heaven messed with his brain waves, he said. They tried brewing hooch to stabilize Cyril's bummed waves, but that plan went tits up.

Then things got weirder. Voices in the woods. Shapes, some even claimed. But nothing you could point a finger at and say: *This here, this is messed up.* Just a feeling. Everyone started acting hinky, especially the kids. It was sorta like that movie he'd watched at the Presidio a few years back after filching some coins out of a blind beggar's cup—*Invasion of the Body Snatchers.* As if the whole damn camp had been taken over by pod people. Virgil half expected to find a bunch of oozing, cracked-open pods down in the kitchen cellar.

Then the outsiders showed up—Virgil hadn't minded so much, because at least there was nothing much weird about them. They came from the world of streetlights and restaurants and roller-disco rinks, from the real world. But soon after, things got unreal when that kid Eli came back looking like something in the woods had sucked the life out of him . . . and then Cy went missing. Virgil was terrified that he'd run off home without telling him. Just took off in the dead of night. *Hasta la vista, Virg, I'll see you in the funny pages, ole buddy ole chum.*

And then just this morning that fucking nigger *cunt* went and stole a motorcycle. When Virgil went to stop it, he got a goddamn wrench chucked at him. It hit him so hard that he tasted metal on his tongue and his skull rang like a church bell. Before he knew it, the rotten pig-fucker was beating the living daylights out of him! And not a damn one of these religious bumpkins stepped in to stop the long-haired spook. They just let the prick whale away. Go ahead, you thieving foreigner, beat the tar out of a goddamn honest American!

Virgil had woken up in Doc Lewis's quarters. His forehead was so swollen he looked like a caveman. His eyes were puffed to slits. That wouldn't have happened if Cy had been around. He would have shot that black bastard dead in his boots. But Cy wasn't around anymore and it broke Virgil's heart.

Presently he got out of his bed in Doc Lewis's bunkhouse and went outside. His face hurt like hell. He walked the fence. Nobody was around. The long-haired English faggot had taken off on the motorbike, he figured. Virgil hoped he'd gotten ripped apart by the things in the woods, that they ate his stringy black ass like beef jerky. Serve him right.

Clouds gathered overhead. The rain started as a light drizzle and built to a torrent, fat drops drumming on the warehouse roofs. Virgil let the downpour soak him to the skin. As a young boy he used to stand at the edge of the desert on scorching summer days watching chain lightning skate over the hillsides, waiting for the rain to come. There was great relief when those swollen clouds finally split open above him.

He watched the forest. Maybe he should run, too. There was another motorbike, right? He ought to get the hell out of here before things got any worse and—

Something or someone was standing between the trees.

Virgil squinted through the sheeting rain. He was still woozy from the beating that jigaboo had laid on him. For an instant, he pictured a gaggle of witches—these old crones with sagging papery skin and cruel twists of mouths shuffling between the tall dark pines clung with eldritch skeins of moss . . . witches, or perhaps just creatures who dressed to look like witches, but who were in truth more ancient and evil than any witch—

But no. It was just one person. A figure standing motionless in the shadowy canopy of the woods.

"Who's out there? Who—"

Whatever it was, it came forward fast—spooky fast. One moment it was fifty yards off and the next it was right there, a few feet from the fence. It was Cyril . . . looked like Cy, anyhow. Except the eyes were off.

And the way he stood there kinda creaky-looking, like his bones were all busted under his skin.

He looks like somebody already dead. This was Virgil's trembling thought. His old pal Cy was dead as a doornail, except that little nugget of information hadn't sunk into his decayed head quite yet. Virgil figured it would have to come as a shock to his dear friend.

"Everything okay, Cy?"

Cyril smiled. His teeth were gray like the dead tooth in his grandma's mouth with a copper wire around it. Except every one of Cy's teeth was gray—you'd think he had painted them with lead or something.

"Fine and dandy, Virg."

"Well, good." Virgil swallowed. Rain washed down his throat. It tasted bad, like water a corpse had sat in for days. "Where you been?"

"Oh, out and about."

That was another worrisome thing. Cy's voice was funny, too. Wet and rattling as if stuff was coming loose inside of him.

"I thought . . . jeez, you're going to call me a dummy, but I thought maybe you'd left, Cy. You couldn't stand another minute and skedaddled."

"Aw, hell." Cy hawked back and spat. The oyster of congealed phlegm just kinda fell out of his mouth like a dead slug and dribbled down his boot, black as clotted oil. "You think I'd leave all this happy horseshit?"

"Sure. No." Virgil tried to smile, but the muscles of his face didn't feel like they were working so hot. "You bet."

Right then, Virgil felt like running. Yep, turning tail and sprinting away from his old buddy Cy. His heart was bappity-bapping inside his chest, and there was a tightness in his crotch as if a hard little balloon were swelling up behind his bladder.

"They all ought to pay, don't you think?"

"Who's that, Cy?"

Cyril motioned at Little Heaven with his chin—the pitiful whole of it. "Everyone. All these fuckers. Pay for disobeying the Lord."

Since when did Cy give two shits about the Lord? "Well now, I don't really see how they've—"

"Shut up, squirrel head," Cy said. Virgil zipped his lip. "Shouldn't they pay for what they let happen to you? That fairy nig beating on your head like a bongo drum while they all stood around with their dicks in their hands?"

Virgil caught a smell coming off his compadre. He nearly gagged. It would be rude to puke on account of Cy reeking so bad. A strong sense of unreality washed over Virgil; he felt light-headed, like when he used to huff gasoline in Mission Dolores Park.

"They could have stepped in, yeah."

"Bet your ass, buckaroo," said Cy. "Now let me tell you—clean the shit out of your ears, dim bulb, and listen up good—the Reverend's got a plan."

Virgil smiled dozily, "Is that so?"

"That's a fact, jack. And all you got to do is exactly what he says. Figure you can manage that, or will following simple instructions make your fool brains squirt out your ears?"

"Aw, come on now, Cy . . ."

Virgil's thoughts were swimmy and remote. It was as if his brain was trying to sprint away from him, away from Little Heaven and everything that was happening. But where could it go? It was trapped in his stupid skull, just like Virgil was trapped here.

"Can you help, Cy? I'd feel a lot better if you were helping. You always were the—"

"The brains of the operation. Yeah, Virg, I know. Lord knows I do. But not this time. You're on your own."

"Why?"

"Because I can't anymore."

"Why?" Virgil repeated stupidly.

Cyril opened his mouth. Virgil took an instinctive step back. The inside of Cy's mouth was all black, but things were moving in the pit of his throat. Bugs, it looked like. But it couldn't be. Roaches scuttling over one another . . .

Virgil said, "Oh."

Cyril shut his mouth. He had begun to drift away from the fence, back toward the woods. Virgil couldn't see his feet moving. That was odd, wasn't it?

I hid a gun in our bunkhouse, Cyril said . . . Actually, he didn't *say* anything. His lips were shut. But Virgil could hear him just fine.

A long bladelike insect—a centipede?—slid out of Cyril's nostril. It curled around the rim of his nose, its legs skiddle-skaddling and antennae twitching, crawled between his eyes and up his forehead to vanish into the tangled nest of his hair. Virgil did not scream, but if his throat hadn't been so dry all of a sudden, he surely would have.

Look under the bed, Virg. Take the gun. You'll need it.

Cy kept on floating back toward the trees. To be honest, Virgil couldn't say he was all that sad to see him go. Cyril's body knitted into the gloom of the woods. A few minutes later, the rain stopped entirely.

Virgil walked through the muddy slop to their bunkhouse. The gun—a Bulldog .38 revolver—and a box of ammunition were stashed under the cot in a hole dug under the clapboards, just like Cyril had said it would be. Good ole Cy, always looking out.

Virgil stuck the pistol into his waistband. Then he crossed the square to the chapel and knocked on the door. The Reverend answered. He didn't look so hot. His hair fell over his forehead in greasy strings. He stunk like a polecat in July.

"Come in." He smiled—a gruesome sight—his eyes flicking edgewise. "We have much work to do."

Reluctantly, with the same dread a man might feel stepping into his own casket, Virgil Swicker went inside.

6

EBENEZER FLED the ruin of Grinder's Switch and hit the interstate, gunning the Oldsmobile's engine hard as he piled up the miles between himself and Little Heaven.

The big-bore engine sent a soothing vibration through the whole car. He flicked on the radio and caught the Sonics singing "The Witch" on KIOT 102.5—"*Spinning platters without the chatter!*"—out of Albuquerque.

The blood on his scalp and ear had coagulated and turned crusty.

He stopped at a Texaco station and cleaned himself up in the bathroom—the gas jockey had looked like he was going to withhold the lavatory key, but something in Eb's demeanor convinced him to hand it over. When Eb emerged, he looked somewhat presentable. He got on the road again and pulled into a roadside diner sometime later. A bubble of polished glass and steel made dull by the constantly blowing dust. He could see a few people inside at the counter or sitting in padded booths. A pie case revolved at the end of the counter—huge, three-inch-thick wedges peaked with meringue or whipped cream. He wiped the drool off his lips and considered his state. He was in no shape for public viewing, not without having to answer a lot of questions. What he needed was a motel room, a bath, and to sleep in a real bed for roughly fifteen years.

A pay phone stood near the diner's entrance. He flipped open the car's ashtray and found a crumpled dollar bill, plus a few dimes and nickels. His back was welded to the upholstery with sweat; he peeled off the seat like a giant Band-Aid and made his way to the phone.

"Truth or Consequences Police Department. Do you have a crime to report?"

Eb cleared his throat. "I do, yes."

The line clicked. A series of buzzes, then a man picked up.

"Detective Rollins speaking. What's the problem?"

The man sounded as if he was expecting an elderly woman to tell him that her cat, Mr. Buttons, was stuck up an elm tree.

"Er, yes . . ." Ebenezer was unsure how to proceed. He should have rehearsed. "I believe something's happening in the woods and hills up past the town of Grinder's Switch."

"That so, buddy? What kinda something we talkin' about?"

The detective sounded fat. Eb pictured him leaning back in a wooden chair while an electric fan stirred the squad room's humid air around. He saw rolls of flab cascading down the back of Rollins's neck to his too-tight collar, balls of sweat rolling down his forehead to dampen his caterpillar eyebrows above a pair of small, piggy eyes.

"I was hiking around that area and I came across—"

"Where you from, pardner? You don't sound local."

"I'm English, if that matters."

Rollins's voice grew hard. "What matters is what I say matters. We clear on that, pard?"

"Crystal."

"Go on, tell your story. I don't got all day."

Ebenezer gazed through the dusty window into the diner. The waitress—an old battle-ax named Flo or Marge or Betsy, no doubt—was gawping out at him. The pie case spun enticingly at her elbow.

"I was hiking in the hills," Eb said tightly. "Came across a camp. A survivalist setup. Little Heaven, I believe it's called. Have you heard of it?"

"Nope." The detective popped the *p* in a way that conveyed his total boredom.

"Yes, so, about thirty or forty of them. Living on their own in the woods."

"That's not a crime. Weird, but not a crime."

"Right, well . . . I think some of them might have died."

He heard a loud *scriitch*—the sound of Rollins pulling his chair closer to his desk, perhaps. His voice was suddenly bright with interest.

"Go on."

"I don't know how it happened, or what happened. All I know is that—"

"What did you see?" Rollins said.

"A body. Maybe more. Some dead bodies."

"You sure? How close did you get to them bodies? You positive whoever it was wasn't just sleeping or knocked out or—?"

"Sleeping? No. Dead."

"Dead how?"

"I beg pardon?"

"*How* were these bodies *dead*? Bullet in the head? Knife? What?"

What use was it to tell this man the truth? That Charlie Fairweather and Otis Langtree and the big redheaded bull had been savagely dismembered by beasts beyond the Sheriff's wildest imaginings—creatures that would wreck his tiny, suet-engirded mind?

Ebenezer sighed. "I . . . I don't know. They're just dead. Either you believe that or you don't." *You shitkicking fathead,* he thought.

A grumbling exhale from Rollins's end. The chair squeaked as his body settled back into what Ebenezer assumed to be its original uninterested posture.

"You know it's a federal offense to transmit wrongful information to a law enforcement officer, don'tcha?"

Ebenezer shut his eyes and rested his head against the phone booth. He should have practiced his story.

"I'm not lying, Officer."

"What's your name?"

"Julius."

"Uh-huh. Julius who?"

"Julius Thriftwhistle."

"Well then, Mr. Thriftwhistle, why don't you haul your ass down to the station and fill out a report for us? Then we can get to work sorting your story out."

Ebenezer wasn't going to any police station. Not in his state—not at all. They would ask for his ID. They might even run his fingerprints, and that would be very bad indeed. Ebenezer and the authorities were on less-than-jolly terms with each other.

"Or why not tell me where you are and I come to you? Pretty sure I heard a big truck blast by a minute ago on your end, so I'd guess you're at a pay phone along the interst—"

Eb hung up. Bloody hell. That had gone poorly. He gazed into the diner. Pure undiluted Americana: bright linoleum and shiny chrome and the smell of delicious starches fried in oil. After a momentary debate, he pushed through the door. A bell tinkled. A father and mother and their young daughter sat in one booth. A traveling-salesman type occupied the counter. Pearl was dishing up them vittles.

He sat on a padded counter stool. He flipped through the miniature jukebox mounted beside his elbow. He slid a nickel in and punched B6. "Stand By Me," by Ben E. King. Eb was surprised to find a black man's song on the jukebox. The waitress approached with an obvious lack of enthusiasm.

"You okay, Mister?" Pronounced it as *misser*.

Eb smiled winningly. It probably didn't help. "Tip-top, my dear. Thank you for inquiring."

She set her order pad down and watched him carefully, the way you'd watch a small but vicious dog that had slipped its leash.

"What kinds of pie do you serve?"

"Sweet potato, blueberry, lemon, shoofly pie—"

"Shoofly?"

"It's a northern thing," she said. "Molasses pie. Our baker came down from Pennsylvania Dutch country. He brung the recipe with him."

"Molasses, mmm? Sounds like treacle pudding. I ate that as a child in England."

Flo clearly did not give a tin shit what Eb had done back in Merry Ole. She tapped her pencil on the order pad, wanting him to eat, pay up, and leave.

"How much?"

"Forty cents."

"Sold! And a cup of coffee you can stand a spoon up in, if'n you please."

"We don't make that kind of coffee."

His smile widened. "I'll take whatever you've got."

Eb closed his eyes and dropped his skull to the countertop. The ceramic was cool on his forehead. Lovely, such small pleasures. He ruminated. What were his options? He could keep going. That was good, and it suited his temperament. He'd promised them he'd call the police. Well, he *had*. That shitkicking detective gave him the gears, all because Eb had a funny way of talking. He wasn't going to the police station; he'd wind up in a cell. What more did he owe, for Christ's sake?

You're scared, Ebenezer.

It was his aunt's voice in his head. His aunt Hazel, dead nearly two decades now. But Hazel practically raised him. Eb's father did what plenty of rot-ass fathers did—went out for a bottle of milk and a pack of Mayfair cigarettes one fine afternoon and never showed his face again. Not even to bring that tossing milk home. His mother was a sensitive type, prone to bouts of the nerves, as they were known in those days; as such, his rearing fell mainly to her older sister, Eb's aunt, Hazel Coggins. Hazel was unmarried—"Men are as useful as a chocolate teapot," she was fond of saying—and worked at the local butcher shop. A big, handsome woman, and a dab hand with a cleaver: she could draw and quarter a hog faster and cleaner than anyone. Hazel was a *hard* woman: eyes, body, outlook. Life was eat or be eaten, according to her, and better to be hunter than prey.

But as a primary school student, Ebenezer had too often been prey. The first-form boys would surround him in the sandlot after school—eight or ten boys, all of them white—to throw insults and, soon enough, fists. When Ebenezer returned home bloody-nosed on a third consecutive day, his aunt took action.

She was still wearing her butcher's apron, wet at the hem with hog's blood. She took it off, wadded it up, and—while Eb struggled—pressed it over his mouth and nose.

"Smell it!" She shoved it into his face as he choked on the sodden fabric. "Are you a hog, boy? Are you *meat*?"

She let him loose. He sucked in a great breath and stared at her warily, suspecting she'd spring on him again.

"Or are you made of sterner stuff, Ebenezer?" she asked. "You have to be, or you'll never make it through this life."

"What do I do?" he asked her.

"Tomorrow, you fight back. Until you can't stand, if that's how it must be." She took his face in her callused palms. "If you bend to them now—if you let them cow you—then you'll get used to the feel of the yoke around your neck."

The next day when his tormentors assembled in the sandlot, Ebenezer said: "Well and good, lads. Let's tussle." He had nobody on his side; his teachers must have known of this abuse by now, but none of them stepped in. If nothing else, this solidified in Ebenezer the fact that his lot in life was to be a man alone—and if his isolation was to be an ever-present part of existence, he'd better learn how to function within that cold circle.

The first boy who rushed at him was a fat and beery-faced son of the local banker. Ebenezer curled his hand into a fist and struck back—and he was shocked to discover he was quicker and much more powerful than his antagonist. The boy's fist struck him with the sting of a mosquito bite; meanwhile, his own fist hammered into that porky, satisfied face with a meaty *smack*. The boy reeled away with a strangled cry. Ebenezer pressed his advantage, throwing venomous punches at the boys ringing him—even the boys who had never struck him, who had only thronged him for the sport of it. *You trifle with the bull, you get the horns*, he'd thought, swinging vicious roundhouses at the wide-eyed white faces flocked around him. In time, the boys began to hit back—he was hammered hard, repeatedly, but this time, instead of turning tail, he'd hit back, again and again, giving almost as good as he got and relying on his ability to continue sucking up punishment while his adversaries lost their gumption, one by one, and fled.

That night he'd staggered home. His eyes were swollen shut, his nose broken, several knuckles crushed. He did not go to school for days. His aunt nursed him back to health. Even she seemed amazed at the punishment he'd taken. But when he returned to school, the torments ceased.

"You will never be scared again," Aunt Hazel said proudly. "You'll never be the hog."

And he hadn't been. From that day forward, he'd been the butcher. That had persisted until the night, only days ago, when he'd seen the boy with the slug-gray eyes all covered in roaches. Then—for the first time in over twenty years—he'd felt the blade on his neck. He was the hog again, his heart filled with that quailing, weak-kneed fear he'd fought so hard to push from his soul.

You were scared, Ebenezer, his aunt spoke inside his head. *Come clean.*

Of course, this was true. As scared as he'd ever been in his life.

That stuck in his craw. He realized it now, many miles from the seat of that fear. He did not like being made to feel scared. More to the point, he was disgusted to find that flaw still dwelling within him—one he'd fought so hard to dispel. But that fear had returned.

Surely it was natural, considering what he had experienced.

Still. *Still*.

He could not live with it. Nor with the abandonment of his compatriots, which left an unaccountably large hole in him—Minerva and Shughrue and the woman and the boy were not his obligation, were they? Lord no! Yet he felt now as if they had been a part of something together, however awful, and he . . . he couldn't believe he had come around to this way of thinking.

But by God, he *owed*.

Bigger than that, though, was the fear. He had been chased off by it. He had allowed himself to be cowed by whatever lurked in the woods surrounding Little Heaven.

And that . . . that simply would not do—

The pie plate clattered next to Ebenezer's ear, breaking his reverie. A fork clanged down beside it. A mug of coffee touched down next, hot droplets sloshing over the rim and burning his scalp.

He lifted his head. There it was. The shoofly pie. Dark, with a flaky crust. He picked up the fork and meticulously cleaned the tines with a paper napkin from the dispenser. Then he flicked the fork away sharply—it *pinged* off the steel coffee cistern—picked up the pie with his bare, blood-stained hands, and shoveled it into his mouth. Eb ate the thick wedge in five wolfish bites, barely chewing, just stuffing it in until his cheeks bulged, then swallowing with a sinuous motion like a snake devouring a gerbil.

"Christ on a dirt bike, Flo, that's some good pie!" he roared with such force that bits of filling sprayed from his mouth. "Shoofly, you don't bother *me*!"

He pushed himself up and rocked back on his heels. He took a big swig of coffee, burning the top of his mouth in the process, shouted, "Ye gods, Myrtle, that's some hot joe!" then pulled the dollar bill from his pocket, smoothed it out over the counter's edge, and set it down primly on his empty plate.

"I shall tell my friends of this place, Darla!" he informed the startled waitress. "I'll sing its praises to the high heavens! *Come for the pie*, I'll tell them, *but stay for the delightful fucking hospitality!*"

The woman in the booth covered her daughter's ears. Her husband—a square-jawed clodhopper in dungarees—appeared as if he might make something of it, but he took a good look at Ebenezer and must have figured his daughter would hear worse in her life.

"Good day to you," Eb said, booting the door open, "and God bless!"

LATER THAT AFTERNOON, Ebenezer pulled into Jimmy's Gun Rack. It was closed. Either Jimmy had knocked off early or folks around here didn't purchase elephant guns past four o'clock. Either way, Eb's task would be much easier with the shop empty.

He knocked on the front door. No answer. He knocked harder, in case Jimmy was asleep in the storeroom. When that got no response, he walked around back. No car. He returned out front and drove the Olds around back. The mesa stretched away behind the shop—nothing but miles of sand studded with scraggly cacti.

The delivery door was locked, but not with a dead bolt. Instead, steel collars were attached to the door and the cinderblock wall, clasped with a heavy padlock.

Eb popped the trunk and peeled back the floor upholstery. The scissor jack sat atop the emergency spare. He grabbed the jack handle—a two-foot steel rod—and approached the door. He threaded the handle through the shackle U and levered his body against it.

"Come on, you old slapper," he grunted, putting his full weight on the jack handle.

The lock popped. The jack handle swung up and cracked Eb in the forehead. He staggered back, dazed, and fell on his ass in the dirt.

The lock fell to the earth. The door swung open and—

BOOM!

The heavy steel door blew open like a screen door caught in the wind, slammed the shop's brick wall, the knob chipping the cement, and ricocheted back.

Eb staggered up and peeked around the door frame. The inside of the door was shredded with pock-holes. A Mossberg shotgun was parked five feet within the entryway, strapped to a mount of welded steel. Copper wire was wrapped around the trigger, the trailing end looped through a series of metal eyelets along the ceiling to a hook on the door.

"Jumpin' Jesus Christ, Jimmy," Eb whispered, shaken. "Some might call that excessive."

He eased past the homemade booby trap and into the storeroom. He flicked a light and gazed over the halogen-lit interior. There didn't appear to be any other nasty surprises—not obvious ones, anyway.

He grabbed a Beretta 12-gauge pistol-grip shotgun and ten boxes of shells. To this he added a pair of Colt M1911s, a hundred rounds of ammo, and six spare clips. He stashed everything in the car trunk, then went back inside. He shed his shirt and pants. His chest and arms were cut, but apart from his ear the damage was superficial. He donned a camouflage hunting outfit he found in the main showroom.

Then he went back for the flamethrower he'd pointed out to Micah when they had first come into the shop. He hefted the canisters. Something sloshed inside the left one—jellied gasoline. The right one would be full of nitrogen propellant.

He found a few other items—a bowie knife, a flare gun, some stout rope, and a Zippo lighter in a desk in Jimmy's office. The lighter sat next to some cigars. Once he identified them as genuine Cubanos and not the trick exploding kind, he slid two of them into the chest pocket of his spiffy new hunting outfit.

He muscled the flamethrower into the Oldsmobile's backseat. He considered leaving a note for Jimmy, telling him his store had been looted by the forces of good . . . but he did not do this, because he was not an especially good person and felt no compulsion to lie about it. He did close the back door. The least he could do.

Ebenezer followed the highway until he found a deserted access road. He drove a mile down it and stopped. He opened the trunk, loaded the guns and the spare clips. A scorpion sunned itself on a flat rock nearby.

He got into the car and drove back to the head of the access road. A big store sat on the side of an otherwise deserted stretch a few hundred yards off. *Big Al's Bargain Village.* He swung into its parking lot. The dusty bay window showcased the store's wares. Blenders and fondue pots and tennis rackets and sterling silver tea sets—*Al's got everything under the sun!* the display boasted.

A seventeen-inch Magnavox TV was broadcasting an episode of *The Andy Griffith Show.* Bug-eyed Barney Fife was giving Opie advice. Someone was always giving Opie advice. The carrot-topped, weedy idiot. Eb closed his eyes and rested his head against the glass. *Are you really going to do this?* he asked himself. *Are you that much of a damned fool?* He pictured those monstrosities skulking through the woods; he recalled the charnel stink wafting off the one that had swooped down and aggressively relieved him of half his ear.

He didn't owe any of them a Christly thing. It had been a business arrangement, nothing more. He'd fulfilled his end of the bargain, hadn't he?

"Can I help you, fella?"

A fat man in a seersucker suit stared at him from the store entrance. Big Al his own self, by the looks of it. He had the flat-hanging, shiny red face of a carnival barker—but he didn't look all too impressed to see a black man in a camouflage outfit mooning around his display window.

"Just reflecting on life," Eb said.

"That so, Alec Guinness?" Big Al bit his thumbnail; his teeth *crunched* on the calcified enamel. "Does that reflection include a desire for mid-quality consumer goods?"

Ebenezer smiled. "I guess not."

"Then I'll kindly ask you to fuck right off."

Ebenezer laughed. "And the horse I rode in on, yes?"

"That's about the size of it. I don't need your nose prints all over my glass."

Still chuckling, Eb walked back to the car. Big Al glared after him. Eb slid behind the wheel and fired up the Olds. "Eve of Destruction" was playing on the radio. He cranked the volume knob and peeled out of the lot, heading back in the direction he'd come.

7

DARKNESS HAD NEARLY FALLEN by the time Minerva and Micah reached the rock. They stopped twenty yards from its southern face. It was black as obsidian. Its outcroppings were sharp as cut glass, impervious to the scourings of wind and rain. Its sheer face climbed nearly two hundred yards before reaching a flat apex. Micah wondered if there was a route to the summit—and, if one existed, did they really want to see what was up there?

They circumnavigated the rock, working eastward. They kept their distance from it, walking through the clingy sand that carpeted the slope. The sun's dying rays washed the woods, but did not lighten the monolith itself. It was as if the sun's light was consumed by it.

It took half an hour to cut around to its eastern face. The monolith was carved sharply, its angles nearly as neat as those on a skyscraper. The new face rose even more sheerly: a black mirror that, instead of reflecting, swallowed the reflections of anything set before it.

The sun set behind the firs. The woods were quiet. The only sound came from the rock itself: a low bristling hum, as if, behind its edge-less face, trillions of flies were filling its core with the seethe of their industry.

"This place is terrible," Minerva said, standing off Micah's shoulder.

Micah could not disagree. It was dreadful to encounter such spots: places that appeared to have experienced horrors that, while unseen and ages-old, were still trapped there—held there by whatever malignancy had minted them. But there was no visible evidence. No sacrificial altar, no open graves or moldering skulls mounted on pikes. Just the implacable rock and the fearsome chill it gave off.

They came upon an entrance of sorts: an inverted V in the rock face, about twenty feet tall at its apex. Darkness crawled out of it. It gave off a more profound cold, too: Micah's forearms broke out in gooseflesh. He removed a flashlight from his pack and shone it into the cleft. The beam gave no indication how far in it went or where it might lead.

"Think the kids are in there?" Minerva said. Her voice was tight with strain. "We could keep walking around the whole—"

"This is the place, Minny."

"Yeah. Feels like it."

The cleft was five feet wide at its base, but it narrowed quickly; they had to duck to get inside. The cleft gave way to a cavern carved through the rock. The flashlight picked up a scattering of pebbles on its uneven floor. Mineral deposits jagged down from the cavern's ceiling: they were two feet long, skinny as soda straws. These weird rock icicles. One raked the top of Micah's scalp like the scrape of an emery board. The rock was wet here, with a popcorny appearance: it resembled a vast exposed brain.

The tunnel was set on a gradual decline, almost too imperceptible to discern. The air was stale with an alkaline undertaste—the taste that comes up off hot pavement after a storm. Micah swept the beam over the walls and ceiling, which was no longer carbuncled but instead perfectly rounded, as if it had been smoothed with a grinder. Their breath filled the cramped space, creating vibrations that flitted against the sensitive apparatus of their inner ears.

A sly squirming noise emanated overhead. Micah stopped. Minerva ran into his back and let out a squawk. He pressed a finger to his lips. The squirming was wet, unctuous, *lush*. He swung the beam up to the cave ceiling. Minerva dry-heaved in revulsion.

The ceiling was covered in a seething mass. Eelish creatures, each roughly three inches long, carpeted the rock. They were pale yellow, the color of margarine or the fatty tissue of an excised tumor. Their pencil-thin bodies were belled at one end and tipped with a flagellate tail at the other. Thousands of them squirmed on the rock above.

"Olms," Micah said quietly. "A kind of salamander. They are not native to this part of the world."

The creatures massed into large balls the size of grapefruits. The balls quivered pendulously, threatening to fall and splat on the floor—or on their upturned faces.

"What the hell are they doing?"

"Breeding," said Micah.

They moved past the olms, deeper into the cavern. The flashlight swept over something . . . Micah registered it the next instant and swung the beam back. A hair barrette. Dull pink. The sort of thing a girl wore. The little Rasmussen girl, for instance.

The cavern narrowed until they had to walk single file. Minerva grabbed ahold of Micah's belt loop. The blackness pushed back at them, almost a physical presence; if he shut off the flashlight—or if the batteries suddenly died—Micah imagined it slipping over them, inside of them, sliding around their eyeballs and between their lips, a predatory darkness seeking something to feast upon. He stumbled and set a hand on the wall to steady himself. The rock was not cold to the touch, at least not this deep inside the monolith: it was warm and slick, like the flesh of a sleeping giant.

The floor dropped away five feet ahead; the flashlight beam picked up motes of dust swirling in a mammoth darkness.

"Hold up," said Micah.

They had reached the lip of a precipice. There was just enough room to perch at its edge. Micah shone the light down. The drop was nearly straight. Micah guessed it was a thirty-foot fall. At the bottom was a basin with a ten-foot-wide base. He could make out the mouth of a tunnel down there; it was more cramped than the cavern they had already traversed—the tunnel looked to be about four feet in height, three feet in diameter. It must lead deeper inside the rock.

A rope ladder traveled down the face of the drop; the rope was sturdy but old, the wooden rungs worn smooth with age. Micah shone the light upward. The ceiling bellied a few feet above them. There was just the precipice, the drop, and the tunnel mouth below.

"Who would put a ladder here?" Minerva said.

Micah grunted. It wasn't a question worth contemplating. The ladder was here. That was the only thing that mattered. He kicked a pebble over the edge and followed it with the flashlight. It bounced off the rocks at the bottom of the basin and skipped toward the mouth of the tunnel—

Micah's breath hitched, then whistled out on a near-silent note.

Four sticks. Craggy and white as driftwood. Four sticks were latched around the top of the tunnel's mouth. At least, that's what they looked like on first blush. So much so that Micah's mind tried to immediately dismiss them as such. Except for their placement. How would sticks get to such a place? How would they find themselves latched round a tunnel mouth so deep within this place? Maybe they were exposed roots—but if so, roots to *what*? What tree or weed could grow down there? And how would those roots push themselves out of solid rock?

Then it dawned on him that those sticks were moving ever so slightly. They were vibrating minutely, in fact, the outermost stick lifting and coming down again on the rock. Tapping, almost . . .

. . . almost like a finger.

Four more sticks materialized close to that first bundle. They crept out of the darkness at the tunnel's mouth and latched around its upper curvature. Micah stood frozen. The fingers were long and wiry like insulated electrical cables. Well, isn't that odd? Dreamily, Micah wondered what they could be attached to. He tried to picture the wrists and arms, the body . . . Next, his brain went dark, his synapses dimming like a cityscape during a rolling blackout.

Then came the sounds. They traveled up from the tunnel below them. The laughter of children. A charmless sound, full of mocking malice.

"*Come.*"

A child's voice. But not exactly. More the voice of a child who had lived in this sunless place for a minor eternity. A child whose eyes were yellow as a cat's eyes and whose flesh has the look of old parchment. A wizened and corrupted thing whose throaty chuckling drifted up from the bowels of the earth.

"*Meat for the feast,*" the voice called.

The strain of terror that entered Micah's heart at that moment was unlike any he'd ever felt—even worse than anything he'd experienced in Korea, though he had been scared an awful lot over there. But those were understandable fears. Fears about what war—and the machinations of his fellow man—could do to your body and mind. He was ripped back through time to a cold night in Korea when he'd been walking past the medic's tent; the flap blew open in a high wind. He saw a young soldier—still a boy, really—lying on a makeshift bed. His arms and legs had been blown off. All that was left were these rags of flesh that swung and drooped from the stumps of his legs like thick moldering curtains. The boy wasn't screaming. The shock put him beyond all that. Micah had glimpsed the surgeon's eyes above his blood-spattered mask: they reflected a dull emptiness, as if he wasn't seeing the patient in front of him. A single word drifted out of that open flap before the wind blew it shut again: *Mommy*. One of those men had called out for his mother—and Micah was almost positive that it hadn't been the soldier's voice.

The terror of war was a bodily one—the fear that you might die in the shit and muck or, worse, get blown apart and live and have to continue on in a horribly reduced capacity. But at least it was a known horror, and your enemy was clear. He shared your same skin.

But right now? Those fingers curled round the rock and the sound of that laughter . . . it was a rip in the everyday fabric. A glimpse in the roiling heart of something impossible to comprehend. Even those things in the woods were dangerous only to a point: they would rip you to shreds and make an end of you. Tear your guts out like they had done to poor Charlie and Otis, who were beyond suffering now.

"Shug?" Minerva said from someplace over the mountain and far away.

Micah's eyes remained on those fingers. They tensed as if in preparation to propel the rest of its body forward the way a spider pushes itself from its hidey-hole: the legs coming first, spanning all around the hole, then the fat black nut of its body surging forth—

The laughter dried up . . . Then it returned even louder than before. Minerva gripped his wrist. *"Please."*

8

BE PENITENT. *Be remorseful. Be the father they need.*

Reverend Amos Flesher sat cross-legged on the chapel floor. A chapel built to his exact specifications and erected by his flock. For months, he had sermonized from its pulpit. His people had received his words with the lamblike docility he had entrenched in them and thus come to expect.

But now, their trust in him had been shaken. At first he had been angered by their treachery—his rage had been such that he'd pictured bashing their heads in until their skulls resembled broken, bloodied crockery . . . but then the Voice spoke, and he listened. Now he understood that the best way back into his people's hearts was through atonement. He had to grovel on his belly.

Be humbled, Amos. Humbled before God and humbled by these ungodly circumstances. They will welcome you back into their hearts.

He stood and walked between the pews. He inhaled the lemony scent of the wood wax—he had insisted upon the brand, as he had insisted on the tiniest detail at Little Heaven. He stood before the chapel window. Night hung over the compound. His face was reflected in the glass. His cheeks were furred with a three-day beard, his eyes set deep in his sockets. No matter. He would feel so much better soon. He had been promised, hadn't he? All he had to do was fulfill his end of the bargain. And Amos would have help in this, he knew. It was in the water now, in the food they ate and the air they all breathed. They were helpless against the forces marshaling against them. They were mindless *insects*. But then, in Amos's eyes, they always had been. They would come back to him, slaves to the sonar in their meek little brains that carried them to Amos like ants back to a poisoned hill.

He fixed his hair, setting it just so. He set his shoulders and straightened his spine, drawing himself up to his full height. A showman must always hold a sense of the moment.

He walked between the pews to the front doors. His hands gripped the brass knobs—*L* imprinted on the left, *H* on the right.

"Showtime."

He threw the doors open. Then he signaled Virgil to ring the bell. It tolled steadily, rolling over the compound and into the inhospitable woods. He spread his arms.

"Come, my children," he whispered. "Come back to me."

He watched them stumble into the square. Single worshippers at first, but they were soon joined by entire families. They were fearful and bruised of spirit. Amos would salve them. It was his gift. His voice was their balm. His people stood before his chapel like frightened animals. Its beckoning light spilled over Amos's shoulders. He saw that light reflected in the eyes of his flock.

"I stand penitent before you. I want to say that I am sorry," he said. "Truly I am."

NATE WAS WITH ELLEN when the chapel bell began to toll. Each ring shivered the bunkhouse walls. Nate went to the window. The Reverend was standing at the chapel door with his arms outspread.

Ellen opened the bunkhouse door. She and Nate stepped onto the grass. The things in the woods hadn't been heard from all day. But it was night now, and that was always when monsters came out.

People began to filter into the square. *They look so lost*, Nate thought. A lot of them wore timid, hopeful smiles. They walked with their heads tilted forward and their fingers pointing back. They looked cartoonish, like Porky Pig drifting toward a pie cooling on a windowsill: they all had that same dozy, dopey expression.

His father passed by. "You coming, Nate?"

Nate gave him a flat stare. "Maybe later."

His dad shoved his hands in his pockets. He tried to smile, but his face wouldn't cooperate. "Things will get better, buddy. You just watch. The Reverend will—"

Nate grabbed Ellen's hand. His father saw it. He dropped his head and nodded once, a tiny bob of his head, then followed the others.

"You don't want to go with him?" Ellen asked once he was gone.

Nate shook his head. "I don't trust him."

"The Reverend or your father?"

Neither of them, Nate thought.

"COME IN, COME," Amos said. "Enter the house of the holy."

Nell Conkwright—the leprous *cunt*, the scheming bitch the sea hag the *whore*—stopped at the chapel threshold. She licked her lips, as if physically hungry for everything that lay within. But she couldn't quite force herself through. She eyeballed Amos coldly.

Amos waited. A bubble of tension formed. His heart rate quickened. Nell's husband stepped forward, brushing past his wife, entering the forgiving warmth of the chapel. Nell reached for him—he shrugged her off with an inelegant, brusque move, as if swiping dandruff flakes off his sleeve. His eyes were focused inside the chapel, on Jesus up on His cross where He suffered eternally for the sins of mankind. Nell Conkwright gaped at Amos, that coldness giving way to a submissive helplessness. Amos smiled at her, mild as milk. Nell Conkwright dropped her head and followed her husband inside.

Amos knew right then that he had them. All of them, mind and soul. They were his to hold and hone, as they had always been. He tamped down a grin. His smile had begun to look manic lately.

They came. Some eagerly, some hesitantly, some even angrily, which was not wholly unexpected—but they all came. The spell had been cast. That old black magic. Amos stroked the odd shoulder as his worshippers filed in, laying hands on his people. He had to physically stop himself from squeezing too hard—if he did that, his hands might take on life of their own, tearing at fleshy spittle-wet lips and gouging at eyes filled with gaseous idiocy. *Bastards and bitches, traitors and heretics, scum-scum-scum-scum* . . . Most of them smiled at him gratefully, the way a whipped dog will still wag its tail when a cruel master pets it.

When they had all come inside, Amos stepped outside the doors. The woods pinched in from every angle. The generators sputtered; they were down to the last few gallons of gasoline by now. The spots dimmed and flickered.

Amos stared into the forest. He could not see anything, but he felt it—something watching. Something black and primitive, built of blood and old bones, breathing back at him. *Encouraging* him, oh yes. That something, whatever it was, wanted him to succeed and would aid his efforts to make that success a reality. His silent benefactor.

"Thank you," he said quietly, to no one at all.

Amos shut the doors and ushered himself to the pulpit. He basked in the warm, approving gaze of his congregants. Whether it was approval of him or simply approval of this ritual—the chapel, the uncomfortable wooden pews under their asses once again, the biblical verses they would move their bloated lips to like cows chewing cud—mattered very little to Amos. Whatever the cause, he soaked up their abject need like a sponge.

"Brothers and Sisters," he said, "the devil has come to Little Heaven."

They made no noise at this. It was obvious, wasn't it?

"I've been in deep palaver with our Lord these past hours and days," he said. "It has taken me to the edge of sanity—sometimes, just for a moment, I felt it slip. Now, I'm going to be just as plain as I know how to tell you. I've never lied to you," he lied. "I *never* have lied to you. An evil has come down on our heads. An evil blacker than anything you could possibly imagine. It's out there in those woods. Now, I know what you're thinking— you're thinking: *Rev, wasn't it you who led us here in the first place?* And yes, it was. Perfect, or as perfect as we can expect in this fleshy realm. I tried to give that perfection to you." His voice grew deeper and slightly wrathful. "I laid down my *life* for you. I've practically died every day to give you peace. And do you have that peace? Sister Conkwright, do you feel it?"

"I do not," Nell Conkwright said, startled to have been called upon.

"And you blame me—no, no, don't answer that. I *know*. His eye on the sparrow, Sister." Amos set his finger below his eyelid and pulled down, exposing the bloodshot white. "Now, why and how did this evil descend upon us? We who are the chosen, our lives given to the pursuance of good and holy matters? But *aaaah*, the devil, he is sly. He hunts for apathy and sloth and dines out on it. He peers deep into our hearts and finds the evil lurking there. It is his sweetest nectar, oh yes."

The chapel began to warm. Sweat collected on the upper lips and foreheads of the congregants. Their eyes had that dull sheen Amos knew well. They were enrapt. They were practically drooling. Amos smiled inwardly. He was going to make them pay for their disobedience. He'd make them squirm for what they had done to him. For scaring him and stripping his power away, even for a moment.

"I'm here to talk *corruption*, Brothers and Sisters! Corruption of the spirit. The insidious sort, the corruption that rusts you from the inside out. From the *outside*, oh yes! Once you let it in, *aaaaah*, ain't it a devil to root out! And I'm here to tell you, corruption wormed its way into Little Heaven well before those things in the woods showed up. Oh *yes*! They just followed the stink of rotten souls, drawn like flies to a trash heap. How did that corruption get here, you ask? It was smuggled in the only way it ever can be—in hearts and minds and in *souls*. *Your* soul, Brother!" He stabbed his finger at Reggie Longpre, who flinched. "And *yours*, Sister!" Stabbing that same finger at Nell Conkwright, relishing her agonized expression. "And yours! And yours! And yours!"

He slammed his palms down on the pulpit. His followers jolted in the pews.

"A person's a fool who continues to say that they're winning when they're losing," he said, switching registers, turning calm. "At first I didn't want to see that poison. I wouldn't credit it. How could my own people, my *chosen*, welcome such filth into their souls? But I prayed that the Lord remove those scales from my eyes so that I could see clearly. And yeah, God did, and yeah, I did—oh, terrible clarity! I saw the bubbling river of spite flowing through the heart of Little Heaven. The paradise *I* built for you! The paradise I nearly died finding for you! The paradise some of you have defiled through treachery and sin!"

Nobody spoke against him. He knew their secret hearts. Who had stepped out on whom, who had stolen and lied and cheated and done villainy against their fellow man. That had always been the price of entry to join his inner sanctum—*Tell me your secrets, my child. As God knows, so must I.* They had all paid that price, willingly.

"Sister Redhill. Stand up."

Maude Redhill rose from the pew. Her husband dead, her boys missing. Her face looked washed out and used up, like burnt pot roast with a wig on it. Amos almost grinned at this mental image.

"What do you deserve, Sister Redhill?"

"What do I—?" she parroted back bewilderedly.

"*Deserve*, Sister. And *ooooh*, ain't that a slippery slope? When it stops being about what we can give to the Lord and our fellow man and starts to be about what we need, *deserve*, in our hungry little hearts? So what is it, Sister? Tell me true."

After a while, the stupid bitch spat out, "We deserve peace. We all came here for peace."

"And we've— Have we had it?"

"No. Not for some time, Reverend."

"And you blame me for that. Don't you, Sister?"

She started to twist, her hands knotted at her sides. Amos favored her with a death's-head grin.

"Oh yes, you do. You, and the person next to you, and the person next to him. All of you. Your hearts turned calloused against me. Your prophet. Your daddy. The one true mouthpiece of the Lord. You abandoned me and threw in with the outsiders. After all I did for you," he said furiously, flecks of spittle leaping from his lips. "You ungrateful *wretches*."

You will see, deceivers. You will see what you have wrought, all of you.

He closed his eyes, becoming peaceful. "Could I detach myself? Of course, yes. I could detach myself from all of you. Why not?" He shook his head. "No, no, no, no, *no-no-NO!* I never detach myself from any of your troubles. I've always taken your troubles right on my shoulders. And I'm not going to change that now."

The eyes of his congregation shone up wetly at him. A powerful loathing ripped through his guts at the sight of their cringing, craven need, their faces looking like a bunch of stepped-on dog turds.

"You must wonder where I've been these last hours. Well, I'm gonna tell you. Last night, at my lowest point, I heard a Voice," he said. "It was not the voice of the Lord. It was unspeakably cold. *Cruel.* I followed that Voice out into the woods."

A low murmur flooded through the congregation.

"Was I scared, Brothers and Sisters? Yes. Did I go anyway? *Yes.* To protect you. *My* children." He let this sink in. "I walked in a daze. I came to a small clearing. A creature stood there. A figure of pure darkness."

The current of unease rippling through the congregation intensified. Amos let their fear ferment and ripen. He savored the dread that sat plainly on their faces—the sniveling children's faces most especially.

"Its smell washed over me. The stink of corpses in a charnel house. It spoke. Never have I heard its equal. Scabrous, sharp as a razor. It *hurt* just to listen to it. I asked it what it wanted. It lifted one hand and pointed. But not at me. Oh no."

Amos let it sit. He withheld it. Tension mounted inside the packed chapel.

"Who?" said Doc Lewis in wretched agony. "*Who* does it want?"

Amos pitched his voice at the perfect octave: almost a whisper, but still loud enough that the peanut gallery could hear.

"The children. It wants your *children*."

The congregation erupted. Mothers threw their arms around their snot-nosed offspring. Grown men whimpered in their seats like petrified infants.

"It wants your *babies*, mothers. It wants your sons and daughters. It wants to take them into the woods and"—the mildest of shrugs—"engage in deviltry."

"You can't let it take the children!" someone shrieked.

"What did they ever do?" shouted Brother Conkwright.

"The sins of the father . . ." the Reverend gravely intoned.

They were whipped into a frenzy. Bug-eyed and quivering, all of them. The children were blubbering in their mothers' arms. *Oh, how perfectly fitting*, thought Amos.

"It asked for the children," Amos went on over their donkey-like bleats. "It said that if we gave them to it, the rest of us would be spared."

A collective wail went up, shuddering the roof beams. Amos laid his head down. To the congregants, it might have looked as though their prophet had become overwhelmed. But he was smiling, and he couldn't let them see it. His body shook. Was he crying? No, he was laughing, hard enough to shed tears.

He raised his head. Tears of mirth stained his cheeks, but his buffoonish congregants surely mistook them for those of sorrow. He set his face in an expression of sadness . . . Slowly, he let it change into one of steely resolve.

"Do you think I accepted its terms? Would I not have been justified, considering your venomous behavior towards your loving prophet? Or should I turn the other cheek, as our Lord commands? Well . . .? *Well?*"

They goggled at him, expecting something. Watery eyes, drool-wet lips. They revolted him. He might as well have been sermonizing to a writhing mass of maggots.

"Brothers and Sisters, I quaked. My soul was at stake. But I stared right back at that foul thing and I said, *No!*" He thumped his fist on the pulpit. "*NO!* No, you will not take our children! NO! *NO!* I will not let you have them, demon from below!"

His people broke into rousing applause, clapping so hard Amos was sure they'd break their spastic hands.

"Praise be!" someone shouted.

"Shelter us in your arms!" cried someone else.

"*NO,* demon, you won't win this battle!" Amos thundered. "For we have the *Lord Almighty* on our side! He is watching from His heavenly seat, and He will not let an abomination such as you take our most treasured prize!"

"We raise our hands to the Lord!" Maude Redhill screamed, her thick suety face awash with tears. "Daddy, we love you!"

"We will fight you on the battlements, hell spawn!" Amos said.

"Hallelujah!" the congregation responded.

"We will fight you on the plains!"

"Praise our prophet!"

Amos shushed them. "Say. Say. Say *peace,* my children."

"Peace," they intoned.

"And finally the hell beast said, *I will have them!* Then it was gone, leaving a sour note of brimstone. I then returned to Little Heaven. My task was clear."

The lips of a worshipper in the third row moved in a silent plea: *Help us, prophet.* Amos could scarcely recall the man's name. Earl something-or-other. Earl or Merle. Earl or Merle was stumpy, with a prematurely bald, ovoid head. Earl the Pearl. Amos did not care about Earl. Earl was weak. They were all weak. They were broken and expected him to fix them. They were human *trash.* Wasted lives, wastes of skin. He was everything to them, and they meant nothing to him. There was not a thing worth harvesting from them anymore.

And so, the field had to be razed. In a way, what was about to happen would be the best thing for them all.

He gripped the pulpit. "What are you without me?"

He needed to hear them say it.

"Nothing," said Reggie Longpre, his voice clear as a bell.

"Nothing," went the echo.

Amos said, "Without me, what meaning would your lives have?"

"None at all," spoke the people of Little Heaven.

"That's right. I'm the best thing you'll ever have."

Wild applause. Nell Conkwright shouted, "Thank you for everything, prophet! You are the only. The *only*. I am sorry for my trespasses."

"Sit down and be quiet," he told them all coldly. They sat at once, like some sentient organism of wretched servility.

Amos signaled to Virgil, who wheeled in a cart from the vestry. On it sat a stack of plastic cups and two jugs of liquid, one red and the other purple.

VIRGIL HAD USED a lot of sugar. An entire bag, holy jeez. The Reverend said it needed to be real sweet.

Why so goddamn sugary? Virgil wondered. He didn't ask. Followers did as they were told. Virgil had followed Cyril for years, and when Cy up and vanished, well, the Reverend was right there to fill the gap. And the good Rev—who was used to telling his followers what to do—never bothered to tell Virgil what he'd mixed into the Kool-Aid after Virgil had made it.

Virgil used to drink the stuff as a kid. It was all his mother could afford. She mixed it so weak that it didn't quite cover the sulfur taste of the well water. *Redneck lemonade*, she called it. Virgil and his brothers and sisters would sit on the porch, guzzling watery cherry Kool-Aid until the skin above their top lips was stained pink.

He'd dumped in double the amount of sugar the recipe called for. The Reverend gave it a taste and said, "More." Eventually it stopped dissolving—

no matter how much Virgil stirred, the sugar crystals just sat at the bottom of the jugs like beach sand. The Reverend took the jug into the vestry and closed the door. When he came out, it looked the same, but there was a slight chemical odor to the Kool-Aid.

"Don't touch it," the Rev had told him. "It's for the children."

Virgil wouldn't drink that shit on a dare. Just thinking about it made his teeth ache.

"Now do the same with the wine," the Reverend told him.

"You want me to sugar up the wine, too?"

The Reverend sneered. "Did I stutter?"

Virgil dumped a sack of Domino sugar into the sacramental wine. The stuff was pretty much unsweetened grape juice, not a drop of booze in it—if so, Virgil and Cy would've necked it long ago. He tested it. He just about got diabetes from a single sip. The Rev disappeared with the wine for a couple of minutes. When he returned, it also had a chemical tang—but different from the Kool Aid.

Now, on the Rev's cue, Virgil wheeled in the cart with the jugs sitting on it. The people in the chapel seemed happy. The Reverend had trotted out the old dog and pony, put on a real whizbang of a show. Now they all wore the goony grins of lobotomy victims.

"We will fight this abomination," the Rev was saying. "We will save the children. We will restore Little Heaven to what it was—the home of the chosen people!"

"Hallelujah!" the crowd yelped.

"We will beat back the scourge!"

"Hallelujah!"

"I alone can do this."

"Praise you, Father!"

They linked hands and swayed in the pews like hypnotized cobras.

"Come forward, all of you, and accept your offering," said the Reverend. "Wine for adults and juice for the children, as always."

Virgil poured wine and Kool-Aid into the cups: only a few mouthfuls in each, just as the Reverend had instructed earlier. The worshippers stumbled up with those dozy grins pasted on their faces. They looked like moths flying into a bug zapper. They each took a cup and sat down. If they had children, they took cups of juice for them. The Reverend watched closely. Virgil noticed the bead of sweat on his nose and the way his fingers trembled.

As Virgil poured, his gaze drifted to the window. Cyril was standing outside in the dark. His face was white as lard. He was grinning, but it wasn't dopey, like those of the worshippers. More of a leer. Cyril pressed his face to the window. It went flatter than skin ought to—

Virgil kept pouring, managing to not spill a drop. Cy's lips were moving like he was speaking, but it didn't look like talking so much as chewing. Then poor Cyril's left eye burst and a thick black runner leaked down his cheek and—

Virgil closed his eyes, hoping Cy would be gone when he opened them. But he was still there a few seconds later. Was Virgil the only one who could see him? The black goo running down Cy's face started to curl upward—it was then that Virgil realized his eye hadn't burst at all. His eye was already gone and a centipede had been coiled up inside the empty socket; the insect scurried down under Cy's jaw, then up around his ear before tucking itself back inside his socket, neat as a pin.

Groovy trick, huh? Cy's voice chimed in Virgil's head.

Sure thing, Cy, Virgil thought queasily. *A real screamer.*

Soon the drinks were poured and everyone was sitting again. Their eyes had that docile glaze. The eyes of ritual junkies.

The Reverend said, "We shall drink the purifying tonic of the Lord. The children first, then the adults. In that order. This is as He wishes. As your prophet wishes."

The children raised the cups to their lips. Some of them coughed a little on account of the sweetness. But none of them spat it out. Watching them, Virgil understood. If Cyril asked him to drink that Kool-Aid, Virgil would have done it in a New York minute. That was what followers did, after all. No questions asked. Who would dare question the Lord? Why question fate?

The Reverend leaned forward. A smile touched the edges of his lips.

"Now you, my older children. Drink. To the very last . . . drop."

9

EBENEZER REACHED GRINDER'S SWITCH as the sun was setting. He wheeled the Olds into the sundry store where they'd stocked up a week ago.

The bell tinkled when he kicked the screen door open. The sick-looking shopkeep who had told them how to get to Little Heaven stood behind the counter. Eb snatched a bottle of Yoo-hoo from the cooler. He drank it and dropped the bottle on the floor. He burped loudly, grabbed another one, and started to drink it, too.

"You think I'm running a food bank here?" the man said peevishly.

Ebenezer held one finger up—*Hold on, I'll get to you*—tipped the bottle to his lips and drained it. He dropped it and grabbed a box of Goobers off the candy rack. He ripped the top off and walked toward the counter, tossing chocolate-covered peanuts in the air and catching them in his mouth.

"Remember me, my fine fellow?"

The man squinted. "You figure I should?"

"Oh, who knows? I'm sure you meet a lot of sophisticated people."

The man was reaching for something under the counter. "You got some kind of mental problem, boy?"

Eb dropped the box of candy and grabbed the man's wrist before it could clear the counter. He lifted the man's arm up and brought it down sharply on the ledge. The gun fell out of the man's hand—a .25-caliber popgun with hockey tape wrapped around the butt. Ebenezer brought the man's bony wrist up and down on the counter again and again until something went *snap*. The man shrieked and fell, hitting his head on a box of Manila Blunts cigars on a shelf behind the counter.

"You knew," Eb said while the man mewled and clutched his broken wrist. "It was death up there and you let us go anyway."

"I don't know nothing, you black sonofabitch," the man whined.

Eb hurdled the counter and dropped down beside the cringing wreck. He punched the man in the face, quite hard. The man squawked.

"There's more where that came from," Eb promised.

Blood poured out of the man's nostrils and bubbled over his lips.

"You mentioned a track machine."

"Wh-what?" the man blubbered.

"A track machine, you called it. Some kind of retrofitted tank."

The man bared his teeth . . . then dropped his eyes and nodded.

"Where can I find it?"

"Why the hell would you go back?" the man said. "You got away, crafty prick."

Ebenezer restrained the impulse to pummel the man into unconsciousness.

"An address, please. And if you call the police after I leave, rest assured I will come back and slit your throat before they take me to jail. Are we understood?"

"Yeah . . . understood."

"Good. That wrist will heal up fine. You will be up and grease-monkeying again before you can say Jack Robinson."

THE TRACK MACHINE sat in the yard of a farmhouse along the western flank of Grinder's Switch. Eb parked a ways down the road and approached on foot.

It was an honest-to-goodness World War II tank, the M2A1 or perhaps the M3, stripped to the treads. A bed had been installed over its back end, same as on a pickup truck, with wood-slat sidings all around. The cab of a Ford pickup had been chopped down and welded to the front end.

Ebenezer slunk through the long grass, climbed the treads, and stole a look through the driver-side window. The interior looked nearly the same as any truck, except instead of a wheel, a pair of steel steering rods protruded from the floor. The original roof had been removed and a zippered flap installed, turning it into a convertible of sorts. It even had an automatic transmission.

Ebenezer glanced at the farmhouse. The kitchen light was burning. This wouldn't be your garden-variety thievery. He would need a few minutes to figure out how the track machine drove, which meant he could count on a visit from its owner. He tried the driver's door. Unlocked. God bless the trusting rubes who populated this scratch-ass town. He slid into the cab. Gas and brake pedals, same as a car. There was no wheel, which meant no steering collar, which was what he would normally break open to access the ignition wires for a hot-wire job.

He flipped down the visor. A pair of keys fell into his lap. People were stupid, hallelujah.

The ignition switch was located under the seat, between his legs. He slid the key in. The machine rumbled to life. The enormous engine sent a shiver through his body. He popped the manual brake and pressed his foot on the gas pedal. Nothing. He frowned and tried the brake pedal. The machine trundled forward. So the brake and gas were reversed. *Good to know.*

He pulled the rod on his left side. The rod on his right shifted forward automatically. The machine turned on its axis until it was pointed at the farmhouse. He caught frantic movement behind the drapes.

He swung the machine around and set off in the direction of the Oldsmobile. The tank rampaged across the yard. The left tread hit an ornamental rock at the edge of the driveway; the machine tilted, throwing Eb against the driver's door as it scraped over the rock, and hammered back down.

"Oh, I *like* this!"

He pulled up beside the Olds. When he hopped out, he saw someone running across the field. Next he caught a flash of something streaking across the ground toward him, much closer. He managed to scramble back into the cab the instant before a dog hurled itself against the door, growling and slavering.

Eb pulled a pistol from his waistband. He could see the owner of both the dog and the machine drawing near. The man was carrying a pitchfork. Who did he think was stealing his property, Frankenstein's monster?

"Get after 'im, Pepper!" Eb heard the man shout. "Tear his trespassin' ass a new one!"

Eb unrolled the window a few inches. He slid the barrel of the pistol through the gap and angled it at the leaping dog. The owner froze.

"You wouldn't—"

"Oh, but I would," Eb said. "Unless you bring it to heel."

The man whistled sharply. The dog immediately quieted down.

"You just stay calm, Mister," the man said.

Ebenezer shut the machine off and hopped out. The man could have been forty but looked much older, his face prematurely ruined by drink or too much sun or simply life in Grinder's Switch. Either way, he seemed to be taking the theft of his machine with good grace. That probably had something to do with the gun pointed at his face.

"I just paid that sucker off," he said. "You wouldn't go stealing it from me, now would you?"

His appeal to Ebenezer's better nature was uplifting, if completely misplaced.

"I will be taking it," Eb said. "But I'll bring it back, as I have no use for this kind of contraption in my day-to-day life—and if I don't return with it, you can come find it in or around Little Heaven. You know where that is, don't you?"

The man scuffed his toes in the dirt. "Guess I do, sure."

"Those people helped pay this great walloping beast off, didn't they?"

"You could say."

"I'm going to toss my equipment in," Eb said. "Then I'll be off. If you and Chopper there play nice, I won't have to shoot you."

The man jabbed his pitchfork into the lawn. "We'll be plenty nice, Mister. And her name's Pepper. Goddamn it."

Eb hurled the guns and flamethrower into the bed of the track machine. The gormless man and his dog observed with matching expressions of tight-lipped impotence—Eb wasn't one hundred percent sure about the dog, but it did look quite pissed.

"You planning on starting World War Three?"

Eb gave the man a look. "How many times have you been to Little Heaven?"

The man shrugged. "Four, maybe five."

"When was your last visit?"

"Month ago, coulda been."

"Did you ever find anything strange about the place?"

The man appeared to seriously consider this. "They take their faith a little too sincerely, you ask me. Me and my wife go to church on Sundays, and Maggie—that's my wife—she bakes vanilla squares for the annual bake sale. But if someone said to me, *Hey, Arnie, guess what? God needs you to live in the middle of the woods as a test of faith* . . . Mister, I don't think the Lord much cares where we practice our faith."

Eb nodded. "You seem a decent bloke. Steer clear of the place."

Ebenezer clambered into the cab. He popped the manual brake, and the machine thundered off toward the trail leading to Little Heaven.

10

LITTLE HEAVEN'S COOK, an old shipwreck named Tom Guthrie, was the first to start choking. His face went pink, then brightened to red as he clutched at his throat. The chapel quickly filled with the sound of hoarse gasps and the frenetic swinging of limbs. By the time Guthrie started coughing up blood, the rest of the adult congregants were either in paroxysms of their own or staggering around wide-eyed as their throats closed up to pinholes.

Seeing it, Amos was relieved to note that he had selected correctly. He had considered weed killer, but had ultimately settled on drain cleaner. A wise choice, it turned out.

Ammate Weed Killer, by Du Pont. *Better things for better living . . . through CHEMISTRY!* read the tagline on its label. Effective against poison oak, sumac, and ivy. Charlie Fairweather had suggested they buy a drum of the stuff; better to douse the grounds than have the kids scratching themselves crazy and having to run back to civilization for tubes of calamine lotion. Amos had snuck into the equipment shed yesterday and read the ingredients on the drum carefully. Ammonium sulfamate was the active chemical. My, that sure *sounded* dangerous. He put a handful of the coarse white crystals in a paper sack and took it to the kitchen, where he mixed it with sugared water. It sent up a powerful smell. He was unsure they would drink it, even with the sugared-wine overlay. He cut a potato in half and doused its weeping flesh with the sugary weed killer. The reaction was mild, only a faint sputtering. That probably wouldn't do.

After this dispiriting test, Amos rummaged under the kitchen sink. He found a gallon jug of drain cleaner. Sodium hydroxide. Ooh, *that* sounded promising. He read the warning label. Breathing difficulty due to throat swelling. Severe burns and tissue damage. Vomiting. Rapid drop in blood pressure. Loss of vision. At the bottom: *Do not administer vinegar or lemon juice. Will cause more severe burning.*

He mixed the cleaner with sugar water. It foamed up in a mad froth. The smell wasn't overpowering. He poured the mixture on a potato. It sizzled, reducing the spud to starchy liquid. Okeydokey. Drain cleaner it would be.

Amos stood at the pulpit as his congregants drank the toxic brew. Most did it in one gulp; a few of them grimaced as if it was bitter medicine, then finished the dose. It wasn't so odd. He'd known rummies in the Tenderloin to drink Sterno or hair spray or worse.

After the initial wave of choking commenced, Amos surveyed the crowd. Virgil Swicker's eyes were wide with shock. Amos clambered down amid the tormented wheezes of his worshippers and jerked the pistol from the waistband of Virgil's trousers. The gun was small but heavy—it felt thrillingly powerful in his hands. Virgil let him take it without issue. Bright penny.

The flighty screams of the children pealed off the roof beams. Their Kool-Aid had been spiked with a powerful barbiturate. Nell Conkwright suffered night terrors. She had confessed this to Amos years ago. Dreams where her children were eaten by fanged things right before her eyes. The doctor prescribed sedatives of increasing potency. The ones she took were powerful enough to put an elephant to sleep. He had instructed Virgil to liberate the bottle of pills from her bunkhouse. More than enough to do the trick. Amos only hoped it wouldn't put the children into slumberland permanently.

The children shrieked as their parents shuffled about with their mouths opening and closing like fish suffocating in the bottom of a boat. Their mothers' and fathers' eyes were full of childlike fear; many of those eyes were completely bloodshot from the force of their vomiting, which they began to do uncontrollably shortly after swallowing the toxic vino. At first their puke was the candy-apple red of the cheap wine, but it turned increasingly thick and frothy, with the deeper red tinge of blood. Many of them were hacking up pulpy shreds of tissue as well; these spongy bits fell from their mouths in moist rags, where they lay steaming on the chapel floor.

"People!" Amos shouted. "You must drink the antidote! Take God's cure!"

He reached under the cart and produced a tray of plastic cups filled with clear liquid. The congregants who heard his voice—the ones who weren't already thrashing on the floor—made their tortured way toward him. The first was Leo Gerson, a bowlegged man with a pockmarked face, which was now red, and his neck horribly swollen, as if someone had stuffed a thrashing cat down his gullet. He grabbed two cups, the second for his wife, who lay on the floor between the pews with her legs jutting into the aisle, her modest unpatterned frock rucked up to display her enormous—yet still modest—white cotton panties. Gerson tipped the cup to his lips with hands that trembled so badly he spilled a mouthful down his chin. He turned back to his wife, but his legs abruptly went out from under him. He crumpled to the floor, spasming in pain.

Seven or eight other congregants drank from the cups; none of them noted the tang of white vinegar. By the time they glugged it down, Leo had managed to crawl back to his wife. The floor behind him was streaked with blood and fuming chunks of meat. The smell inside the church was utterly foul—the stink of acidified flesh.

Virgil stared at Amos helplessly. "What . . . ? What the hell did you *do* to them?"

"I purified their souls."

Nell Conkwright stood in the middle of the aisle. Her face was an angry purple shade, her throat a distended bulge as if she'd swallowed a baseball. Her hubby, Pious Brother Conkwright, was slumped over a pew; his buttocks were facing Amos, and the Reverend saw a dark stain on the seat of Pious Conk's sensible trousers. Nell's eight-year-old daughter clung to her mother's leg, shrieking. Nell cradled the girl's face with gentle affection, as if knowing exactly what was happening; she coughed up thick knotty structures from somewhere deep in her guts; those structures wriggled between her lips like worms and hit the floor with moist splats. Her daughter continued screaming, but even then her eyelids were drooping.

"Oh my God," Virgil said. "Oh my Gooooooo—"

Amos grabbed Virgil's collar and shook him until his teeth rattled.

"This is *happening*." He pointed the pistol at Virgil's chest. "Now is not the time to go soft. If you're not with me, Brother Swicker, I am afraid my use for you is incredibly limited."

Virgil gawped at him openmouthed. Numbly, he nodded. "Okay."

"Go to the vestry and hold the door open. Wait for me there."

Obediently, Virgil retreated. Amos turned to the congregation in time to see Doc Lewis staggering toward him, arms outflung as if in mimicry of some horror show boogeyman. His eyes bulged so far from their sockets that Amos could see their underswells pooled with blood. Lewis's lips were skinned back and his teeth gritted; he vomited but didn't open his mouth, so the bloody pulp came out his nose, twin jets of ropelike red.

Lewis's hands closed around Amos's throat; his mitts were so big that they encircled Amos's beanpole neck entirely, fingers touching at the back. He squeezed with amazing force, considering he was choking to death on tatters of his own throat lining. His breath bathed Amos's face, rank as meat seared in stearic acid. His eyes looked comical, yet they were filled with swarming hatred. They were the eyes of a man who could see, truly *see*, for the first time.

Lewis was steadily crushing the Reverend's windpipe; if Amos couldn't twist free, he was convinced the man's fingernails would punch through his skin and rip out his windpipe. Amos brought the pistol up. The barrel dimpled the underside of Lewis's chin. Lewis grunted quizzically, blobs of bloody tissue ejecting from his nose as he squeezed tighter—

Amos pulled the trigger.

The bullet tore Lewis's face open from bottom to top. It cleaved his chin, splitting bone and muscle, then blew his nose apart in fleshy wings, burrowed through the skin between his eyes and bisected his forehead before continuing upward to bury itself in the chapel roof. The pressure on Amos's throat relented; he stumbled back, gagging. Lewis reeled in a drunken circle, blood geysering from his exposed nasal cavities, staring cross-eyed at the tragic ruin of his face. He sat down on his ass dejectedly and inelegantly, an infant taking a tumble. He gazed up at Christ on His cross, his eyes pleading, before his head dipped to touch his chest. He slumped steadily forward until his skull was resting on the waxed boards.

Amos backed toward the vestry, giggling now—a shrill loony note, *Ah-hee-hee-ah-hee!*—as the congregants shuddered through what he assumed must be their death throes. The smell of blood perfumed the chapel; the temperature seemed to have zoomed up twenty degrees in the last minute. The children continued to scream; a few of them had lurched to the main doors, which were locked, in an attempt to get help. From whom? Who *wasn't* here?

The outsider woman with the burn, the Reverend realized—Virgil said the other three had left the compound, but she was still here. There was also the very slim possibility that a few others hadn't attended. No matter. Amos would deal with them soon.

He walked backward to the vestry, still facing the pews. He took it all in. His flock—the deceitful scabs, the filthy betrayers—were dying in wretched agony, coughing up scraps of their guts as their children lay on the floor insensate or still clinging to their parents as they expired.

God's will be done, he thought with tremendous satisfaction.

Another man was tottering down the aisle toward him. His face was plastered with blood to the point that Amos could no longer identify him. *Earl the Pearl, is that you? Why the long face, Earl?* Oho-o-*ho*! Amos backed into the vestry and locked the door. He turned and saw Virgil sitting in the corner, shivering. Amos grimaced. He hoped the blubbering clod could hold it together until his usefulness dried up.

Amos crossed to his desk and removed the claw hammer stashed in the drawer. Somebody hit the vestry door.

"Earl the Pearl, don't interrupt!" Amos said, and hooted laughter. "Can't you see I'm busy in here? Make an appointment with my secretary!"

A pair of fists pounding . . . . but as the seconds drew on, their force ebbed. Soon nothing but a kittenish scratching could be heard from the other side of the door.

FIRST, NATE HEARD THE SCREAMS. Then the gunshot.

He was outside the bunkhouse with Ellen. They had watched everyone file into the chapel. Soon after, they heard the Reverend sermonizing. Nate pictured everyone inside, eyes closed and swaying. Things might turn out okay, he thought. Maybe God really was watching over them again.

Shortly after that the screaming had started. Ellen went stiff. She grabbed Nate's hand. The shrieks inside the chapel ascended to a shrill peak and stayed there. Next came the loud *bang*. Nate wouldn't have been sure a year ago, but by now he'd heard enough gunshots at Little Heaven to know that sound.

"No" was all Ellen said.

They stood in the chilly night with the woods silent beyond the fence. Who was doing the shooting? His father was in there. And the Conkwrights, whom Nate liked a whole bunch. And some others he guessed were decent enough.

Neither Nate nor Ellen moved. Nate's legs were locked up—someone might as well have bolted his knees together. Clearly something horrible was happening. Could he help? He yanked his hand away from Ellen's— "Nate!" she cried out—and stole toward the chapel.

He crossed the square as if in a dream; the momentum was sickening, unstoppable. The screams intensified, pulsing against his eardrums. As he got closer, he heard other noises: choking, wheezing.

He crept around the side of the chapel. The blood pounding in his skull made him dizzy. He had to brace himself on the wall so he didn't faint. A terrible pressure inside his head pushed against his eyeballs and nose so hard that he had to breathe through his mouth, which had gone dry, his lips glued together with pasty spit. He curled his fingers over the windowsill and peeked inside.

WHEN AMOS OPENED the vestry door again, a blood-slick body slumped forward to hit his shoes. Amos roughly kicked it aside and passed down the aisle, pistol in one hand and hammer in the other.

A strange light had entered his eyes. A mincing, eager refraction that had lain dormant for his whole life, really, apart from a few brief and secretive incidents where it had been allowed to glow brightly. There was nothing to stop it now. That light was free to stoke itself into a gleeful inferno.

He high-stepped down the aisle over the twitching bodies of his worshippers. A few of the older children were still conscious, beating their fists weakly against the doors. The younger ones were already insensate.

A hand manacled around his ankle. Amos followed it to the body of Nell Conkwright, the rancid sow, lying facedown next to her unconscious daughter. The flesh of her fingertips had been eaten away by the acidic vomit she'd hacked up. She was mumbling something. A prayer, a curse—who cared? Amos shook his ankle free in disgust. Then he set his foot on her shoulder and shoved her onto her back. Her eyes were milky, flecks of bloody vomit smeared on her face. Her skin sizzled as the drain cleaner continued to eat into it. She kept mumbling even though most of her teeth had fallen out, her gums stripped back to the bone, her mouth sagging inward like an old pumpkin left to rot on a front stoop.

"O ye of little faith," Amos whispered. "You did this to yourself, heathen. And to your child, too."

The woman's face wrenched into an expression Amos took as mortal terror. She reached blindly for her daughter. Amos raised the hammer and brought it down on her skull. He'd never hit someone with a hammer, so he didn't know how hard he ought to do it—as hard as possible seemed wisest, but at the last instant he quailed, so the hammer impacted Nell Conkwright's head with a flat *smack*, taking away a coin-sized blot of skin. She moaned and retched again. Amos gritted his teeth and flipped the hammer around to the claw end and brought it down again much harder. It punched through the top of Nell Conkwright's head. Success! Now she thrashed and yowled; Amos felt the thrum of her body all the way up the hammer's wooden shaft. He wrenched the claw free and continued on. He did not notice the horrified face of Reggie Longpre's boy hovering at the window.

Movement to his left. He marked someone crawling toward the doors. He expected it to be Bart Kennick or Shane Weagel, who were among Little Heaven's hardiest specimens—but land sakes alive, if it wasn't Reginald Longpre. Reggie was near the exit on his bloody hands and knees. Saying something, too, though it came out all mush-mouthed. *Nate, I'm sorry*, it sounded like.

Amos stepped over a half dozen bodies as if they were sandbags, making his way to the front. Only one boy was trying to open the doors now; Amos tucked the hammer under his armpit and cupped his hand over the boy's face and pushed hard; the boy groaned and fell, curling into a fetal ball. Amos unlocked the doors and threw them open with a flourish.

"Monsieur," he remarked to Reggie, "you look as if you could use some fresh air."

Reggie crawled past Amos, perhaps not even cognizant he was there. Amos took no offense at this, seeing as Reggie was likely blind from the cleaner burns. Sturdy ole Reg made it all the way out the doors, struggling down the swaybacked steps onto the trampled grass. His palms slipped, and he sprawled on his belly. He wormed around on the ground; the sight filled Amos with revulsion. He stepped forward, set his foot firmly on the back of Reggie's neck, and shoved him down into the dirt. Then he cocked the pistol and—

ELLEN WATCHED THE CHAPEL DOORS swing open. She caught a brief glimpse of the insides—bodies lying on the ground or slumped over the pews—before her attention was stolen by the sight of her sister's ex crawling out the doors. By the light streaming out of the chapel, she could see that Reggie was covered from head to toe in gore. He squirmed awkwardly, chest heaving, strings of bloody drool swaying from his lips. He clawed his way down the steps and made it a few more feet before collapsing.

The Reverend followed Reggie out. He walked with a purpose, seemingly unhurt. He held something in each hand. Ellen watched, awestruck with horror, as the Reverend stomped on the back of Reggie's neck, forcing a sad bleat out of the servile mailman, then cocked the pistol in his right hand and fired it point-blank at Reggie's head.

The gun issued a sharp crack. The feathery fringe of hair at the back of Reggie's head—it must have been months since his last haircut—puffed up as the slug drilled into his skull. Reggie grunted softly, as if in mild disagreement with something the Reverend had said. The bullet corkscrewed through his head and made its exit above his wide gaping eyes, blowing a window of bone out of his forehead. *It looks like the box the little bird pops out of in a cuckoo clock,* Ellen thought in a daze of fright.

The Reverend leapt back, loosing a giddy shriek like a boy who'd gotten a jolt from his uncle's joy buzzer. Reggie's boots drummed the earth. Virgil Swicker emerged from the chapel doors; he stood transfixed with shock. The Reverend raised the hammer in his other hand and swung it into the broken bowl of Reggie's skull. Wet clots spattered his face. He hooted as he brought the hammer down again, again, his pompadour unraveling as he sweated through the pomade, his hair hanging in lank wings over his ears like a hardcover book opened in the middle.

Ellen did not move. She was physically unable to. The world fractured into shards like an enormous mirror shattering, and behind it lay a black hopeless place teeming with madness and suffering and death.

The Reverend looked up. He saw her. He grinned. He raised the pistol and fired. The bullet zipped past her head. An instant later she heard the *pop!*

She turned and ran. The gun went off again; the slug drove into the siding of a bunkhouse ten yards ahead. Ellen ducked, zigzagging. She flashed around the side of the nearest outbuilding, noticing an uncapped drum of weed killer sitting half shadowed inside. Another gunshot. She flinched but kept running.

Her mind buzzed; it was hard to think, to plan anything more than putting one foot in front of the other. The gates loomed into view. The woods were menacing, yes, but who was to say things hadn't become more dangerous inside Little Heaven now?

She skidded to a stop at the main gates and wormed through the gap.

The forest lay a hundred yards off. She checked up, her shoes scuffling in the dust—then she saw a shadow elongating around the shed and knew the Reverend was hot after her. Trapped between the devil and the deep blue sea.

After a moment's hesitation, she bolted. The woods reached out for her. Another shot rang out. Ellen hit the woods at a dead sprint; the temperature dropped as soon as she entered the canopy of trees. Her feet went out from under her; she crashed down on the carpet of pine needles. She got to her knees and cast a panicked glance behind her; the forest was too dark to make out anything beyond the ten feet of trees and bush. She hoped to God those *things* might leave her alone, at least for the next few minutes.

She peered through the trees at the compound. The Reverend stood at the gates, squinting into the trees. He pulled the pistol's trigger again and again; all he got was a dry click. He bared his teeth, which gleamed amid the bloody canvas of his face. He smashed the hammer against the gate in frustration, then set off toward the chapel.

Ellen waited thirty seconds. She couldn't be sure the Reverend wasn't still watching. Perhaps he'd taken the time to reload the gun. But she couldn't just sit here.

She crept out of the woods but remained in the shadows of the trees. She slunk around the perimeter of Little Heaven to the woodpile, which was stacked ten feet long and six feet high, covered with a burlap tarp. Her mind was still reeling. What the hell had happened? The Reverend had gone mad—that was the only certainty. Unless he had been crazy from the start, which was not entirely impossible to conceive.

Her next panicked thought: *Nate!* Ellen could only hope he hadn't seen the slugs driving into his father's head.

She crept around the woodpile and slipped under the burlap tarp. The air was laden with the smell of pinesap. She crawled to the front and lifted the flap, peeking out. Her vantage provided a view of Little Heaven; she could see clear across the square to the chapel. Its doors open, light spilling out. The Reverend came into sight again. Ellen saw him speaking with Virgil. Then they went inside and began to drag bodies out. They didn't look like adults. Too small for that.

Had everyone been slaughtered? Ellen crouched under the tarp, her hands cut and bleeding. It didn't seem possible, and yet . . .

What kind of devil would do such a thing? If only Micah and Minerva were here. They wouldn't let the Reverend get away with it. They would—

Something crashed into the burlap, nearly knocking her down. She shoved herself back on her heels until her spine sat flush with the timber pile as something blundered around on the other side of the tarp. She stifled a scream, expecting a bullet or a knife or talon to pierce the burlap and shut her lights out for good—

The tarp rose. Nate peered in at her. "Hey," he whispered. He crawled under. They hugged. Nate was trembling. They both were.

"How did you find me?" she said.

"I saw you running. I hid behind the big warehouse."

"The Reverend didn't—?"

"See me? Don't think so."

"Did you see . . . ?"

"Inside the chapel?" Nate let out a choked sob. "They're dead. The Reverend killed Nell Conkwright. I saw him do it . . . They're all dead, I think."

"Everyone?"

"The grown-ups. The other kids . . . I don't know. Maybe not. I saw some of them. They weren't as bloody as the grown-ups."

They lifted the tarp and peeked out. Virgil and the Reverend were dragging the children's bodies out and lining them up on the ground.

"What the hell are they doing now?" said Ellen.

VIRGIL WAS UTTERLY LOST.

Never did he imagine it could go this way. He wouldn't ever have agreed to come to Little Heaven if he had thought, for even one second, that things could—

Blood. More blood than he had ever seen. More than he thought bodies could possibly hold. *You look like ten pounds of shit in a five-pound bag*—Cyril had once told Virgil this after a string of hard-drinking nights. That had been Virgil's thought while gazing over the bodies in the chapel. *Ten pounds of blood in a five-pound bag.* Where had it all come from? Some horrible magic trick. It was as if extra blood, buckets of it, had leaked through the chapel floorboards—*And up through the ground came a bubblin' cruuude. Oil, that is. Black gold! Texas tea!*—to mix with the stuff pouring from the worshippers' mangled bodies.

Virgil hadn't liked any of them to begin with. Shrill Goody Two-shoes, the lot. He would happily take their money, but not their lives. They didn't deserve this. Nobody deserved this.

"Brother Swicker!"

Virgil turned to find the Reverend crossing the square toward him. The gun was pointing at Virgil's chest. His own gun.

"Bullets," the Reverend said. "Do we have more?"

Virgil stood at the chapel entrance. The smell of blood was hot and slimy in his nose. He wondered if this was what slaughterhouse workers inhaled all day—a mist of blood like the air on a foggy morning. How did the stench not drive them batshit? It wormed into his mouth and ears until he was drowsy with it. He wanted to crawl into the darkest space he could find, curl up, and close his eyes.

"Bullets?" he said dazedly. "I think . . . uh . . ."

The Reverend's face swarmed out of the night, so close that Virgil could see the oily blackheads on his nose. His features were alive with tics and flutters, as if drumstick-legged locusts were trapped desperately under his skin. The Rev's arm swung in a big loop and the gun cracked Virgil on the side of the head. He sprawled on the chapel floor, dimly amazed at the change in the short-assed fraudster. The Reverend now terrified him worse than Cyril ever had.

"Up," the Reverend said curtly. "*Up-up-up!*"

Virgil woozily heaved himself to his feet. His hand made contact with the cooling limb of a dead worshipper and he cringed. The Reverend grabbed him by the collar.

"We must hurry." The Rev's breath stunk of bitter bile. "It will be here soon."

"What'll be here?"

The Reverend did not answer. His fingers tightened. "Bullets, Brother. *Now.*"

Virgil wasn't sure he wanted to give the man more ammo. He got a sense the next round the Rev chambered might be earmarked for Virg's noggin. But with the whipped-dog servility that had been knit to his nature for years, he went into the vestry and got the bullets. His eyes fell on the shape of the Conkwright woman with her brains bashed in.

When he returned, the Reverend handed him the gun. "Load it."

Virgil did as he asked. It was so much easier this way. Just follow instructions. Virgil always got into trouble when he tried to think for himself. Better to put it in someone else's hands. His mind relaxed as he thumbed the rounds into the pistol. The Reverend led; Virgil obeyed. Easy as peach 'n' pie.

He handed the gun back. The Reverend jammed it down the front of his trousers. He chuckled.

"Look at me. Johnny Six-guns!"

Virgil managed a tinny laugh. It *was* kinda funny. The Reverend with his fancy hair sweated flat as a pancake and hanging over his ears, with a roscoe peeking out of his pants. He couldn't help noticing the Reverend also sported a huge erection. It jabbed against the tight material, hard and somehow bladelike.

Is that a gun in your pocket, or are you just happy to see me, sailor?

Virgil laughed again, a little hysterically. Man, life moved fast, didn't it? One day this, the next day that. Go with the flow, Joe.

The Reverend wrapped his hand around the back of Virgil's neck and pulled him forward until their foreheads touched. "These next twenty minutes are the most important ones of your life. Do you understand?"

"Uh-huh," Virgil said, not understanding at all.

"If you stay the course, your reward will be infinite. Would you like that, Brother Swicker?"

"Sure, I guess."

The Reverend grinned. "Bless your pea-pickin' heart."

The Reverend then went to the nearest child, a girl of about eight. He grabbed her ankles and pulled. The girl's dress hiked up. Her panties were wet on account of her pissing herself. The Reverend dragged her out the door down the steps—her skull made a hollow *bonk* on each stair—and laid her on the ground not far from the fence.

When he came back in, Virgil hadn't moved. The Reverend frowned.

"Are you waiting for an engraved invitation?"

Virgil hopped to it. It didn't take long—about twenty minutes, like the Rev said. At the end, the kids were lying side by side all in a row. They were asleep, not dead, their legs twitching. Most of them had peed themselves, and they began to involuntarily shiver when the piss cooled on their thighs.

"Yes, oh yes," the Reverend cooed. "We have done good works today."

"Why . . . ?"

The Rev cut his eyes at Virgil. "Why what?"

"Why . . . the kids?"

"Because," the Rev said, "it has always been the children."

The Reverend's headlamp eyes were staring into the woods. His body was motionless as if he'd been frozen. Virgil stared in the same direction.

Something was coming, just like the Reverend promised. No, not just one thing—*many*. Virgil rubbed his eyes—he really did that, just like an actor in a movie who thinks he's seeing a mirage. It didn't make sense, was why. This all felt unreal, same as a movie.

The shapes drew closer. Virgil saw them . . . but it couldn't be. There was something else behind those shapes, too—something larger, draped in shadow. Gooseflesh climbed the knobs of Virgil's spine and spread around his neck in a pebbled collar. His breath came in small, whiny gasps like a hurt dog.

"For you," the Reverend said to the shadowy thing. "All for you."

Virgil's mind broke a little at the sight—or maybe broke a lot. It was hard to tell with minds, because the world didn't change. Only the way you processed it did.

Hey! Just go with the flow, Joe.

11

EBENEZER PILOTED the track machine up the path leading to Little Heaven. The high beams illuminated the pines. The machine lumbered over stumps and downed logs, charging through the river without issue. He drove it with ease; the steering levers required only small adjustments. Not a single bug splattered the windshield. It then came to Eb: he'd been in the woods for days and didn't have one mosquito or blackfly or tick bite.

He set the brake and idled at the base of a shallow rise. From here, the path ran straight to the gates of Little Heaven with no aggressive turns or bends.

He let out a shaky breath. "Right. Hop to it, my son."

He unzipped the cab's roof. The sky was salted with muted stars. He stood on the seat and hopped over the front panel into the bed. Working quickly, he laid out the shotgun, the Colts, the spare clips. He strapped the clips to the front panel of the bed with duct tape. Then he cut three lengths of rope and tied them around the topmost slat of the panel. He fastened the shotgun and the pistols to the end of each rope—shotgun on the left side, pistols on the right. The guns hung from the ropes and clinked lightly against the panels, all within reach.

He cut a longer length of rope and threaded it through his belt loops. He pulled one of the Cubanos from his pocket, unwrapped it, and nipped the nub off with his teeth. He spat it out and flicked the Zippo and thumbed the flywheel and lit the stogie. A deep inhale, a cough, then he hopped down from the tailgate.

The forest did not stir, but ahead—and not far, either—he could sense them. The skin tightened up in his throat.

He found a stick that looked like it might work and opened the driver-side door. He set one end of the stick on the gas pedal and wedged the other end under the seat; the engine growled. He tested to make sure it wouldn't jar loose, then locked the steering levers so the machine would drive straight ahead. He puffed on the cigar and blew a few smoke rings. It had been ages since he'd had one of these. Why in blazes had he quit? Lovely habit.

He licked his lips. His mouth was dry as a wood chip. Ebenezer's entire life boiled down to the following few minutes. Well, hell, couldn't the same be said of any man? There was that handful of minutes that really mattered, and then there were all the other minutes that made up that man's life. And those minutes had led him here, hadn't they? That big clock in the sky was always ticking against fate.

"Fortune favors the brave," he whispered. "Or does it favor the lunatics? Either way, Ebenezer, my son, you've got a coin flip's chance."

He popped the transmission into drive. The track machine lurched forward. He swung himself over the front panel into the bed. He twisted the knobs on the flamethrower's canisters and heard a hiss; he lit the nozzle with the Zippo—a small blue flame like a furnace's pilot light. He shrugged the weapon over his shoulders.

Steadying himself as the machine clattered up the incline, he tied one end of the rope around his waist to the wood slat on his left side of the front panel, then knotted the other end on the right side. He leaned back, testing the makeshift harness. He could sway his body a foot to the left or the right along the rope, close enough to cut his guns loose if the flamethrower petered out.

Ebenezer fired a flare into the trees ahead on his right. It traced a low orbit and dropped, sputtering, into the woods two hundred yards ahead. He reloaded the gun and shot another flare into the woods to his left. By their fitful glow, he could see things moving, their bodies crossing the flickering light in an agitated manner.

He sucked on the cigar and cracked his neck to drain his sinus cavities. His heart was pounding, but his hands barely shook. He would kill them all if possible, or he would die in the midst of killing however many he could. They would not scare him ever again.

That's my boy, he could hear his aunt Hazel say. *My Ebenezer, he's no hog.*

"*Git aloooong, little dawwww-gies, git alooooooong*," he crooned.

The machine rumbled over the rise. The lights of Little Heaven winked in the distance.

"Come on, you bastards."

The machine rumbled ahead. The wrecked pickup came into view. The windshield smashed, some luckless sonofabitch's headless body still tilted against its rear wheel. The flares brightened in the wind that scoured the woods. They were there—Christ, he could *see* them now. Some large, some smaller, all of them hunched and ungodly. He charted the air above, concerned one of them might plummet from the sky, like the one that had mangled his ear. But they remained where they were.

The machine charged steadily toward the gate; it stood less than a hundred yards off, moonlight glinting off the gilded *L* and *H*. Eb glanced behind him and saw nothing in pursuit. He had not really anticipated reaching the compound—he'd half expected to be ripped to pieces before reaching the gates, although it had tickled him to picture the track machine crashing through it, propelling his mangled corpse straight to and then through the chapel doors. But he was alive, less-than-miraculously so, and had to step lively now.

He grabbed for the bowie knife. The machine hit a dip, jostling him; the knife slipped from his fingers.

"Shit!"

He stretched for the blade as it clattered on the metal bed. The rope threaded through his belt loops prevented him from bending down any farther. The flamethrower dipped; the scorching nozzle brushed his leg and he let out a screech. The gates were fifty yards away. If he didn't cut himself free and get into the driver's seat, the machine would—

His fingers closed on the knife. He sawed through the rope. When he was free, he shrugged off the flamethrower and clambered over the front panel, toppling into the cab just as the machine hit the entrance to Little Heaven, tearing through the gates like Tinker Toys; the iron squealed as they tore off their hinges, crumpling under the machine's determined progression.

Eb sat up, blinking a trickle of blood out of his eye. The machine was making a beeline for a utility shed. He didn't see anybody, but figured they should be awake by now, scurrying to the nearest window to see what fresh hell had invaded their midst. *It's the cavalry, you miserable sods!*

He grabbed the stick pinning the gas pedal down; it wouldn't budge.

The machine hit the shed broadside, reducing it to matchsticks. He kicked at the stick until it snapped. With no pressure on the gas pedal, the machine slowed immediately. He stomped on the brake pedal. The track machine jerked to a stop.

He crawled up into the bed and hacked the shotgun free from the rope. He swung around with it, ready to blast anything that had a mind to barrel through the gates after him. But the path was empty. Far off, the flares continued to gutter on the forest floor.

He hopped off the tailgate. The spotlights flickered around the compound; some were now going dead for several seconds before struggling back to life. Though he couldn't see well in the fitful light, Eb could tell that nobody was out. A vague sense of dread zephyred through him. He'd come back. Jesus, what a fool. He palmed blood out of his eyes; it trickled steadily down from the cut on his head. His cigar had remained clamped between his teeth all this time, but it was snapped nearly in half. He tore off the dangly bit.

A restless silence overhung the compound. He stared at the chapel—door open, lights weakly glimmering. A body lay on the grass ten yards from the door, bathed in the jumpy spots. He gripped the shotgun and headed toward it. Ebenezer's dread intensified with each step. The inside of the chapel came into view.

"Good Christ . . ."

His feet ground to a halt. The cigar slipped from his lips. What in the name of—

"Ebenezer?"

He swung around to see Ellen and the boy. Their shoulders were carpeted with wood chips.

"What happened here?"

"He killed them," the boy said quietly. "The Reverend."

". . . Everyone? Micah and Min—?"

Ellen shook her head. "They left after you did. In the afternoon. To search for the missing kids. They went deeper into the woods, moving north. Towards—"

Eb held up his hand. Micah and Minerva's whereabouts were of less integral importance than what the boy had just said. "The Reverend killed them? Who? How many? How did he—?"

"*All* of them, Ebenezer. His entire flock. In the chapel during the sermon." Ellen ran a trembling hand through her hair. "I'm not sure how he did it."

"They threw up blood," the boy said hollowly.

"He must have poisoned them," Ellen said. "You can almost smell it."

Poison, Eb thought. *The madman poisoned his own people.* Part of him wasn't terribly surprised. He'd sniffed a hint of lunacy in Amos Flesher the first time he'd set eyes on him—the itchy gaze, that switchblade smile. The line between prophet and lunatic was a thin one indeed. And his followers were just that. Every lemming off the cliff. He could see it happening. Yes, all too easily.

"And you didn't attend the service?" he said.

Ellen shook her head. "I wouldn't have been welcome. And Nate stayed with me."

"Tell me what else happened," Eb said.

"After he killed them, the Reverend came out of the chapel," Ellen said. "He shot . . ."

She nodded to the body on the grass but would not say who it was. Ebenezer could guess. Nate didn't look as if he'd been crying, though his eyes were compassed by swollen red flesh—as if tears were lurking close to the surface, but he was wise enough to know this wasn't the time to grieve the loss. That, or perhaps he was mildly glad his father was gone. Ebenezer didn't know the boy well enough to say.

"After that, Flesher shot at me," Ellen continued. "So I ran. Hid in the woodpile. Nate found me. The Reverend gave up trying to find us. Other things to worry about, I guess."

"Other things?"

Neither of them answered.

"The children aren't dead. At least I'm pretty sure," Ellen told him. "They dragged them out of the chapel."

"Who?"

"The Reverend's hired man. The one you beat up this morning."

"Virgil. He and the Reverend are the only ones left?"

Ellen nodded.

Eb said, "So they dragged the kids out and . . . ?"

Ellen and the boy exchanged a look.

"Something came," the boy said, his voice nearly inaudible.

"What was it?"

"Out of the woods." The boy stared at his feet as if he couldn't bear to look at the chapel. "It . . . took them. Or . . ."

"Or *what*, boy? For Christ's sake, wh—"

"Or they went with it willingly," Ellen said softly. "Anyway, they all went."

"The children?"

Ellen and the boy nodded, neither one meeting Eb's eye.

"It took the children," Ellen said.

Something always wants the fucking children, Eb thought. "And the Reverend and Virgil with them?"

More nods. Eb swiped a hand across his mouth; he felt hot, his skin clammy, first signs of the flu. "What took them?"

They did not speak for some time. Finally Ellen said, "It wasn't human."

"Or an animal," the boy said.

"Or one of those things in the woods," Ellen said. "It was something else entirely."

Ebenezer's hands clenched on the shotgun. The track machine's engine ticking down was the only sound in an otherwise still night.

Not human, hmm? he thought. *Well, there's hardly much surprise in that, now is there? Not a lot of humans left in these here parts. Outnumbered, outgunned. Last of a dying breed. We've trapped ourselves in the killing jar, all of us for one reason or another. I may be daftest of all because I escaped, only to fly back in. And something's pumping in the ether now.*

His shoulders slumped. What else could he do? In for a penny . . .

"Which way did they go?"

12

THEY WERE ON THEIR WAY back to Little Heaven when it came.

Minerva felt a dry electrical tang at the back of her throat that reminded her of those hot afternoons during her childhood when the sky would scud over with clouds: the taste of a thunderstorm gathering over the horizon.

She checked up in the middle of the ashen path.

"What?" said Micah.

She flicked her head toward the trees. Micah got the hint. They moved quickly, hiding in the heavy dark of the firs ten feet off the path.

The notes of a flute drifted through the air. Jangling, discordant, yet possessed of a rhythm that touched a hidden center in Minerva's chest, a second heart within the main organ.

She didn't see much of it. Only a flurrying of legs—the low-hanging branches, laden with needles, prevented her from viewing anything in its entirety. The first pair of legs were abnormally long and stork-like; they passed in a mad dervish, spinning and pirouetting and high-kicking like a court jester. The flute music intensified, sharp notes invading Minerva's skull and itching at her brain. Other, smaller sets of legs followed. Pale legs streaked with blood. Feet clad in dusty boots or buckled shoes with ruffled socks. They passed silently, only the crunch of their soles on the dead gray earth, their movements manic as they jigged and capered toward the black rock.

Neither Micah nor Minerva moved for some time after the procession passed. Their breath rattled out of their lungs where they knelt under the trees. Micah's eyelids were squeezed shut. When he finally opened them, she saw a new hardness in his working eye.

"We have to go back," Micah said. "I have to get down there."

Her chest tightened. "Into the . . ."

"That is where they will be."

Minerva started to shiver. She couldn't stop.

"Shug, I don't think I can."

"I understand."

"That cave," she went on, feeling the need to explain. "Those . . . *fingers*. Those noises. I want to help. I just don't think . . ."

"I understand."

She put a hand on his leg. His muscles jumped. "Do you have any clue what's down there, Shug?"

In time he said, "I know it is a bad thing. But then . . ."

"Then what?"

"I have done bad things, too."

"You're talking about human evil. It's different."

He did not appear to agree. "We all owe, Minerva. We owe and we are all paying, every day. What else is life but the repayment? But them, what could they owe?"

"Jesus, Shug. What is it you think you owe?"

"They are children, Minny. Only children."

"Yes."

"All lives are not equal. Some are worth more than others."

She said, "I won't argue it with you."

"You could return to Little Heaven."

"I could, yeah," she said. "But I won't. I'll go with you. But I'm telling you right now that I don't know if I can follow you all the way down there, right to the bottom."

Micah pressed a finger to his lips. Minerva held her breath. She heard it then—footsteps.

These came from the same direction as the others had—from Little Heaven. Two sets of legs passed this time. An agonized wheeze accompanied them, two sets of lungs heaving.

Micah and Minerva waited until those legs had passed before crawling out from under the trees. Minerva pulled Ellen's pistol. Micah shone the flashlight up the path, pinning the backs of two men in its beam fifty yards ahead. The men froze. Slowly, they turned.

"Greetings, fellow travelers," the Reverend said with sunny good cheer.

Bloody as butchers, the two of them. The good Reverend's hair was slapped on either side of his skull like a muskrat pelt. He was smiling, wide-eyed. Virgil looked like he was ready to burst out crying.

The Reverend reached into his waistband and put something in Virgil's hand. He stood on his tippy-toes, whispering into Virgil's ear—

"KILL THEM, MY SON," the good Reverend said.

The weight of the pistol in Virgil's hand. A good weight—the weight of finality. Virgil could end it all now. For himself, the Reverend, the one-eyed wonder, and the skinny dyke bitch. End them all. *Him*, Virgil Quincy Swicker. He had that power now. Maybe that would be the best thing. Better than following that abomination deeper into the woods.

It was all Virgil could do to not put the barrel in his own mouth and pull the trigger. He *wanted* to do that. He couldn't get the image of it out of his head. Its enormous body with its flap-a-dangly arms and long, cartoonish legs. Its head and its mouth and its horrible, terrible eyes. How the notes of its flute—a bleached femur bone, it looked like, with holes riddled through it—roused the children from their drugged sleep. They had all gotten up as one, linked hands, and danced into the woods following that horrific piper.

Seeing that, something in Virgil gave over to the madness. He followed the piper into the woods, blood storming through his veins. It didn't even feel like he was walking—more like he'd stepped onto an enormous buried conveyor belt that was stubbornly pulling him along. At some point, he stared up into a tree and saw, or thought he'd seen, a body glossed by the moonlight. Cyril's body, just maybe—Cy, his brother from another mother!—spinning bonelessly, lifelessly, at the end of a thick bough. Cy looked like some awful Christmas tree ornament hung by a giant malicious child. Seeing this, a trapdoor sprang open inside Virgil's head; beneath that door was a stinking yellow room whose bristling and undulating floor suggested that something huge was moving quarrelsomely beneath it . . .

Things had gone a little hazy after that. The minutes or hours slipped by until . . . until . . . until . . .

And now here he was. In the woods with the Reverend and a gun in his hand.

"*Kill them* both." The Reverend's honeyed voice in his ear. "End them."

Virgil was crying. The tears came easily. He barely realized it. When was the last time he'd really sobbed? As a teenager, when he found the body of a stray dog under the bushes in Union Park, kicked to death by some sadistic shitheel. He hadn't cried since. Never seemed a deep enough need. But he did so now—for the dead fools at Little Heaven; for their children, who were fated for something far worse; for his buddy Cyril, who had been turned into a fucking tree ornament; and for his own dumbshit self, who didn't have the brains to see a way out of this awful muddle.

The gun came up. He saw it there at the end of his arm, but it didn't feel like part of him. He pulled the trigger. It was as easy as breathing, it really was.

The bullet creased the air inches from Minerva's skull. The *pop!* filled her ears. Her own gun jerked up automatically. She fired. Virgil didn't go down. He was walking toward her, sobbing the same words over and over. *I'm sorry*, it might have been. He was bawling like a baby.

He shot again, missing his mark. *Pop!* She fired and also missed. Her hand trembled. *Stop it, goddamn it, stop shaking just st—*

A bullet smashed into the ash between her spread legs. She couldn't stop the shakes. Virgil was walking and firing. He was half blind from crying, but it wouldn't matter; a few more strides and it would be pretty much a point-blank proposition.

Her finger froze on the trigger. She couldn't—couldn't—

Micah snatched the gun out of her hand. *Bang.* Virgil's head snapped back in a mist of red. His body was flung with such force that his left foot was ejected from his boot. He rolled bonelessly to the edge of the path. He did not get up.

"Shug, I'm sorry." A wave of adrenaline shakes rolled through her. She stared at her gun hand, the one that had betrayed her. "I don't know what . . ."

She read it in his eyes. *You are not made for this, Minny.* There was nothing cruel in his appraisal. It wasn't a slight on her toughs or spine— simply that, in the cut, she couldn't pull the trigger. And he could.

They walked over to Virgil. His big toe poked through a hole in his woolen sock. Merciless, what a bullet could do. There was no need to check for a pulse. The top of Virgil's head was missing. Everything above his eyes, which were still filmy with tears, staring blankly into the cold night sky.

13

THIS IS ONE BLUBBERING NINNY *who's better off dead* was Amos's thought as he put the gun into Virgil's hand.

The idiot's eyes were all swimmy as he made with the waterworks. Amos had to swallow his revulsion. Virgil had been useful in a pinch, but now he was deadweight. In fact, Amos had been speculating about how to get rid of the dummy. And now, out of the blue, the perfect opportunity— two birds with one stone.

Virgil nodded at the Reverend's simple instructions, docile as a lamb. Then he began to fire. Amos didn't wait to see the result. He scampered up the incline, slipping on dead pine needles. He laughed thinly—*a-hee, a-hee-heeee*—because there was something deliciously funny about the events of the past hours . . . and because he couldn't stop laughing, even when he bit his lip so hard that the skin tore and blood gushed—he just kept on howling, the shrill gasping notes pouring out of him.

Job 8:21, he thought. *God will fill thy mouth with laughing, and thy lips with rejoicing! Hallelujah, praised be, and pass the spuds!*

He ran as fast as his legs would carry him as the gunshots continued to ring out from behind. *Pop-papop-pop-poppoppop!* The shots abruptly stopped; the woods ran thick with silence. Good-bye, Virgil! See you in the funny pages, Skinny Bitch! Farewell, One-Eye! Godspeed to none of you, and may Satan feast on your genitals in hell!

He hurried toward the black rock. He was not tired, and his pace did not flag. He was filled with a limitless reservoir of energy. Even though his legs were leaden and his chest searing, he felt like those niggers in Africa who had developed incredible cardiovascular endurance from being chased across the veld by hungry lions. He could run a million miles!

His eyes momentarily slipped shut. The wondrous creature lay there, imprinted on his eyelids. Oh, what a sight that had been.

You are beautiful.

This had been Amos's awestruck thought. The thing had to be twelve feet tall. Long, articulate legs and arms. Its flesh was smooth as porcelain. Its belly was cask-like, as if pregnant with some unfathomable offspring. Amos's heart quailed at the sight of it easing through the trees. Its head was enormous. Its mouth stretched across the entirety of its face; it looked to be smiling, but as its mouth followed the upward curve of its skull, a smile must be its default expression. Its eyes were ineffably black and lusterless, like buttons: Amos pictured the four little holes in their centers where a seamstress could loop her thread.

It had come through the trees slowly and somehow playfully. There was a hint of shyness in its movements. Amos's eyes had quivered in their sockets, as if his peepers were under some enormous pressure, jittering like roaches in a hot pan. He knew why his eyes were struggling, too: they were trying to see the shape *behind* the shape. The creature had another face, and it lurked beneath the one Amos was allowed to see—but his frail human eyes and his inadequate and too-literal mind were preventing him from seeing its more breathtaking true shape.

It had bent over the sleeping children, sniffing them as a coyote might a moldering carcass; the slits in the middle of its face dilated. Its black tongue made a sandpapery note as it slid over its fleshless lips. It had no teeth to speak of; rags of wet tissue dangled and swayed in its mouth, reminding Amos of the fibrous pith inside a pumpkin.

It then produced a flute. Its fingers danced nimbly along its length, coaxing from it notes that raised the hairs on the nape of Amos's neck. The children had stood up all at once. Their eyes were still closed, but their bodies were alert. They linked hands. The creature began to dance. It was both horrible and magnetic: the strange articulation of its limbs, the mad glee with which it jigged. The children mimicked it, their legs and arms moving unnaturally.

The thing danced into the woods. The children followed. They went quickly, their feet seeming not to touch the ground. Virgil only stood in a slack-mouthed stupor. Amos shook him—when that failed, he slapped Virgil hard across the face. The dimwit's eyes unfogged, the faintest glimmer coming back into them.

"We must follow, my son."

Virgil swallowed with effort. "Yeah. Follow. I can do that."

And they had done so, shuffling along in pursuit of the thing. Until they had been set upon by the troublesome outsiders—but those two ended up doing Amos a great service by erasing a vestigial player from the proceedings and hopefully wiping themselves out in the bargain. Everything was coming up Flesher!

The trees now gave way to a clearing. The moonlight settled across an empty expanse—sand scalloped by the wind and the black rock standing watchfully in the distance. In that same moonlight, he could see small footprints in the sand. He followed them, his heart singing.

He had done his duty. Now he would reap the reward. What form would it take? He had no use for money or renown, the common ambitions that common men spent their common lives pursuing. He desired knowledge. An understanding of how this world—or the worlds beyond it—operated. A peek behind the curtain. He wanted to see God—not the one his worshippers cowered before, either. The God that had led Amos out here in the first place. The God of Flies and Blood. He wanted to thank that God for making Amos Flesher just the way he was.

The footprints led straight to the black rock. A quiet hum emanated from it. He followed the footprints around the rockface, glancing back to see if anyone was in pursuit. He paused. There—far away but visible. The sweep of a flashlight? He bared his teeth. The outsiders. The bastards. He could only hope that Virgil had killed one of them and perhaps hurt the other. But the one-eyed man struck Amos as a fellow who'd be calm in a shoot-out. No matter. Once he had claimed his just reward, Amos would deal with them. Oh yes, he could take his time with it. There was nobody out here to help them.

Amos picked up the pace, swallowing the blood from his torn lip. The rock tilted ninety degrees as it opened onto a fresh face. He jogged along it. His sweat mixed with the lanolin in his pomade and slid down his cheeks in gooey runners. He wiped them away absentmindedly and crooned an old gospel ditty.

> *The Father sent the Son*
> *A ruined world to save;*
> *Man meted to the Sinless One*
> *The cross—the grave:*
> *Blest Substitute from God!*
> *Wrath's awful cup He drained:*
> *Laid down His life, and e'en the tomb's—*

Amos tripped and stumbled, arms outflung. He found his feet again and carried on, singing a new song that he made up as he went. His rich baritone carried out over the wastes.

> *Fuck the Father, fuck the Son, and fuck the Holy Ghost;*
> *Fuck the bearded carpenter, and fuck his lordly host;*
> *Fuck the baby Jesus, that wormy little runt;*
> *And fuck the whore of Baby-looooon, yes fuck her greasy*
> *cuuuunt—*

He reached a cleft in the rock. An odd glow poured from its mouth. The footsteps carried on into the enveloping darkness that existed past the entry.

"*You have been fiddling. Fiddling, fiddling, fiddling . . . ,*" said a familiar voice.

It sat twenty feet to Amos's left, crouched on the sand. The moon touched its awesome contours, reflecting off the egg-like dome of its skull. It spoke in a perfect mimicry of Sister Muriel.

"*You always were a filthy boy, Amos Flesher. The filthiest, by far. Do you know what will happen if you keep fiddling with your dirty stick, hmm? It will fall off. That's right! Snap off like a winter icicle, it will. And you will be so ashamed, won't you? You will have no choice but to bury it in the yard, as a dog does with a bone. Your uuuu-rhine will simply fall from the hole where your little stick once poked, Amos. Yes, as sure as Christ sits in Heaven.*"

Amos took a step back. He realized right then how alone he was, miles and miles from anyone. "I did what you asked."

The creature made a sound like the chittering of an insect. *"I didn't ask anything of you,"* it said as Sister Muriel.

A thin wire of unease threaded into Amos's heart. The thing chittered on and on. It was too dark for Amos to tell if the sound was coming from some part of its odd anatomy or if this was its version of laughter.

"Not me, no, no, no," it said, this time in a voice that might have been its own: high and breathy, the voice of a baby who had learned to enunciate its words. "My father asked . . . my father, my father, my daddykins . . ."

"Your . . . your father?"

The thing squatted in the sand, repeating those two words over and over. "My father, my father, my father . . ."

The understanding rocked Amos. This thing was no more than the lapdog of a far greater entity. Comprehending this, the sight of it—its bloated belly, its bird legs and button eyes—now filled Amos with disgust. Hunched in the dark, babbling the same two idiot words: *My father, my father*. It was nothing but an overgrown mynah bird with a gift for impressions. It made Amos sick to look at it now—no different from those soft-brained children at the orphanage he'd delighted in jabbing with a pin.

"Where?" he said to it. *"Where,* you filthy thing?"

The thing raised its arm, one exquisitely long finger pointing at the cleft.

"My father is waiting."

MICAH ROUNDED THE BLACK ROCK. Minerva lagged behind, still shaken from the encounter with Virgil. He pressed on without her. Maybe it was best she stay out of it.

Micah's mind was cluttered; he lacked a great deal of information, and under normal circumstances he would retreat and regroup. But there was no time for that and he was fueled by a rage more profound than anything he'd experienced in years. Worse than what he'd felt for Seaborn Appleton or even his old Captain Beechwood.

He would kill the Reverend. He should have done it the first time he'd laid eyes on the man. He had practically smelled the crazy seeping out of him—it had a scent, true craziness did: the stench of old flooring rotted through with cat piss. Micah had sensed the malice festering in the fuming wastes of the Reverend's soul, and he should have put a bullet in his brain right then and there . . . but Charlie and Otis had taken his sidearm, robbing him of the opportunity.

Abruptly, Micah came to the cleft. He had been so taken up with thoughts of vengeance that he lost track of time. He shone his flashlight into the crevice. Moody blue shadows gave way to deeper enveloping blacks. He spun on his heel, alerted by a klaxon blaring in his unconscious mind—

Something loomed motionlessly out in the sand. A huge humanlike form plated in moonlight.

"Fine evening for a perambulation, eh, Private?"

It was the voice of Captain Beechwood. The thing issued a terrible flapping sound like an enormous cockroach beating its wings.

"My father is waiting," it said in Beechwood's voice. *"My father will just let some air into those children, Private Shughrue. Just a little air. My father is thirsty. So thirsty. Hungry. Yes. Meat."* Its mouth stretched wide, splitting its entire face in two; then its jaws snapped shut with a sound like wood planks spanked together. *"Meat for the feast. My father, my father, my father . . ."*

It pointed at the cleft. Micah took a few steps in that direction, his eye never leaving the thing. It did not move or try to stop him. In fact, it appeared to be urging him inside. Micah aimed his flashlight into the gap again. Dust sifted down, sparkling in the beam.

"My father is waiting . . ."

He entered the cleft. Beads of sweat popped on his brow. He held a hand out for balance; it brushed the cave wall and he recoiled, disturbed once again by the soft and somehow fleshy character of the rock. It felt like the skin of a sick old man, smoothed and made clammy with age and disease. The darkness sucked in on him with unnatural avidity; it hungered after the feeble beam shed by his flashlight, nibbling at its glow with invisible black teeth.

He passed under the colony of olms and came to the precipice rather quickly. The rope ladder clattered against the rock, down and down, stirred by a subterranean wind—or by someone who had recently climbed down it. He stared down to the tunnel below. An odor drifted up, almost too faint to credit. A smell that spoke of childhood. A mix of bubble gum and dime-store perfume, the blood off skinned knees and chocolate coins wrapped in shiny foil. It was all of those things, but corrupted somehow. Mixed with the smell that permeates an old folks' home: sickness and dust and the yellowing reek of bodies rotting from the inside out. The smell of living death.

Staring down, Micah pictured something hunched just past the mouth of the tunnel. His mind couldn't entirely compass it. But the outline was of a person of unfathomable age: two hundred, three hundred, a thousand years old. He pictured this corrupted thing quivering in the darkness below, leering with its young-old mouth, its gums black as tar—

Micah's jaw tensed. "I am coming," he whispered.

He stuffed the flashlight into his pocket and dropped one foot down until it touched the first rung of the ladder. He gripped the ropes as the ladder swung out from the rock, throwing him off balance. He stabilized himself and followed it down. The flashlight shone inside his pocket, its tepid glow illuminating the space directly below him.

It came then. Thick, throaty—the laughter of a child.

Shapes swarmed in the darkness below. Alien, twisting movements. Micah's bladder clenched. Fear poured into his brain; he stood rooted for a span of time he could not judge, then slowly pulled the flashlight from his pocket. When he shone it down, nothing was there.

The ladder slapped the stone. His foot found the basin floor. He released the ladder and turned, kneeling, shining the flashlight into the tunnel.

The beam outlined the start of a cave system carved through the rock. Micah crept to the tunnel mouth. It stretched twenty feet or so before hitting a bend. The tunnel was honeycombed with holes—some small, others big enough to accommodate a person's body. He wondered just how large this network of tunnels could be, and where they all might lead.

Body tensed, head throbbing, he forged into the alkaline dark.

14

"DO YOU LIKE TO PLAY . . . GAMES?"

Minerva stopped. The voice belonged to a small child. She turned toward it, summoning every ounce of her willpower. Something squatted in the dark not far from the cleft, which she had arrived at some minutes after Shughrue. The moon gave only a hint of this thing's contours.

"Games," the voice called. "Shall we play?"

Her paralysis was absolute. With a fervency she hadn't felt since she was a girl, she wished she could squeeze her eyes shut and just disappear. Wink out of existence and appear somewhere else, ten thousand miles away where the sun was shining and the world made sense.

"We *will* play."

The voice became stern. Minerva could see it better now. She wished she couldn't. She wished she were blind. It sat in the moonlit sand with its long legs crossed, knees flared out so as to resemble wings. Its pendulous stomach spread across its thighs.

"Come," it said.

Minerva went to it. There was no option. Its voice was a summoning. She sat before it and crossed her legs in kind.

"Do you like games?"

She shook her head numbly.

It smiled. A repellent sight. "I thought all children enjoyed games."

"I'm not a child," she managed to say.

"You are all children of eggs," it said.

She said, "What are the rules?"

It tittered. "My rules."

"What are the stakes?"

"Everything you owe, my dear."

A seed of terror planted itself in her stomach. "What do I owe?"

Another dry titter. "Everything. Nothing. The game decides."

A cloud scudded over the moon. The landscape went dark. The creature's eyes glimmered wetly.

"*Let's play, Minny! It will be ever so much fun!*"

Its voice had changed. Gone were the breathy baby syllables. Now it spoke in the voice of Minerva's dead brother. Little Cortland Atwater.

"AND THE NAME OF THE STAR is called Wormwood: and the third part of the waters became wormwood; and many men died in the waters, because they were made bitter . . ."

Revelation 8:11. Wormwood, Wormwood, the name of the star is called Wormwood . . . It was a favorite passage of the Reverend's. The waters turned bitter; many people died. He had always liked the sound of that.

He was inside a burrow carved into the rock. *He* was the worm now. But not a worm in wood, oh no. A worm in its wormhole. No roots to get in his way. No birds pecking at him with their sharp beaks. He was hidden safely, deep within the rock. It was dark down here, though. So very dark. That scared him a little. But this was a quibble. The father would pay him what he had earned soon.

Laughter drifted through the rock, coming from everywhere and nowhere. Children's laughter. He'd never cared for it. No matter how many shrieking infants he'd blessed or how many apple-cheeked little shits he'd kissed on the forehead, he couldn't stomach kids. Their sticky hands and gap-toothed smiles and their stupidity—everything that people seemed to love about them, Amos loathed. All children were useless until they had grown old enough to contribute to his coffers.

But currently, that laughter sounded quite sweet to his ears. Angelic, even.

It was hard to say how much time had passed since he had climbed down the rope ladder to the secondary tunnel system. There was no natural light at all, but the rock held a strange glow. He had begun to crawl through the main tunnel, scraping his knees, inching toward the hum that emanated from someplace ahead. The tunnel walls were pocked with holes—burrows, it almost seemed. *Big* ones. They reminded him of termite boreholes, or honeycombs where bee larvae might pupate. But the bugs that would nest in holes of that size would be . . . no, they were not bug burrows.

He'd kept crawling toward the heart of that hum. Yet the closer he had gotten, the more scared he became. The fear pulsed in his brain, taking on terrible forms. He pictured an enormous chalice inside the rock—a bowl teeming with massive insects. Beetles the size of border collies. Bloated roaches with wings fanned out like garbage can lids. Millipedes with legs thick as a baby's arm. Tens of thousands of them, blind from lack of sun, their bodies either transparent or foggy white so you could see the queer workings of their guts. Skittering madly inside the smooth rock basin, trundling over the corpses of their dead. The basin was studded with huge bean-shaped sacks that burst with wet pops, spewing forth flabby larvae with skin that sweated like gray sickly cheese, these revolting grubs that mewled like newborn babes. The bowl was too steep for any of them to escape; all they could do was squirm and shuck madly, waiting for an unassuming visitor to tumble down from above . . .

The image entombed itself in his head. He couldn't shake it. Suddenly frightened by that hum, he had crawled into one of the burrows off the main tunnel. It was so tight that his shoulders brushed the sides. He couldn't say how far or deep he pressed into the hole. At some point, it had swollen into a bubble. He curled up. The rock was warm as flesh. It felt like a womb. The darkness pressed against his eyeballs. He was careful where he set his hands—in some silly chamber of his mind, he thought he might touch the resting shape of . . . well, *something*. Whatever might slumber deep in this rock. He pictured a hairless rat with yellowed teeth like shards of broken crockery; he pictured his hand closing on its tail, thick as a garden hose, a whip of oily flesh . . .

The image spooked him. Still, at least a giant rat would be of this world—a common enough sight, even if blown up ten times its normal size. What he really feared was that he might encounter something not of this world. Something he wouldn't find in his worst dreams, because, after all, those dreams were still culled from the sights and sensations he would have experienced while waking.

He let go of a jittery laugh. The rock sponged up the sound so quickly it was as if he'd never made a peep.

The breath whistled out of his lungs. He was safe here. He would wait and recite some scripture to calm down.

"The name of the star is called Wormwood . . . Wormwood . . . Wormwood . . ."

The laughter came again. Dancing and sprightly, tickling the hairs of his inner ear. Almost a song, holding lyrics that he couldn't quite make out.

Distantly, he heard something or someone pass the mouth of his burrow—he already thought of it in that possessive way: *his* burrow. Was it one of the outsiders? Rage flooded through him; the air flared red before his eyes. They would not take his gift. The father owed him. He had given it what it wanted. But Amos was too terrified to move. It was as if he had crawled to the very bottom of the earth, down with the hiss of unseen voices and the punch and seethe of machines made from bone and teeth, machines whose purpose he could not understand. The father's beautiful instruments.

"Wormwood," he whispered hoarsely. "The name of the star . . ."

MICAH FORGED DOWN the tunnel. He wasn't focused on the Reverend anymore; that bloodlust had sluiced out of him. His every muscle was tensed and screaming. A tiny voice inside his head yammered for him to stop, for God's sake, *go back*.

The smell was stronger as he navigated toward its source. He gagged on the putrid stench, a smell like rotted offal marinating in mothballs—so powerful that it was more a taste. The rock seemed to throb—*thu-thump, thu-thump*—shuddering slightly like a thick artery.

His boot brushed something, making a metallic jangle. He shone the flashlight on a manacle, hand-forged and browned with rust. How old could it be? A hundred years? The sort of thing a slave would have worn . . . except it was too small to fit around a man's wrist.

He continued on. He was scared, oh yes—terrified—but that rested easily within his mind. It was a perfectly natural reaction, so he did not try to fight it. He came across a shoe next. A child's size, incredibly old. He picked it up, trembling. Faded but still legible on the bottom of the vulcanized rubber sole: *Charles Goodyear, 1871.*

He encountered other artifacts: tatters of clothing, a busted pocket watch. A wooden doll with the eyes scratched out.

The tunnel bent gently, the rock running smooth as alabaster. He shone the flashlight along its upper curvature, which was so low his head brushed it even as he crawled. It was carpeted with an odd fungoid growth, black and spiky. He raised the flashlight beam to it. The fungus broke apart. What he had mistaken for fungus was in fact a dozing ball of sightless spiders; they scuttled down the tunnel's circumference, dancing lightly on the rock, vanishing into tiny holes in the floor. Micah noticed that the floor and walls were pocked with thousands of similar holes, tiny pits of darkness the flashlight beam could not penetrate. What else was hiding in there?

The father the father is so thirsty so hungry meat for the feast . . .

The air got progressively more rotten. He pulled his shirt over his nose and mouth, breathing shallowly. He spotted a bone. Bleached white, picked clean. It could belong to an animal. But animals were too wary to venture down to such a place, weren't they?

He stared closely at the bone—a long, elegant filigree, the tips polished smooth by time or by . . . by something sucking on it until the ends went smooth.

Which is when he heard them. The worst, the most awful sounds.

"THERE ARE CALIBRATIONS *of the nerve endings, Minny, that you have never known to exist,"* the thing said in little Cort's voice. *"There are registers that you have never felt, the way dogs can hear sounds humans cannot. I can help you reach them. It will be my pleasure."*

The thing's long-fingered hands moved in graceful patterns, its nails tapering to sharp points. Their movements were hypnotic. Minerva felt as if she'd chugged codeine cough syrup.

"*Lay your hands out,*" it said as Cort. "*Palms up, Minny, pretty please.*"

Helplessly, she obeyed. It touched a fingernail to a spot on her wrist where the veins ran blue under the skin. The pain was instant and exquisite, like nothing she had ever known. Too painful to scream, even. Its finger withdrew. Her skin had not been broken. There was no mark.

"*I can open you up,*" it said in Cort's voice. "*I can make you feel as you have never felt before, Minny. Things precious few of your kind have ever known. Would you like that?*"

"No," she said. "I don't want you to."

The creature made a frowny face. Its voice was now a babyish coo: "Why-sy why-sy, pudding and pie-sy? We could have such fun, you and I-sy."

It reached again. Minerva flinched. Its finger slowly retracted. Its head was cocked on its thin neck, its eyes reflecting the moonlight.

"*It hurt,*" it said in her dead brother's voice. "*When the snake ate me. It hurt so much, Minny. You didn't do anything to help.*"

She let out an airless gasp. "Cort, no, I wanted to—"

"*But you didn't,*" the thing said spitefully. "*Wanting to isn't doing, Minny. And now what am I? Shit. Snake shit.*"

"Stop," she whispered.

"*It was pink, Minny. The sun shining through the snake's skin. The light was pink inside its mouth. Pink with black threads where its veins ran. There was the smell of squashed grasshoppers. I suffocated, but it took a long time. A lot longer than you'd think. My ribs were broke and my lungs filling with blood, but I think I screamed. Do you remember how my screams sounded? I bet you heard me. You weren't far away. Just up that tree. Safe and sound.*"

"Please stop," she begged.

The creature touched her other wrist. The pain was immense, world-eating. Its finger withdrew. It blew gingerly on her flesh. The pain receded.

"Shall we begin, my love?"

"No, please no . . ."

It shook its head with what appeared to be true sadness, as if to say the following events were beyond its power to control. "We must."

"No, no, no . . ."

It said, "If it's information you seek, come and see me. If it is pairs of letters you need, I have consecutively three."

"Wh-what?"

A macabre smile. "The game, my dear."

This horrid thing wanted her to answer riddles? She almost laughed at the banality. Then she remembered the words scrawled on the wall back at the Preston School for Boys.

Why is 6 afraid of 7?

789! 789!

"What if I don't play?"

"You will, my dove." It spoke as one might when an answer exists beyond all doubt. "And you will lose, because your kind always does. The pain you experience will exist beyond your wildest conception; your purest amazement will be in just how deeply you can feel." A forlorn sigh. "Your suffering will show me nothing new or novel. I have played this game too many times. There are no secrets your kind has left to tell me."

"So why even play?"

An expression crossed its face that in the embalmed moonlight could have passed for sorrow. The thing was revolted at itself for what it was— what it couldn't help but be. But aren't we all prisoners of our natures, deep down?

SSSSSLLLLLLLLLLLLLLUUUUUHHHH . . .

A sucking, slurping sound. Prolonged and somehow chunky. There was a hideous eagerness to it.

These noises drifted through the tunnel and slid into Micah's ears. He was unprepared for the blast of panic that filled him. He sensed an opening ahead. He clapped his fingers over the flashlight lens, letting just enough light seep through to illuminate the rock directly in front of him. He did not want to announce his presence to whatever might be lurking ahead. He crept forward, blood blitzing through his heart—he was dizzy with the pulse of it.

The sounds intensified. Good Christ, what could be making them?

The tunnel ended. He was able to stand up again. He had entered some kind of vault. Some kind of—*lair* was the word that skated uneasily through his mind.

He was in a bubble deep inside the rock, perhaps at its very center. He could not intuit its size, but by the frail light leaking through his fingers he saw the walls on either side of the tunnel running upward to give a faint impression of scale. It was less a bubble than a cube.

Or a . . . a box.

The sucking sounds were louder. Whatever was making them was in here. Carefully, heart thudding, he lifted one finger off the flashlight beam. A slice of light fell across the chamber's floor. The rock was black as obsidian. The sounds stopped. There was a pregnancy to the pause; Micah pictured a thousand eyes swiveling in his direction.

Amos Flesher, he thought. *Is that you?*

But he knew it wouldn't be the Reverend, much as he dearly wished it. There was only so much threat Flesher could pose. The noises in the dark unlocked a far more potent terror. They whispered directly into his veins, mainlining fear into his heart.

The father . . .

He lifted another finger off the flashlight lens. He could see the odd bone fragment and moldering tatter of clothing. Uniforms? The flashlight dimmed briefly, the contact points on the batteries failing for an instant. Oh Jesus. Not now. Don't let that happen.

He lifted a third finger. A crease of light cut across the chamber and touched the rock wall thirty-odd yards away—

Something skittered across the beam. A white, wormish fluttering. A network of tubes or something—his instinctual impression was of a gargantuan maggot hacked into sections, the segments stitched into a vaguely humanoid form.

He lifted his final finger clear as dread knotted in his throat. He swept the beam across the chamber, trying to take in as much as he possibly could in hopes of understanding what he was dealing with—

He saw it then.

15

THE STRANGEST POSSIBILITY trip-trapped over the surface of Minerva's brain once the game had started. She thought: What if God or Buddha or the Creator or who-the-fuck-ever had come to her as a freshly conceived zygote; what if the Creator had said: *Listen, you, this is how your life is going to unspool. Dead father, dead brother, sadness and rage and regret aplenty, and the whole shebang's gonna end on the far side of the desert with some unearthly creature making you answer riddles. Knowing all this, chum, you sure you want to ride this merry-go-round?*

What would she have said, knowing the shape of her life to come?

"If it is information you seek, come and see me. If it is pairs of letters you need, I have consecutively three."

The thing chanted this riddle in Cort's voice. She had always gotten an F in classes where deductive reasoning was taught. That stuff maddened her. When would she ever need to know *What has four eyes but can't see?* or *What has hands but can't clap?*

The thing licked its lips. Its corrugated black tongue slipped out, sopping up the drool that threatened to cascade down its chin. Its body trembled with tension, although its eyes remained dull and dead.

Far off: the sound of trees snapping.

"Please," it said. "An answer."

"Give me a few minutes. Isn't that fair?"

"Fair has very little to do with it, Minny," the thing said in Cort's voice.

Minerva's brain synapses burned up, smoke practically pouring out her ears. *If it is pairs of letters you need, I have consecutively three.* She pictured six envelopes, six stamps, six addresses, all in a neat row. *If it is information you seek . . .* The letters held important information, but she couldn't open them. Each envelope was fastened shut. Goddamn it, *open*!

The tree-snap sounds grew louder. A new sound joined those snaps: a low rumble. The creature must have heard it, too.

"Tick-tock," it said in its own voice.

Minerva squeezed her eyes shut. *Information you seek . . . pairs of letters . . .*

She laughed mirthlessly. "I never was any good at these."

The thing chuckled. "*Should have paid more attention in school, big sis.*"

Minerva gave it a sunless smile. "Fuck off. Stop talking like that."

"You have fire," it said, no longer in Cort's voice. "I like that. It will take time to extinguish."

The rumble was unmistakable now. The sand trembled under Minerva. The creature unkinked its legs and stood. It towered over her, its limbs throwing shadows across her face.

The rumble became the metallic rattle of an engine. A pair of headlights burnt through the trees. The thing's attention was diverted. She took that chance to skitter away.

Some kind of vehicle bore down on them. The driver blared the horn. The thing took a step back, its perplexity deepening. Was it some kind of . . . tank? A figure stood on its hood. A familiar English voice rose over the churn of the engine.

"*Git aloooong, little dooooogies . . .*"

The thing lifted one arm, a spindly finger pointing.

"Father—?" it said questioningly.

A concentrated stream of fire ripped through the night. It hit the thing square in the chest. Ebenezer's face was lit by the glow off the igniting gasoline. The creature went up like a kindling effigy. Illuminated by the brilliant light, its face held an expression of puzzled wonderment. Then it began to scream. A high trilling shriek that ascended through several octaves before dropping to a searing howl. It gibbered in many voices, a few of them recognizable to Minerva.

Ebenezer let his finger off the flamethrower. The thing stood in a flickering column of orange, crackling and hissing. It craned its head toward Minerva; its eyes were unchanged, black as lumps of coal in the melting tapestry of its face. The fire had peeled its mouth even wider. It issued a mocking titter and began to jig in place, its legs kicking crazily, flinging gobbets of roasting skin from its shanks.

It took two steps toward Ebenezer. He let loose with another burst. The thing shrieked in what seemed to be true pain. Then it fled down the slope toward the forest. A mesmerizing sight: its fiery limbs carrying it swiftly through the night, twenty yards in a single stride. It reached the woods and monkeyed up the first tree, then began to leap from treetop to treetop. It left a point of flame at the tip of each fir; the trees began to burn, the fire spreading rapidly.

Minerva approached the machine. Eb remained on the hood, a nitrous blue finger dancing from the nozzle of the flamethrower. Ellen was driving. Nate was there, too.

"The cavalry has arrived," Ebenezer said grandly.

Minerva grinned. She couldn't help herself.

"Ah!" Eb said. "Finally, a smile! What was that god-awful thing?"

"That was what took the kids," Ellen said to Eb.

"Ah-ha!" Ebenezer said, full of overadrenalized good cheer. "Mystery solved!"

Minerva pointed at the cleft. "They're in there. The children are."

"We better go find them," said Ellen.

"Oh, I don't think you want to do that," Minerva whispered.

MICAH SHUGHRUE knew it wasn't the Reverend. But the man's face was familiar.

Even by the most charitable definition, this could not be considered a man anymore. He hung in the center of the box buried deep within the black rock. He was suspended on a network of red ropes resembling wet sinews; the ropes were attached to various points of the man's anatomy but primarily his shoulders and head and neck, bearing him aloft. The ropes issued a faint thrum like high-tension power lines.

This man was grotesquely shriveled, and human only insofar as he had a pair of driftwood legs and arms that were no more than bones clad in the barest stretching of tissue. His chest was so withered that the skin had shrunk around every rib, his innards encased in a yellowish sack in the center of the rib cage. His head was a grinning, fleshless skull, nose a blade of cartilage. His legs were pulled up tight to his body, the kneecaps visible as saucers, the bones of his feet jutting like gruesome sticks. His posture was that of a sickening fetus curled up in its womb.

The flashlight beam hung on its terrible face for an instant. As wasted as it was, Micah had seen it before. But where? Something in the flinty slope of those cheeks, the jut of those calcified ears . . .

It finally registered. He'd seen this man's portrait on a desk in the Preston School for Boys. It was Augustus Preston himself.

Preston's appearance encouraged a gruesome fixation. Much as he wanted to, Micah could not look away. It was as if the man had been devoured from the inside out, the way termites remorselessly harvest an oak tree. If Micah were to touch him the wrong way, he was certain Preston's innards would spill out—parched, desiccated, sawdusty: his lungs and liver and heart all pulverized and turned to powder. And still, the annihilations of the man's soul seemed somehow worse, if less obvious, than the ruin of his body. There was nothing inside him anymore. This was Micah's dread sense. Not even sawdust. Only a yellowing, howling emptiness that his soul had fled years ago. The essence of his humanity had been irretrievably lost, boiled away like steam off a hot pan.

How had Preston arrived at this place? How many years had he been hanging here? For nearly a *century*—was that in any way possible? What were those ropes? What was the purpose of this vault and—

Sssssllllllllllluuuuuhhhh . . .

Micah swung the flashlight. The light bled beneath Preston's suspended feet. He saw something, and followed it up to Preston's body. Micah had somehow missed it on the initial sweep.

A tube ran out below Preston's bottom rib. It was white and wrinkled, like the milky intestines of a gutted fish. The tube trailed down to the floor and wormed into the dark. It flexed and cramped the way a garden hose does when fed water from a tap; it swelled in places as if something larger, more solid, were passing through it.

Micah followed it without wanting to.

His blood ran cold. Micah had never been much for books, but he did enjoy a dime-store paperback from time to time. *The Feasting Dead.* That had been a pretty good one. *The Body Snatchers*, too. In such books, he had read that phrase a dozen times. *His blood ran cold.* He didn't know much about writing, but he knew that was a lazy cliché, right up there with *water through a sieve* and *a deer caught in headlights.*

Yet this was his exact sensation. A paralyzing chill swept through him—it was as if his blood had been sucked out and stashed in a deep freeze and injected back into his veins. A coldness that made his lungs lock up and his bowels throb with the urge to be voided.

The tube ran out of Augustus Preston and into a small body. A boy's body. Could that be Eli Rathbone—?

If it was Eli, there was precious little boyish about him anymore. Eli lay limp on the floor, eyes open in an expression of unending horror. The tube—*the umbilicus*, Micah thought; *that is what it looks like, a huge elongated umbilical cord*—expanded into a funnel, which was latched over the boy's mouth. The cord rippled at its tip as if tiny insects were trundling under its surface; Eli's body jerked helplessly as the cord cramped and flexed, as that awful slurping sound filled the air.

Not wanting to but unable to stop himself, Micah followed Eli's body with the beam. Eli's hand was linked with that of a small girl—Elsa Rasmussen? Who else could it be? Their hands were melted into a carbuncled knob. The girl was welded to the boy behind her in the same manner, and that boy to another boy, and him to another, and another, and perhaps ten more after that. Their bodies rag-dolled into the nether recesses of the vaulted box, chained together through some hideous alchemy. Eli looked the worst by far; Elsa was a bit better, and the two boys a bit better than her. It was as if something was feeding on them in turn: First Eli, who was almost used up. Then Elsa, then the two boys who looked like brothers.

The most recent additions appeared relatively unmarked. Micah was looking at a food chain in the most literal sense.

The children behind the two boys were still clothed. Their eyes were open, too—their pupils constricted when the beam touched them—but they were unmoving and unspeaking, as if they had been injected with a paralysis toxin from a giant spider. Micah shone the beam to chart the upper reaches of the chamber, expecting to see a huge shaggy arachnid hanging from the ceiling, rappelling toward him eagerly on a skein of gossamer thick as a steel cable . . . but there were only those red ropes rising to knit with the rock.

Micah forced himself to approach Preston. It was only a few steps, but scaling Everest would have been easier. He had no idea how big the man had been before, but whatever process his body had been subject to had altered it horribly. Now that Micah was up close, he could see that Preston wasn't just thin—he had *shrunk*, his arms and legs shortening, the bones dissolving or something, until he was nothing but a twisted effigy. He was no more than four feet tall, an emaciated dwarf.

The chamber was silent except for that *suck-suck*, and even that had quieted. He stopped a foot from Preston. The man's body did not give off any sort of smell—not of age, or rot. He looked almost mummified: the topmost layer of his skin was crackly, the crust of a flaky pie. Micah was sure the faintest touch would cause it to crumble away entirely, exposing the bleached bone. Dear Auggie had been consumed by some relentless hungering force—and now, with Preston used up, that same force had reached out for other sustenance. The sweetest, youngest delicacies it could find.

Preston's eyelids were shut. Micah wasn't certain he would find eyes behind those lids; if anything, they might resemble putrefying grapes. He had no intention of finding out. The red ropes radiated a pleasant warmth. A vein of solid light shone inside each of them. He gingerly shifted around Preston, shining the flashlight to make sure nothing lurked out of sight. Then he trained the beam on the gruesome cord running out of Preston's body to attach to Eli's face. Micah's free hand gripped the hilt of the bayonet he'd taken from the Preston School days before—

Watery voices drifted in from the tunnel. Minerva? He wanted to shout out to her—*Stay away!*—but he might need her help, and selfishly he did not want to face this alone.

His gaze fell on Preston's spine. Preston's right arm was tucked behind his back in a chicken wing that would have snapped his bones under normal circumstances; his forearm was shielding something on his lower back. Biting down on his revulsion, Micah used the flashlight to lever that arm up; it moved with the dry creak of ancient leather. There was a long slit across Preston's spine, six inches above his buttocks. A full foot long, running from hip to hip. The lips of the wound were dry and hard as cured meat. The flesh inside those lips was bright pink. The wound looked somehow fresh.

The voices drew nearer. Micah barely heard them. He was fixated on the wound . . .

Without much thought, he unsheathed the bayonet. He touched the tip of it to one edge of the wound in Preston's back. It split the gummy surface; clear fluid burped through. *Now* there was a smell coming from Preston, almost indescribable—the stink of pure putrefaction and death. He let the nausea pass. The lips of flesh opened and closed as if breathing. Mesmerized, disgusted, he reinserted the bayonet tip into the wound. The blade sank into ripe, squishy softness. Preston did not stir. Micah ran the blade through the wound lightly, slitting a translucent layer gluing the lips together. They pulled apart in a pink leer—

Micah could see something inside. Runneled and warty like a diseased brain.

It . . . Did it *move*?

The enormous umbilical cord jerked, spastically. Micah's consuming urge was to step on it, crimp the line—would the pressure build until it ruptured, spewing . . . ?

Breathing shallowly, trying to inhale as little of the stench as possible—the air swam with the fumes wafting from the slit—Micah inserted the knife again. The blade dimpled the pink and carbuncled thing inside. It twitched hectically, somehow gleefully. The cord whipped and spasmed; the sucking intensified, and Micah could hear the children's bodies shucking and jerking in the darkness.

The blade opened a one-inch secondary cut in the pink flesh inside the wound. Micah pulled the bayonet away. Whatever lay inside the smaller cut was black and shiny. It radiated a powerful sense of malice that Micah could feel physically—it felt as if burning ants were crawling over every inch of his flesh.

Oh Jesus, what is that what is that what IS that—

The pinkness closed over the black bulb momentarily before opening again. That blackness radiated an ageless festering rage.

With a thunderclap of understanding, Micah realized what it was.

An eye. Purest black. And that eye had just blinked. Or winked.

In the same instant, Augustus Preston's head cranked around to face Micah. It should not be anatomically possible, as Preston had been hanging in the opposite direction—but it happened all the same, his neck making horrid snapping sounds as it twisted, the skin of his throat tearing like cheesecloth to display a papery tube that could have been his trachea. His eyelids flew open; Micah had been mistaken in thinking Preston's eyes must have shriveled away; they stared at him now with a bright malignancy and a profound insanity—the look of someone whose brain had been utterly ruined. And yet there was hatred in that gaze, too, the loathing that can accrue only in the mind and heart of any creature that has had to exist in such a place for so long—a hatred for anything that has experienced love, humor, and the simple pleasure of sunlight on its face.

"*Meeeeeeattttt . . .*" Augustus Preston whispered through his ruined vocal cords, his voice like a razor drawn down a strop. The children began to laugh.

Fear flocked into Micah's brain on dark wings. The flashlight slipped from his grip and spun on the ground; he stumbled, bellowing in surprise, then reached up instinctively—

—his fingers closing around one of those trembling red ropes.

MINERVA HEARD SHUG BELLOW somewhere in the tunnel system. A short, powerful burst that quickly faded.

She and Ebenezer had already climbed down the rope ladder when she heard Micah hollering. Nate and Ellen were still at the top of the drop, where they had agreed to wait.

"Keep watch," Minerva called up to them. "Do you have a flashlight?"

A grim nod from Ellen. Clearly she didn't want the creature Ebenezer had set aflame and chased off to return with them all alone. None of them wanted that. Minerva turned to join Ebenezer at the tunnel mouth. Ebenezer shone his flashlight into it. Micah's voice had come from wherever the tunnel led, deeper into the rock.

"There's only enough room to go single file," said Minerva.

"I'll go first," Eb said.

They crawled inside. The flashlight beam bobbed on the walls. It was studded with holes, some shallow and small, others wide and deep. Minny got a chill when passing the larger ones—it seemed conceivable that some hungry thing with sightless eyes might dart out and snatch her. The smell she had noted at the mouth of the cleft intensified. She could not describe it, but it raised the short hairs on her neck.

Their breath filled the tunnel. The weight of the rock pressed down. They rounded a bend. Was the Reverend down here somewhere? Had Shug found him in this confounding warren? Or had the Reverend gotten the jump on Shug—was the bellowing they'd heard the result of Amos Flesher driving a knife into his heart? . . . It couldn't be that. The Reverend was no match for Micah Shughrue; if Minerva was sure of one thing in life, it was that.

Still . . . it was so dark down here. Disorienting. The perfect element for a reptile like that crazy-ass preacher.

"There's an opening ahead," Eb said.

The tunnel emptied into a huge darkened space. As soon as Minerva stood up, she saw Micah's boots lit by the glow of his flashlight. They were jittering madly, as if he was being electrocuted.

"Shug!" she cried.

WARMTH. That was Micah's first sensation upon touching the living rope. Glorious, comforting warmth.

Harmony. That was the second sense. A feeling of satisfaction and well-being more profound than any he had ever known.

"Shug!"

He heard his name, but could not respond. He was bathed in this bliss. He didn't *want* to respond. He wanted to stay this way forever, perfectly content.

Hands on his shoulders and arms. They pulled remorselessly. *No, you bastards! No, no, stop, please sto—*

He stumbled into the arms of Ebenezer and Minny. The beautiful fog lifted. He was back in the black box with Augustus Preston. He tore himself from their grip. He dropped to the floor, his muscles not wanting to cooperate with him.

"You all right?" Minny asked.

"Yes," he said. He picked up the flashlight where it had slipped from his fingers and stood up again.

"What happened?"

"I do not know. But I am fine. Stand back," he said, his voice a bit shaky.

"Shug, what—?"

"I said *stand back.*"

They did, all three training their flashlights on Preston's body. It jerked roughly, as if a pair of huge invisible hands was jolting it. Then something began to push itself out of Preston's back. His spinal cord ripped through the paper-thin flesh. The children writhed beyond the light, their bare feet *whushing* on the stone. Preston's toothless mouth was open, withered eyes alight with horror.

"Faaaaather," Preston breathed as he bucked like a giant revolting newborn in the girdle of red ropes. "Father, noooooooo . . ."

All of them watched, horrified, as a wriggling shape emerged from Preston's squandered flesh. It perched for a moment on a flap of hardened skin before toppling gracelessly to land with a *splat*. The fibrous tendrils attached to its body snapped as it fell; those tendrils must have been mooring it to Preston at some unseen root.

That connection severed, Preston began to thrash even more animatedly. His mouth opened so wide that the skin split at its edges, stretching it into a gruesome bloodless slash. The red ropes anchoring him to the ceiling began to snap one by one; Preston jerked awkwardly, like a snarled parachutist getting cut down from a tree. When the second-to-last rope let go, Preston swung on the final cord, a gibbering pendulum. When that last one disconnected, Preston hit the stone with the unmistakable snap of bone.

Preston mewled as he tried to crawl toward whatever had pushed itself from his body. His arms were shattered, the sharp edges of bone shorn through his papery flesh. He issued a pitiable cry—not of pain, but of abandonment. The wail of a milksop boy left in the woods by his callous parents. It was terrible to gaze upon a body lacking a true animus, a *soul*—at least Micah prayed so, even for a man as horrible as Preston surely had been—as it squirmed and thrust on the cold stone floor of this inhospitable place. It was like watching a wooden marionette stir to ghastly life, its legs kicking in feeble paroxysms, its lifeless marble eyes rolling wildly in their beveled sockets—

"Faaaaaather. Oh please, my faaaaaather . . ."

The gunshot was deafening. Preston's head did not explode so much as crumple like a dry bird's nest. The brain inside the blown-open skull case was arid and chalky as an old cow flop.

Ebenezer holstered his pistol. The three of them stared through the haze of smoke at the shape that had deposited itself on the stone.

16

WHEN THE GUNSHOT THUNDERED UP from the tunnel below, Ellen flinched. She exchanged a glance with Nate: *What should we do?*

She shone her flashlight over the ledge. The gunshot's echo continued to ricochet through the cave system. Who had done it—and why? Was someone hurt?

"Wait here," she told Nate. "I'm coming right back, okay?"

Nate's face was pinched with worry. "Hurry."

Ellen slid her flashlight into her pocket and climbed down the ladder. Nate peered over the ledge, watching the darkness swallow her. She reached the floor and crept to the tunnel.

"Ellen?"

"I'm okay," she called up to Nate.

She crawled into the tunnel carefully, the rock smooth under her knees. The tunnel was pocked with holes. She shone the flashlight into one. The light turned grainy, giving no sense of its depth. She crawled on, ears straining for a human voice. All she could hear was a dull hum. She wondered where it could be coming fro—

A pair of hands shot out of the hole she was passing, one that was deep and vaporous. A cheese-white face swarmed out of the darkness.

"Wormwood!"

The Reverend's hands closed over Ellen's mouth before she could make a sound. He jerked her skull with terrific force, slamming it into the rock.

"ELLEN?"

No reply. Nate knelt at the ledge. He felt a point of concentrated cold at the nape of his neck, as if he had been touched with a dead man's finger.

He looked behind him. Nobody was there. Just the faintest glow of fire on the rocks. He was scared that the thing—the huge prancing monster the Englishman had set aflame—would come stomping down the cave next, its skin crackly black and its eyes full of hate. He had seen the thing's face as it went up in fiery incandescence. It had looked, at least momentarily, like his own father's face. His father saying, *I'm so sorry, Nate. So, so sorry . . .*

Please, Ellen, he thought. *Come back.*

———————

A BABY. Could it possibly be?

For all the world, it appeared to be just that. An infant, cherubic and chubby, its flesh a clean-scrubbed pink. A healthy eight pounds, six ounces, if any of them were to hazard a guess.

This was what had tumbled from the slit in Augustus Preston's back. What had been nesting inside of his body for God knows how long.

It squirmed from its gelatinous sheath—a placental sac of sorts, splattered with the contents of Preston's skull. It wriggled out of its translucent membrane and writhed on the stone like a fat, contented grub. Michelin Man arms and legs, plump fingers grasping at the air. It could have just fallen from the stork's blanket. It was as cute as a bug's ear, it really was. A thousand photographers would line up to snap a shot of the little darling.

The three of them stepped around the shriveled mess that was Augustus Preston, drawing nearer to the baby. Its aspect shimmered; it was almost as if it was clarifying and solidifying its own shape before their eyes. For an instant Micah saw a prawn-bodied fetus with a bulbous rotted-melon head crawling spastically over the stone; its eyes and mouth and nose were horribly compacted, as if it had been born under immense pressure that had wrenched its features monstrously out of shape—

The next instant, those deformities disappeared. The baby was cute, angelic.

The compulsion to touch it was irresistible. Each of them felt a powerful stirring in their sex organs—but there was nothing lustful in this feeling. It was a straightforward, procreative urge. They each wanted to *have* a baby. Desperately. Right that minute. A baby just like this perfect dewdrop, right here.

The creature shimmered again; in that shimmer, its perfection dissolved for a few stuttering heartbeats. The child had no sex organs; the space between its legs was studded with inflamed nodes that looked a little like misshapen nipples. Its skin was faintly wrinkled—the crepe-like folds that grace the backs of an old woman's hands. And its eyes were not those of an infant: black as tar, glinting with an ancient cunning.

But these obvious malformations quickly dwindled to irrelevancies.

This infant was purest beauty, sheerest love. It made a display of its na-
kedness, angling its body to show off its buttery curves. Inviting them to
touch it—just one finger, the barest brush of its skin. It humped awkwardly toward Eli Rathbone, who lay a few feet away. The baby's tongue
popped out of its too-plump lips, licking them lasciviously, obscenely—
an infantile come-on that made Ebenezer ill. But his revulsion was a distant thing, far less powerful than his urge to touch or even kiss this child.
He was not a fan of babies. Shrieking, shitting, life-ruining creatures. But
this child . . . oh yes, he wanted to sweep it up in his arms and shower it
with kisses, even though he felt certain those kisses would taste of old
death.

It is not a baby was Micah's own desperate thought. *It is something terrible, something that wants to have its way with all of us . . .*

Minerva's knees gave out; she sank down in front of the child. "Such a
pweeetty bayyyy-beeeee," she cooed.

She reached out a trembling hand. Micah batted it away. The baby's
eyes rolled, trapping Micah in its baleful glare.

"We have to kill it," Micah heard himself say.

"And why would we ever consider doing that to such a cutie-pie?"
Ebenezer said in a breathy voice.

Micah was distantly aware of the horror of the scene: the three of
them in a box made of rock with a dozen emaciated children, doting over
something that looked for all the world like a baby but was in fact something far older and infinitely more hostile.

The Father.

Micah drunkenly swung around. He had surrendered control of his
limbs. This thing on the floor was robbing him of his motor skills somehow. The beam of his flashlight fell upon the bayonet. He approached it
clubfootedly, swaying like a wino. He managed to pick it up. He swiveled
to spot Ebenezer and Minerva reaching for the baby again.

"No!"

He blundered toward them. His feet got tangled with Preston's legs as
he lurched past the corpse. Eb's and Minny's fingers were only inches
from the baby's piglet-pink skin—Micah swept his arm in a rude chopping

motion, hitting their grasping hands away. He shouldered them both aside, hearing the wind whoof out of Ebenezer.

"Close your eyes," he said. "Don't look at it."

He knelt next to it. He lifted the bayonet and stabbed down, aiming for its chest. The thing's eyes widened in shock. The bayonet zagged sideways, nicking the rock an inch left of the baby. Micah raised the blade—it took an enormous force of will—and tried again. This time, the bayonet zagged in the other direction. It felt like trying to touch two giant magnets with matching polarities; he would get close—so, *so* close—only to miss with his strike.

Ebenezer grabbed his elbow. "*Heeeeyyy*, don't hurt the—"

Micah shrugged him off. The baby was squalling pitiably, eyes squeezed shut as saliva bubbled between its lips. It looked more like an infant than ever: perfect, pristine. Micah positioned the blade directly over its flaccid chest. He hunched his shoulders, using the full weight of his body to bring the bayonet slowly and remorselessly down—

The baby's eyes widened. For the first time, Micah saw fear kindling in those fuming black pits.

No. Don't you dare.

The voice that filled Micah's head was the dreadful rasp. Micah shuddered . . . then, summoning all his will, bore down again.

Stop, the thing spoke inside his head with a rising note of concern.

Micah glanced at Minerva and Ebenezer. So they could hear it, too. It wasn't just him.

No, Micah thought back at it. *You die now.*

Anything, it said desperately. *Whatever you desire . . .*

AFTERWARD, WHEN THEY THINK ABOUT IT, the shape of those moments will never be quite clear. Their thoughts become hazy. Did any of them truly *ask* for anything? Did they wish in the traditional sense: a plucked eyelash, a whispered hope before blowing out their birthday candles? Was it ever so cut-and-dried?

Or was it more that the Father had reached into their hearts and found their deepest longing, and in that moment granted it? Was it that they didn't even understand what they had wished for—and would that be so unbelievable? How many of us truly know the beat of our hidden hearts?

None of them will be able to find any certainty. It simply occurred. All three of them felt it. Their bodies filled with the terrible, overpowering certainty of it happening.

Anything. Whatever you desire.

One wish. A terrible one. They were granted their heart's desire. Unconsciously and involuntarily. And from that moment forward, they would be forever burdened with it.

WHEN THEIR MENTAL HAZE BEGAN TO LIFT, they found that they were still in the chamber. The baby was crawling toward Eli.

"No," Micah said.

He shook his head to clear the cobwebs. What had just gone on? He felt like a dinner party guest who had entered a room where everyone had been talking about him and now they had all lapsed into an uncomfortable silence.

The baby continued humping toward Eli. Its fingers were elongating, becoming less plump and coming to resemble twitching pink wires.

"No," Micah said, more forcefully this time.

I neeeed them, the thing's voice wheedled in his mind. *I gave you what you wanted . . . gave you everything . . .*

Gave him what? Micah shook his head again. He couldn't clear the fog; his skull felt as if it was stuffed full of cotton balls.

"Not the children," he said.

You must give me someone, it groveled. *You must must must—*

Micah took two big steps, pistonned his leg back and punted the hateful infant as hard as he could. His boot sank into the marbled tissue of its chest. The baby tumbled pell-mell into the darkness, arms and legs flapping. Silence . . . then a squalling cry that rose to a petulant shriek.

The children at the back of the chain were beginning to stir. Their hands came unstuck as they entered wakefulness. Their movements were clumsy, as if they'd been drugged. Minerva and Ebenezer helped them up. They were scared and shaky, like children who had just come out of a coma—and perhaps they had, of a sort. None of them cried. They were too shocked for tears, though those would surely come before long.

"Where are we?" asked a little girl.

"We're in the dark," Minerva told her gently. "But we're going to find our way back out, okay? You stick tight with me."

The girl rubbed her eyes. "Why is a baby crying? I can't see it."

"It misses its mom, I guess."

"Oh."

Eli, Elsa, and the Redhill boys did not stir. Their hands were welded together, the flesh melded and seamed. The other children had not suffered this same fate. Those ones—who Micah had to assume had only recently arrived here—seemed to be recovering already. He hoped so. He shook Eli's shoulder; flies buzzed from the rotten hole under his armpit. Wordlessly, Micah held his hand out for Ebenezer's pistol.

"Take the rest," he said. "I will follow directly."

Ebenezer and Minerva led the children to the tunnel. Ebenezer said: "Hop lightly, boys and girls."

They trailed him into the tunnel. Minerva waited until they were all through before bringing up the rear. She hesitated.

"You sure, Shug?"

"Go on, Minny."

Once she was gone, Micah sat with Eli. The baby's keening screams shot acid through his veins. Biting back his disgust, he gripped the umbilical cord fixed over Eli's mouth. It clung to his face as if attached with fishhooks. He pulled, terrified he'd rip the boy's skin off or discover some giant leech projecting from his mouth—

The baby's cries abruptly cut out.

Take them, then, it said spitefully.

Eli shuddered upright. His eyes shone black and he was screaming; his gleeful, lunatic cackles traveled through the funnel of opaque skin. The other children staggered up, too. Their stick-figure bodies began to prance in the flashlight's beam as their ghastly laughter filled the darkness. Their hands were fused together in those ulcerated florets; they swung one another around as if playing a hellish version of "Skip-to-My-Lou."

There was no longer anything recognizably human about them. Some essential quality had been cleansed away. The thing living inside Preston hadn't simply eaten their flesh—it had eaten their spirits, their sanity . . . their almighty souls, if those existed.

Micah stifled a scream, his own sanity threatening to go right along with them. There was no saving them. There was only one final mercy he could offer.

He raised Ebenezer's gun. It should have taken four bullets. But it took a few more. It was so dark.

And Micah's hands were shaking so damn bad.

17

WHEN MICAH MET THEM outside the black rock, his hands were still trembling.

The night was cool. The children who had been saved were standing around a strange vehicle. Micah figured it must be the track machine the shopkeeper in Grinder's Switch had spoken about. Ebenezer was helping them into its bed. Micah caught snatches of the children's anguished speech—"Where's Mommy and Daddy?" and "What did the Reverend do to my momma?"

Down the slopes, the forest was burning against the night. A fire was spreading quickly, urged on by the wind blowing over the mesa.

"We have to get out of here," Minerva said.

"We can still make it," Eb said, "but the fire is curling down the hillside to Little Heaven. Our only shot is to outrun it."

Nate rounded the edge of the machine. His face was peppered with ash.

"Where's Ellen?" he said.

"Wasn't she with you?" Micah asked the boy.

"No. She followed them down." Nate pointed at Minerva and Ebenezer.

Jesus. Ellen was still in there.

"Go," Micah told Minerva.

"We can wait, Shug. We'll go back together."

Micah shook his head. "If you do not get the children out now, it will be days before help comes."

Minerva cast a glance at the fire gathering along the hillside.

"Five minutes," she said. "Then we go."

Micah nodded. He walked back into the cleft.

WORMWOOD WORMWOOD WORMWOOD *the star's name is called—*

Amos Flesher lay in his rocky burrow with the burn-faced woman. Their bodies were pressed together. He could smell the blood from her wound, warm on his nose. He giggled. He had hit her quite hard. Had he fractured her skull? He hardly knew his own strength anymore! Something about the darkness, the smells, and the dripping rock gave him an immense sense of power. Wonderful voltages coursed through his bloodstream.

He had been tucked safe in his hidey-hole when the gunshots rang out. Four or five, he couldn't count, as they had come so fast. Then three more, spaced out with some deliberation. The woman jerked with each shot, but she did not regain consciousness—just nerves, he figured, the way a fish will flop when you drive a knife into its brain.

Next came the sounds of passage through the tunnel. Someone was exiting, following the children he'd heard leaving already. Things went silent again. Had everyone gone? Were they all alone, finally?

Aaaaaamos.

The Voice filled his skull. Oh! Painful. Like putting his ear next to a huge stereo speaker. Warm wetness coated his lips. Was his nose bleeding? He could feel it trickling from his ears, too.

Come to me. Worship.

Yes, Father, Amos thought. *Anything for you.*

He squirmed out of the burrow. Gripping the woman's ankles, he dragged her into the tunnel with him. He flicked her flashlight on. Oh my! That *was* a lot of blood. Doc Lewis could have stitched up that gash on her head, but Lewis was now dead in a pool of his own blood. Ah, well. Fiddle-dee-dee.

It was hard work dragging her through the tunnel, but Amos labored with a song in his heart. After all the struggle and compromise amid his inferiors, his day of reward had arrived . . . or night—he could no longer tell. Time had lost all meaning. Only the darkness, heavy and unending.

The tunnel bellied into a vast vault. The floor was scattered with items of clothing . . . The beam swept over what appeared to be a body, but it was so ghastly that he could scarcely credit it as being human. Its head had been blown apart.

The children's bodies were here, too. Eli, the Redhill brats, the Rasmussen urchin—

From somewhere in the nether reaches of the chamber: timid, fluttery inhales. A small pair of lungs drawing delicate sips of air. He shone the flashlight toward that sound. He saw or thought he could see a small shape heaved up against the far wall, its legs cycling uselessly—

He caught sound behind him, from the tunnel. Someone was approaching.

He flicked the flashlight off and left the woman on the floor. He hid.

MICAH FOUND ELLEN in the chamber. Her face was a mask of blood.

He rushed over to her. Inspected her head. The wound was bloody but superficial. He shone the flashlight on the bodies of Preston and . . . the others. Nothing moved now, and nothing had moved since he'd been here.

Ellen was breathing regularly. He pinned one of her eyelids open; her pupil dilated when the light touched it. Okay, okay, she wasn't—

A hand slid around his hips. He tried to knock it away, but it was too quick; the hand unsheathed the bayonet. Someone crashed down on him.

A pudgy, antic body wriggling on top of his chest. The Reverend: Micah could tell by the reek of his goddamn pomade.

THE FIRE WAS CONSUMING ever-greater swathes of the forest.

"How much longer?" Eb asked.

Minerva checked her watch. Seven minutes had passed. The children were waiting in the track machine. Eb sat behind the wheel.

Every man jack of us has to make his own decision in this nasty old world. Minerva figured Shug had made his. She hoped his was the right one for him, and she hoped the decision she was about to make was right for everyone else.

Please, Micah. Just get your stubborn ass out of there alive.

"Fire it up," she said to Ebenezer. "Let's cut and run."

"WORMWOOD!" AMOS SCREECHED, stabbing frantically with the bayonet. "The star's name was called Worm-wooOOood—!"

Micah's hand closed around the blade. Amos jerked it away, raised it to stab down again. Micah's palm and fingers opened, blood pissing from the gash. Micah managed to corral the Reverend's wrist as he brought the bayonet down; the tip of the knife struck his glass eye; he felt the glass splinter all through his skull bone as the knife *scrrrrriiiiitched* across its surface.

"Wormwood!" Amos yelped, and laughed like a schoolboy.

Micah knocked the bayonet away. The Reverend was still on top of him. Micah jabbed upward with his thumb; he felt it sink into the Reverend's eye, which burst with a ripe pop. Vitreous jelly spilled down the back of his hand. The Reverend fell away, shrieking. Micah grabbed his ankle. *Oh no. You're not going anywhere.* Micah's rage was overwhelming. He skinned up Amos Flesher's thrashing body—"My eye!" he was screaming. "My eye my eye my eye!"—grabbed twin fistfuls of his stinking hair and rammed his skull into the ground again and again.

The Reverend soon went limp. Micah crawled over to the flashlight and shone it on Flesher. He was knocked out, his nose shattered, blood bubbling from his nostrils.

He pinned Ellen in the beam. Her eyelids were fluttering. He crawled over to her.

"Can you stand?"

"Micah?" She blinked, squinting into the light. "Where are we?"

"Nowhere we want to be. Can you stand?"

"I think so."

Micah retrieved the bayonet. He swept the flashlight around until it fell upon the baby. It lay facing him now, its eyes focused on him with feverish need.

Give that one to me, it said. *The trickster.*

Yes, Micah thought. *You deserve each other.*

Micah stalked over to Flesher. He jammed his knee into the Reverend's spine. Flesher moaned and spat up blood. Micah slit Flesher's shirt with clinical skill, exposing his pallid back. He pinned him easily to the stone; the Reverend bleated and cried out.

"Father! Don't let him hurt me!"

But the thing that the Reverend beseeched offered no aid. Its saggy mouth opened and closed as it watched both men with eager, feral eyes.

Micah stabbed the bayonet into the Reverend's back a few inches above his hips. The Reverend squealed like a stuck pig. Micah then proceeded to hack a trench into Flesher's back. He set about his task efficiently, the way he had always worked at such grim bodily matters; he grunted with strain as he sawed through flesh, but that sound was drowned out by the Reverend's screams.

When the trench was deep and long enough, he backed away. He wiped the blood off his lips with the back of his hand, watching as the Reverend crawled into a corner of the chamber. Micah followed him with the flashlight. Flesher curled fearfully against the wall. His trousers were heavy with blood. His face had become childlike in its fear.

"Please," he whimpered. "Don't hurt me anymore. Be merciful."

"You stay here," Micah said.

"I will." The Reverend nodded, exaggerated bobs of his head. "It's all I ever wanted."

Micah left him in the vaulted room. He and Ellen traced their way back through the tunnel. At first they could hear the Reverend mewling, and then—like a bully trying to regain some of his old bravado—he began to scream: "I'll kill you! Kill you all! *Wormwoooood!*" They ignored him. Micah told himself he would not return to that black box, not for all the money in the world. Not if God himself gave the order.

They came to a fork in the tunnel labyrinth. Micah began to crawl to the left—

"No," Ellen said. "This way."

He followed her. Their breath knocked harshly inside the cramped space. Micah tried not to think of the children's faces lit by the muzzle flash: innocent again in the final reckoning, their expressions a mixture of bewilderment, anguish, and fear.

They reached the tunnel mouth. The ladder hung down the side of the basin. Ellen climbed it with obvious difficulty, her balance wonky from blood loss. Micah followed her up, steadying her when needed. When they reached the top, he pulled the ladder up. He did not want the Reverend following them—or anything else, for that matter.

They made their way through the cleft. There came a soft, moist pattering. The olms—those weird salamander things—were falling from the roof. A disgusting shower of albino amphibian flesh.

"They will not hurt us," said Micah.

"I know," Ellen said. "They're just . . ."

"Gross?"

"That's the word, Micah."

They tucked their heads and raced through the falling olms. Micah felt one wriggle down his collar—it felt like a cold, thrashing wad of snot. Ellen made a noise of revulsion as they plopped in her hair. When they had passed their nesting ground, they shook the piggybacking amphibians from their hair and clothing. Ellen picked one off Micah's shoulder and set it gently on the ground.

"They never hurt anyone," she reasoned.

A few minutes later, they reached the entrance to the cleft. The track machine was gone. Micah was glad. The forest was already engulfed in flames. The fire was reflected in Ellen's wide awestruck eyes.

"I don't do well with fire."

Micah said, "It will not reach us. The sand."

She turned to face him. "Your eye."

She reached up, gingerly fingering his glass eye. It crumbled from his socket at her touch; the Reverend's blow had shattered it to pieces. He blinked to clear the pebbly shards, which fell to the ground like crushed ice.

"I'll make you another one, okay?"

"I would like that."

"Your hand," she said.

"Your head," he said.

By the light of the raging forest fire, he inspected her wound. The ragged cut was a few inches long, just above the ridge of her burn tissue.

He said, "It will leave a scar."

She waved his concern off. "What's a scar? They give a person character, don't you think?"

They stood close but not quite touching, watching the world burn.

18

THE TRACK MACHINE raced down the path, and the flames raged after it.

Nate was shocked by how loud the fire was—it growled and hissed, and when the wind gusted, it made a ripping-screaming sound like some huge beast without a body. The trees didn't stand a chance: in the side-view mirror he watched the fire eat towering pines in a matter of seconds, sucking them into its molten heart; they went up in sizzling flashes, the trunks glowing white-hot—*It's their souls* was Nate's bizarre thought; *that's the shape of a tree's soul just as it winks out*—before the inferno rolled right over them.

The Englishman steered them down to Little Heaven. The ashen path was wide enough that the machine could fit; any tree in the way got snapped and ground up by the treads. The Englishman glanced at Nate. His face was shiny with sweat.

"You watch how I'm driving, son. I may need you to take the helm soon."

"*Me?*"

Nate knew how to pedal a bike, sure, but a *tank?* He could hear his old playmates crying in the back of the vehicle. He wanted to cry right along with them. They were dead. Everyone's parents. Even people who had no kids like Doc Lewis and the grouchy cook. His own father. Nate shut his eyes. He could still see the scene inside the chapel: people screaming with blood all down their chests, shrieks and moans, the Reverend standing at the pulpit with his arms in the air as if this was all God's will.

"What was that thing?" he asked the Englishman.

"What thing are you talking about, precisely?" the Englishman said in the manner of someone who had seen a lot of strange things lately.

"The thing you set on fire."

The Englishman worked the steering rods. A tree snapped under the treads. "There are details of this world that exist beyond understanding," he said. "I never would have expected to say such a thing. But there it is. I don't know what it was, son. Try not to think about it."

"I can't help it. I will see it for the rest of my life."

"I will, too, if it's any consolation."

They were nearing Little Heaven. Ebenezer had no intention of driving *into* it—could you imagine the looks on the kids' faces at the sight of their dead parents? Better those bodies get burned up, he figured. Better the kids recall their folks in a less traumatic light.

But those things might be lurking in the woods leading back to civilization. No, they *would be.* He was sure of it. They had let him back in because—well, why wouldn't they? Another lamb to the slaughter. But he was sure that the slaughterhouse door only swung in one direction, and that they would shortly have to force their way back out.

To that end, Eb would have to be wielding a weapon. Minny, too. It was the only way they'd stand half a chance—and if he were a wagering sort, those were the best odds he'd give them right now.

Little Heaven came into view. Ebenezer drove around the fence, skirting the chapel and the terrible sights it held.

"The woodpile!" Minerva yelled.

He drove to it. When he got out, he saw the fire tearing through the woods to the north. It was advancing with stunning speed: points of flame dancing across the treetops, which swiftly burned down to the forest floor, igniting the browned needles. Christ, he could hear it now—a low, wet, gnashing sound, like a hive of insects chewing and eating as the fire fed on the forest. Minerva hopped down and hauled the burlap tarp off the woodpile.

"We need to wet this!" she said to Eb.

They carried the tarp to the pump. Eb feverishly worked the handle; it took a minor eternity before water began to splash out. They dragged the sopping cover back and wrangled it into the bed of the track machine.

"Get under it!" Minerva instructed the kids.

They did as she said. They all fit underneath the tarp, which would provide at least some protection from the fire that was now bearing hungrily down. Sparks blew all around them, whipped on the wind; they swirled around the track machine like fireflies, fizzling in Eb's frowsy hair.

Eb clambered back into the cab and angled the machine until it pointed directly down the path leading out of the woods.

"Have you been watching me?" he said to Nate. The boy nodded. "All right, then, come sit where I'm sitting."

Dutifully, the boy slid over. Eb took Nate's hands and put them on the steering rods. "You don't have to adjust these at all, yes? Just keep them steady. Now, you see this pedal? That's the gas. I want you to put your foot on it."

Nate pressed down on it with his toe.

"A little harder."

Nate did. The motor growled menacingly.

"There. That's the perfect weight. Now put your foot on the brake." Nate did. Eb slid the transmission into drive. "When I tell you, take your foot off that pedal and put it back on the other one, the gas. We'll start to move. I want you to keep your foot on the gas pedal just like you did there, okay? And you keep going, no matter what."

The boy said nothing.

"*Okay?*"

The boy said, "Okay."

Ebenezer clapped him on the shoulder. "Good lad."

He clambered into the bed with Minerva. The fire was nipping at their heels; the skin tightened down his neck, sweat darkening his collar. He glanced back and saw the shimmering wall of flame advancing in a breathtaking wave—breathtaking in a literal sense: the fire ate the surrounding oxygen, leaving him with precious little to fill his own lungs. Ebenezer wondered if it would crash over them that same way—a fiery tidal rip curl picking them up, pushing them forward, charring their bodies to ash before they had even a moment to scream—

He slipped the flamethrower tanks over his shoulders. He could see the things massing ahead. They weren't going to make it easy.

"You ready?"

Minerva nodded. There was a hardness in her eyes he hadn't seen before.

"Go," he told the boy.

With a jerk, the machine trundled forward. A few children cried out under the tarp. Eb lit the flamethrower's pilot light.

The forest fire was closing in; looking back, he saw a vein of white flame rip out of the woods toward the chapel. It would soon climb its roof and set that mighty cross on fire. After that, the bodies inside would begin to blister and char.

"That's perfect," he called down to the boy. "That exact speed."

They hit the first cut of woods. The things attacked.

It happened quickly. A frenzy of activity. They came in multiple surges. Time fractured, and what Eb recalled came in flashes.

FLASH: A shaggy brutish *something* lumbering out of the trees, many-limbed and growling. Ebenezer hit it with the flamethrower. It went up in a soaring cone of fire, its legs continuing to saw toward the track machine until Minerva shot it twice with the shotgun, blasting gobs of flaming tissue across the dirt. A fresh horror dodged in from the opposite side: a wet, shimmering, torsional creature of outrageous length, the wiry fibers of its anatomy braided together in some living, livid rope—

FLASH: A pack of smaller things rushing at them, a dozen or more, the size of house cats but much faster; Minerva picked a couple of them off as they advanced, and a few more got squashed under the rumbling treads. But two managed to scale the machine and clamber into the bed; their oily skin was covered in wart-like growths, their mouths studded with needle teeth. The first one attacked Eb's boot, tearing a chunk from the leather. Minerva kicked it into the corner and blasted it into red hash. She wheeled around to grapple with the second monstrosity as—

FLASH: Something swooped down from the sky to land on the hood. An enormous bat-like thing—black wings spread across the whole hood, claws hooking it to the grille. Its body was the size of a big dog, a madcap mishmash of parts. It snapped at the windshield as its claws scrabbled on the hood, trying to climb the glass like some friendly puppy that only wanted to lick the boy's face. Nate shrieked; the vehicle slowed and he shrank back in the seat, his foot slipping off the gas. Eb pulled the flamethrower's trigger and got a sad hiss. The fuel tank had run dry. He cut a pistol lose from the slat and shot the thing at point-blank range; it hissed and screeched. He emptied the clip into it, but it clung tenaciously to the hood, scraping its way up the windshield. Minerva turned the shotgun on it. The gun boomed twice, and then the thing was carried off the edge of the track machine, hanging to the hood by the claw on its wing. It shrieked pitifully as the treads caught the flapping edge of its other wing, chewing it underneath the vehicle, where its body crunched with a sickening sound . . .

Then, seemingly moments after it started, it was over. The track machine shunted down the slope, leaving the things behind. They had escaped the kill zone, and nothing appeared to be following. The forest fire was now a faint glow across the bottomlands, though it wouldn't be long before it caught up to them again.

Eb threw his arms up. "You beautiful bastard, you!" he shouted at Minerva.

The track machine ground to a halt. Ebenezer took a peek under the tarp to make sure the children were okay; then he turned to Minerva with a boyish grin—

She kicked him in the chest and sent him crashing off the tailgate. He hit the ground hard, the wind knocked out of him.

"Get up," she said coldly, hopping off the tailgate herself.

It felt as though his chest had caved in. He was able to pull in a few shallow heaves and drag himself to his feet. What the hell was she on about? They had survived by the skin of their teeth and now—

"Get your gun," she said once he was up.

She walked to a spot thirty yards away. Then she turned to face him, waiting.

"I'm going to shoot you now, Ebenezer Elkins," she said calmly.

He was still doubled over, sucking wind. "Wh-what?"

"I'll give you a moment to check your weapon and catch your wind. You tell me when you're ready."

He stared at her, baffled. "Minerva, for Christ's sake."

"Check your load, pal. We don't got all day here."

Fire collected along the curve of the earth. Minerva closed her eyes and waited. She had felt it by then, for the first time ever: the sensation she would come to know as the Sharpening. She'd felt it during the firefight just passed. Everything had slowed down, and she was able to operate calmly within the cool center of chaos. Right at that moment, it felt the most natural thing in the world.

Ebenezer dusted himself off. "You can't possibly be serious."

She closed her eyes, feeling her newfound capacities surge through her. "Oh, I am. As a heart attack."

His voice changed—became accepting, as men such as him tended to be under even the most unreasonable circumstances. "May I ask why?"

"No. You ready yet?"

She opened her eyes. Eb stared searchingly at her across the starlit path.

"I'm not ready, no. Not hardly. Minny, I don't understand."

"You don't have to understand, Ebenezer. You just have to skin that pistol, point, and shoot. Should be easy enough for you. Made a tidy living off it, haven't you?"

Ebenezer saw something then. A thin band of gold rimming her irises—though it was too dark and he too far away to note it with such precision—but yes, something deep-set and ineffable in her eyes. Something ticking ever clockwise, sharp and pure.

"If we do this, I—I don't shoot to wound," he said. "I'm not built that way."

"You better do what you do, then."

The children peeked from beneath the tarp, their eyes wide and curious.

"I don't want to, Minerva. I will kill you. I'll have to. Why end everything like this when we've been so lucky?"

She didn't answer him. Her hand fell to the Colt at her waist. Ebenezer tucked his own pistol into his waistband. His fingers danced above the grips. The fire was set to scream over the rise, devouring everything in its path.

"Ready?" she said.

"No. But I'm afraid I'll be ready well before you are, milady."

They drew.

She's so fast was Ebenezer's amazed thought.

Minerva's first shot tore through his leg just below his knee. He'd managed to clear the gun from his waistband, but her next shot clipped its barrel, sending it flying through the air. He uttered a shocked cry and fell back, clutching his knee. Blood pulsed through the neat hole in his pants.

"Ah-*fuuuuuuuuu*—" was all he could get out.

She hopped into the track machine again and came back to him with something in her hands. She flung it at his feet. He was in such pain, tears swimming in his eyes, that he could not make it out. She toed it a little closer. Some kind of dried reptile head. A snake, if he had to guess.

"You killed my father in a shack near Yuba fourteen years ago," she said simply.

He stared at her gape-jawed, unable to comprehend.

"And because you killed my father, my brother died. All on the same day."

"Who?" he managed to ask through gritted teeth.

"Charles Atwater."

"But I didn't . . ."

Minerva cocked the pistol and pointed it between his eyes. "Think on it."

In time, he nodded. "Ah. A gambler . . . yes?" He winced, the pain in his knee drilling up and down his leg. "I was hired . . . to collect his debt."

"You were just doing your job, right?"

"Of course. Had I known . . ."

"How could you have known?" she said, softening just slightly.

He dropped his head. Then he began to laugh. His shoulders hitched softly with it.

"All this time, Minerva. You've been waiting on this moment?"

She didn't answer. What was the point? When Ebenezer looked up, he was smiling. "You got it out of your system, I trust?"

"I don't figure so, no."

"That would have been my guess." He laughed again. "The whole time! Oh, but you are a patient viper."

Minerva walked to the machine and slung herself into the cab. "Scoot over," she told Nate. She put the vehicle in gear. The fire glinted in the side-view mirror, bearing down.

"What just happened?" Nate asked.

"He said he wants to walk home."

Ebenezer's voice rose over the onrushing fire: "Are we all square now, Minerva? Tell me we're even now, at least!"

She didn't bother answering that, either.

19

THE REVEREND AMOS FLESHER screamed out of unconsciousness.

It was dark. So very dark. Had he been dreaming? The dream itself was gone, but its outlines still clung to his mind: an inky spillage roiling with unseen bodies. He shivered. He was shirtless, his belly spilling over the waistband of his trousers.

He was still here. His father's room. The house of treasures. He saw a light a dozen yards off. A flashlight lay on the floor, pointing at the wall. The rock met at a perfect ninety-degree angle. Puzzling. His initial sense of this space was of a huge bubble inside the rock. But seeing the way the rock met, his mind reoriented its parameters: not an orb but a cube.

Hell is a box.

He recoiled. The voice had come from his own head—mirthless, a flat, deadened tone—but the words were so powerful that it felt as if they had been whispered into his ear. But when he turned and looked, only the darkness peered back.

His legs were tacky with blood. How? It came back to him. The one-eyed bastard! Amos's fingers roamed around to his spine. His fingertips touched flayed meat. He cried out in pain. Jesus Lord, merciful provider. The fucker had quartered him like a hog. He would bleed to death! He tried to call out, but his lips were waxy and his vocal cords shredded. Had he been screaming in his sleep?

He tried to stand. Impossible. His legs were numb and useless; they might as well have been made of wood. Had the one-eyed fuck severed a nerve cluster in his spine?

He hauled himself forward, fingers seeking purchase on the rock.

One of his fingernails peeled off with a gluey snap, but it didn't hurt one bit. He laughed again—what's a fingernail? what's a finger? what's a toe?—and hauled his body on, singing an old hymn:

O that day when freed from sinning, I shall see Thy lovely face;
Clothed then in blood washed linen, how I'll sing Thy sovereign
  grace;
Come, my Lord, no longer tarry, take my ransomed soul away;
Send thine angels now to carry me to realms of endless day.

He was near the flashlight when the first rope descended. He could identify it by the thin thread of light running through it, like an electric eel darting in a dark sea cave. The rope danced hypnotically in front of him. He smiled and laughed; he wanted to clap, it was such a neat performance. The rope grazed his shoulder. He gasped. What a *wonderful* sensation. Indescribably lovely. His mind burst with colors. Flowers holding hues that did not exist in nature bloomed in his head.

This is Heaven, he thought rapturously. *I must have died; this is my everlasting reward.*

The ropes spooled down from above. Dozens of them alighted on his flesh; his mind expanded with wonderments so massive that he struggled to contain them all. The ropes lifted him up. He had never felt such a profound sense of love and tenderness. They hoisted him effortlessly, his body drawn to a standing position in the center of the chamber—the *box*. His legs hung under him, useless deadweight; his arms were also immobilized. He could barely move except to wriggle his torso a little, but it hardly mattered. He was safe and warm and loved.

Next: sounds from the far edge of the chamber. The moist shucking of a body across the stone. He stared around blearily, a kittenish smile on his face.

Where was that coming from? What was—?

It crawled through the flashlight beam. *A baby . . . ?* was the only conception his mind registered. Something determinedly dragging its pulpy pink body across the beam. Flesher blinked, peering closer. Its body shimmered, and he saw a different shape entirely. Something that reminded him of a wet, wadded-up dish towel. Grub-like, but with a lean articulation of limbs up and down its body—the legs of a centipede. Fat and ribbed with skin that was not baby pink but a rotted-banana black, with seeping boils all over. Its eyes were pinned on the Reverend with a malignancy of purpose, a singular hunger, and a hatred deeper than human fathoming.

Then the shimmer ebbed and it was simply a baby again, chubby-cheeked and cute beyond belief. It humped through the flashlight beam, its feet pushing eagerly. He could hear it advancing toward him with a slick suction. A chill broke out over his body. He began to convulse in the harness of ropes, which held him in a gentle but stern embrace. He did not want that thing touching him. There was nothing in the world he could possibly want less. Better to let crows peck out his eyes; better to set wasps loose inside his mouth. Anything would be better than that horrible thing with its ancient shriveling stare.

Hell is a box, hell is a box, hell is a—

Something touched his naked calf. Now *that* he could feel. He tried to jerk his leg away, but it was useless. He couldn't move an inch.

Nonononono—

The thing began to mount his leg. It skinned its way up gradually, as if savoring the ascent. Instead of a baby's slack limbs, the appendages climbing his flesh felt more like a lobster's spiny legs. Before long, the flashlight's batteries would die. After that, the darkness would be total.

The thing was at his knee now. It was making loud sucking sounds like an infant hungering for a big fat tit.

Father must fill its belly, spoke a voice in his ear.

Being eaten wouldn't be so bad, would it? Not in the grand scheme of things. It would be absolutely horrible, of course, to be eaten alive by the thing now licking its way up his inner thigh, pausing to tease the head of his dangling fear-shrunk cock; it would be excruciatingly painful to be eaten piece by piece, and the pain would amplify until he was driven mad with it, in all likelihood . . . but still, there would be an end to it. There was only so much of him to consume.

I have made the most terrible mistake, the Reverend thought.

Amos Flesher sensed this thing would do something far worse than merely devour him. Something that sat well outside the rational bounds of human pain or madness. Its feasting would be deliriously slow and torturous in a way that would eclipse all taxonomies of pain known to flesh or mind. All he knew was that the suffering would be immense and utterly lonely—trapped in the despairing dark, no way to mark the years as they bled into decades while this thing broke him down piece by relentless piece.

Please, he thought frenziedly. *Don't hurt me I'll do anything be anything for you just don't hurt me please God I don't want you to hurt meeeeeee . . .*

I will not hurt you, came the cooing reply. *I will love you. You will be loved deeper than you ever imagined possible.*

Love. Never in Amos's life had a word held such a sinister undertone.

The thing was muscling around his hips now, moving toward the wide slice in his back. The Reverend thrashed madly, his dead legs slapping together to make comical sounds. The ropes held him in place. Their warmth and wonderments had retreated. They had become but dutiful tools of restraint.

The thing slipped inside his opened flesh. Teasingly so—inching just a cunt's hair inside of him, as if wishing to savor it this first time. The pain was monolithic; his brain shrieked, every synapse shuddering. The Reverend squealed breathlessly; the sound fled up into the darkness to die. The thing was squirming inside of him rather energetically now, a birth in reverse; the Reverend felt his organs being displaced as the thing pushed doggedly inside—

Finally, its little feet sucked through the slit, which then closed over, the lips gumming shut on their own. The thing shuddered contentedly inside of him, its body flexing minutely as it enjoyed its new home.

For a long empty moment, nothing. Then: the smallest and most timid voice.

Let us begin, shall we?

MICAH COULD HEAR THE SCREAMS over the roar of the forest fire. They boiled out of the black rock. They were followed by silence and then—most chillingly—by a prolonged laugh.

"Did you hear that?" Ellen asked.

Micah nodded.

"The Reverend?"

"I suppose."

They spent the night at the mouth of the cleft as the forest burned. The wind was gusting and the trees dry; Micah wouldn't be surprised to hear that half the state had gone up. The heat intensified. They were forced to retreat into the cleft. It was much cooler inside the rock. Micah had a sense that even if the fire was raging right outside, it was always cool and wet inside this particular rock. He closed his eye, his eyelid lit by the mellow orange of the distant inferno. He hoped Minerva had made it out with the children.

The fire swept north and west the next day. Ellen managed to sleep for a few hours while Micah kept watch. The burned trees continued to glow until a heavy rain bucketed down. Columns of steam rose from the blackened forest floor. When the downpour cleared, they walked the wet sand to the edge of the forest. The tusks of what had been fifty-foot pines jutted from the earth.

"Should we start walking?" Ellen wondered. "We shouldn't get lost, at least."

"The fire could still be burning underground. In the tree roots."

"Well?"

They agreed to set off before evening. They had no water or food; their lips were cracked and white, the first stages of dehydration. Maybe the well at Little Heaven had survived the blaze. They could draw a few ashy mouthfuls.

They had just set off when the air filled with the *thacka-thacka* of chopper blades. A search helicopter crested the western horizon, bearing steadily toward them. Ellen waved her arms. The pilot swooped low over-head, buzzing their position.

"He must have seen us," Ellen said.

Micah nodded. "He will bank around and land nearby."

"You don't seem all that happy."

"I do not wish to talk to the authorities."

He began to walk toward Little Heaven again.

"Micah?"

"You go with them," he said.

She trotted over to him. "You're not serious." When he did not reply: "Micah, you could die. After all this—"

But she could see he was resolute. Mule-headed to the end, this man.

"Then I'll come with you."

He shook his head. "Go with them. I will be fine."

"How will I know that?"

He took her hand. The gesture seemed to surprise both of them.

"You will know because I will come find you, Ellen."

"You promise?" She held a hand up. "Don't answer that."

"I will not. But you know the answer."

She nodded. "I'll see you then, Micah."

"Yes. You will."

She watched him walk into the landscape. He did not melt into the trees, there being no living trees left. But the fabric of his trench coat liquefied into the blackness surrounding it, becoming one with the charred earth after a few hundred yards.

"You better get your ass back to me!" Ellen shouted.

Twenty minutes later, a helicopter cut down from the pristine sky. And by then Micah Shughrue was only a name.

PART SEVEN

THE IN-BETWEEN TIME

1966–1980

High-Alert Bulletin from the New Mexico State Forestry, October 21, 1966:

WILDFIRE IN SOUTH-CENTRAL NM

BLAZE RAGING ON HILLSIDES AND DENSELY WOODED ZONES IN BLACK MOUNTAIN WILDERNESS AREA ABUTTING LINCOLN NATIONAL FOREST . . . UNKNOWN CAUSE . . . THUNDERSTORMS PRECEDING. LIGHTNING STRIKE POSSIBLE. WINDS GUSTING TO HIGHS OF 70 MPH . . . CATASTROPHIC BLAZE POTENTIAL . . . ALL EMERGENCY FIRE PERSONNEL ARE TO REPORT TO . . .

Excerpt from US Department of Agriculture Report: "Black Lands Fire Summary," published January 15, 1967:

OVERVIEW

The Black Lands fire was believed to have been started by a lightning strike in the Black Mountain Wilderness Area on the evening of October 21, 1966; suppression activities were initiated by US Forest Service firefighters based in Lincoln National Forest. The fire raged through that night and the day following, aided by high winds that lifted embers beyond the initial fire line, leading to a catastrophic blaze that claimed a total of 53,890 acres (36,922 on Lincoln National Forest, 4,355 on Mescalero Apache tribal land, 3,002 of New Mexico land, and the remainder on private land), plus 354 private dwellings and 43 larger structures.

Primary entities involved in responding to the fire were the US Forest Service, Lincoln County Sheriff's Office, Lincoln County Office of Emergency Services, and the State of New Mexico (NM).

Somewhat strangely, the town on the southern edge of the Black Mountain range—a small village, Grinder's Switch—was left unscathed. The fire burned down the eastern and southern flanks of the range, crossing a wide river running through the lowlands, but failed to reach Grinder's Switch.

No emergency workers perished fighting the blaze. But several civilian casualties were later reported; the documented circumstances of those fatalities can be found in Federal Bureau of Investigation (FBI) Reports G-55A and G-55B, and Central Intelligence Agency (CIA) Dossiers 0-99[A-G], which are available to authorized personnel upon approval.

News Item from the *Clovis (NM) News Journal*, October 23, 1966:

MASSACRE AT BACKWOODS RELIGIOUS SETTLEMENT? UNCONFIRMED REPORTS SUGGEST DOZENS DEAD, CHILDREN SOLE SURVIVORS

Tragedy appears to have struck an isolated religious compound located in the Black Mountain Wilderness Area.

The compound—dubbed Little Heaven by its overseer, the Reverend Amos Flesher, most recently of San Francisco—sat in the hills of the Black Mountain range. The compound was accessible via an access road or a secondary footpath that wound up through the hills.

Information remains spotty in the wake of the Black Lands fire, which emergency crews continue to battle in the southernmost reaches of the state. The compound burned in the fire, along with tens of thousands of neighboring acreage. Details emerging in the aftermath come from the remaining eyewitnesses—the children of Little Heaven, who appear to have been rescued by an unknown Good Samaritan or Samaritans.

The children arrived in the town of Grinder's Switch yesterday, in the early-morning hours. They showed up in a specialized vehicle that had been used to transport goods and equipment to the compound. The unidentified driver left the vehicle at the Grinder's Switch police station, where a single constable, William Jeffers, was on duty. The driver and any confederates were gone before Jeffers could confirm their identities.

According to Jeffers, the children were in a state of shock. He was unable to get much out of them about their ordeal.

"Only one of them had anything to say," said Jeffers. "A girl, six or so, name as yet unconfirmed. She said they were all dead. The grown-ups. When I asked how, she said the Reverend killed them all. Every one."

It is unclear if this witness's story is factual or the product of shock. Nor is it yet known exactly how many people resided at Little Heaven.

The *News Journal* will diligently update this story as details emerge.

HOSPITAL GENERAL INCIDENT REPORT FORM

Cibola General Hospital
1016 Roosevelt Ave.
Grants, NM 87020

Prepared by: Rhonda Popplewell, HR Liaison
Date of Incident: October 23, 1966. Approx. 2:15 a.m.
Location: Hospital pharmacy, basement level
Nature of Incident: Assault/forcible imprisonment

Description of Incident
At approx. 2:15 a.m. on October 23rd, George Lennox, 55 y/o, night-shift pharmacist, was violently assaulted by

an unknown man. According to Lennox, his assailant approached in a wheelchair. Quoting Lennox: "Black fellow. He was wet and filthy and covered in blood, wheeling himself down the hall." When Lennox informed said assailant that he would need to go upstairs to the emergency ward, his assailant replied, quote: "Can't do that, old chum. I'm behind in my insurance payments." When Lennox insisted sharply that the man comply, going so far as to grip his wheelchair, the man sprang upon Lennox and beat him roundly about the face. Subdued and now fearful for his life, Lennox allowed himself to be led into the pill lockup. The man directed Lennox to fill a bag with various pharmaceuticals, plus items liberated from the general dispensary. A comprehensive itemization is attached. Lennox noted that his assailant had a bullet wound near his left knee; the items taken would seem to address the treatment of such a wound.

The assailant was roughly six feet tall and a hundred and eighty pounds. Black, with long unkempt black hair. Brown eyes. In his mid- to late thirties. He spoke with an English accent. He did not evidence signs of drug addiction. Lennox describes the man as being cordial, with a sunny disposition despite his injuries; still, there was never a moment where Lennox did not actively fear for his life.

The man carried on a spirited conversation while Lennox collected his items. He seemed especially focused on the negative behavior of a certain woman; Lennox suggested to me that this woman could have been the man's wife or girlfriend, and that she may have been the one who shot him. I have shared this information with the sheriff's department.

After Lennox had put the items into a sack, the man tied him to the lockup cage with Tensor bandages. The knot work was quite good; it took Lennox thirty minutes to twist free, by which point his assailant was gone. The wheelchair was found by the laundry exit.

Report submitted to: Donald Grubman, Chief Executive Officer

Letter postmarked December 15, 1968. Old Ditch, Arizona:

Dear Minerva,

How goes the war, milady? Are you sleeping well?

Hah.

I survived. But I suppose you must know that. You can feel it, as I can feel you. And Micah, too, when the wind blows a certain way. It's blowing that way now. Cold, yes? Winter, though not anything like the winters of my youth. Winter in Arizona means you might want to stop taking ice in your tea. But it's the Yuletide season and I suppose I'm maudlin. Or wistful. Such a fine thread between the two. They don't celebrate Christmas with much gusto in these parts. It's an old folks' town and Christmas is for the young, isn't it? But there are lights, garlands, the odd tree. Another year gone past. Ah, well. God can take all the years I've got left. I cannot see much use for them.

I wish to say I'm sorry. I know that will mean nothing to you. I know that it fixes not a goddamn thing. I wish I had that capacity to go back in time, back to when I was a churlish child, a WISEASS, as you Yanks would say, and just...be better. Set myself down a proper path, one that didn't lead to so much bloodshed and regret. I had people in my life who tried to put me on that good path. Shame I didn't listen to them nearly enough.

George Orwell wrote that at fifty, everyone has the face they deserve. But some of us get our just deserts earlier than that.

I killed your father. He was a gambler. A common enough vice. Nothing a man ought to be killed over. But I did. I shot him. I could tell you that I did it as a function of my work, that I was no more than an automaton fulfilling its purpose, but every man has his own agency. I didn't have to kill him. But I had the ability to and he had sinned in a very small way and I felt it fair at the time to take his life for that.

I do not know how my killing your father caused your brother to die. We did not have much time to discuss it, me with your bullet in my leg and you with those children to drive to safety—which you did, as I was heartened to read about. They all lived. I hope they have grandparents and aunts and uncles to take them in. I hope they forget everything they saw. Children's minds are supple, isn't that what the headshrinks say? A child's mind can be erased and rewritten, fresh. Little Etch A Sketch brains. I hope so.

The fire almost got me. It was a near thing. I dragged myself down to the river. It was running four feet deep. I submersed myself and breathed through a reed—a REED, my dear, like some cartoon character! Ash

fell on the river's surface; it ran so thick
and black that I couldn't see up, like being
sunken in a river of ink. But the fire raged
past quite quickly and when it was over I
managed to drag myself down to Grinder's
Switch. My knee—ha! A flesh wound. I've had
worse. Sometimes I wonder if you shot me in
the perfect manner, Minerva my dear. Enough
to hurt me and leave me with a constant
reminder, but not quite kill me. Were you
merciful in the cut? Or was it just luck? I
like to think it was the former. If not, don't
wake the dreamer from his dream.

In the commotion, nobody made much note of
me. Just another wide-eyed survivor. It was an
easy enough matter to steal a car. And later,
some medical supplies to patch me up until I
could visit Shughrue's veterinarian friend. I
passed out a few times from the pain, but I
survived. I don't know what business I had doing
so, but I did.

I think about those days, my darling. What
we saw. What we did. What was done to us. I
think about evil. Our own and the evil of things
ineffably larger than us. Incomprehensible
evil, yes? It cannot fit inside my mind. I
cannot find the space for it, so it finds its way
out in my nightmares. I wake up screaming
night after night. But I live alone far from
any neighbor, so I doubt I am much bother to
anyone. Hah.

We did the right thing, didn't we? We acted

rightly when the chips were down, to use the old cliché... didn't we?

I wonder. I suppose all my life I will wonder.

In any event. Now you know for a fact. I EXIST. I am still sucking breath.

So if you are still feeling raw about... all that. Well. You know where to find me.

Yrs,
Ebenezer

From "Little Heaven's Prisoners" (as published in *Esquire* magazine, January 1970) by Chris Packer:

He was a devious worm."

Sister Muriel Hanratty remembers Amos Flesher all too well. His birdlike eyes. His fleshy lower lip. The pale strip of flab that ballooned between his waistband and the bottom of his shirts, which were always a size too small.

His nasty habits.

"He was a fiddler," she tells me in the atrium of the Wooded Nook Rest Home outside of San Francisco. "Not a violinist," she clarifies archly. "He touched himself. All the boys did, of course. No stopping that. You could cut their dirty sticks off and they'd still play with them, surely to Christmas. But there's your garden-variety pawing and then there's *fiddling*. It's a wonder he didn't whittle the thing away like a bar of soap in the shower, that's how much he twiddled with it."

At eighty-seven years old, Sister Muriel isn't one for niceties. But I have little doubt that she was always a straight shooter. She worked at the San Francisco Catholic Orphanage for fifty years, until its doors shut for good. Budget cuts, Muriel says. A few of the other nuns were moved to Wooded Nook with her, but they have since passed on. She misses them, she says, as well as her time at the orphanage.

But not Amos Flesher. Him she does not miss one bit.

"He poked kids until they bled," she tells me. "We had a ward full of boys and girls who were soft-headed. Our Children of God. The purest, most open smiles. We put Amos in charge of them during naptime. Amos was old enough; he ought to sing for his supper, we figured. Well, he stuck those poor kids. With a darning needle or a big pin. Most of them were restrained; it's terrible, but it was for their own good. I started to see blood on their jammies. Their bums, their thighs. First I thought it was bedbugs. But it went on a while. I never caught him doing it. Amos was a sly boy. I don't know that I'd call him smart—*cunning* is the word I'd use. Why would he want to hurt those poor children?" She shook her head. "When I heard about what happened out in the woods, I thought: *Amos Flesher went and got himself a whole camp full of soft-brains so he could stick them all with pins.* He was bloody-minded, Amos Flesher was. Bloody as anyone I've known."

Bloody-minded. It would seem so. In the three years that have passed since the Little Heaven fire (it is properly known as the Black Lands fire, but hardly anyone refers to it by that name), precious little is known about the circumstances preceding it. No adult from Little Heaven lived to tell the tale, including Amos Flesher himself; the children who survived can recall very little of their experience. By the time I was able to arrange interviews with some of them—navigating a web of protective caretakers and foster parents and aunts and uncles—their stories held little in common. It would seem that their minds have embarked on a purposeful act of erasure. They can remember almost nothing, which is likely for the best.

About all that links their stories is a thread of stark, almost unimaginable terror. They talk about seeing their parents covered in blood—flashbulb memories, these searing mental images—though they can no longer recall how that happened. They've surrendered the connective tissue between these vivid recollections, the necessary bridgework. One girl talked about "a dark place where a dead baby wouldn't stop crying." Noises in the woods. A ghostly giant with the black eyes of a doll. The stuff of childhood nightmares, all of it. The kids' minds and memories seem to be playing tricks on them, putting the faces of imaginary boogeymen on horrors too real to cope with— the evil of men. The evil of their own mothers and fathers, just maybe.

Survivor trauma, the shrinks call it.

Fire is the grand reducer. The heat of a forest fire can reach 2,672 degrees Fahrenheit—hot enough to melt carbon steel. Little Heaven disappeared in the most conclusive way: it burned, carbonized, and drifted away on the wind. Every structure, every body, everything. Gone. There is no way to sift the leavings and make much sense of what happened there. Only questions remain. Were they all dead already when the fire swept over the hillside? If so, how? If not, why didn't they flee when the fire began to burn down upon them? They would have had time to abandon everything and run. They might have even made it out at a brisk walk, had they seen the fire early enough.

But that didn't happen. Every adult died—or if not, they are nowhere to be found. They have not resurfaced anywhere and have yet to reclaim their children. The only sane reasoning is that they are gone. The hows and whys may never be known.

"I hope he's burning in hell," Sister Muriel says when I ask after the fate of Reverend Amos Flesher. She has a highly developed sense of divine retribution, and she lets it be known that God would not have it any other way. "Sure as I have breath in my body, that boy is roasting in the fiery pit. I hope the Devil gives him a few extra pokes with his pitchfork for me. Evil little bastard. The dirty fiddler."

———————————

Letter postmarked June 8, 1969. Girdler, Kentucky:

Dear Slimeball
   So. I guess I'm glad you're not dead. Congratulations on living.

                                             Minny

2

MICAH FOUND ELLEN AGAIN, just as he said he would. And she was sure he'd come, though it took longer than she would have liked. She had made him a new eye by then, which was good, because he showed up wearing that ratty old patch.

"You'd go to pieces without me" was the first thing she said to him.

It became a familiar refrain. *You'd go to pieces.* In time, it proved to be true. A man can go his whole life never needing anyone. But when he finally finds the one, he can't live without her.

Ellen had been living with Nate in the town nearest her sister's jail. By then, Ellen had put it all out in the open to her nephew. Ellen was his aunt. She had been sent by Nate's mother to check in on Nate at Little Heaven. Ellen had hired Micah and the other two.

Nate took it all pretty well. Kids didn't suffer so much with cognitive dissonance. He missed his father, despite how badly Reggie had unraveled in his final days. It wasn't his fault, Nate reasoned privately to himself. It was a lot to ask, and more than his father had been fit to bear. Nate wished his last memories of his father weren't so negative. He wished he hadn't seen his body on the grass in front of the chapel, his forehead . . . He wished he hadn't seen that, but he knew, having seen it, that he always would.

He went back to school. His teachers remarked on what a pleasant, thoughtful boy Nate was—though they might have said in the privacy of the teacher's lounge, over a quickly puffed cigarette, that he was more remote and somehow *harder* than a boy his age ought to be. As if Nate had suffered extreme pressures that had diamondized him. And those sparkling, diamond-like aspects of Nate were just a little off-putting. They made a person feel nervous, even when the boy gave you no good reason to feel that way in his presence.

Micah rented a room in the same town. Nobody there knew their histories.

At one point, a reporter came rolling in. Fussy guy with a Virginian accent, always wore a crisp vanilla-white suit. With one of the big-city dailies, he said. Had a hot tip that one or more of the survivors of the Little Heaven fire might be living right here. Well, that put a bug up the town's collective ass. But Micah was glad that the reporter wasn't much good at his job, and that he went away empty-handed to pursue some story about astronauts.

The three of them spent every waking minute together. Before long Ellen's sister earned an early parole, time served for good behavior. Ellen helped her get reacquainted with life outside the walls. Then Nate moved back in with his mother. After that, it was time to go. Ellen had a new life to get on with. One that now included Micah.

For Micah's part, he left it all behind. The gun-for-hire work. He had no other skills, but he was willing to learn. They got married in a small chapel in Santa Cruz. They bought a ranch and settled down. Micah wasn't much of a herdsman or a farmer, but still, things had a way of working out. Money flowed to him, easy as water. Some said he had the devil's own luck. If they only knew.

They were never far from the black rock. At first, they saw themselves as guardians of a sort. Sentinels. It was only a matter of hours to reach it, though neither of them had the smallest desire to make that journey. That place lived deep inside their minds, implacable as a pebble in their shoes. In time, though, they forgot about the rock—their conscious minds did, anyway. But it twisted away in their under-brains, as such things are wont to.

They had a child. Their greatest joy. Micah wept the day Petty was born. When she got sick as an infant, he sat up all night beside her crib, rocking her when she cried. And if, as she got older, Petty sensed a distance from her father, well, he was distant with everybody except her mother. He was not cold or unloving with Pet, and he was wildly protective of her—just, he seemed unable to open himself to her completely, as other fathers might. He carried an inarticulate sorrow that a man of few words was incapable of expressing.

Then one morning Micah's wife, Petty's mother, didn't wake up.

Micah rose that morning to find her still sleeping. He got up to make breakfast. He found it strange that she would be asleep, as she was usually up before him. When he came back, she had not woken. He laughed under his breath—he was not a man for laughter, but Ellen could provoke it in him for almost no reason at all—and ate his breakfast alone. Petty woke and dressed and ate and went outside to play. Micah watched her run through the field, the crisp morning light falling through her spread fingers.

He went into the bedroom. Ellen was still sleeping. Her chest rose and fell; her eyeballs zipped around under her lids. There was something profound about her sleep. A seam of worry split Micah's mind. He gripped her shoulder gently.

"Ellen?" He shook her. "*Ellen?*"

Her eyes opened then. Relief washed through Micah. But it soon faded. Ellen's eyes were open, yes, but her chest rose and fell with the rhythm of sleep. Her body was warm and vibrating like a tuning fork that had been struck moments ago.

Their long waking nightmare began that day. Ellen's eyes would remain open, often for days at a time—but she would not wake up. The doctor tried the standard techniques: loud noises, pinching the flesh between her thumb and forefinger. Nothing. A coma, or something like it. *Locked-in syndrome*: Micah heard the doctor speak this phrase over the phone. The doctor asked questions: Had they been out of the country recently? Had she been bitten by anything? Suffered a bad fall? Eaten some foreign delicacy for the first time? No, no, no, no, no.

Specialists came next. Sleep-disorder doctors and nerve-disorder doctors and doctors who administered to maladies Micah had never conceived. All useless. Ellen slept with her eyes wide open. She got thinner and thinner. The doctors plugged feeding tubes into her. She developed bedsores; they swelled and burst. Micah dressed them and turned her over often to prevent them from festering. As she rarely blinked, Ellen's eyes would get as dry and tacky as peeled grapes. Micah had a specialist create moisturized eyeball shields made out of breathable fabric; he would put them over Ellen's eyes and keep them wet with a special solution squeezed from an eyedropper.

Ellen's sister and Nate moved to the nearest town. There wasn't much they could do. They sat by Ellen's bed and talked to her. They read books out loud; Nate would record himself reading books on cassettes, which Micah would play on the tape player in her room. The doctors said that might work; they said that Ellen might follow a familiar voice up out of the fog.

He slept beside her at night. Sometimes she turned to him, one of the moisture pads slipping off the convex of her eyes. Staring at him in the moonlight bleeding through the curtains—the light's on, but nobody's home. Or *was* somebody home? Was Ellen behind those eyes, trapped inside her own skull, screaming to be let out? She did not make a noise on those nights—except sometimes, in a whisper so hushed he could barely make it out, she would say: "Please, no. Please stop." Those words iced his heart. What was happening inside her head? What horrors was she living through? He whispered to her: "Please wake up." But he knew, in a complex chamber of his heart, that she would not—because of him. He had wished this upon her.

My dearest love will never leave me.

Had that been it? His wish? It must have been something like that, if not those words exactly—it hadn't been anything expressible in words, anyway, and the creature hadn't needed him to say it. It had simply reached into his heart and plucked it out.

You'd go to pieces . . . Never leave me.

And the creature had delivered, hadn't it? Oh yes, in full. He wanted

Ellen to be with him forever, never leaving his side. That had been his cowardly, heartsick wish. And so he'd gotten it. Lock, stock, and barrel.

"I am so sorry," he whispered into her ear. "I never wanted this."

And yet he had done it. His wish had put her there in that bed, beyond all remedy.

He thought about it. Going to the black rock. Asking that thing for Ellen's release. But he had his daughter to consider, and he sensed it didn't work that way. He had to wait. Suffer, as Ebenezer and Minerva were surely suffering. That was part of it. Perhaps the most crucial part. The suffering.

So they lived there—a man and his daughter and the woman they both loved—on the edge of some greater catastrophe that never quite arrived. But Micah understood that someday it would come to drag him back into the fray.

And then, one lonely night when the stars shone especially bright, the black thing's henchman had come and taken his daughter.

Which is when it began all over again—because such things never truly ended, did they? The wheel went around and around. You rode along and it changed you. You didn't change the wheel. It kept turning and turning until it was time to take that final spin.

3

FIRE IS THE GREAT PURIFIER.

The woods came back. The flames died down and the ashes nourished new life. It was not long before green shoots were pushing through a crackling layer of slag.

The shoots became trees and shrubs; the forest thrived as it had before. The woods climbed the hillsides and filled out the valleys in crisp chlorophyll green. Long alleys of undergrowth cast sprawling shadows so dense that it was chilly in their shade on even the warmest summer days. Wildflowers scattered knolls between sweeping boughs of oak and cottonwood; foxgloves and bracken shone redly in the broad sunshine. Deep thickets and spongy undergrowth sprang up; bramble and buckthorn and tangled knots of poison oak lay over the ground in heavy abundance, dank and choking.

The animals returned in time. The woods teemed with the smallest forms of life at first. The industry of ants, the scuttling of beetles. Then the chirp of birds and the scamper of rodents. Soon the animals that made a meal of those lower orders of life returned, too—the foxes and opossums and lynxes and wolves. Everything grew and spread and became whole again. The shadows stretched, and in them, life went on as it always had.

The black rock was there, too. It had been there forever.

No living creature approached its sheer cliffs. The animals and even the insects steered clear—something warned them off. Nothing grew upon the rock, or even near it. In the deepest hour of night, a sound could sometimes be heard emanating from it. A prolonged sigh. Was it of contentment, or of unspeakable pain? Impossible to tell.

The black rock stood within itself, brooding and implacable.

It waited as it always had. For that wheel to come round again.

PART EIGHT

THE RETURN

1980

1

YOUR DADDY OWES MY DADDY.

The Long Walker traveled on. Petty followed helplessly, her hand engulfed in its own. *The woods are lovely, dark and deep*—that was a line from a poem her mother read to her years ago, before slipping into her big sleep.

The trees creaked in a gentle breeze that ruffled the hem of Petty's nightgown. She wasn't cold or hungry or thirsty, though she should be all of those things by now. Here and there the boughs dropped away to give a view of the sky salted with bright stars.

Your daddy owes my daddy . . .

The Long Walker had told her this at the start of their journey. What had her father done, and to whom? Her dad was a strong and clever man, but she doubted he would double-cross anyone, especially anything that might count the Long Walker as its son.

The Long Walker spidered up the side of a cliff, its feet finding hidden grooves in the rock. It cradled Petty lovingly; with her ear pressed to its chest, she could hear the strange workings of its insides: a cresting buzz, as if its chest was all honeycombs crawling with wasps.

The trees grew sickly and sparse. A huge formation came into view: darker than the night sky, with a density that made her body shrink inside her skin. Was the Long Walker taking her there? She couldn't even imagine it.

I will go crazy, she thought simply.

She knew that wasn't how it happened. People didn't "go crazy," not all at once. It was something that occurred more slowly. A person starts to hear voices, or she thinks people are looking at her when really they're not. Those worries get worse, and that person slowly slips into insanity. But Petty could see it happening another way, too. A person experiences something so horrible that it tears her brain in half—a crack zigzagging across a frozen river, the black madness pouring in all at once.

The trees gave way to a sandy slope leading to the monolithic rock. She tried to jerk her hand out of the Long Walker's grip. It laughed softly at her struggles.

"Please," she said. "I don't want to go."

"*One two three four five six seven*," it said in a voice Pet recognized as her own mother's. "*All good children go to heaven*."

"Don't." Her cheeks flushed with anger despite her fear. "Don't you talk like her, you . . . you *asshole*," she said, summoning the vilest word she knew.

The Long Walker grinned, perhaps admiring her spunk. The towering shadow of the rock cast over them even in the dead of night. Coldness seeped off of it, and a faraway sense of panic wormed into her veins.

"Have you ever heard a newborn cry as it awakes from a nightmare?" the Long Walker asked. Petty was too stunned by its question to reply.

"A newborn, only a few days old," it went on. "They have nightmares, but not as you would understand. Their minds are unformed, as was your own at that age. A newborn baby can still see the world behind the world, you see? The world where my daddy lives, and me and a few others like us. They can still see us. That's why they scream as they do."

Petty swallowed hard. "Because they're . . . they're scared of you?"

"No, precious. Because they don't want us to leave them."

They reached a cleft in the rock. The Long Walker guided her inside. It had to stoop to make its way through the dark and twisting cavern. They went deeper and deeper, until the light died. The Long Walker was untroubled by the darkness, though—it navigated as if by some kind of sonar, never stumbling, bearing Petty quickly along. There came a faint squishing from overhead, but that quickly dwindled. The mineral smell of the rock invaded Petty's nostrils. She stepped on something that made a metallic rattle under her feet. She caught a glimpse of a child's toy browned with rust.

They came to a drop. A rope ladder was rolled up at the ledge, its rungs salted with dust that had accumulated over a period of years. The

Long Walker sat, its legs dangling over the edge. It had no need of the ladder; it skinned down the rocks, carrying Petty effortlessly. At the bottom was another tunnel. The Long Walker urged her inside of it—Petty had stopped fighting, realizing it was useless to try. It swept in behind her, its body filling the entire tunnel. She couldn't see a thing, yet she never bumped a wall or hit a dead end. She might as well have been moving through outer space.

They crawled for some time. Petty didn't even think she was crawling—she was motionless, her limbs made sluggish with worry, and yet she moved. The Long Walker propelled her forward through some manner of infernal mechanics; she felt as if she were on a moving walkway, or had been harnessed to a remorseless winch that was pulling her toward . . . likely nothing she'd ever want to meet.

The tunnel emptied into what her senses told her was an enormous vault—the air wasn't as tight, and she got an impression of vastness, as if she'd stepped into a warehouse. But she still couldn't see anything. That was frightening enough. It was like waking in the middle of the night in your bed and waiting for your eyes to adjust. But at least then you're still in your warm bed, in your house, with your parents not far away. Here she was totally alone . . .

No. There was something else in here.

That's what was raising the hackles on her neck, what was making the flesh crawl up her throat.

"I'm home, Daddy." The Long Walker danced, limbs swinging and kicking. "Home again, home again, jiggety jig."

It pranced into the center of the space toward whatever it was that inspired fright to flutter like a bird's wings in Petty's chest. Its body kicked off a weird deep-sea glow . . . and that's where Petty may as well have been right now: a hundred miles under the surface of the deepest sea, hopelessly alone.

The light of its body touched the shape of another shape. Petty staggered back with a scream rising in her throat.

I will go crazy in a second was the thought that rabbited through her mind. *And maybe that's for the best.*

2

MICAH, MINERVA, AND EBENEZER set off from the godforsaken cabin before daybreak. Minerva was plagued by worries that its luckless occupant might peel himself from his perch upon the wall and shamble forth, blood spluttering from the severed stump of his neck, to avenge the loss of his head—which was by then a roasted, hatchet-cleaved husk in the stove.

They had debated burying the poor man's remains, but that was a problematical proposition, owing to the fact that his body, while indeed headless, was still *moving*: the legs quivering, the arms spasming against the heavy pelt tacks pierced through his flesh. Even trying to bury a motionless body would tax both their energy and sanity, which was already somewhat on the trembling edge—as such, they regretfully opted to leave him hanging on the wall.

Having made their decision, they hunkered down a couple hundred yards from the cabin. But the proximity was too much for Minerva: she kept hearing the choking, garbled laughter of the hunter's decapitated head as it baked in the stove; she swore that she could overhear his spiteful chuckles spindling up through the tin chimney and atomizing into the air like so much lunacy-inducing smoke.

"Let's go," she said to them before dawn had even broken.

They walked, resolutely. Their bodies ached, joints screaming. They were fifteen years older than they'd been the last time they made this trek. The land was unchanged, but they were different. Gray hair, wrinkles, shot nerves. Ebenezer's knee felt as though it had been hollowed out and packed full of fire ants. As the hills grew steeper, Minerva regretted every belt of gutrot whiskey she'd drunk and every unfiltered cigarette she'd smoked in the interceding years. The fear was what wearied them the most—fear had a terrible way of getting inside your chest, sucking at you like a vampire until every step became a misery.

But the nearer they came to the black rock, the more their pains receded. Exhaustion and thirst and hunger deserted them. Their pace actually picked up. Micah had heard that people who perished of hypothermia felt the same way: their brains kicked out a powerful natural narcotic that caused a rosy glow to settle over their minds as their organs froze inside of them.

They spoke as they walked. The darkness unlocked their lips—they spoke, if only to drive that blackness away. They raised questions of an unanswerable nature that had dogged them the last fifteen years.

"What do you think it is?" Minerva asked. "I've always wondered. A demon?"

"Mammon," said Ebenezer. "Demon of greed. A minor demon, but even a minor one is cause for alarm, right?" A wan laugh. *"No man can serve two masters: for either he will hate the one, and love the other; or else he will hold to the one, and despise the other. Ye cannot serve God and Mammon.* Scripture of Matthew. I saw an old painting in a book. This hunched, goblinny thing. For a while I'd thought . . ."

They followed the shadowed path. Creatures stirred faintly in the underbrush.

"But I don't think so now," Eb went on. "If I believed it was a demon, then I would have to believe in its opposite, in God, the pantheon of angels and all the rest. And despite the fact that I see His face every night— or what that thing will have me believe is His face—I do not trust in God's existence."

"What about the other thing?" said Minerva. "Ole daddy longlegs that you lit up like a Roman candle?"

Ebenezer shrugged. "A familiar? Same as a black cat to a witch? What I want to know is why it doesn't leave. Think about it. What it did to all the animals in these woods—what it turned them into. What it must have done to the minds of Amos Flesher and just about everyone else at Little Heaven. It is an immensely powerful entity, is it not?"

Neither Minerva nor Micah would dispute it.

"So why does it live in that rock?" Eb went on. "Why feed—is that what it does? Feed? Let's assume so. Why not set up shop someplace where the pickings are more plentiful?"

Micah had thought about this, too. Perhaps the thing was not so insa-

tiable as Ebenezer suspected. Perhaps it was like a snake. It ate plenti-
fully, dining on the sweetest flesh: on children, as it seemed to have more
of an appetite for them than the older, stringier members of our species.
Though perhaps it wasn't about the quality of our meat, lamb versus
mutton—it was the quality of a child's spirit, its virginal state, versus the
corrupted and corroded worldview of an adult. Once it had eaten, it had
no need to seek prey again for possibly decades—so long as it had a host
like Augustus Preston or Amos Flesher, something to suck on slowly like
an after-dinner mint. If it were to migrate to some more populated place,
it might be found out. This thing had been plying its trade a long time,
and this was its happy hunting ground.

But there was another possibility—one that had dawned years ago,
when Micah fleetingly touched those glowing ropes that had borne Augustus Preston aloft. He'd felt such warmth and wonderment in that instant. Those ropes felt . . . heavenly. So perhaps those ropes held both
Preston *and* the thing in thrall . . . ?

Maybe the black rock wasn't the thing's home. What if it was its
prison?

The trees bled away. They came to a spot where the foliage grew
sparsely. A rough circle of blast. The vegetation was thinner, struggling to
thrive. The leaves of the shrubs were a sick shade of off-white, eaten
through with disease. They checked up, a signal pinging in their primal
brains.

"Little Heaven," said Minerva. "We're standing on its remains."

The diameter of the patch mimicked the size of the compound. Although there was no clear sign that Minerva was correct—they did not
see the rusted ribs of the main gate poking up from the grayish dirt, or
the flame-scoured remains of the massive crucifix that had once topped
the chapel roof—they were each certain of it. Something emanated
from the ground, seeping up like poisoned oil: the curdled, blighted mi-
asma of Little Heaven. The fire-eaten bodies of its worshippers stirred
in with the earth. Their ghostly voices drifting up, lamenting, searching
for something—relief, perhaps even revenge. Against whom? Whom
could they pin the blame on except themselves? Or had their souls

ascended heavenward at the moment of their death, as Amos Flesher must have promised? Had they died in a state of grace?

Micah and Ebenezer followed Minerva across the circle of barren ground. The wind scudded at their heels, raising cones of dust. Quite suddenly, Minerva had to tamp down the powerful urge to cry. She swiped her cheeks, certain her fingers would come away wet with tears. But they were dry as bone, dry as the cracked earth under her boots.

"I'm sorry," she said, though she could not say for whom this apology was meant.

They entered the thicker tree line at the edge of the perimeter. They felt it sucking at their spines—the grieving, implacable tug of Little Heaven, its grim memories, its souls interred beneath the sunbaked dirt—until that tension released, freeing them with almost an audible sigh.

"How do we know the world isn't full of such things?" said Ebenezer later.

"What things?" said Minerva.

Ebenezer stared up at the sky, pricked with guttering stars. "A man descends into madness, a family goes missing, a backwoods religious compound burns to ashes—how do we know that the cause is earthly? *Known?* Often we never find out. But we tell ourselves it must be so because to invite other possibilities is to invite madness into our hearts, isn't it?"

They walked for quite some time in silence, pondering this. Ebenezer had exhausted his capacity for speech. He dragged his leg behind him like a curse.

"There's one thing I've always wondered, Shug," Minerva said.

Micah made a questioning grunt.

"When we were all there in the rock, you menacing it with the knife like you were going to hack it to pieces," Minerva said. "This is weird to say, it being so small and weak-looking and all, but . . . did you get the impression it was all that scared, really?"

This had occurred to Micah as well. At the time, he had believed it was frightened, the way it flinched and mewled. But over the years, he had come to wonder if it had merely been pretending. How could anything like that have any fear of man? Perhaps it had been an act. One facet of the grand game it had played with them all.

"I cannot say."

"Because it's not weak, is it?" said Minerva. "Not at all. Christ, it won't let me die. I can't even . . . It won't even let God take me. Or the devil."

"I have a theory about that," Ebenezer said. "What if its power over you is directly influenced by how close you draw to it? Picture a nuclear reactor with a leak. If you're ten thousand miles away, you'll feel nothing. If you're right next to it—if you stick your hand into it—then you're dead. The closer you get, the more power it has over you. You carry that sickness the rest of your life, okay. But in order for you to truly be at its mercy, you'd have to enter the black rock."

Minerva nodded, accepting this. "Why did it grant us those wishes, then—because it knew they would cause us more pain than not granting them?"

Neither Micah nor Ebenezer answered her. The truth seemed all too plain.

They hiked until the trees thinned out. The creatures that had plagued them all those years ago—the ones that had torn off Terry Redhill's head and Ebenezer's ear, that had ended Otis Langtree's and Charlie Fairweather's lives—were not in evidence. They had no use under present circumstances: Micah and the others were making their way to their master's lair willingly, if not eagerly.

Dawn began to gloss the horizon. They staggered, their legs failing—and then, quite suddenly, they were there.

The gray sand and paling sky. The black rock.

"Dypaloh," Micah said. "There was a house made of dawn. It was made of pollen and of rain, and the land was very old and everlasting. There were many colors on the hills, and the plain was bright with different-colored clays and sands."

Ebenezer and Minerva looked at him, confused.

"Read that somewhere," he said. "Exact opposite of this."

They rounded the face of the rock where it sheared on a ninety-degree scaling. It was the same as ever—towering, featureless, obsidian.

There were no crags or outcroppings where birds might build nests, but then, it would seem an unwise choice for any living thing to dwell upon it. The rock was cold, though the day itself was heating up; a chill radiated off it, as if the coils of a refrigerator were humming behind a quarter inch of stone. The polished surface reflected their features with a funhouse-mirror warp: they somehow looked younger in that shadowy reflection, as if their old selves were trapped in there, too. In many ways, that was true, as a part of them had never left this place.

They hiked around the sheer obsidian angles, and in time they reached the cleft. Though it was now daytime, the sun was blanketed by thick gray clouds. But even if the sun had been shining at full wattage, its light would not have penetrated far inside the rock.

Micah unpacked the last of his gear. He lit the kerosene lantern and tested his flashlight. He patted his pocket to make sure his Buck knife was still there. He shouldered his backpack again. Minerva noticed him wince under its weight.

"You can stay out here," he said to them.

"Shut up," Minerva said. "You know we damn well can't, so quit saying it."

"We can't?" Eb said.

"You can," said Minerva.

Eb seemed to consider taking her up on the offer, but ultimately he shook his head.

"In for a penny," he said, squinting up at the sky.

THAT OLD SMELL—the smell of living decay—hit their noses the moment they entered the cavern. Darkness swiftly closed over them. The lantern threw wavering shadows on the smooth, dripping rock walls. Their footsteps made no sound: they could have been stepping across an enormous wet sponge. They were filled with terror—as stark as the silvery flash of minnows in a dark pool—but they had no choice. They had surrendered that choice years ago.

"Olms," Micah said at one point.

He held the lantern above his head; its light fled up to a domed ceiling bubbled within the rock. "There were olms up there last time."

"The hell are those?" said Minny.

"Salamanders of a sort," he said. "Thousands of them. White ones."

Minny said, "Well, ain't it a crying shame they're gone."

Micah managed a smile. If this had an endgame feeling to it—and yes, it surely did—then why not have a few laughs before the curtain came down?

They reached the ledge. The darkness yawned. The rope ladder was still there, rolled up right where Micah had left it. The strangest thing. He remembered watching Ellen climb it fifteen years ago, the backs of her legs trembling in exertion. He recognized that some part of her must still be here, too.

Micah kicked the ladder over the edge; its rungs clattered against the stone as it unfurled. They climbed down. Ebenezer stopped halfway, his knuckles white on the rope, breathing in short doglike pants.

"I'm okay," he said, to himself more than to the other two. "I'm not, actually, but that's okay. That's perfectly acceptable."

They clustered in the basin facing the tunnel mouth. A sound emanated from it: a languorous exhale, as if the rock itself were breathing. Their faces were pale and sweat-stung in the lantern's light.

Micah unshouldered his pack and put it on backward so that it hung from his chest. He crawled in first, holding the lantern. The tunnel was peppered with other holes, both small and large, holding teeming knots of darkness. Not a goddamned thing had changed. It was like crawling through an old dream that got progressively worse, narrowing to a perfect speck of darkness—the center of the nightmare.

The kids, Micah thought. *We saved them. They would still be down here otherwise. That is the only change—they are not here. That is a good difference.*

Ooooh, but wait, whispered a silky, devious voice in his ear. *Some of them are still here, aren't they?*

The tunnel ended. One by one, they crawled out and stood within the great, dark vault. Micah set the lantern down and shrugged off his pack. He found his flashlight and swept it through the inky—

"No" was all he heard Minny say. One word, flatly stated. Her voice full of horror.

3

FIFTEEN YEARS. One-fifth of the average human lifespan, give or take. Yet time tended to behave oddly; it was never static, and people felt it differently depending on circumstance. For a child squirming in his desk on the last day of school, those final minutes before the bell rang could seem endless. When that same boy passed through adulthood to old age, those same minutes could pass without his knowing.

Fifteen years. For the Reverend Amos Flesher, they must have been an eternity.

He hung in a web of scintillating red ropes. His body had shrunken and seized up; his feet, which had once touched the ground, now dangled nearly a foot above it. His skin was as brown and dry and moistureless as a chunk of liver forgotten in the back of a freezer. He looked somehow wooden. His toes were curled and hooked upward in grisly curlicues, like awful genie shoes. His lips had thinned away to transparencies, his teeth brown and cracked. The fretwork of ropes creaked softly like the hull of an old Spanish galleon on the night sea.

Micah swept the flashlight past this horrible sight, moving left . . . His breath caught.

"Pet."

His daughter stood behind the Reverend. Motionless, her face crawling with dread. Micah stepped toward her. The flashlight disclosed another shape behind her. Its fingers curled possessively on Petty's shoulder, its upper body swathed in darkness.

The Big Thing. The Flute Player.

"Daddy, *please*."

Micah could not tell if it was his daughter who had spoken or the thing behind her—it was an uncanny mimic, as he recalled. He held up his hands in surrender.

"She is all I want."

"*Ass, gas, or grass,*" the Big Thing said in his daughter's voice. "*Nobody rides for free, Daddy-o.*"

Micah nodded. Instinctively, he knew what to do. He pulled the knife from his pocket and unfolded the blade. He approached the Reverend. The slit in his back, the one Shughrue had carved into it all those years ago, was still wet, still . . . weeping. Gingerly, Micah touched the tip of the knife to its edge. A membrane burst, spilling noxious nectar down the Reverend's flesh. The smell was that of a cracked-open coffin. Micah glanced at Amos's face, wondering if any of this was registering; the Reverend's eyelids were fissured with tiny dry cracks that seemed on the verge of ripping open, spilling his eyeballs down his cheeks.

Micah turned his attention back to the slit. He drew the blade across it, severing the protective sac. Something turned inside the wound, fat and slug-like; the sight was reminiscent of a cat stretching itself on a warm windowsill.

"Micah, what are you . . . ?" Minerva said somewhere behind him.

The thing began to push itself out forcefully, with hard flexes and shoves. The Reverend shook helplessly; a second rip spread across his abdomen, and a desiccated loop burped through the split. His crotch—which was essentially sexless by now, just a flaccid free-hanging tube like a spent condom and a terribly distended and elongated sack with a pair of BBs rolling around inside—swayed lewdly, parodically. Micah stumbled back, the sight so overwhelming that his knees buckled, fear rushing through his brain as the thing muscled its way out with determined thrusts and the other thing, its helpmate, laughed the same way his daughter did at Scooby-Doo and Scrappy on the Saturday morning cartoons—

The thing slid out of the Reverend's back and landed on the floor. At nearly the same instant, the ropes mooring the Reverend let go. The Reverend fell gracelessly and crumpled to the floor in a boneless heap . . .

Then Amos Flesher began to shriek.

His screams drilled through the air and ricocheted off the walls. They started out hoarsely, his vocal cords seized from disuse, but built to a lung-rupturing pitch. They were the gibbering bleats of a lunatic—a madness so profound it was all but unimaginable.

"No, Daddy!" he squealed as he bucked and writhed on the stone. "You don't love me anymore you don't love me never stop loving *meeeeeee!*"

Micah was overcome with pity. Amos Flesher was a devil—the cruelest man he had ever encountered, and he had run across many in his lifetime—but to see him there, naked and wizened as he shuddered on the floor with a kind of horrid, lascivious glee . . . Micah wanted to do something, if only to shut him up and end his misery. But he could not. He was completely paralyzed.

The Reverend's hands—brown and sinewy and hooked into talons— danced in the air. His legs moved as if he was trying to climb an invisible staircase. He began to rip at his wasted body. His skin tore all too easily. Chunks of his chest and arms ripped free like enormous scabs. He screamed and laughed until he ran out of breath and began to gag helplessly as his hands rose to his face, scrabbling at his cheeks and nose and finally his eyes, which burst dryly, like spore bags, releasing splintered puffs of matter.

"Daddy!" he mewled, crawling blindly toward the thing that had lived inside of him for fifteen years, feeding on him in some terrible way, wrecking him in a manner no human should have to experience. "Pleeeeeaase, oh pleeeease, don't *leeeeave* me, Daddy!"

He scrabbled toward the wet pink baby-thing, moaning and spluttering. The Big Thing left Petty's side; it strode forward, and with quick, methodical ease, it stepped on the Reverend Amos Flesher's skull. A sickening crunch. The Reverend's reedlike legs jittered. Then they quit moving.

Micah waited, his breath whinnying out of him. When the Big Thing did not move, he took a wide berth around the squirming baby-thing and went to his daughter. The Big Thing knelt, fingering the remains of Flesher's broken skull case. The Reverend's brain was pale and dry, leeched of moisture, like some kind of cheap, crumbled cheese.

Micah knelt in front of Petty, inspected her for injuries. "Did it hurt you?"

She shook her head. She seemed both alert and hazy at once, as though trapped in a very vivid dream she was helpless to wake from.

"Are you okay?"

"Are you here?" she said. "*Really* here?"

"You are not dreaming, Pet. I am here."

"I'm scared."

"Me too. More than you can imagine."

"It said you owed its daddy. What do you owe, Dad?"

Everything, Pet. Everything I can possibly give.

Micah turned to the things, the father and its doting son. "I know what you want. But you have to let them all go."

The Big Thing squatted beside the baby. For some time, they held a silent palaver.

"What if we want . . . everything?" the Big Thing finally said.

"You do not want them," Micah said evenly. "You never did."

The two things conferred further. The Big Thing appeared to chuckle. "Yes," it said. "Just one of you will do."

"And you must lift the curse. Take it back."

A smile touched the corners of the Big Thing's mouth. "Curse? My father should be outraged. Was it not exactly what you wished for?"

Micah said nothing. In time, the Big Thing nodded. "As you wish. My father is merciful."

Micah turned to Ebenezer and Minerva. "Take her," he said. "Quickly."

"Micah, no," said Minerva. "What are you—?"

Micah turned away. He couldn't stand to look at them. He had known from the outset that it would come to this. He had realized—in the deepest, most honest chamber of his heart—that it would have to end like this. It was the only way. The creature would take all of them, or it would take Micah alone. But Micah had to give himself willingly. And he knew the thing wanted him so, *so* badly. For he was surely the only member of his species who had ever caused it true fear, true pain, in its vast and fearsome life.

Micah turned back to confront his daughter's agonized face. He hugged Pet tightly. With her arms pinned to her sides, she was too surprised to return it. He felt the heat of her body and the rapid beat of her heart. He tried to imprint it in his mind: her warmth, her innocence, all the love pouring out of him into her.

"I love you, Pet." She shimmered before him. "I love you so much. And your mother, of course. More than anything on earth. You be sure to tell her that, okay? You tell her how much I love you both. Will you do that?"

His daughter nodded obediently. He wondered if she had any idea of just how much he loved her. Does a child ever understand the irrational, endless love of a parent?

"Go, then," he said. "And do not *ever* come back. Do you hear me?"

"No, Daddy. I won't go without you."

"It cannot be any other way, my love. You do not understand, but you have to trust me. I am begging you."

Minerva and Ebenezer stood in the sputtering light of the lantern. Micah appealed to them next. "Go. Now. What in hell's name are you waiting for?"

"We can't just—" Minerva started.

Micah stilled her with a look. She knew, too. As did Ebenezer. This was the only possible way. The cards were stacked against them. Those cards had begun to stack the moment Micah had accepted Ellen Bellhaven's request to take her to Little Heaven to find her missing nephew.

Micah tried to let go of his daughter. His arms wouldn't unlock. He wanted to hold her forever. But he had to let go.

His arms wrapped around her, the comfort he felt with her in his hands—his *hands*. He saw them now in the flickering lantern light. Hard, callused. A killer's hands. At first, he hadn't wanted to hold Petty when she was an infant. This memory came to him, clear as spring water. He had been afraid that some of his evilness might invade her tiny body. But he sensed a change in himself the moment she was born, right in his very atoms. His arms, his hands, his entire body was changing in subtle ways in order to accept this sweet burden he'd been given. *She fits perfectly in my hands*, he remembered thinking when the doctor gave her to him. *They have shaped themselves to her without my even knowing—*

He let his daughter go. It was the hardest thing he'd ever had to do. "Go, my Pet."

"No!" the girl screamed, clutching at him.

The Big Thing chuckled, enjoying the touching family moment.

"We can accommodate two," it said.

"You will have to take her," Micah pleaded with Ebenezer and Minny. "Please."

They grabbed his daughter's arms. Her screams intensified as they dragged her away, legs kicking wildly. Ebenezer whispered something into her ear. At that, Petty stopped kicking. Her eyes shone in the dim, the brightest spots in the chamber.

"I love you, Daddy" was all she said.

"Blow me a kiss, darling."

She did. He watched it float through the dark air, then reached out and snatched it. Micah put his daughter's last kiss in his pocket. "Thank you, baby. I will need it." They left him, Petty trembling, still disbelieving, her body limp as a wrung dishrag. Minerva followed her, stunned and softly weeping. Ebenezer was last; he departed with a terse but compassionate nod. The three of them crawled into the tunnel. The Big Thing followed them out, leaving Micah with its daddy.

Micah exhaled. He pulled himself together. He unbuttoned his shirt in the flickering glow of the lantern. The baby made gluttonous sucking sounds. His hand trembled as he stretched the skin of his stomach taut. Old flesh, wasn't it? It had felt a lot, carried him through so much. It bore the nicks and scrapes of its service.

It is not an easy thing, stabbing oneself. Micah had scarcely considered how it ought to be done, never having harbored those thoughts. Fast and declarative seemed best. Cut fast, cut deep.

Micah heard the rope ladder banging against the rock as Petty and the other two climbed up it. *Go on, baby. Keep going. Never look back.*

He hissed through his teeth as the knife slid into his belly. He jerked the blade across in a straight and bitter line; his flesh readily opened up. He dropped to his knees, swooning as blood soaked into his waistband. Deep enough? He sensed the thing would have its own methods of opening him up.

A delicate touch on his shoulder. A red rope had descended from the ceiling to alight upon him. It wasn't painful. The warmest kiss. He batted it away. That couldn't happen yet. He had one final task to complete.

He dragged his bleeding body over to his backpack and rooted inside. His hands closed around the bricklike object he'd carried many miles. He pulled it out. The baby issued a quizzical burble.

Micah had purchased it from an acquaintance from his sad old, bad old days. He had purchased it before heading off to find Ebenezer, meeting the man in a parking garage and paying in cash. Such transactions should carry no trace. The man he had bought it from asked no questions regarding its usage—men like the seller made it their business to proffer product without moral consequence. He only told Micah that it was enough to do the trick, which had sounded about right to Micah.

He turned to the baby. Showed it what he was holding.

"I hope," he said laboredly, "you are not afraid of enclosed spaces."

"DADDY!" the Long Walker shrieked.

Petty—who was up the ladder by then, although her progress had been slowed by her tears—looked down at the thing, which stood at the bottom of the basin watching as they ascended. Pet was startled by the childish pitch of its voice. Its huge moonface was split in a rictus of rage—the expression of something that had been tricked most awfully.

It turned and fled back into the tunnel, its huge legs sawing through the dark air.

"Move," Minny said to Petty. "As fast as you can, little girl."

SEVEN STICKS OF TNT wired together in a bundle.

"How many seconds do you want me to rig the timer?"

This was the question the man Micah had bought it from had asked. A cheap plastic egg timer, the kind you'd find in kitchens all across America, was wired to the fuses and strapped to the dynamite with duct tape.

"Three seconds," Micah told him.

"Three? Jesus, man. That's not nearly enough time to run clear of the explosion. That's barely enough time to blow your nose."

"Three," Micah said again.

Micah twisted the knob on the egg timer as the baby-thing watched him. He could sense its worry—though perhaps it was faking again? It began to hiss menacingly as it crawled toward him. In the lantern's glow, Micah at last got a sense of its true shape: the light shone through its fatty covering to display a network of brachial and spiny limbs. It moved quickly, its nails clickety-clacking on the rock. Its voice filled his skull.

Oh no no don't you dare do not DARE—

Micah could hear the other thing coming now, too. He pictured its mouth opened in a tortured leer as it raced through the tunnel to protect its precious father. It was getting closer, steaming toward him—

You had to be calm in the cut. That was the key. You had to hold your mud for that extra half second, even with the hammers of hell pounding down on you. Everything hubbed on that. It really did. If you acted too soon, you could lose it all.

The Big Thing tore into the chamber, its body billowing up and out to blot the lantern's light. Micah waited until it was fully inside; then he hurled the TNT down the tunnel it had just vacated. He turned to face them. The baby's fleshy face twisted in rage. The Big Thing stood rooted, momentarily perplexed. Micah opened his hands to them as blood sheeted down his stomach.

Sorry, fellas, but it had to be done.

Micah wore a blissful smile. He looked less threatening when he smiled. So much less the badass. Ellen always said he ought to smile more often. And right now he did. For her.

THE EXPLOSION ROARED out of the cavern. A hail of black dust and rock splinters shotgunned from the cleft to spray the sand in a wide radius.

Minerva and Eb and Petty were clear of the blast zone by then. They stood three abreast, staring gape-jawed as more dust and rubble sifted from the cavern. They could hear the rock giving way as the interior began to cave in.

"No," Minerva whispered. "Micah, oh, Micah, what did you do?"

MICAH CAME TO some time later. He was still alive. It came as a shock. Not an entirely welcome one, under the circumstances.

The lantern continued to burn. Squinting, he could see it was partially covered in a coating of black, coal-like dust. Someone had scraped some of the dust off and relit it.

He saw chunks of stone on the floor, their jagged contours swimming in the light of the lantern. A fine haze of soot hung in the air. He looked down at himself. The edges of his gaping stomach wound were crusted with the same black soot. The ragged, bumpy edges looked like a dog's gums. The smell of explosives was sharp in his nose.

But he was still alive. The chamber was still here. It had not caved in. *Naughty boy.*

The voice sent a spike of panic through him.

You must be punished.

He rolled onto his side. The tunnel was gone—in its place a solid fall of rock, a few chunks of which had rolled across the chamber's floor. So it had worked. He was dimly amazed that the cavern hadn't collapsed around him. But this thing had immense power, so it was not absurd to think it had found a way to protect its lair from the blast. At least Micah had sealed them all inside.

He stood dazedly. He couldn't see anything past the apathetic light shed by the lantern. He flinched as something touched his shoulder. A red rope had descended from the ceiling to lick at his flesh. He did not fight it this time. It felt too good. The ropes spooled down in great multitudes, all with shining inner cores. They attached to his flesh and gently lifted him up. He almost laughed—even as the blood sheeted down him. Such a delightful sensation. They held him in a loving embrace. He could not move. In that moment, he didn't want to.

The lantern light fell upon the Big Thing, which had moved into a corner. It produced a flute, which it raised to its lips. The flute made no sound, but the Big Thing danced anyway, legs kicking and feet shuffling, happy in whatever way it could be.

The baby mewled somewhere behind Micah. It, too, had survived the blast. Of course it had. Micah heard it slapping closer to him, though he could not chart its approach.

A chill raced through his body when a cold tongue brushed his calf. He flinched, unable to help it. *No,* he thought. *Do not get weak-kneed already. It will get worse.* His eyes fell upon the Reverend's body covered in a dusting of black soot. *So much worse.*

The Big Thing had stopped playing its flute. It seemed to bear Micah no ill will for the explosion that had trapped it here. Perhaps it could get out easily enough. Perhaps a few tons of blown-apart rock and a lack of breathable air meant nothing to it. The thing stared at him in the fluttering light.

"It must be said, you are strong," it said in obvious appreciation. "Stronger than any of your kind we have encountered."

The baby made a gargling rasp—a note of agreement? Something coiled around Micah's ankle and constricted mercilessly.

"That does not matter, does it?" Micah asked.

The Big Thing shook its head almost sadly. "Time and pressure will split the strongest rock," it said distantly. "In fact, time alone is sufficient."

The baby slid between Micah's spread legs. In the lantern's light— which was now dying out, Micah noted with worry—it didn't resemble a baby at all. It was much older and more unspeakable. His eyes couldn't grasp the true shape of it, or didn't want to; his gaze skated off its awfulness, shying from it like a nervous horse. It began to mount him. Micah moaned. He couldn't help himself. The Big Thing retreated to the far side of the chamber. A chalice had been grooved into the rock. It folded its enormous body into that indentation, tucking its legs up to its chin. It closed its eyes and went still: a toy in a cupboard waiting for its owner to take it out and play with it again.

The lantern's flame blew sideways, frayed by an unfelt wind. It would go out soon. Micah was terrified at the thought of being alone in the dark with this thing. The light made it slightly less maddening. Would he die when the air ran out? He hoped to God it would be so.

The thing had reached his knee now. Its body was wet and hard like a naked tendon. It made a snuffling noise that a dog might make rooting for scraps under a dinner table. This, too, almost made Micah laugh. Instead he cried. He realized he'd actually been doing this on and off for some time. It was of no matter. He could cry all he liked.

The flame *whumphed* and spluttered, the kerosene nearly gone. The thing was slipping inside of him now. It didn't hurt so bad. The red ropes might have something to do with that. He didn't dare look, but he could hear his insides shifting with a soft squelch. He took a few hiccuping inhales, the sort a boy makes before he dunks his head underwater to see how long he can hold his breath.

Oh God, he thought wildly. *Please let them be safe. Please let them live without wondering, without too much burden, without without without—*

The lantern's light winked out. Darkness overtook him.

In that darkness, a voice:

Shall we begin?

HOMECOMING

1980

1

ELLEN SHUGHRUE reentered her own body at five minutes past ten on the morning her daughter returned home.

She would never remember the dream she was roused from. All that remained was a sense of darkness and the incessant fluttering of wings. And inside that swirling turbulence, her husband's calm and ever-present voice:

Without without without . . .

She did not crack her eyelids. As usual, her eyes were already open. Ellen simply fled back into consciousness like a person flung out of a mine shaft. The sunlight streaming through the window was so powerful that she let out a pained hiss. She blinked—*Mother of Christ, that hurt!* Her eyelids grated against her eyeballs like fine-grit sandpaper, causing tears to flood down her cheeks. When was the last time she'd slept in late enough to have the sun wake her? It was her habit to be up before dawn. Had she had a few drinks with Micah last night? Her head throbbed like an abscessed tooth.

A wave of guilt swept over her: here she was lying in bed with a hangover while Petty was up and no doubt wondering why her mother was still lollygagging in bed. Didn't they have something this morning? Ellen struggled to recall. A piano lesson, soccer practice, or—?

Her sister came into the bedroom. Sherri's hands fluttered up to her mouth. Her eyes were wide with shock.

Something was wrong. Ellen realized this all at once. Her sister shouldn't look that damn old. Sherri, she . . . Lord, she was an old biddy. Her sister's hands were bony, the skin stretched tight over the bones. The fine lines at the edges of Sherri's eyes had become deeply trenched crow's-feet.

"Are you . . . ," Sherri said, awestruck. "Ellen, are you awake?"

Why the hell wouldn't I be awake? I know I slept in a bit, but let's not make a capital case out of it.

This was what Ellen was going to say. But when she tried to speak, her voice was a papery rasp. Her mouth was dry as dust. Her vocal cords felt rusty, a bit like an engine in a junkyard that had seized up from disuse.

She groaned and rolled onto her back. Oh! That hurt, too. Fuck a duck. She tried to sit up. Couldn't. She nearly laughed—how *weird*. Her muscles were slack. She managed to lift her arm off the coverlet. She would have screamed, were she capable. Her arm was a fleshless stick— Christ, what the hell had happened to her? Who had stolen her life, her body?

"Calm down," she heard Sherri saying. "It's going to be okay."

Hands shaking, Sherri picked up the phone on the dresser and worked the rotary dial.

"Doctor? It's Sherri Bellhaven. She's awake." Shaking, nodding her head violently. "I don't know—I just came in and she's up. Okay, okay, okay-yup-yup-yup."

She hung up. "The doctor's going to be here soon. You need to keep your eyes open, El. *Please*, just keep your eyes open. Stay awake."

What are you so worked up about? Ellen wanted to ask, resisting the urge to panic. *I don't feel the least bit tired. I've had a full night's rest. The sleep of the damned, it feels like.*

A twentysomething man came into the bedroom. Ellen wanted to snatch the covers up, feeling somehow naked, but her arms wouldn't obey. The boy was handsome and trim with sandy hair. He was staring at her in disbelief.

"Aunt Ellen?"

No. It couldn't be. *Nate?* Nate wasn't old enough to drive a car or smoke cigarettes. This *couldn't* be her nephew. It was someone else. An imposter. Someone was playing a filthy, mean-spirited trick on—

Ellen experienced a sickening whiplash sensation. Just how the hell long had she been asleep?

"The doctor wants you to sit up," Sherri said. "Nate and me are going to help you up, okay? Now, this might hurt a little."

Ellen managed to nod. Fear was crawling over her scalp now. Not fear of falling asleep—she wasn't sure she'd ever fall asleep again—but fear at how much time was gone from her, this terrible sense of loss, of her life having been snatched away from her.

"What time is it?" she rasped at her sister. Then, suddenly terrified: "What *day* is it?"

Where's Petty? Where's Micah? Why weren't they here?

Sherri gripped her right arm and shoulder; Nate gripped her left. As gently as they could, they sat her up and rested her against the headboard. The pain was monstrous. Her muscles were atrophied, her body horribly shrunken. She became aware of a fungal, unwashed smell; it took a few moments before she recognized it as her own. She boggled at the wrecked canvas of her body, the lower half of it mercifully hidden under the sheets.

Propped up, she could see out the window. The front yard with its barren flower beds. The sun glinted off the mailbox at the base of the long graveled drive. Squinting, she watched a car approach. A big bastard. Cadillac. Her chest jogged as she tried to laugh again. Had Micah bought himself a Caddy? That wasn't like him at all. Next he'd be stepping out in rhinestone cowboy boots.

The car pulled into the driveway. Her heart took a funny hop as a vision flashed through her mind, impossible to grip—a premonition, the tarot card readers would call it.

Oh please, she thought as the car doors swung open. *Oh please please . . .*

MINERVA THREW THE TRANSMISSION into park. Petty remained asleep in the backseat. Her face was wrenched in a troubled expression, as if the girl was suffering through a night terror.

"Hey," Minerva said, reaching back to give her a gentle shake. "Thanks for giving us directions. We're home now, honey."

The girl woke up. Her face smoothed out, serene. She rubbed her eyes and sat up.

"I was dreaming."

"Oh yes?" Ebenezer said. "Not a pleasant dream?"

She stared at him in confusion. "I don't remember."

"Could be that's your good fortune, my dear."

The three of them sat in the car with the engine ticking down.

"Thank you," Petty said finally. "For coming to get me."

They opened the doors and stepped out. The day was warm, considering the season. Petty walked toward the house in bare feet, the hem of her nightgown swishing around her ankles.

"Are you coming?"

Ebenezer said, "In a minute, dear. You go on in. You have been missed."

Petty turned back to the house. "Hey," Minerva called to her. "You know how much your father loves you, don't you?"

The girl turned again, and nodded. "Where is he?"

Minerva wondered if she was already forgetting, the same way Minerva had heard the survivors of Little Heaven had forgotten. Could be so. Maybe that was the best and only way of soldiering on.

"He's coming, I'm sure," Minerva said, meeting Petty's questioning gaze directly. Was it a lie or a hopeful truth? She had no idea.

Minerva and Ebenezer walked toward the house in tandem.

She said, "You figure that was his intention all along?"

"Micah, you mean?" said Eb. "To have it just be him?"

She nodded. Ebenezer kicked a pebble.

"I have no idea. His aims weren't always easy to assess."

"He did save us."

"Yes."

"You figure we're worth saving?"

Eb smiled. "Not really. But maybe he thought so. And his daughter was at stake, too."

He was limping badly. Minerva slowed down to let him keep pace. "Do you think he's dead?" she asked.

"After all that? I can't see how it could be otherwise." Ebenezer went silent a moment. "I hope so. I . . . I'll pray it was so."

Minerva nodded. "I don't know if I can just leave him back there, though, Eb. Not without knowing for sure."

Now it was Eb's turn to nod. "Yes. We may have to go back. I cannot believe I'm saying that, but . . . Ellen might force the issue."

"If she ever wakes up."

"Yes. If."

"I think I can die now," Minerva said suddenly. "I feel it, you know? Of any old thing. A bloody nose. A bee sting."

"So does that mean you want to die, milady?"

She turned her face up to the sky. The sun was uncommonly bright today.

"I'm gonna have to think about it."

He clapped her on the back. "Think long and hard, my dear."

PETTY STEPPED INTO the bedroom.

Oh, my little girl was all Ellen could think. *Oh, my baby, where have you gone?*

Petty threw herself on the bed. She grabbed Ellen fiercely around her threadbare waist.

Gentle, baby girl. Your old mom's not the woman she once was.

"Where have you been, Mom?" Petty asked.

"Where have I been?" Ellen croaked, noticing the dirtied hem of her daughter's nightgown "Where have *you* been?"

They shared a look, one that said, *I don't know where I've been. But I'm so happy to be back.*

Sherri and Nate stood with gobsmacked grins on their faces. Ellen's gaze carried over to the window. Two figures were walking up the drive. She recognized them dimly—she had the sense of knowing them from long ago, as friends perhaps . . . although *soldiers* was the word that skated across her mind. These were people she had been in some terrible battle with, the exact nature of which she could no longer recall. The woman turned her face up to the sky to drink in the sunlight. She smiled and said something to the man, who patted her on the back hard enough to raise a plume of dust off her clothing.

"Put my arm around you, Pet," she said. "I can't lift it at the moment."

Petty took her mother's arm and draped it over her shoulder. It lay there like a bit of driftwood. It was okay. The feeling would come back eventually. Only one thing was missing.

Come back to me, Micah. For Christ's sake, you come back.

It came to her then. A second premonition, but much worse this time. A hellish snapshot from her buried past, walled off behind an impenetrable barrier her mind had constructed to keep it from doing any further harm.

A black rock. A monolithic buzzing. The spiteful laughter of children. And a presence deep within that rock, cold and vile and relentless—

She recoiled. Then she began to cry. The sobs wracked her frame in painful waves, but she was unable to stop. She hadn't cried with such ardency since she was a girl.

"What's the matter, Mom?" she heard Pet say.

"I don't know, baby. I don't *know*."

2

HELL IS A BOX.

Micah hung in emptiness. No top or bottom. All darkness.

He had surrendered all memory of his body. Eventually he would surrender everything else, too. His sanity, his humanity, even his name. This certainty rested easily within him.

Dypaloh. There was a house made of dawn. It was made of pollen and of rain, and the land was very old and everlasting. There were many colors on the hills, and the plain was bright with different-colored clays and sands.

He tried to hang on to this, among a few other things. That image—a house made of dawn—and the shape of his wife's mouth and the warmth of his daughter's body pressed to his. But it was so goddamn hard. It was all fading, all failing, taking him with it.

What do we truly know of hell?

The thing nested contently within him. It . . . pulled. A slow, remorseless withdrawal. Sometimes he tried to fight back. Not physically, as he had irrevocably lost that control. But he would wall off his mind and *think* at it. Think good thoughts, affirming ones. The thing seemed to enjoy Micah's feistiness. Time alone will split the strongest rock.

While his mind was still intact, Micah dwelled. Such was some men's nature, as it was his. He reflected that this thing inside of him called out to evil men—or it called out to the evilness in men, which was essentially the same thing. It drew in those like Augustus Preston and Amos Flesher; perhaps over the course of its history, it had drawn dozens more. And now, it had drawn Micah into its web.

What did that mean? Was Micah as evil as those others had been? There was abundant evidence to support that argument. He had killed his fellow man without mercy and at times without cause. Old men, young men . . . yes, even children.

And yet.

And yet . . .

Dypaloh. House made of dawn. My father's house has many rooms, each more splendorous than the last. Jesus loves me, this I know, for the Bible tells me so—

It's all so goddamn fragile. Your life and the thread you carry it on. And the more love you carry, the more stress you put on that thread, the better chance it will snap. But what choice do any of us have? You take on that love because to live without it is to exist as half a person. You give that love away because it is in you to give, not out of a desire for recompense. And you keep loving even when the world cracks open and reveals a black hole where all that love can get swallowed.

He had a sense of the thing inside of him now. It was distilled evil. Vast, unknowable. But it was elementally itself, as it had always been. The wasp stings. The jackal bites. That is the nature of those creatures, just as evil was this thing's nature. Could anything be faulted for its nature?

I forgive you, he sometimes thought. This angered the thing to no end. It would shift within him, sending out needlefish of pain. But it was worth it.

Other times, he was able to cast his mind out of the black rock. Only for a few seconds before the thing caught him and reeled him back; it had become harder to do the more the thing fed upon him. In time, he would not be able to do it at all. But for now—if he marshaled all his will—he was still able to make that flight.

He pictured it as a jump. He coiled and sprang. His unconscious fled out of his body, up through the black rock to its peak. It was like swimming up through suffocating oil. He broke through into the clean sunshine, fresh air, birds trilling . . .

. . . and he could hear her.

Petty. His daughter. He could hear her—the wild, reckless laughter of youth. And whatever was left of him swelled to bursting.

Was evil a static commodity? He wondered this, too. Perhaps there was no more or less evil on earth now than there had ever been. It was like any other element. You could not manufacture any more of it than already existed. It got passed around from body to body, from death to new life. We all inherited a little bit of it. He had seen plenty of it. In the eyes of the men he'd fought beside in the war and in the eyes of the men he'd killed afterward . . . He'd seen it in his own eyes in the mirror. This being the case, perhaps it was not possible to erase evil from the lives of those you care for. All you could hope to do was divert it away from your loved ones, focusing it on another, equally profound evil. Failing that, you take it on yourself. Take that bullet, even if you have to take it for a hundred years.

Evil was fundamentally weak. Micah understood that now. It was cowardly and dreary and it sought the darkest spaces between the beams to make its home.

I forgive you for what you are, he thought at the thing.

Needlefish. *Needlefish.*

Still worth it.

Micah Shughrue hung in emptiness, curling the remains of his mind around the sound of his daughter's laughter, defending it like a mother bear protecting her cub in the deepest, blackest reaches of her den. Sooner or later the thing would snatch this from him as well—he could already feel it slipping through his fingers, and with it the most essential element of his soul—but until then he would nurse it, bite and claw and scrape to keep hold of it.

My name is Micah Shughrue, he thought. *I have sinned, I have committed great awfulness, but I am loved. I live with my wife and daughter in a house made of dawn. The house is made of pollen and rain and laughter . . .*

pollen and rain . . .

and rain . . .

rain . . .

ACKNOWLEDGMENTS

MY THANKS TO THE USUAL SUSPECTS: my rockin' agent, Kirby Kim; my kickass editor, Ed Schlesinger; Jennifer Bergstrom and Stephanie DeLuca and everyone at Gallery Books. To my father, who read and offered his thoughts on the first draft; my mother, who's always pulling for me; my wonderful wife, Colleen, who supports me through this strange and meandering journey; and our son, Nicholas, who just does what he does and makes us smile every day. To artist extraordinaire Adam Gorham, who provided the awesome illustrations throughout this book—*grazie mille!* To the fine writers who were willing to read the manuscript and offer their kind words, I'm deeply appreciative for your generosity.

Now, if you're one of those readers who skip to the end of the book and check out the acknowledgments before finishing, I ought to post a warning here.

SPOILERS! SPOILERS! SPOILERS!

. . .

. . .

REALLY, I'M DEAD SERIOUS. SPOILERS AHEAD.

OKAY?

YOU HAVE BEEN WARNED.

So. Amos Flesher. Anyone with a passing knowledge of religious fanaticism and cults will see where I drew inspiration for that character's portrayal—the aviator shades, the fussy hairdo, hell, even the method by which Amos dispatched his unruly worshipers. In fact, it's even more depraved than you might suspect: for Flesher's final speech, delivered to his flock minutes before their demise, I liberated the odd snatch of dialogue from the transcripts of Jim Jones's own speech to the disciples of his People's Temple—the one where he compels his followers to drink the Kool-Aid. You can find it online, if you've got a mind to read it. When Flesher says, "I'll never detach myself from any of your troubles. I've always taken your troubles right on my shoulders" and "Say, say peace"—those were lines spouted by Jones his own self as he prodded his people to drink up. The rest of it, okay, I pulled that out of thin air. But a few of those lines belong to ole Jimmy, the crazy rat bastard. So, uhhhh, I guess credit where credit's due?

Thank you most of all, dear reader. Obviously no writer would be able to do what they do without an audience out there to receive his or her words, so I'm especially grateful for the support of those who take the time to read the Cutter books. *Merci!*